EXIT
WOUNDS

BOOKS BY J. A. JANCE

Joanna Brady Mysteries

Desert Heat

Tombstone Courage

Shoot, Don't Run

Dead to Rights

Skeleton Canyon

Rattlesnake Crossing

Outlaw Mountain

Devil's Claw

Paradise Lost

J. P. Beaumont Mysteries

Until Proven Guilty

Injustice for All

Trial by Fury

Taking the Fifth

Improbable Cause

A More Perfect Union

Dismissed with Prejudice

Minor in Possession

Payment in Kind

Without Due Process

Failure to Appear

Lying in Wait

Name Withheld

Breach of Duty

Birds of Prey

and

Hour of the Hunter

Kiss of the Bees

Partner in Crime

EXIT WOUNDS

J. A. JANCE

 HarperLargePrint

An Imprint of HarperCollins*Publishers*

EXIT WOUNDS. Copyright © 2003 by J. A. Jance. All rights reserved. Printed in the United States of America. No part of this book may be used or reproduced in any manner whatsoever without written permission except in the case of brief quotations embodied in critical articles and reviews. For information address HarperCollins Publishers Inc., 10 East 53rd Street, New York, NY 10022.

HarperCollins books may be purchased for educational, business, or sales promotional use. For information please write: Special Markets Department, HarperCollins Publishers Inc., 10 East 53rd Street, New York, NY 10022.

FIRST HARPER LARGE PRINT EDITION

Printed on acid-free paper

Library of Congress Cataloging-in-Publication Data
Jance, Judith A.
        Exit wounds / J.A. Jance.—1st ed.
            p. cm.
        ISBN 0-380-97731-1 (Hardcover)
        1. Brady, Joanna (Fictitious character)—Fiction.
2. Fourth of July celebrations—Fiction. 3. Policewomen—
Fiction. 4. Sheriffs—Fiction. 5. Cochise County (Ariz.)—
Fiction. 6. Arizona—Fiction. Title.
PS3560.A44 E88 2003
813'.5421

                                                        2002035891

ISBN 0-06-054549-6 (Large Print)

03 04 05 06 07 WBC/RRD 10 9 8 7 6 5 4 3 2 1

This Large Print Book carries the Seal of Approval of N.A.V.H.

EXIT
WOUNDS

PROLOGUE

The woman lay in her bed, tossing and turning, and tried to sleep. It was hot, but southern Arizona in July is always hot. Due to unpaid bills, the power company had shut off electricity to the shabby mobile home months ago. By now she was pretty well used to sleeping without benefit of a cooler or even a blowing fan.

The heat **was** a factor, but more disturbing than physical discomfort was thinking about the approaching interview. She had kept her mouth shut for almost thirty years. For that long, other than pouring her heart out to her grandmother, she had been part of an ugly conspiracy of silence. No more. Tomorrow—today, in fact—she was going to talk. To strangers. To reporters. She was going to let it all hang out. The question was, what would happen then?

Someone had told her once—wasn't it that same grandmother?—that the truth will set you free. The story she was about to tell was the truth, but would it really free her of the demons that plagued her? The terrible sense of dread she felt wasn't at all like being set free. What if she only made things worse? What if telling damned her forever?

Finally, around four, a slight breeze ruffled the frayed curtain over her bed, and she drifted off. A scarce three hours later, awakened by a recurring nightmare, she staggered out of bed and into the bathroom. When she turned on the water faucet in the lavatory, nothing happened.

"Damn!" she muttered. "What a time to run out of water."

Pulling on a pair of shorts and a T-shirt, she hurried outside into the relative cool of the early morning. The dogs, locked in the straw-bale shed, heard the back door slam and set up a terrific racket. If she was outside, they wanted to be outside, too. She went over and opened the door on the make-do shed where she kept her motley collection of dogs overnight. As soon as the door opened, the dogs cascaded joyfully out into the early-morning sunlight.

As always, Streak, the fleet-footed beagle, led the way, followed by Jasper, a mutt who was more German shepherd than anything else. There was FiFi, the three-legged poodle, followed by Donner and Blitzen, the two malamutes the woman had found as tiny puppies left in a box outside Wal-Mart on Christmas Eve two years ago. Fat Albert, the dachshund, raced through the doorway carrying a ball and wanting her to throw it. Razzle, Yo-Yo, and Pansy, three rescued greyhounds, pranced out daintily, with Yo-Yo stopping long enough for a leisurely stretch and to have his ears scratched. Angel was an ugly, wrinkle-faced chow and Roger a doberman whose ears had been mangled in an amateur attempt at cropping. Mikey, the boxer, gave his owner a slobbery-faced greeting while newcomer Hombre—a black-and-tan hound—sidled shyly past her as if still unsure about whether or not he could trust her.

The older dogs came later. Chief, a collie mix of some kind, had lost several teeth, and Mopsy was a black Lab with a developing hip problem. The Lab had recently given birth to a batch of pups, only one of which had survived. The woman hoped that with money from her upcoming interview, she'd be able to afford to get the dogs not only their shots and licenses, but some veterinary care as well. Lester, a happy-go-lucky black cocker with an age-grizzled muzzle, was virtually blind due to cataracts that had dimmed both his eyes. Expensive canine cataract surgery would far outstrip his owner's meager ability to pay.

Last in line was her favorite, a beloved mongrel

named Oscar, who was evidently the result of an unfortunate mating between a German shepherd and a dachshund. Oscar's large shepherd body tottered around on legs barely six inches tall, but what he lacked in height, Oscar more than made up in love.

Four of the dogs—Chief, Oscar, Roger, and Streak—had been with the woman for years, through a series of dingy apartments and humiliating evictions and, finally, at the very end, before her grandmother had let them come here, the dogs had lived with their owner in her Datsun 710 wagon. That was the wonderful thing about dogs—they loved you no matter who you were or where you lived.

After Oscar emerged, the woman glanced inside the gloomy shed to see if she had missed anyone. She didn't remember having seen Shadow, Mopsy's eight-week-old pup, but she was sure he must have come out with the others. Shutting the door while the dogs wandered off to relieve themselves, the woman turned resolutely toward the pump.

When she first moved in, she had cursed her grandfather for stubbornly continuing to use an old-fashioned rope-pull gasoline-powered pump on the well rather than switching over to an electric one that would have operated automatically or with nothing more than the touch of a switch.

But now that same rope-pull pump, hard as it might be to start sometimes, was a blessing rather than a curse because it continued to work without benefit of electricity. The woman hoped that maybe, after she took care of the dogs, there'd be enough money left over to make up those months of unpaid bills and have her power restored.

The mobile home was parked on three acres just east of the San Pedro River. Sheltered on three sides by mesquite and brush and on the river side by a grove of cottonwoods, it was so isolated that, once the noisy pump had water flowing into the storage tank, the woman had no qualms about bathing outside under an outdoor showerhead her grandfather had installed between the tank and the house. She had finished and was toweling off when the dogs began barking and racing toward the gate.

The woman's heart pounded in sudden panic. Most people weren't pushy enough to drive past the bullet-riddled No Trespassing sign wired to the gate. And, although the two reporters weren't due until eleven—she had told them not to come any sooner than that—she was dismayed to think they might have decided to arrive early.

Dreading seeing them and hoping vaguely for some other stray visitor, she grabbed up her discarded clothing and raced toward the back door, calling to the dogs as she went. Hearing the distress in her voice, the dogs came as one. She stood just inside the door and pulled on her shorts and T-shirt as they bounded past her. Once Oscar, always the slowest, had lunged his way up the wooden steps and into the house, she slammed the door shut behind them.

Even though it was still early, the inside of the house had never cooled off overnight and was already terribly hot. The woman knew that neither she nor the dogs could stay there very long. In order to keep vermin away from the place, she always fed the dogs inside the mobile. Milling around her in the kitchen, that's what they expected now— breakfast. She had planned to feed the dogs and then return them to the relative cool of the tree-shaded shed while she met with the reporters.

But the dogs were oblivious to her uncertainty and concern. They simply wanted to eat, and so she fed them. At first her quaking hands fumbled clumsily as she grabbed for dog dishes and filled them with food, but gradually that simple task had a calming effect. By the time all the dogs were happily munching through their dry food, she rushed into the bathroom to peer at her reflection in the mirror.

She looked at herself so seldom that she was shocked by what she saw. Her face seemed gaunt and pale. There were deep shadows under her eyes from lack of sleep. Her lank, uncombed hair flopped in wet tangles around her face. In other words, she looked like hell. She had desperately wanted to make a good impression on her visitors. Since they had mentioned videotaping the interview, she had hoped to sit in the sun long enough to dry her hair. She had even planned on putting on some makeup, if she still had any, that is.

Now, though, by arriving early—while the dogs were still underfoot and before she could make herself presentable—her visitors had ruined everything. No one would take her seriously if they thought she was nothing more than a madwoman living in a house overrun by a pack of unruly dogs. The reporters would probably take one look at her and write her off as a hopeless nutcase.

She was still staring in the mirror when a car door slammed outside. Streak, always the first to finish eating, abandoned his dish and raced to the front door, barking furiously. Leaving their food uneaten, the other dogs followed suit in a raucous, noisy chorus.

"Quiet," the woman urged. "It's all right."

Milling in excited circles, the agitated dogs paid no attention. The woman waded through them as far as the front window. Tweaking one corner of the curtain, she peeked outside. She recognized the familiar truck as soon as she saw it.

"What are you doing here?" she demanded, without moving toward the door.

The dogs had quieted briefly. At the sound of her voice they resumed barking. "Quiet," she ordered once more. This time the dogs didn't stop. Their deafening barking continued unabated as her unwelcome visitor began pounding on the front door.

"Open up," a voice called from outside. "Let me in. I need to talk to you."

"No. Go away. Leave me alone. Please."

The woman watched spellbound as the front doorknob jiggled. Fortunately the door was locked. She always kept it that way. After a long moment, the jiggling stopped abruptly. Creaking footsteps retreated across the rickety front porch and down the steps. As they started around the side of the mobile, the woman realized in dismay that she had been in such a rush when she came into the house with the dogs that the back door might still be unlocked.

Alarmed, she headed there. Her overly excited dogs impeded her progress at every step. No matter how she tried to maneuver, one or another of them was in her way. She reached the back door just in time—just as that doorknob, too, began to turn. When the door started to open, the woman sprang against it and slammed it shut. First she twisted the small button on the knob that locked the door. Then, for good measure, she shoved home the dead bolt as well.

"Let me **in!**" her visitor complained. "I have to talk to you."

Breathing rapidly, the woman leaned against the door and closed her eyes in relief. "I don't want to talk to you," she retorted. "Go away."

She was still standing just that way when the first of the bullets ripped through the door's thin aluminum shell and slammed into her midsection. The powerful .45-caliber bullet ripped into her flesh and propelled her backward until she came to rest against the flimsy paperboard wall behind her. As the wall collapsed under her weight, another bullet found its mark and pounded into her shoulder. She was already off balance and falling, and the force of the second bullet spun her around so that when she landed she was facedown. Other bullets were fired as well, but they flew harmlessly overhead. The fallen woman wasn't conscious of any of them. All she heard was the sound of her dogs, barking, and barking—trying to protect her. But it was too late for that—much too late.

Sometime later, she came to. Oscar was pressed to her side, whining and licking her face. In the background she heard the other dogs as well, whimpering and whining. Drifting in and out of consciousness, she tried to reach out to pet Oscar, but her right arm was useless. She saw that the dog was covered with blood. At first she thought Oscar had been shot as well, but as soon as she attempted to move, she knew the truth. Wounded, bleeding badly, and in need of help, she was the one who was in trouble.

Using only her left arm and with terrible effort, she inched her way along the linoleum-covered floor, down the hall, through the kitchen and into the living room. All the while the dogs continued to race around her as if trying to understand if this was some new game. The woman knew that the phone was there—in the living room. All she had to do was reach it and dial 911. If she did that, someone would come to help her.

And they would have, too, but the woman never made it that far. She dragged her bleeding body as far as the living room, where the telephone sat on a corner table next to the couch. It was no more than a foot away from her grasping fingers, but it might just as well have been on the moon.

Weakened by loss of blood, she dropped onto the orange shag carpet and didn't move again. Hours passed. Some time later, with her overheated dogs still hovering anxiously around her, the woman died. All through the day, the temperature in the closed mobile home continued to soar. And, with their mistress dead, one after another, the dogs, too, slowly succumbed to the heat.

ONE

Late on Tuesday afternoon, Sheriff Joanna Brady sat at her desk, stared at the pages of her calendar, and knew that Butch Dixon, her husband, was absolutely right. She was overbooked. When he had mentioned it at breakfast that morning, she had done the only reasonable thing and denied it completely.

Coffeepot in hand, Butch had stood looking at the week's worth of calendar he had finally convinced Joanna to copy and tape to the refrigerator door in a vain attempt at keeping track of her comings and goings.

"Two parades on Friday?" he had demanded, studying the two pages of copied calendar entries she had just finished posting. "According to this, the parades are followed by appearances at two community picnics." Butch shook his head. "And you still think you'll be at the fairgrounds in time for Jenny's barrel-racing event, which will probably start right around four? You're nuts, Joey," he concluded after a pause. "Totally round the bend. Or else you've picked up a clone without telling me about it."

"Don't worry," she told him. "I'll be fine."

Butch had poured coffee and said nothing more. Now, though, late in the afternoon and after putting in a full day's work, Joanna studied her marathon schedule and worried that maybe Butch was right. How would she cover all those bases?

The Fourth of July had always been one of Joanna's favorite holidays. She loved going to the parade, hosting or attending a backyard barbecue, and then ending the evening in town watching Bisbee's community fireworks display.

But this wasn't a typical Fourth of July. This was an election year, and Joanna Brady was an active-duty sheriff trying to do her job in the midst of a stiffly contested reelection campaign. Rather than watching a single parade, she was scheduled to participate in two of them—driving her Crown Victoria in Bisbee's parade starting at eleven and in Sierra Vista's, twenty-five miles away, starting at twelve-thirty. She was also slated to appear briefly at two community picnics that day—in Benson and St. David. The day would end with her making a few introductory remarks prior to the annual fireworks display eighty miles from home in Willcox. Stuffed in among all her official duties, she needed to be at the Cochise County fairgrounds outside of Douglas at the stroke of four o'clock.

After years of practicing around a set of barrels positioned around the corral at High Lonesome Ranch, Jennifer Ann Brady had declared that she and her sorrel quarter horse, Kiddo, were ready for their public barrel-racing debut. That Fourth of July would mark Jenny's first-ever competition on the junior rodeo circuit. Joanna's showing up for the barrel-race rodeo had nothing at all to do with politics and everything to do with motherhood.

Be there or be square, Joanna told herself grimly.

Looking away from her calendar, Joanna walked across to the dorm-sized refrigerator Butch had brought back from Costco in Tucson and installed in her office. She retrieved a bottle of water. Taking a thoughtful drink, she stared out the window at the parched hills surrounding the Cochise County Justice Center. The thermometer perched in the shade under the roof of a covered parking stall just outside her office door still hovered around 103 degrees. Summertime temperatures in and around Bisbee seldom exceeded the low nineties, so having the temperature still that hot so late in the afternoon was bound to be a record breaker.

Inside Joanna's office, things weren't much better. The thermostats at all county-owned facilities were now set at a budget/energy-conscious 80 degrees—too warm to think or concentrate. She had a fan in her office, too, but she hated to use it because it tended to blow loose papers all over her desk—and there were always loose papers.

The radio, playing softly behind her desk, switched from music to bottom-of-the-hour news where the weather was a big concern. All of Arizona found itself in the grip of a severe drought and what was, even for July, a fierce heat wave. The radio reporter announced that flights in and out of Phoenix's Sky Harbor airport had been grounded due to concerns that the heat-softened runways might be damaged by planes landing and taking off in the record-breaking 126-degree temperatures. The announcer's running gag about its being a dry heat didn't help Joanna's frame of mind. Bisbee, situated two hundred miles southeast of Phoenix, was a couple of thousand feet higher than Phoenix and more than twenty degrees cooler, but that didn't help, either. Deciding to ignore the weather, Joanna switched off the radio and returned to studying her calendar and its self-inflicted difficulties.

Months earlier, one of her least favorite

deputies, Kenneth W. Galloway, had officially announced his intention to run against her. Bankrolled by a wife with a booming real estate business in Sierra Vista, Ken, Jr., had resigned from Joanna's department within weeks of announcing his candidacy. Minus the burden of a regular job, Galloway had been on the stump ever since. He spent every day on the campaign trail, crisscrossing the county with door-belling efforts and public appearances.

And that was where he had Joanna at a disadvantage. With a department to run, she couldn't afford to doorbell all day long. She had done her share of rubber-chicken banquets and pancake-breakfast speeches for local civic organizations, but she'd had to squeeze them in around her regular duties. Which was why she had said yes to appearing at all those various Fourth of July events. She'd be able to cross paths and shake hands with far more people at those holiday get-togethers than she would have been able to see under ordinary circumstances. But now, at the end of a long day, the prospect of keeping multiple far-flung commitments seemed nothing less than daunting. She wished she had said no more times than she had said yes.

The phone rang. Thinking Kristin would answer it, Joanna let it ring several times before she realized it was a quarter to six. Her secretary,

Kristin Gregovich—a young working mother with both an eight-month-old baby girl and a baby-sitter waiting at home—punched out each afternoon at the stroke of five. Sighing, Joanna picked up the phone.

"Hi, Joey," Butch Dixon said. "How's it going?"

Just hearing her husband's cheerful greeting lifted Joanna's sagging spirits. "My head aches and my feet hurt," she told him. "Other than that, I'm fine."

"So it's off to Sierra Vista?" he asked.

"That's right," she said, reading from the calendar notation. "Seven p.m., Karen Oldsby, **Sierra Vista Tribune**. Interview."

"You don't sound very enthusiastic about it," Butch said.

"I'm not," Joanna agreed. "It's so hot in this office I could scream."

"Couldn't you do the interview by phone?"

"Ms. Oldsby prefers doing interviews in person, but while I'm driving out there I'll turn the air-conditioning on full blast. That way, by the time I get there, I'll have had a chance to cool off. Maybe I'll feel better."

"Do you want me to hold dinner for you?" he asked.

Other husbands might have suggested Joanna cancel the interview and come straight home.

She appreciated the fact that Butch did no such thing. He understood as well as she did that politicking had to be done during off-duty hours, during what should have been considered family time. It was clear to her that it was Butch's backstopping of her—his being at home, doing chores, cooking meals, and looking after Jenny— that made Joanna's run for office possible. It had also given her a new understanding of and respect for her mother, Eleanor Lathrop Winfield, who, years earlier, had supplied the same kind of priceless but unpaid behind-the-scenes labor for Joanna's deceased father, D. H. Lathrop, when he had run for and won the same office Joanna now held. However, Joanna's newfound respect for her mother didn't make the woman any less annoying.

"Joey?" Butch asked. "Are you still there?"

"Yes," she said quickly, embarrassed to have been caught woolgathering. "I'm here."

"You never answered me about dinner."

"Sorry. No, don't bother keeping anything warm. If I'm hungry, I'll grab something on my way to Sierra Vista. Otherwise, I'll dig through the fridge when I get home."

"Or have a bowl of Malt-o-Meal," Butch said, making no effort to mask his disapproval. For years Butch Dixon had run a Phoenix-area restaurant—the Roundhouse Bar and Grill in downtown Peoria. He had hired cooks, but he was also a respectable short-order cook in his own right. Joanna's propensity for coming home late and having a bowl of cereal or cocoa and toast for a supper drove him nuts.

"Drive carefully," he said. "See you when you get here."

"I will," she said. "I love you."

"I love you, too."

In the aftermath of the Twin Towers tragedy, where so many police and fire officers had died, those were words they exchanged without fail every single day. They said the words, and they meant them.

Joanna put down the phone and then scrounged around under her desk for the pair of low heels she had kicked off in the course of the afternoon. Her feet squawked in protest as she tried to slip the shoes back on. Was it possible her feet had grown a full size in a matter of hours? Shaking her head, Joanna limped over to the mirror on the back of the door and did a quick hair and makeup check. Her short red hair would need to be cut soon, and there were deep shadows under her bright green eyes.

I'm a mess, she thought grimly. **And, with my luck, they'll probably want a photo**. After all, the possibility of having her picture taken for the paper was the reason she had chosen to wear a skirt and blazer that morning rather than her uniform. She had wanted to look businesslike and not too official. But that was also **before** she had put in a full day and then some in her anything but cool office at the Cochise County Justice Center.

Joanna had picked up her purse and was on her way to the door when her phone rang again. She hurried back to her desk to answer. "Sheriff Brady."

"Oh, good," dispatcher Tica Romero said. "You're still there. I was afraid you'd already left the office."

"Why?" Joanna said. "What's up?"

"Manny Ruiz is on the line," Tica said. "He's out near the San Pedro and needs assistance. I'm sending him some backup, but I thought you'd want to talk to—"

"Put him through," Joanna said.

Early in the year, the head of Cochise County Animal Control had left the county to take a better-paying job elsewhere. Struggling to come to terms with an out-of-balance budget, the board of supervisors had decided against replacing her. Instead, they had folded the Cochise County Animal Control unit into Joanna's department. Now, in addition to her law enforcement duties, Sheriff Brady was responsible for running the local pound as well. Fortunately, the core members of the Animal Control unit had stayed on when their supervisor left. Joanna may have been less than thrilled with her additional responsibilities, but at least she was supervising a group of people who knew what they were doing.

"What is it, Manny?" she asked when Animal Control Officer Ruiz came on the line.

"Sorry to bother you, Sheriff Brady," Ruiz said. "I'm out off the Charleston Road. You know, where Graveyard Gulch runs into the San Pedro? I came out to check on that hoarder, Carol Mossman. You remember her, don't you? The one with all those dogs? I gave her a citation two weeks ago. But they're dead, Sheriff Brady. All dead."

Manuel Ruiz was usually a very slow talker, known for a ponderous delivery that tended to hold back far more information than it passed along. This time his words tumbled over themselves in a rush.

Joanna did indeed remember Carol Mossman. In the last six months, thirty-seven rabid skunks and three rabid coyotes had been found inside the boundaries of Cochise and Santa Cruz counties. As a result a rabies quarantine was now in effect in those two adjoining southern Arizona jurisdictions. Carol Mossman had come to the attention of Animal Control due to complaints that her loose dogs had been chasing some of her neighbor's horses.

Two weeks earlier, Manny Ruiz had driven out to the Mossman place expecting to find one or two unlicensed and unvaccinated dogs. Instead he had discovered a total of eighteen, most of them confined to a dog-crate-lined straw-bale shed out behind a run-down mobile home. The crates had been shaded by a makeshift roof constructed of discarded lumber and delaminating cast-off doors. When Carol Mossman had been unable to produce valid vaccination records for any of her animals, Officer Ruiz had issued a citation. Yesterday had marked the end of her two-week compliance period. Today he had returned to see if the animals had now been properly licensed.

"The dogs are all dead?" Joanna asked, trying to clarify what Manny Ruiz had said. "Are you telling me she chose euthanasia over licensing?"

"I don't think she chose anything," Manny replied. "I think she's inside the trailer along with all her dogs. I looked in through one of the living room windows. There are dead dogs everywhere and no sign of movement. The door's locked from the inside, and there's a bunch of waist-high bullet holes punched through the back door. In the living room I can see a foot, sticking out from behind the couch, but I can't tell if whoever's there is alive or not. Should I break in to check on her, or what?"

Joanna closed her eyes. If Carol Mossman was

already dead, then it was important not to disturb the crime scene. If, however, there was the smallest chance the woman was still alive, saving an injured woman's life automatically took precedence over preserving evidence.

"Is there another door?" Joanna asked.

"Yeah, the front door. I already checked. It's locked, too."

"Open it if you can," Joanna said. "Break it down if you have to. If Carol Mossman's still alive, call for an ambulance. If she's dead, don't touch anything."

"Yes, ma'am," Manny Ruiz said.

"Call right back and let me know what you find out," Joanna added. "I'll wait here until I hear from you."

As soon as she ended the call, Joanna dredged her calendar out of her purse. She had been scheduled to meet Karen Oldsby at the **Tribune** office on Fry Boulevard at 7 p.m. Whether or not Carol Mossman was dead, what had happened at her mobile home constituted a more compelling demand on Sheriff Joanna Brady's time than a newspaper interview.

Joanna dialed the phone number she had scrawled in the calendar next to Karen Oldsby's name. When a canned, computer-generated voice mail announcement came on, it gave the dialed telephone number only. There was no way for Joanna to tell whether she had dialed the reporter's home or office number. She left a brief message anyway.

"Karen. Sheriff Brady here. There's been a possible homicide out near the San Pedro. I'm sorry, but I won't be able to make our appointment this evening. Please call my office tomorrow and reschedule."

Ducking into the coat closet just inside her back door, Joanna ditched her heels and changed into jeans, a T-shirt, white socks, and tennis shoes. She was finishing tying the second shoelace when the phone rang again.

"She's dead," Manuel Ruiz announced flatly when Joanna answered. "Shot in the belly."

"And the dogs?"

"They're all dead, too," he replied. "I counted seventeen in all. The place was like a goddamned oven. No air-conditioning. The windows were open, but the mobile was sitting in direct sun most of the day. Must be at least a hundred and twenty inside. I'm sure that's what killed the dogs. Heat prostration. Dogs can't take it, you know. Coop 'em up inside a hot building like that or in a car, and it kills 'em every time."

The dead woman may have been Joanna's problem, but the dead dogs were Manny Ruiz's primary concern.

"Are you back in your vehicle?" Joanna asked.

"Yes, ma'am."

"Wait right there," Joanna told him. "I'm on my way."

After putting the phone down, Joanna stared at it for an indecisive moment, then picked it back up and dialed Tica's number.

"Officer Ruiz told you what's up?" Joanna asked.

"Yes."

"So who all's heading to the scene?"

"Detective Carpenter's on call tonight," Tica replied, naming Joanna's lead homicide detective. "Dave Hollicker's on his way. So is Casey Ledford."

With her investigative team—a detective, her crime scene investigator, and her latent fingerprint tech—all en route, Joanna nodded. "What about Doc Winfield?" she asked.

"The ME will be heading out in a couple of minutes," Tica replied.

"Good," Sheriff Brady said. "So am I."

Grabbing her purse, Joanna hurried outside. As she stepped through the door, late-afternoon heat hit her like a physical blow. Her shiny Crown Victoria was parked in a shaded spot right outside her private back-door entrance, but knowing she was headed for a less than perfect road, Joanna bypassed that vehicle. Instead, she vaulted into her much dented but entirely trustworthy four-wheel-drive Blazer. As soon as she started the engine, she turned on the air-conditioning as well, although for the first several minutes the only thing blowing through the vents was nothing but more overheated air.

Pausing for traffic at the entrance to the Justice Center, Joanna searched the sky for some sign of the few stray clouds that had poked their puny tops over the edge of the horizon earlier in the day. Now those wisps of cloud had disappeared entirely, leaving behind not so much as a single drop of moisture. Cochise County old-timers swore the rainy season always started on the Fourth of July, usually just in time to drown out the municipal fireworks display. If that was going to be the case this year, weather conditions would have to change drastically in the course of the next few days. Joanna Brady didn't hold out much hope. The summer monsoon rains would come when they were damned good and ready and not a day before.

Convinced she'd encounter less traffic by going through Tombstone, Joanna headed in that direction. As she drove, her mind began sifting through the officers at her disposal and considered what additional assets she'd need at the crime scene. She clicked on her radio.

"Which deputies from Patrol are en route to the crime scene?"

"Raymond and Howell," Tica Romero replied.

"According to Manny, we've got seventeen dead dogs to handle," Joanna said. "That being the case, we'd better call out Jeannine Phillips, too."

Jeannine Phillips was Joanna's second full-time Animal Control officer. "We're going to need another pair of hands. Tell her to bring along the Animal Control equivalent of body bags. We'll need a bunch of those."

Joanna dreaded what would happen when word of the canine fatalities leaked out. Arizona was a state where it was legal for unrestrained children to ride as passengers in the back of moving pickup trucks, but it was against the law to have an unrestrained dog riding there. Obviously the dog lobby was far more powerful than whoever was supposed to be looking out for little kids. Joanna was convinced that the deaths of seventeen dogs would create far more outrage than Carol Mossman's apparent murder. And, since the deaths had occurred in Joanna's jurisdiction and on her watch, she suspected that any public outrage would be aimed squarely in her direction.

As the miles ticked by, she tried to remember the exact sequence of events in which she had first been made aware of the Mossman situation and what actions she should have or could have taken to prevent this from happening. Manny

Ruiz's initial report had shown up in a mid-June morning briefing.

"What's a hoarder?" she had asked Chief Deputy Frank Montoya.

"Jeannine tells me they're people who are a couple of bubbles out of plumb," Frank replied. "As long as their lives are going along normally, they're fine, but once they go off the tracks, they start 'saving' animals. They usually mean well, but they often end up taking in far more animals than they can care for properly."

"And they don't have them vaccinated," Joanna offered.

"Because they don't take them to see vets," Frank added. "With that many dogs, it's too expensive. Same thing goes for buying decent food."

Joanna had skimmed down Manny Ruiz's report. "It says here that the dogs seem to be well cared for."

Frank nodded. "And when he went by that day, none of the dogs were loose. They were all in their crates in a shed. That's why Manny issued a citation rather than taking the dogs into custody."

"And gave her two weeks to comply," Joanna added.

Which she probably didn't do, Joanna thought.

As she left Tombstone on the Charleston Road and headed west, the glare of the setting sun was blinding. Even with the help of her visor and sunglasses, it was almost impossible to see oncoming traffic.

She crossed the spindly bridge across the San Pedro River—the same river Cortés had followed north in search of the Seven Cities of Gold—and turned right. She knew from Manuel Ruiz's previous report that Carol Mossman's single-wide mobile home was about half a mile north of the intersection. As soon as she turned off, she could see the clutch of vehicles that meant some, if not all, of her officers had already arrived.

Slowing the Blazer, Joanna steeled herself for what was to come. Crime scene investigation wasn't one of her favorite things. As sheriff, she certainly wasn't required to be a part of every homicide investigation. Nonetheless, ever since taking over the helm of the department, she had insisted on being present and accounted for each time a homicide had occurred inside her sixty-four-hundred-square-mile jurisdiction.

Andy, Joanna's first husband, had been a deputy sheriff campaigning for the office of sheriff when he was gunned down by a drug dealer's hit man. Despite Joanna's own lack of law enforcement experience, she had been asked to run for office in his place. To everyone's surprise, including her own, she had been elected by a wide margin in what her detractors called a "sympathy" vote. Those same naysayers had expected her to confine herself to administrative duties only. Instead, in the course of those first few treacherous months in office, she had sent herself off to take police academy training and had made it her business to be personally involved in the process of fighting crime at its most basic and gut-wrenching level. Her active personal involvement in each of her department's homicide cases had gone a long way toward winning her the grudging respect and cooperation of the career police officers under her supervision.

She came to the grim task of homicide investigation with the clear knowledge that every murder affected far more than a single victim. The dead were already beyond help. As someone whose husband had died as a result of violent crime, Joanna was focused on helping to bring closure and comfort to those who were left behind. It was far more than just a job for her. It was a mission—and a calling.

When Joanna arrived at the address, she went in through an open gate and then followed a gravel track until she reached a run-down fourteen-by-seventy mobile home baking in the full heat of the late-afternoon sun. A covered wooden porch had been tacked onto the front of the mobile. Off to one side was a lean-to carport with a dark green Datsun 710 station wagon parked under its sagging roof. Whatever else might have happened here, attempted car theft most likely wasn't part of the program. A chain-link fence separated the mobile and shed from the surrounding desert.

Joanna tucked her Blazer in amid the collection of other official vehicles, identifying each and taking informal attendance. Manny Ruiz's pickup with its cage-laden bed blocked the opening to the carport. Parked nearby were two Ford Econoline vans belonging to Detective Carpenter and Crime Scene Investigator Dave Hollicker, who was already busily casting tire tracks. Casey Ledford's aging but dependable Taurus was parked directly behind the vans. The medical examiner's van was notable by its absence. The only officer visible other than Dave Hollicker was Manny Ruiz. With his head resting on his arms, the Animal Control officer leaned heavily on his pickup's hood.

As Joanna approached, Manny straightened up. Joanna noticed at once that he looked uncommonly pale. "Are you all right?" she asked.

"I've seen gut-shot animals before," he murmured. "But never a person." He broke off.

You get used to it, Joanna thought. "It's pretty bad then?" she asked.

Ruiz nodded. "It's bad, all right. She must've been right in front of the back door when she got hit. There's blood everywhere and a trail of it through the kitchen and into the living room like she was dragging herself along on her belly. I think she musta been trying to get to the phone to call for help. She never made it."

Concerned over Manny's unnatural pallor, Joanna took him by the arm. "Come back and sit with me in the Blazer for a minute," she said. "You don't have any animals stuck in your truck, do you?"

Ruiz shook his head. "Nope. This was my first stop of the day. I was afraid I'd be bringing all of Carol Mossman's dogs back to the pound with me. I wanted to have plenty of room. Even starting out empty, I figured it would still take two trips."

Once Manny Ruiz was seated in the Blazer, Joanna handed him a bottle of water. He drank half of it without pausing for breath.

"And the dogs?" Joanna asked.

"Heat," Manny replied. "If the cooler'd been turned on, the dogs would probably be okay. If they got thirsty, they could have drunk water out of the toilet. And if they'd gotten hungry enough, they could've . . ." He left the sentence go unfinished. Joanna saw where he was headed with that bit of speculation. With an effort she managed to prevent her own mind from completing the image.

Manny took another drink. Polishing off the contents of the bottle with his second gulp, he handed the empty back to Joanna. They were sitting in the front seat of her Blazer with the doors open and the radio chattering in the background. The radio was silent for the space of a moment or two. Suddenly, Manny sat up straight. "Did you hear that?" he demanded.

"Hear what?" Joanna asked, thinking she had missed an important radio transmission.

But Manny Ruiz had already vaulted out of the Blazer. Rumbling along with the gait of an upright grizzly bear, he charged past the mobile home and headed for the river. Once Joanna was outside the car, she heard what he had heard—the unmistakably mournful cry of a bereft puppy. Running to keep up, Joanna followed Manny around the trailer to the jury-rigged hut where Carol Mossman had confined her pack of dogs.

The building was exactly as Manuel Ruiz had described it in his initial report. It was approximately the size of a two-car garage. Walls of straw bales covered with a thin veneer of stucco rose from the ground to a height of about ten feet, at which point the builder ran out of money, patience, or both. The roof consisted of a shaky collection of two-by-fours held up by several interior four-by-four upright posts. On top of the skeleton of two-by-fours lay a collection of scavenged lumber and doors, all of which would have toppled down at the first hint of a monsoon-driven wind.

While Joanna paused long enough to examine the exterior of the building, Manny Ruiz disappeared inside. He emerged a moment later cradling a tiny ball of black fluff in one of his massive fists. "Look here," he announced. "Here's one little guy that made it." He passed the whimpering puppy to Joanna. "And I'll bet he's starved," Manny continued. "I've got some milk in my thermos. If you'll hold on to him for a minute, I'll go get it."

Joanna was still holding the puppy when Dr. George Winfield, the Cochise County Medical Examiner and Joanna's relatively new stepfather, showed up behind her. "Looks like a single survivor was pulled from the wreckage," he observed, peering over her shoulder for a closer look at the squeaking ball of fur still squirming fitfully in Joanna's hands.

"He wasn't in the wreckage," Joanna said. "If he had been, he'd be dead by now, too, right along with the others. Somehow he ended up being left in the shed when all the other dogs went inside the trailer."

"Lucky for him," George said.

And for us, Joanna thought. Crime scenes were usually places of utter desolation, yet here was a little life-affirming miracle, a scrap of hope. She clutched the puppy more tightly and cradled him to her breast.

About then Manny Ruiz showed back up with his thermos. He poured some milk into the cup of the thermos, then he gently removed the puppy from Joanna's grip and held its nose to the milk, which it lapped up hungrily. The puppy may not have been old enough to be weaned, but with his mother likely numbered among the dead dogs inside the mobile home, he was weaned now.

The puppy drank until he seemed ready to pop. He would have drunk more, but Manny took the cup away and poured out what was left. "That's enough, little fella," he said. "You drink any more right now, you'll make yourself sick."

Manuel Ruiz put the puppy down on the ground, where it staggered around in circles for a moment or two, then dropped onto Manny's booted foot and fell sound asleep. The heavyset officer stared down at the puppy with a look of such tender concern on his face that Joanna was almost embarrassed to have seen it. Somehow she had fallen victim to the kind of stereotypical thinking that assumes Animal Control officers don't like animals. Clearly that wasn't the case with Officer Ruiz.

"He is a cute little guy," Doc Winfield agreed. "And I could stand here watching him sleep all day, but I'd better go have a look at my victim. Your detectives will be pissed at me for holding up the show."

He strode off, leaving Joanna and Manny looking down at the puppy. "He's so little, I hate to take him to the pound," Manny said thoughtfully.

Joanna looked at the contented wad of sleeping puppy. It was months now since Jenny's blue-tick hound, Sadie, had succumbed to cancer. Neither Joanna nor Butch had brought up the subject of getting another dog, and Jenny had seemed content to divide her time and attention between Kiddo, her horse, and her remaining dog, Tigger, a comical half pit-bull, half golden-retriever mutt. Now, though, seeing this homeless puppy, Joanna knew this was the right dog at the right time.

"Don't worry about it," Joanna said, reaching down and plucking the sleeping puppy off Manny Ruiz's boot. "Lucky's going home with me."

TWO

Finished making his tire- and footprint casts, Dave Hollicker had disappeared into the mobile home while Joanna spoke to Manny. Now, as the CSI emerged once more, Joanna went to meet him. Dave's face was flushed and his clothing was soaked with sweat.

"What's up?" Joanna asked.

"It's hotter'n hell in there," he said, wiping his streaming forehead. "No electricity, so there's no air-conditioning, and we're losing the light. Doc Winfield's wondering if you have an extra trouble light with you. And where'd you get that cute little puppy?"

The puppy, cradled in Joanna's arm, was still fast asleep. Stuffing the sleeping animal inside her shirt, Joanna fumbled the Blazer keys out of her pocket and handed them over. "Manny found him out in the shed," she explained. "There's a trouble light in the back of the Blazer. Doc Winfield is welcome to it, but what's the matter with the electricity? Can't you replace a fuse or pull a breaker and get the cooler running again?"

Dave shook his head. "We've placed a call to the power company. They told us the juice is turned off due to lack of payment. We've requested that they switch it back on as soon as possible, but they don't seem to be in any particular hurry."

Two more patrol cars and a second Animal Control vehicle drove up. "That'll be Deputies Raymond and Howell," Dave said. "What do you want them to do?"

"The shots came through the back door, right?"

Hollicker nodded.

"And you've done all the footprints?"

"All I could find."

"While it's still light enough, then, have Raymond and Howell start a preliminary foreign-object search," Joanna said.

"Will do."

Jeannine Phillips walked into the yard lugging a large box.

Dave started away, then turned back to the two Animal Control officers. "Doc Winfield also said that he'd like you to remove those dead dogs as soon as possible. There are dog dishes and dead dogs everywhere. The ME needs them out of the way. Since there's so little room to work in, maybe one of you could go inside and ferry the dogs as far as the door. Remember, though, this is a crime scene. Whoever goes inside needs to wear booties and sign in on the crime scene diary."

"I'll go," Manny offered. Wordlessly Jeannine handed him the box with its load of large plastic bags.

During the next half hour, Joanna watched as Manny carted one heavily laden bag after another to the door, where he passed the burden along to Jeannine, who then hauled it out to the waiting trucks. It offended the dog lover in Joanna to see all those dead animals carted off like so much unwanted garbage. Mentally keeping track of the number of trips, Joanna was doubly conscious of the tiny heart of the contentedly sleeping puppy beating a feather-light tattoo against her lower ribs.

Which one of those black bags holds Lucky's mother? she wondered. **And how come he's still alive when all the other dogs are dead?**

Jeannine Phillips was a strapping young woman who had once, as a junior in high school, gone out for boys' football. Bisbee High School's football coach had let her try out for the Pumas' JV team, but a broken leg during a pre-season workout session had put an end to her football-playing ambitions. It had also left her with a slight but permanent limp. After only a year or so of junior college, she had started working Animal Control on a part-time basis and had never left. Now the situation was reversed, however. She worked full-time for Animal Control and was a part-time student at the University of Arizona's satellite campus in Sierra Vista, where she was within twenty or so units of completing her bachelor's degree.

Clearly the situation that afternoon offended Jeannine Phillips every bit as much as it did Joanna Brady.

"This never should have happened," Jeannine grumbled as she returned to collect yet another bag. "If we weren't so damn shorthanded, maybe one of us could have gotten back out here earlier to check on things. Maybe all these dogs wouldn't be dead now."

On her best days Jeannine Phillips was a naturally taciturn loner. On occasion she was downright surly. This time, as far as Joanna was concerned, the woman's complaint and attitude were both entirely understandable, and although Joanna tried not to take the criticism personally, she knew some of it was justified. With all the other demands on her time, Sheriff Brady **was** too busy to give Animal Control the kind of attention it deserved. It was hardly surprising that they viewed themselves as unwelcome stepchildren inside Joanna's department.

As for Jeannine Phillips, she had more grounds

for dissatisfaction on that score than all of her compatriots put together. When the previous head of Animal Control had resigned the position, Jeannine should have been the logical choice for promotion. After all, she had worked in the unit longer than anyone else. She knew the procedures and understood how things were supposed to work. Now, with Joanna's time and attention often focused elsewhere, Jeannine had been forced to assume the unenviable position of unofficial acting manager. As such, she supervised the unit's day-to-day activities without the added credibility of an official title or any additional pay to compensate her for the extra work.

"I was under the impression it was handled properly," Joanna offered. "Manny told me when he came here earlier today, it was at the end of Carol Mossman's two-week compliance period."

"Right," Jeannine muttered. "But if we'd been doing the job we should have been doing, we would have known about this woman a long time ago. Maybe we could have done something to correct the situation long before she had a chance to work herself all the way up to eighteen dogs."

There was no arguing with that. Just then, Manny emerged carrying one last bag. He paused next to Joanna. "This is it, Sheriff Brady," he said. "If you want to go in, it's clear now."

Manny trudged away toward his truck, still

wearing his crime scene booties. Steeling her heart for whatever gruesome sight awaited her inside the overheated mobile home, Joanne went looking for a pair of booties of her own. Before she could put them on, however, a cab drove down the gravel driveway and stopped in front of the gate in the chain-link fence. Moments later, the driver hopped out of the cab, opened the back door, and reached in to help his passenger exit.

While Joanna watched, a pint-size white-haired woman, moving with the aid of a walker, emerged from the backseat. Impatiently shaking off the cabdriver's helping hand, she headed straight for Manny Ruiz, who had just finished loading the final bag into his truck.

"You can't take Carol's dogs away!" she shrieked at the Animal Control officer. Her walker get hung up briefly on a clump of dried grass. For a moment Joanna feared the woman would pitch forward over the handlebars and land on her head. Instead, she righted herself and resumed her tirade.

"Do you hear me, young man? You can't." A moment later she had closed the distance between them. Parking her walker directly in front of the startled Manuel Ruiz, she glared up at him and shook a tiny fist in his face.

"You let those dogs out of that truck right this

minute!" she ordered. "Whatever the fine is, I'll pay it. I have my checkbook right here." Leaning on the walker with one hand, she seized a purse out of the basket on the handlebars and flailed that at him as well. Fortunately for all concerned, Manny dodged out of the way before the purse connected with his chin.

Joanna hurried over to the melee. "Please, ma'am," she said. "Officer Ruiz is just doing his job."

The woman abandoned her attack on Manny Ruiz and rounded on Joanna instead. "His job?" she demanded. "Just because Carol doesn't make enough money to pay expensive vet bills is no reason to come take her pets away. What a heartless, mean-spirited thing to do. She loves those dogs, you see. Loves them and needs them."

"You know Carol Mossman, then?" Joanna asked.

"Know her!" the woman snorted. "Of course I know her! Why wouldn't I? She's my granddaughter, isn't she?" The old lady glowered at Joanna through narrowed eyes. "And who are you?" she demanded. "Another one of these glorified dogcatchers?"

"Hey, lady," the cabdriver called. "How long do you think you'll be? My dispatcher wants to know when I'll be back in Sierra Vista."

Now the woman turned her considerable ire on

him. "You just hold your horses, young man," she snapped. "Can't you see I'm busy? It's going to take however long it takes. I already told you I'll pay for you to hold the cab, so hold it!" She turned back to Joanna. "Now who did you say you are again?"

"I didn't have a chance to say," Joanna said, removing her ID wallet from her hip pocket. "I'm Sheriff Joanna Brady. These are my two Animal Control officers, Jeannine Phillips and Manuel Ruiz."

The woman glanced briefly at Joanna's ID and then handed it back. "Since when is the sheriff in charge of the dog pound?" she demanded. "I should think, as sheriff, you'd have far more important things to do. And since when does it take this many people to pick up a few dogs? But as long as you're here, maybe you can help me get them to let Carol's dogs loose. As I tried to explain to this officer here, I've come with my checkbook. However much the fine is, I'm willing to pay it."

"And your name is?" Joanna asked.

"Mossman. Edith Mossman."

"That's my car right over there," Joanna suggested, pointing toward the parked Blazer. "Maybe we should go sit in it for a few minutes."

"Sit in it?" Edith demanded. "What do you mean, sit in it? Are you placing me under arrest, is that it? Is it illegal for me to try to get my granddaughter's property back? Or are you implying that I hurt that officer in any way? I never touched you, now did I? In fact, I never laid a glove on you."

Manny Ruiz nodded warily but maintained a discreet distance.

"I'm not placing you under arrest," Joanna continued quickly. "Not at all. I just thought you might be more comfortable sitting down while we talked."

"I'm perfectly comfortable standing right here," Edith Mossman insisted. "And I'll be even more comfortable once Mr. Dogcatcher here lets those poor dogs out of his truck. It's inhumane to have them locked up like that on such a miserably hot day. I can't see that there's anything else to discuss."

"Mrs. Mossman," Joanna said gently. "I'm sorry to have to say this, but there's something I must tell you. We're here this afternoon because this is a homicide scene."

Edith Mossman frowned as though she hadn't quite understood the word. "Homicide?" she repeated. "You mean someone's dead?"

"Yes," Joanna said quietly. "Inside the mobile home."

"In Carol's mobile home?"

Joanna nodded. Edith Mossman pointed her

thumb in Manny's direction. "What's he doing here, then?"

"He came to pick up the dogs," Joanna said with a sigh. "They're dead, too, Mrs. Mossman. Except for one, they were all locked inside the trailer with no air-conditioning and no water . . ."

"Are you telling me Carol's dead? My sweet little Carol?"

"I'm so sorry," Joanna said, "but, yes. We're quite certain she's the one who's dead. Officer Ruiz here had encountered your granddaughter before and knew her on sight."

All the spunk and fight drained out of Edith Mossman. Her grip on the handlebars of her walker went flaccid while her eyes rolled up into the back of her head. Seeing her knees crumple, Manny Ruiz leaped forward. He caught the unconscious woman before she could fall to the ground. He lifted her waist-high as easily as he had carried the dead dogs.

"Where to, Sheriff Brady?" he asked.

"To the Blazer," Joanna said. "Put her in the backseat. Jeannine, quick. Bring some water."

Edith was out cold for only a matter of seconds, but the momentary fainting spell seemed to last forever—long enough for Joanna to wonder if the woman had suffered a heart attack or stroke. But by the time Manny Ruiz deposited

Edith in the Blazer the stricken woman had regained consciousness and was struggling to sit
up. Impatiently she pushed aside Jeannine's
proffered bottle of water.

"I have to see her," Edith sputtered, struggling
to clamber back out of the vehicle. "I have to see
Carol. Take me to her."

"That's not possible at this time," Joanna said.
"It's a crime scene, Mrs. Mossman. Other than
the investigators, no one's allowed inside until
they and Dr. Winfield finish their on-site work."

"You mean there's a doctor in there with her?"
Edith demanded. "Maybe he can help her.
Maybe she'll be all right then."

Joanna shook her head. "He's not that kind of
doctor, Mrs. Mossman. Doc Winfield is the
Cochise County Medical Examiner. It might be
best if you went home and waited for them to
finish up inside. At that point, we will need a
family member to make a positive identification,
but there's no sense in your waiting around here.
It could take hours."

"I don't care how long it takes," Edith announced. "I'll wait. I can do the identification
here, can't I?"

"Yes, I suppose you can. But as I told you,
there's no telling how long this will take."

"Can you have someone take me back to Sierra
Vista afterward?"

Joanna nodded. "I suppose so, but . . ."

"Call that cabdriver over here, then," Edith said. "I'll pay the man off and send him on his way. It's already cost me a fortune."

The cabdriver was reluctant to leave his cab in answer to Edith Mossman's summons. His frame of mind wasn't greatly improved by the size of the tip she placed in his hand as she dismissed him. "You said your dispatcher wanted you back, didn't you?" Edith inquired.

"Right."

"So get going then," Edith told him. Shaking his head, the cabbie stalked off.

"Do you need anything else at this time, Sheriff Brady?" Manny Ruiz asked. "It's hot. We should take care of these animals as soon as possible."

"Did Doc Winfield say he wanted to run any further tests on them?"

"No, ma'am. It had to be more than a hundred and twenty degrees in there when I found them. He's sure the heat is what killed them."

"You and Jeannine go ahead then, Manny," Joanna said. "Thanks for all your help."

Nodding, Manny walked away. Meanwhile, Edith Mossman had listened to this entire exchange with avid interest. "Is that what killed Carol too, then?" she asked. "The heat?"

"No," Joanna said. "The information I have says she was shot."

Edith took this news in silence. Moments later, the two Animal Control trucks drove away, taking their tragic loads with them. About the same time Lucky stirred restlessly inside Joanna's shirt.

"What's that?" Edith asked, catching sight of the movement.

Guiltily, Joanna removed the squirming puppy and placed him on the ground. He waddled around sleepily for a little while before peeing. After that, he curled up again on a clump of grass and went right back to sleep.

"One of Carol's?"

Joanna nodded. "He's too young to go to the pound. I decided to take him home with me instead, but of course, if you'd like to have him . . ."

"Oh, no," Edith said. "Not me. I'm far too old for a puppy. I've always been more of a cat person than a dog person, but it doesn't matter either way. I can't have pets at Ferndale anyway. They don't allow pets of any kind."

"Ferndale?" Joanna asked.

"Yes. It's one of those assisted-living places. On Fry Boulevard. Used to be a motel back in the old days, but they changed it a couple of years ago. Remodeled it. Now it's where I live. Number 261. It's nothing fancy, but it's plenty good enough for me. The food's nothing to write home about, but the price is right."

Joanna removed a notebook from her pocket. "I'm sure my detectives will need to speak to you eventually, Mrs. Mossman. If you could give me the address and phone number—"

"Oh, for Pete's sake. Call me Edith. I can't stand all this Mrs. Mossman stuff. And whatever happened to the water that dogcatcher lady was trying to give me? I didn't want it then, but I do now. I'm parched."

Joanna retrieved the bottle of water from where Jeannine Phillips had left it on the front floorboard. She handed the bottle over to Edith Mossman, who took a long, grateful drink. When she had finished, she sighed and stared long and hard at the partially empty bottle as though hoping to find answers there.

"Tell me about your granddaughter," Joanna said quietly.

"Carol?" Edith Mossman asked, taking another drink. "What do you want to know?"

"Was she ever married? Does she have children?"

"No children," Edith said. "Only dogs."

"Boyfriend?"

"Not that I know of. If she had one, she never mentioned him to me."

"Did she work?"

"Oh, she worked all right. It took a while, but she finally got a job clerking at that new Shell station out on Highway 92. Didn't make enough

money to make ends meet. Barely enough to pay
for gas and dog food most of the time. If she'd
had to pay rent on this place, I'm sure she would
have starved to death and her dogs right along
with her."

"She evidently didn't pay the electric bill,"
Joanna observed. "That's why the house was so
hot. No electricity, so no cooler."

"I'm not surprised," Edith said. "She's not the
kind of person to ask for help unless things are
really tough. If I'd known things were that bad, I
would have helped her."

"I'm sure you would have," Joanna agreed.
"But you're saying she lived here rent-free?"

"That's right." Edith was indignant. "You
don't think I'd charge rent to my own flesh and
blood, do you? What kind of a person do you
think I am, Sheriff Brady? I wouldn't do any
such thing!"

"This is your place then?"

"Yes. It's mine until I die. Then it goes to the
Nature Conservancy. When Grady and I—Grady
was my husband, you see. We first bought
acreage and the trailer back in the mid-seventies.
When we lived in it, that trailer was neat as a pin.
Clean, too. Carol's not big on cleaning. I think
she worries way more about the dog runs and
crates than she does the house itself. The last I
saw of the inside, the place was a pigsty. That's

when I decided I wasn't coming back. At least I stopped going inside. Couldn't stand to see it that way. Made me want to haul out a mop and a dust rag and go to work."

"But you did come by today," Joanna said.

"Well, of course. Carol asked me to because she needed help."

"What with?"

"With her dogs, what else?" Edith asked with a resigned shrug. "She never said a word about her electricity bill, but she wasn't too proud to ask for help with the dogs. She said she needed to get them all vaccinated and licensed. The problem is, I wanted to wait until after the first of the month—until after my Social Security check was in the bank. If I had known she was really desperate, I could have done something sooner, but it would have meant cashing in one of the CDs. I didn't want to do that if I didn't have to. Grady wouldn't have approved, you see. He was always warning me about that. 'Now, Edie,' he'd say, 'you watch your money. Whatever you do, you don't want to outlive your money.' And he's right about that. I've seen what happens when people do—outlive their money, that is. It's hell. For everybody."

"So Carol asked you for help with the Animal Control situation?"

Edith Mossman nodded. "She said she wouldn't

be able to get them all licensed and still keep her head above water. Must have been close to two weeks ago now when she dropped by my place to talk to me about it. I can see now, I should have come quicker. It makes me sick to think that just by dipping into one of my CDs I could have prevented all this. I'm sure it's all my fault."

For the first time, the old woman struggled to find words. Tears sprang to her eyes. It was as though, for the first time, the awfulness of the situation was finally sinking in.

"Believe me," Joanna assured her, "it's not your fault."

Edith's lower lip trembled. "Is it a suicide?" she asked softly.

Joanna shook her head. "As I understand it," she said, "one or more shots were fired through the back door while your granddaughter was standing in front of it. All the dogs, with the exception of Lucky here, were locked inside with her."

"When did it happen?" Edith asked.

"We don't know," Joanna replied. "At least not at this time. That's one of the things the medical examiner will be working on—establishing time of death."

"She didn't go to work today," Edith volunteered. "I know that much. I was planning to go by the gas station and take her my check. Since I have to hire a cab to go anywhere, seeing her at work in town would have been a lot easier than coming all the way out here. But when I called to talk to her, her boss said she had taken today off for an appointment of some kind." Edith Mossman paused. "Remind me to call him. I need to let him know what's happened."

Joanna knew that any useful information she could gather now would offer a needed assist for her detectives later on. "If you'll give me Carol's work number and the name of her supervisor," Joanna said, "someone from my department will be glad to take care of that for you."

"Thank you," Edith said. "Thanks so much. That'll be one less thing for me to worry about anyway."

"Would you be considered her next of kin, then?" Joanna asked, after jotting down the information. "Is there anyone else who should be notified—parents, perhaps? Brothers or sisters?"

"Carol's mother is dead," Edith said curtly.

"And her father?" Joanna prodded.

"I can't tell you for sure if my son is dead or alive," Edith Mossman said. "If Edward is still alive, I have no idea where to find the son of a bitch. And I'll tell you this. If he is dead, I'd be first in line to piss on his grave."

The utter fury in Edith Mossman's voice when

she spoke of her son took Joanna's breath away. She considered asking more about him but changed her mind, contenting herself, instead, to making a note of Edith's reaction in her notebook.

"What about siblings?" Joanna asked.

"Three sisters," Edith answered. "You maybe know Stella Adams. She and her family live in Bisbee. Down in Warren, actually, at the far end of Arizona Street. Andrea lives in Tucson. She's not married. She works at the U of A as a secretary in the Chemistry Department. Kelly is still in Mexico, down in Obregón. I doubt you'll be able to get in touch with her there. I'm not even sure if she has a phone, and she most likely won't be coming home for the funeral."

"In other words, she and Carol weren't close."

The rheumy eyes Edith Mossman turned on Joanna were filled with a terrible sadness. "Yes," she said. "I guess you can say Carol and Kelly aren't the least bit close. Besides, Carol preferred dogs to people."

Just then Joanna caught sight of a group of people emerging from the trailer. "If you'll excuse me a moment, Edith, I'll go see how we're doing."

Scooping up the puppy and stowing him back inside her shirt, Joanna hurried over to the small wooden porch that had been built outside the mobile home's front door. The sun had long since disappeared behind the Huachuca Mountains. It wasn't quite nighttime yet, but it would be soon. In the deepening twilight, the entire investigative team stood on the porch, swilling down bottled water. From the looks of the sweat-drenched crew, Joanna was grateful she'd been standing outside, in the relative cool of evening, interviewing Edith Mossman. Clearly, the tough duty was happening inside.

"How's it going?" she asked.

"Hotter'n hell in there," Ernie Carpenter muttered, echoing Dave Hollicker's earlier sentiments. He nodded in the direction of Joanna's Blazer. "Who's the old lady?" he added.

"Edith Mossman," Joanna told him. "Carol Mossman's grandmother."

"Good work," George Winfield said, inserting himself into the previously two-way conversation. "At least I won't have to knock myself out trying to locate the next of kin. But what's she doing here? Who called her?"

"Nobody," Joanna answered. "She came to see Carol without knowing anything was wrong. I tried to get her to go home. She says she's waiting for you to finish up so she can do the identification."

George frowned. "It's really bad in there, Joanna," he said, while Dave Hollicker nodded in somber agreement. "No way the grandmother should see the inside of that house. Can't you talk her out of it?"

"Like I said," Joanna told him, "I've tried, but I haven't made any progress so far."

The medical examiner glanced toward the darkening sky. "We'll probably finish up in another fifteen or twenty minutes," he said at last. "I still think it's a bad idea to do this here, but we'll put the victim in a body bag and bring her out on a gurney so Granny can take a look."

Joanna's cell phone rang just then. Seeing her home number in the screen, Joanna excused herself and walked a few feet away before she answered.

"Where the hell are you?" Butch Dixon demanded. "I've been scared to death."

"What do you mean, where am I? I'm at a crime scene. There's been a murder out by the San Pedro."

"What about your interview with Karen Oldsby?" Butch responded. "She called here a few minutes ago, mad as a wet hen and wondering where you were. She's been sitting in her office for over an hour waiting for you to show up. I told her I'd try to track you down if I could and have you call her back right away."

"Butch, I did call Karen Oldsby," Joanna interjected. "I called even before I left the office to come here. I said in the message that I'd been called to investigate a possible homicide and that she'd need to call tomorrow to set up another appointment."

"The mood she's in right now, I suspect that wouldn't be such a good idea. If Karen Oldsby does the interview at all, she's likely to tear you to pieces."

"Give me her number again," Joanna said. "I'll call and explain."

Karen Oldsby answered after only one ring. "Oldsby here."

"Karen, this is Joanna Brady. I'm so sorry about the misunderstanding—"

"There wasn't any misunderstanding. The appointment was for seven o'clock, right here in my office. I couldn't have been more specific about that."

Joanna could tell from the reporter's tone of voice that Butch was right. Karen Oldsby was pissed.

"As I told you in my message," Joanna said, "something came up. There's been another homicide and—"

"I didn't get any message," Karen interrupted.

"But I called and left one," Joanna said. "I left it on voice mail."

"Not here, you didn't," the reporter replied, sounding less than mollified. "Or if you did, it isn't here now. Where did you leave it? Was it on this number or the one at home?"

Joanna had been carrying her purse with her the whole time she'd been at the scene. Now, holding the tiny phone against her left shoulder, she struggled to reclaim her calendar from the depths of the bag. Once she'd dug it out, she had to walk all the way back to the Blazer and turn on the reading light before she could make out the numbers she had scribbled down next to Karen Oldsby's name. She read them into the phone.

"That's not my number," Karen announced brusquely when she heard it. "You reversed two of the numbers."

"I'm so sorry about this," Joanna said. "Things have been really hectic. I must have been suffering from momentary dyslexia and written them down wrong, but I have my calendar right here with me. If we could go ahead and reset—"

"I'll let you know," Karen Oldsby interrupted. "My week is pretty hectic, too. If it looks like I'll have time to schedule another interview, Sheriff Brady, I'll be in touch. But since we've already missed this week's deadline, I don't know when we'll be able to squeeze you in."

With that, Karen Oldsby hung up. Brimming with indignation, Joanna stuffed her calendar back into her purse. Then she walked far enough away to be out of Edith Mossman's earshot before she redialed her home number.

"Oldsby just hung up on me," Joanna told Butch when he answered. "I evidently wrote her number down wrong, so when I called and left my message, she didn't get it. I tried to apologize, but the woman acted like I committed a federal offense."

"Don't worry about it, Joey," he said. "She'll get over it eventually, but tell me. Who's dead?"

"A woman named Carol Mossman. Her place is out here by the river, just off the Charleston Road. George is inside. The victim's grandmother and I are waiting for him to bring the body out so she can make the formal ID. After that, I'll need to drop her off at her assisted-living facility in Sierra Vista on my way home."

"Can't someone else to drop her off?" Butch asked. "Think about it, Joey. It's late. You've already put in a full day at the office. When are you going to give yourself a break?"

"When Edith let her cab go, I told her I'd see to it that she got home," Joanna told him. "And I will. It won't take that long."

"Suit yourself," Butch said. "I'll see you when you get here." Then he, too, hung up.

Exasperated by what felt distinctly like two separate dressing-downs, Joanna turned her phone's ringer on "silent" and stuck it in her pocket. If anyone else called, she didn't want to talk to them. They could damn well talk to her machine.

After all, Carol Mossman had been murdered. Finding her killer was far more important than chatting on a cell phone.

THREE

While Joanna had been juggling phone calls, Deputy Raymond had removed a gurney from the back of George Winfield's van. Now, unfolded, it sat outside the front door of the mobile home waiting to be taken inside and loaded.

"They'll be bringing the victim out soon and taking her over to the ME's van," Joanna told Edith Mossman. "Do you think you could walk that far, or should I have them bring her over here?"

"I may have to use a walker, but I'm not helpless," Edith said. "I'm perfectly capable of walking from here to there."

As Joanna and Edith started their slow progress toward George Winfield's minivan, Deputy Raymond pushed the gurney into the house. By the time Joanna had guided Edith to the back of the van, Matt Raymond and Debra Howell had rolled the gurney back out through the front door and eased it down the wooden steps. They headed for the van with the medical examiner close on their heels. Once the gurney came to a stop, George Winfield stepped forward and held out his hand to Edith.

"I'm Dr. George Winfield," he said. "I don't believe we've been introduced."

"My name's Edith," she answered. "Edith Mossman. Carol's my granddaughter."

"If you don't want to do this here . . ." he began.

"No. There's no sense in putting it off," Edith replied. "I need to know for sure, and so do you."

"Deputy Raymond," George said, "would you please bring one of the trouble lights out here?"

Nodding, Matt Raymond hurried into the trailer. Back beside the gurney, he held the light aloft while George unzipped the body bag, immediately letting loose the foul stench of rapidly decomposing human flesh.

Joanna knew what to expect. She looked warily at Edith Mossman, worried that the awful odor, combined with seeing her granddaughter's dead face, might cause the woman to faint again, but she didn't. Leaning on her walker, Edith studied the face for a moment. Then she nodded.

"It's her," she said. "It's Carol." With that, she turned to Joanna. "If that's all you need, Sheriff Brady, I'd like to go home now. There are people I'll need to call."

After helping Edith Mossman into the Blazer, Joanna hurried back to the mobile home. Not wanting to have to go through the booties routine, she called Detective Carpenter over to the door and gave him a rundown of the information she had gleaned from talking to Edith.

"Did Deputy Raymond tell you he found several pieces of .45-caliber brass in the backyard?"

"No," Joanna said. "He didn't tell me, but I'm glad to hear it."

"Me, too," Ernie Carpenter said. "It's a start, but he and Debbie Howell didn't have time to do a complete foreign-object search. We'll have to continue that tomorrow."

Joanna nodded. "You'll leave someone here to secure the scene when you go?"

"You can count on it," Ernie said.

Joanna and Edith Mossman drove into Sierra Vista in virtually unbroken silence. The day's trauma had exhausted the old woman's energy, leaving her devoid of speech. Twice Joanna glanced at her passenger, thinking she might be asleep, but Edith was wide awake, staring straight ahead into the beams of oncoming headlights.

By the time they arrived at the Ferndale Retirement Center, Lucky was eager to extricate himself from the confines of Joanna's shirt. In his eagerness to escape, his tiny sharp claws left long trails of scratches in the skin of Joanna's chest. After Edith had limped off down the open breezeway to her unit, Joanna took the puppy out, gave him a drink of water, and let him relieve himself once more. She was grateful that he made no effort to run away.

This time, though, when Joanna tried to return him to her shirt, Lucky was in no mood to be locked back up. He had slept long enough. He was ready to be up and exploring—or chewing. Reluctant to let him loose in the Blazer while she drove, Joanna finally emptied the contents out of one of the plastic carrying cases she used to hold equipment. She moved the plastic carton to the front seat and put Lucky inside that. Standing on his hind legs, he was tall enough to peek out over the edge, but not quite tall enough to scramble out.

It was only as Joanna pulled out of the retirement center's parking lot that she realized she had failed to mention anything at all to Butch about bringing home a puppy. Now, as she headed home, she wished she had given her husband some advance warning.

"Well, sport," she said aloud to Lucky, "you'll probably go over like a pregnant pole-vaulter."

Which immediately brought her to another problem, one she'd been deliberately dodging all day long. Was she or wasn't she? For someone whose menstrual cycles were as regular as clockwork, Joanna Brady was now a whole week late. She hadn't worried about it much for the first couple of days. After all, she was on the Pill, wasn't she? She took one of those every morning right along with the vitamins Butch dished out. But a whole week?

Joanna and Butch had discussed having a child someday, but they had both agreed that now was too soon. They had wanted time to settle into being a married couple. So why exactly had Joanna waited this long to tell him about her suspicions? Was it because she wanted to know for sure before she mentioned it, or was it because she was just a tiny bit worried about how he might react? Was Butch's saying he wanted a baby the same as **really** wanting a baby? During the course of the week, Joanna had examined her own varied reactions to the possible pregnancy. She had determined that she was both scared and exhilarated. Worried and happy. Concerned and thrilled.

But what if Butch's feelings were far more one-sided than hers? What if his reaction was totally negative? What if he turned out to be scared, worried, and concerned without being exhilarated, happy, and thrilled? Joanna wondered if she would be able to look at his face when she gave him such earth-shattering news and know what was **really** going on inside that thick skull of his.

And what would Jenny think once she heard she was going to be joined by a baby brother or sister? She was thirteen and about to enter eighth grade. Joanna was afraid Jenny would be mortified when she found out. After all, what better proof could one have that her parents were actually "doing it" than being presented with the inarguable reality of a baby? Joanna knew that at thirteen she wouldn't have wanted to see either of her parents as a sexual being, so why would Jenny? Even now, as a married adult, she found it difficult to see her mother, Eleanor, making goo-goo eyes at her relatively new husband, George Winfield.

Then, of course, Joanna had her job to think about. Butch had told her early on that if they ever did have a baby, he'd be more than happy to stay home and take care of it. His first novel remained unsold, but he was convinced he could work on a second or third and look after a baby at the same time. Joanna had to acknowledge that Butch was a pretty capable guy. It was more than likely that he'd do a great job of being a stay-at-home father to a newborn. After all, he had negotiated the dicey minefield of stepparenting Jenny with little apparent difficulty. Still, Joanna remembered what it had been like having a newborn baby in the house. She wondered if Butch had a realistic idea of the nitty-gritty involved.

And what about the people of Cochise County, the ones who had elected Joanna three and a half years ago? Would they go for having a sheriff whose newborn baby was being cared for by a stay-at-home father? Outside the metropolitan areas, Arizona voters were a pretty staid and conservative bunch. Could they be persuaded to vote for a sheriff's candidate who was already four or five months pregnant on election day? What if she kept it quiet? Wouldn't it be dishonest to get herself elected without telling her constituents what was really going on? Didn't the voters have the right to know a candidate was pregnant before they marked their ballots one way or the other? Election rules obliged Joanna to fill out any number of financial disclosure forms. Shouldn't she also be obliged to disclose this?

Lost in thought, Joanna turned off Highway 80 onto High Lonesome Road. Then, without thinking, she automatically turned into the driveway that led to High Lonesome Ranch—the old driveway to the old house, the one where she used to live, rather than the new driveway a mile up the road that led to the new house on what had once been Clayton Rhodes's place. Joanna Brady and Butch Dixon's new rammed-earth house had been completed two months earlier. They had lived in it now for almost a month and a half. It was a sign of how distracted Joanna was that she made the wrong turn.

You'd better get a grip, she told herself sternly.

Their old house had a detached garage. The new one had attached garages—two of them, his and hers. Joanna could open the garage door with a wireless remote control and then walk from the car into the laundry room without ever having to set foot outside. Butch had installed a weapons safe next to the laundry room door so she could remove her two Glocks and put them away without bringing them into the house proper. Butch had designed the whole project, down to the tiniest detail. Every part of it had been done with utter practicality and convenience in mind.

And with a new puppy around, Joanna thought as she took the time to remove her weapons, **it's a good thing we have mostly Saltillo tile on the floors rather than carpet.**

Prepared for the worst, she went back to the Blazer, retrieved the puppy-laden carton, and headed into the house. Butch sat at the kitchen counter, laboring over his laptop. There was an office in the house—a spacious, nicely furnished office off the dining room, but that was used mostly as Joanna's at-home office. Butch preferred to work in the kitchen, where he could write and keep tabs on the laundry and the progress of dinner at the same time.

He looked up from the screen when she came in. "What's this?" he asked, spying the carton. "Surely you didn't bring home more work to do—" He broke off in midsentence when Lucky poked his tiny black nose up over the edge of the box. Butch's jaw dropped. "Don't tell me you brought home a puppy!"

"I couldn't help it," Joanna explained quickly. "The woman who was murdered had a whole bunch of dogs, including Lucky's mother . . ."

"You've already named him?" Butch asked. "That sounds a whole lot like we're keeping him."

"Lucky's the only survivor—the other dogs all died, Butch," Joanna told him. "They were locked in an overheated mobile home with Carol Mossman. We think the heat did them in."

"Which is why he's Lucky, I suppose," Butch said, reaching out and lifting the squirming black fuzz of a dog out of the box.

"By the way, where's Tigger?" Joanna asked, suddenly worried how their resident half pit-bull, half golden retriever mutt might react to the interloper's presence.

"In Jenny's room," Butch replied, stroking the puppy's ears. "She has tennis in the morning, so she and Tigger went to bed early. Has this little guy eaten, by the way?"

"Not recently," Joanna answered. "He had some milk earlier this afternoon."

"We're a bit shy on Puppy Chow at the moment," Butch said. "And he's way too little for Dog Chow, so let's see what we can do."

With that, Butch handed Lucky over to Joanna and went prowling in the refrigerator. He returned with a half gallon of milk and some bread, which he crumbled into a cereal bowl. Then he poured milk over it and set the concoction down on the floor in front of the famished puppy, who stepped into it with both front feet.

"That's one thing I love about you," Joanna said softly as they both stood watching the puppy eagerly lap up his milk and bread. "You're totally unflappable."

"I like to think I try," Butch said modestly.

"What say we go for broke, then?" she asked, gathering her courage.

"Wait a minute," he said. "What are you saying? Is there another puppy out in the car that you haven't brought in yet?"

"Not exactly."

"What then, exactly?" Butch prodded.

Joanna took a deep breath. "What if I told you I might be pregnant?"

"Pregnant? You're kidding!"

"No. I'm not kidding. I'm late. Over a week now."

"Are you sure?"

"No, I'm not sure. I mean, I'm sure I'm late,

but I'm not remotely sure if I'm pregnant. It's possible, though."

Suddenly, Lucky was forgotten. Grinning from ear to ear, Butch grabbed Joanna by the waist and swung her around the kitchen in a series of circles. "Joey, this is wonderful news. It's great! I can hardly wait to find out for sure. What time is it?"

"It's nine o'clock. Why?"

"What time does Safeway close?"

"I don't know—nine or maybe ten. Why?"

"Let's go right now and get a pregnancy test. You can buy them over the counter, can't you? I mean, you don't need a prescription or anything, do you?"

"I don't think so," Joanna told him. "But can't it wait until tomorrow?"

Butch shook his head. "No, ma'am. If I'm going to be a father, I want to know it now, not later. Besides," he added with a grin, "we need Puppy Chow anyway. Now, are you and Lucky coming along, or are the two of you staying here?"

In the end, Lucky and Joanna rode along while Butch drove like a maniac. Two hours later, they were lying in bed side by side, giddy and sleepless. "A father," Butch murmured over and over. "I'm going to be a father. I never thought it would happen to me."

Joanna lay beside him as he rambled on and

thought how different this was from when she'd told Andy she was pregnant with Jenny. They'd been at the drive-in theater on Alvernon in Tucson and to this day she had no idea what movie they had gone to see because she had blurted out the news without even waiting for the show to begin. Where Butch was almost delirious with happiness at the news, Andy had been resolved—maybe even resigned. Of course he would marry her. Of course he would do the right thing. But for years, there had always been that nagging little question in Joanna's mind. And, although they had never discussed it, maybe the same question had plagued Andy as well. Would Joann Lee Lathrop and Andrew Roy Brady have married if she **hadn't** been pregnant? Or would they have broken up eventually and lived entirely different lives?

But they hadn't, and thirteen-year-old Jennifer Ann Brady was very much a part of this new equation.

"We should tell Jenny in the morning," Joanna said. "First thing. We don't want her thinking we've been sneaking around, keeping secrets."

"Right," Butch agreed. "We'll tell her at breakfast."

"I thought you said she had tennis early."

"We'll get up even earlier. And, in that case, we'd better try to get some sleep."

And they might have slept. It's possible they

could have slept, except right then, as soon as they stopped talking, Lucky, confined to his bedside carton, set up a mournful wail—the same keening cry that had summoned Manny Ruiz earlier that evening. Within seconds Tigger, at the far end of the hall, began barking his head off and throwing himself against the door to Jenny's bedroom.

Butch sighed. "Well," he said, hopping out of bed, "I suppose we'd better get used to it."

Joanna turned on the bedside lamp. Butch had just grabbed Lucky up and was trying to quiet him when Jenny began pounding on their bedroom door. "What's going on in there?" she demanded. "What's that awful noise? Tigger's having a fit. He woke me up."

Holding the puppy, Butch jumped back into bed and snuggled Lucky under the covers. "All right," Butch said. "You can come in, Jen, but you'd better leave Tigger in the hall."

"How come?"

"Because. Trust me."

Moments later, a pajama-clad Jenny was in their bedroom, looking more than a little cross. "What's going on?" she asked indignantly.

Standing with her hands on her hips and with a disapproving frown on her face, Jenny looked like a miniature Eleanor Lathrop Winfield. **And sounds like her, too,** Joanna realized in dismay.

In answer to Jenny's question, Butch pulled the

wiggling Lucky out from under the covers and held him up in the air. Jenny's blue eyes widened in delight, then she vaulted onto the bed between Butch and Joanna.

"He's so cute!" Jenny exclaimed breathlessly. "Where did you get him? Is he ours? Can we keep him? What's his name? Can I hold him?"

In answer to the barrage of questions, Butch simply handed Lucky over to Jenny. The puppy scrambled up her bare shoulder and buried his nose in her long blond hair.

"His name is Lucky," Butch replied. "And we will keep him—if you can keep Tigger from eating him, that is."

"Tigger won't eat him," Jenny declared. "He'll be fine, I know he will be. Should I let him in now, so we can introduce them?"

"I don't think so," Butch said. "Not right now."

"Why not?"

Taking a deep breath, Butch looked from Jenny back to Joanna. "Because," he said finally, "I think your mother has something important to tell you."

Joanna was already in her office and at her computer when Chief Deputy Frank Montoya came in for the morning briefing.

"What's up?" he asked, placing a sheaf of papers on Joanna's polished wood desk and taking a seat in one of the captain's chairs.

"What do you mean, 'What's up'?"

"Don't play innocent with me, Sheriff Brady. You look like the cat that swallowed the canary."

Joanna got up, walked over to the door that led to the interior lobby and Kristin's desk, and pulled it shut.

"I guess I did, in a manner of speaking," she said. "Swallow the canary, that is."

Frank seemed mystified. Joanna sat back down and looked at him across her desk. "I'm pregnant, Frank."

"Whoa! Are you sure?"

"Yes, I'm sure. I took a pregnancy test last night, and I'm definitely pregnant."

Frank's face broke into a grin. "Well, congratulations, then. That's big news!"

"I'll say." Joanna grinned back at him.

"So who knows?"

"Well, Butch, Jenny, and now you."

"What are you going to do?" Frank asked.

"What do you think? I'm going to have the baby."

"What about the election? Are you going to drop out?"

Joanna was adamant. "And give Ken Junior a free ride? No way."

"So are you going to keep it . . . well, under wraps until after election day?"

"We probably should delay making an announcement, just in case of a miscarriage, but Butch and I already talked it over. I'm going to go public with it. ASAP. I may even give our old friend, Marliss Shackleford, an exclusive on this."

Marliss, a columnist for the local paper, **The Bisbee Bee,** had long been a thorn in Joanna's side.

"Do you think that's wise?" Frank asked. "She's done everything but post 'Galloway for Sheriff' signs at the top and bottom of her column."

"That's exactly why I want Marliss to be one of the first to know," Joanna responded. "It'll be one of her biggest scoops ever in 'Bisbee Buzzings.' Knowing Marliss is solidly in Ken Junior's corner, people are bound to read the column and talk about it for days afterward. I figure, if the voters know about the baby in advance and elect me anyway, then no one will be able to complain about it later on. And if I lose? Then I lose. I'll go back to selling insurance—although that wouldn't be my first choice."

"I take it you and Butch have talked this through?"

"Absolutely."

"All right, then," Frank said. "If you two are okay with it, then I've got no complaints." He picked up his stack of papers. "Sorry I wasn't there to help out last night," he added.

"Don't apologize, Frank," Joanna told him with a smile. "You get to have some time off, and so do I. Now, what more do you have for me this morning?"

For the next twenty minutes or so they went over routine departmental business, including the previous day's incidents reports. They ended with a discussion of the Mossman homicide.

"Ernie Carpenter will be at the autopsy later this morning," Frank said. "Jaime Carbajal will start canvassing the neighborhood around Carol Mossman's place and talking to her supervisor and co-workers. He'll also be organizing an inch-by-inch search of the property. Dave Hollicker believes that since the shots were fired through a locked door, there's a good chance the killer never made it inside Carol Mossman's place. That means any physical evidence left behind by the killer would most likely be outside the trailer rather than inside it."

Joanna nodded. "This whole thing offends me," she said, her green eyes flashing in sudden outrage. "Most people, including Carol's own grandmother, might consider that run-down trailer little more than a hovel, but it was Carol

Mossman's home, Frank—her place of refuge. She and her animals were inside it, unarmed and defenseless, when somebody blew her away and killed all her dogs in the process. It's true that, in trying to help all those strays, Carol Mossman may have broken some of the dog-ownership statutes, but at the time she was killed, she and her dogs weren't hurting anybody."

"No, they weren't," Frank agreed.

"I was on the scene last night. We were all working and doing our jobs. This morning, I realize it was like it was all business as usual. It would be all too easy to write Carol off as some kind of weirdo who was somehow responsible for what happened to her, but if the Carol Mossmans of this world aren't safe in their own homes, nobody else is, either. I want whoever did this caught!"

By the time Joanna paused, Frank Montoya seemed a little taken aback by the strength of her emotion on the subject. "I see what you mean," he said. "So what's the next step?"

"Have Jaime contact that Explorer troop out on post at Fort Huachuca to see if they can help with the foreign-object search."

"Will do," Frank said.

"And we should probably get the Double Cs in here to update us sometime this afternoon." The term **Double Cs** was departmental shorthand for the two homicide detectives, Carbajal and Carpenter.

"Okay," Frank agreed.

"Anything else?" Joanna asked.

The chief deputy looked decidedly uncomfortable. "Well, there is one more thing," he said.

"What's that?"

"It's about the dog."

"What dog?"

"The one you took from Carol Mossman's home last night."

"It's not a dog, Frank," Joanna responded. "It's a puppy—a cute little fuzzy black puppy."

"Jeannine Phillips has lodged a formal complaint."

"You're kidding!"

"I wish I were," Frank said regretfully. "She says you confiscated the dog yourself rather than following established procedures."

"Frank, the puppy's mother was dead. Lucky was practically starving to death."

"Lucky. You mean you've named him?"

"Yes, I've named him. He's not a dog, Frank. He's a baby—barely weaned, if that. Somehow he was left alone when all the other dogs got locked inside the trailer with Carol Mossman's body. It's a wonder he was still alive. I brought him home. Butch fed him bread and milk and then went straight out to buy Puppy Chow.

What's wrong with that? What was I supposed to do, ship him off to the pound so they could keep him for however long they keep animals before they put them down?"

"And how long is that?" Frank asked.

Joanna shrugged. "I don't know for sure—a couple of weeks. A month, maybe."

"You should probably know," Frank put in mildly, "the correct answer is actually seventy-two hours."

Joanna was shocked. "That's all?" she demanded. "You mean, from the time the animals are picked up?"

"That's right. If they're not claimed by an owner or adopted by the end of seventy-two hours, they're out of there."

"As in put to sleep."

"Right."

"That's awful. I was sure they had longer than that."

"I thought so, too, boss, but I checked the statute just this morning. If you care about animals at all, and if those are the kinds of conditions Animal Control is working under, maybe that's part of the reason Jeannine Phillips is so pissed off all the time. I sure as hell would be."

"Do you think she'll take her complaints to Ken Junior?" Joanna asked.

"If she's in a mood to make trouble, what do you think?"

Joanna thought about that. Finally she said, "If I end up losing this election, will it be because I'm pregnant or because I took in an orphaned puppy?"

Frank Montoya grinned and shook his head. "Anybody's guess," he said.

After the chief deputy sauntered out of her office, Joanna sat staring out into the lobby through the open doorway. She thought about the scene in her kitchen earlier that morning, when Tigger met Lucky for the first time. Jenny had put Tigger on a "Wait" command at the door to the kitchen. But the word **wait** meant nothing to the puppy. He had scampered across the room and, despite Tigger's bared teeth, had leaped up and licked the big dog's face. Offended, Tigger had grabbed the puppy by the scruff of the neck and put him down, where he lay stock-still on the floor with his paws straight up in the air. Only the tiniest tip of his tail had moved—a twitch rather than a wag.

After several seconds, Tigger had let his captive go. Lucky had jumped up and gone racing around the room, his tiny claws clicking on the tile floor as he skidded around the corners. Each time he returned to Tigger, the older dog had growled and bared his teeth again, but he made no further move to attack the little interloper. The scene was so comical that Jenny had giggled with delight. Butch and Joanna, too, had laughed aloud. And now, because she had taken in the little rascal to give him a good home, Joanna was suddenly in the doghouse with her Animal Control officers.

Making up her mind, Joanna punched her intercom button.

"Yes, Sheriff Brady," Kristin Gregovich answered.

"I'm going out for a while," Joanna said.

"When will you be back?"

"I don't know," Joanna replied. "I'm on my way out to Animal Control. You might call ahead and see if Officer Phillips is there. Let her know I'm coming to see her."

The several miles between the Justice Center and the Animal Control compound on the far side of Tin Town gave Joanna plenty of time to think about her upcoming meeting. And the more she thought about it, the more she suspected Jeannine Phillips was in the right and she was wrong. After all, police officers investigating crime scenes were charged with collecting evidence connected to whatever crime had occurred. At the same time, they were prohibited from taking any items not thought to be part of the criminal investigation.

Going strictly by the rule book, Joanna had no excuse for taking the puppy. But Lucky was by no means part of the Carol Mossman homicide, and the animal was far too small to be shipped off to a pound. That opinion was underscored when, a few minutes later, she found herself wandering through a maze of dog runs searching for Jeannine Phillips. Joanna's passage set off a cacophony of barking. She found it difficult to look at the sad collection of animals, their muzzles pressed hopefully up against the chain-link gates, watching as Joanna walked by. One in particular caught her eye—a blue-eyed Australian shepherd bitch.

Joanna finally located Jeannine Phillips. Hose in hand, she was cleaning out an empty run. Joanna didn't want to consider what had happened to the previous occupant. The Animal Control officer nodded in greeting when Joanna walked up, but continued hosing down the concrete-floored run.

"What can I do for you, Sheriff Brady?" she asked finally after turning off the hose. "I suppose you're here to bitch me out for lodging the complaint?"

"Not exactly," Joanna said. "Although I did come to talk to you about that." She paused. "I guess it never occurred to me that saving one puppy's life was a breach of procedure."

"If it had been a child," Jeannine said brusquely, "you would have turned it over to Child Protective Services."

"But there were all those other dead dogs," Joanna objected. "Seventeen dead dogs."

"Right," Jeannine agreed. "What's the big deal about seventeen dead dogs? We put away that many every week. And by the time we get through with the Fourth of July weekend—with all the dogs that get scared and run away from home because of firecrackers and are never reclaimed—we'll do double that next week."

Joanna felt sickened. "That's outrageous!" she exclaimed. "We euthanize that many? I had no idea."

"I didn't think you did," Jeannine Phillips said. "But don't feel bad. Nobody else knows, either. Since puppies don't eat much, we can keep them a little longer. And we could probably have placed **your** puppy. It's a different story with older dogs. For one thing, they aren't that cute, and they eat too much. When the board of supervisors dished out the budget cuts, our unit took a ten percent hit right along with everyone else, Sheriff Brady. But so far I haven't been able to convince any of the dogs that they should eat ten percent less."

As the morning sun climbed higher in the sky, the temperatures in the unair-conditioned kennel area was heating up as well. Joanna followed Jeannine back through the kennel, the woman stopping here and there to turn on big industrial fans.

"They help some," she said. "If nothing else, they keep the air circulating."

Inside the building, Joanna and Jeannine walked through a hallway lined with cat cages. Most of those were full as well. Animal Control's ramshackle office was furnished with discarded, mismatched furniture that had seen better days. Joanna soon realized the office wasn't air-conditioned, either. An old swamp cooler half-heartedly blew tepid air and the odor of mildew into the room as Jeannine sat down behind a scarred wooden desk.

"We should have two full-time kennel attendants," she told Joanna. "Since we only have one, Manny and I end up doing kennel duty when we should be out on patrol. If somebody actually wants to adopt a dog, we have to be paged so we can come back and handle the paperwork. It's no surprise that so few dogs get adopted.

"Before she left, Donna Merrick had all kinds of bright ideas. She had met with several local veterinarians and was hoping to get the county to contract with them for low-cost spaying and neutering. Donna thought we'd have better luck finding homes for animals if we brought the animals to the people instead of waiting for people to come to us. She had even talked to some of the local store managers about having adoption clinics on Saturday mornings. Donna wanted to pay for a dog groomer so the animals would be cleaned up and looking good the mornings of the clinics."

"Sounds good to me," Joanna said. "What happened?"

"Donna talked the idea up and the Wal-Mart managers in Douglas and Sierra Vista were all for it. So was the manager of the Safeway store here in town. But when the board of supervisors heard about it, they wouldn't even consider it. Said that running adoption clinics went beyond our 'legal mandate' and that the taxpayers would think it a waste of money. And, once Donna went up against the board, the next thing we knew, she was gone. Now we're part of the sheriff's department, and we're even more short-handed than before."

"So I guess we need to do something about this," Joanna said when she finished.

Jeannine nodded. "Yes, we do," she said, but she didn't sound convinced that anything would change.

"How long have you worked here?" Joanna asked.

"Eight years."

"And Manny?"

"Six."

Joanna nodded. "So what do you want me to do about the puppy? Should I bring him back here?

I offered him to Carol Mossman's mother, but she didn't want him. The place where she lives doesn't allow pets."

"Manny said you'd already named him," Jeannine said.

"I thought he was lucky, so that's what I named him—Lucky."

"Go ahead and keep him," Jeannine said in exasperation. "Since he's already got a home, there's not much sense bringing him back here. You're supposed to have him properly licensed, once he has his shots, and he'll need to be neutered."

"Right," Joanna said. "We'll take care of it."

"Good enough," Jeannine said.

Joanna stood and started toward the door. Then she stopped and turned back. "How long has that little Australian shepherd been here?" she asked. "The one in that last bunch of kennels."

"Oh," Jeannine said. "You mean Little Blue Eyes?"

"Yes."

"Three days," Jeannine replied. "She'll be gone tomorrow."

"Gone as in adopted?" Joanna asked.

"No," Jeannine said. "Gone as in gone."

Sheriff Joanna Brady thought about that, but not for long. **Butch won't mind**, she thought. "My husband and I live on a ranch out on High

Lonesome Road," she said. "There's plenty of room for dogs."

Jeannine Phillips's sullen expression brightened slightly. "You mean you'd like to take her?"

"Yes," Joanna said. "I think I would."

"She'll need to have her shots, too, and be licensed."

"And spayed," Joanna added.

"No," Jeannine said, "you won't have to worry about that. She's already been fixed. But you should know, she doesn't like men much—not even Manny, and he's a real sweetheart when it comes to dogs."

"That's all right," Joanna said. "I'm sure we'll be able to manage."

For the first time in Joanna's memory, the grim set of Jeannine Phillips's face was replaced by a tentative smile. "Great, Sheriff Brady," she said. "I'll get started on the paperwork right away."

And I'll go back to the office, Joanna thought, **and see how much progress we're making in catching Carol Mossman's killer.**

FOUR

alf an hour later, using a bright red disposable leash, Joanna led her new dog out of Jeannine Phillips's office. The Australian shepherd walked in a demure, ladylike fashion. Clearly someone somewhere had taken the time to give her a bit of obedience training. By the time the dog hopped in through the Civvie's back door and settled gracefully into the backseat, Joanna was ready to give her a new name.

"Little Blue Eyes doesn't suit you," she said aloud. "But we'll see what Butch and Jenny want to call you."

On the way back to the Justice Center, Joanna stopped off at Dr. Millicent Ross's veterinary clinic. Joanna emerged from the clinic half an hour later with a properly vaccinated dog and accompanying documentation that would allow her to license an Australian shepherd still officially known as Blue Eyes. Once inside Joanna's office, the dog disappeared into the cavelike kneehole under the desk. Joanna left her there and went looking for a dish and some water. Her search took her to the lab, where her latent fingerprint tech, Casey Ledford, liberated an aluminum pie plate that would work temporarily for dog-drinking purposes.

Joanna peered around the lab. "What are you up to?"

"I've processed the prints I took from Carol Mossman's back door. The ones I have don't match the victim."

"Have you run them through AFIS?" Joanna asked, referring to the Automated Fingerprint Identification System.

"Sure did," Casey replied. "No hits so far."

"What about Dave?" Joanna asked, peering around the lab shared by Casey and the crime scene investigator. "Is he back out at the scene?"

"No," Casey said. "I'm pretty sure he's down the hall on his computer. He's working on the brass they found yesterday."

Taking the pie plate with her, Joanna went to the doorway to the crime scene investigator's cubicle, where she found him staring closely at his CRT. "What's up?" she asked.

"Take a look at this, Sheriff Brady," Dave said, moving aside and allowing her access to his computer. "It's really interesting."

On his screen was a large circle with a much smaller one inside it. Two straight lines went from the outside of the smaller circle to the edge of the larger circle, dividing the larger one in half. At the top of the larger circle was the initial **S.** At the bottom, the number 17.

"One of the casings from yesterday's homicide?" Joanna asked.

Dave nodded.

"Tell me what I'm looking at."

"An antique, for one thing," Dave said. "This is a Colt military head stamp. It was used on ammunition manufactured prior to 1921. See that seventeen?" Dave asked, pointing with the tip of his pencil. Joanna nodded. "That's the year of manufacture—1917. The **S** on top stands for where it was made—Springfield, Massachusetts."

Joanna was astonished. "You're telling me Carol Mossman died after being shot by a bullet that's eighty-six years old?"

"Two shots were fired," Dave replied. "The one to her lower body is the one that actually killed her. The other went through her shoulder. I dug most of that slug out of the paneling on the wall behind her."

Joanna Brady was amazed. "I'm surprised ammunition that old still works."

"I'm not," Dave said. "I suppose you could expect a certain degree of unreliability, but if the bullets have been kept dry, there's no real reason why they shouldn't work."

"And they did," Joanna supplied. "But where did they come from, and where have they been all this time?"

"Who knows?" Dave replied. "That's what I'm trying to find out right now. I can't just call up Colt and ask for records from way back then."

"No," Joanna agreed. "I suppose not."

"I've sent a copy of the firing fingerprint to the NIBIN," Dave Hollicker continued. "So far there's no match."

Joanna was well aware of the National Integrated Ballistics Information Network. Functioning much the same way AFIS does for fingerprints, NIBIN provides a computerized database of weapons signatures collected from crime scenes nationwide. It allows investigators to know when the same weapon is being used to commit crimes in more than one jurisdiction. It also makes instantaneous connections between solved and unsolved crimes that would otherwise be regarded as unrelated incidents. Following the travels of a particular weapon sometimes makes it possible for detectives to track the movements of an individual perpetrator as well.

"You don't really expect them to come up with a match, do you?" Joanna said. "How many eighty-six-year-old homicides do you think have been entered in the system? As I recall, computers weren't even a gleam in engineers' eyes back in 1917."

"That's not true," Dave said.

"It isn't?"

"And you of all people should know it," Hollicker told her. "Have you ever heard of Augusta Ada Byron King, Countess Lovelace?"

"Never. Who's she?"

"Her daddy was a guy named Lord Byron."

"As in Shelley and Keats—Lord Byron, the poet?"

"Right. She was born the year her parents were divorced, and her father never saw her after that, but she was one smart little girl whose mother saw to it that she was trained in mathematics. At eighteen she went to hear a lecture by Charles Babbage on what he called his 'difference engine.' Ada managed to finagle an introduction to the man. When she saw Babbage's machine itself, she was one of the few people who immediately grasped how it worked and could visualize its long-term potential. She and Babbage went on to become more than friends," Dave said. "Not only that, from what I heard, she's the one who created the first punch cards and invented computer programming."

"When was all this?" Joanna demanded.

"Sometime in the mid-1800s, I think," Dave

Hollicker answered. He was clearly getting a kick out of their sudden reversal of roles.

"And how come you know about this . . . What's her name again?" Joanna asked.

"Augusta Ada Byron King, Countess Lovelace."

"How come you know about her and I don't?"

"Because when you sent me to CSI school in Quantico, Virginia, one of my instructors, Agent Amanda Blackner, had a real thing about women doing all of the grunt work and getting none of the credit. You'd better believe it. If you didn't know about Lady Ada in full, essay-answer detail, you didn't pass Blackner's class."

"I might not have taken that class, but I know about Ada Lovelace now. Thanks," Joanna said and then changed the subject. "Did you pick up anything else from the crime scene last night?"

"Some tire casts," Dave answered. "And casts of a footprint or two. Hiking boots. Could be either a small man or a large woman."

"Or a juvenile," Joanna suggested.

Dave nodded. "That, too," he said. "In fact, speaking of juveniles, I need to be on my way. Jaime said that the Explorer troop will be on tap at one to help with the foreign-object search. I want to be there when they do it."

"Good enough," Joanna said. "And good luck."

With that she took the pie plate and retreated to her office, pausing long enough at the hallway water fountain to fill it. Then she continued on toward her office, holding the pie plate carefully in both hands to keep the water from spilling.

"Whose dog?" Kristin asked, nodding toward Joanna's closed office door.

"Mine," Joanna said.

Without having to be asked, Kristin got up and opened the door. The Australian shepherd was waiting anxiously just inside. When the animal saw Joanna, her cropped tail wagged furiously. Joanna set the plate of water down and watched while the dog lapped it dry.

"When I took the mail in, I wasn't expecting to find a dog in your office," Kristin said. "She scared me so much I almost dropped the mail. I guess I scared her, too."

"Sorry," Joanna said. "I meant to tell you but you weren't here when I went by and—"

"Is that the dog from last night's crime scene?" Kristin asked. "Somebody said it was a puppy, but this doesn't look like a puppy."

"Different dog," Joanna said. "This one's from Animal Control. They were getting ready to put her down, so I decided to take her. You and Terry wouldn't happen to want another dog, would you?"

"We've already got Spike," Kristin said, shaking her head. "If we brought home another dog, our landlady would have a fit."

Kristin's husband, Terry, and his eighty-five-pound German shepherd, Spike, constituted the Cochise County Sheriff's Department's K-9 unit.

"Right," Joanna said. "I'm sure she would."

The phone rang, and Kristin reached to answer it. "It's Tom Hadlock," Kristin told Joanna. "He says the jail AC has gone out again. He's done his best to restart it but so far no luck. Now he's asking what you want him to do about it."

Joanna sighed and looked longingly at her desk, where that day's worth of correspondence was already laid out and awaiting her attention.

"Tell him I'll be right there," Joanna said.

Walking between her office and the jail commander's, Joanna found herself squinting in the unrelenting sun. She didn't need a thermometer to tell her that, for the third day in a row, the midday temperature was already over a hundred.

Tom Hadlock sat at his desk with the top two buttons on his uniform unbuttoned and sweat pouring down his face when Joanna entered his office. A small personal fan sat on his desk, facing him and oscillating feebly. The moving fan blades stirred the air slightly, but the resulting breeze did little to take the edge off the heat.

"I'm on hold with the AC company in Tucson," he said. "The first person I talked to said they could probably have someone here the day after tomorrow at the earliest."

"That's not good enough," Joanna said.

Hadlock nodded. "I told her that. She said she'd see what she could do. That's what we get for going with the lowest bidder," he added. "Sammy Cotton here in town handled our AC contract for years. Whenever we called him, he was always Sammy-on-the-spot, but then the board of supervisors decided we needed to put the contract out to bid. This outfit up in Tucson underbid Sammy but . . . Hello? Who's this?"

Tom punched the speakerphone button so Joanna could hear what was being said.

"I'm Alexander Blair, the owner of Anchor Air Conditioning."

"Well, Mr. Blair," Tom replied, "I'm Tom Hadlock, the jail commander down here in Bisbee. You could say I'm a little hot under the collar at the moment. We've got an air-conditioning problem here at the jail—an air-conditioning crisis, actually. The girl who answered your phone told me you wouldn't be able to have anyone here until the day after tomorrow. That's totally unacceptable."

Joanna winced at Tom's use of the word **girl**. As it turned out, she wasn't the only one to take umbrage.

"That 'girl' happens to be my mother," Alex

Blair answered stiffly. "She's been in the business for thirty-some-odd years. If she says that's the soonest we can get to you, then that's the way it is. Like she said, we'll have someone down there first thing the day after tomorrow."

"But," Tom Hadlock sputtered, "I have the contract right here. It says we'll receive 'priority' treatment."

"That **is** priority treatment," Blair returned. "In case you haven't noticed, all of Arizona is in the middle of a heat wave at the moment. Every single one of my technicians is out on calls. We're doing the best we can."

Joanna stood up and turned the speakerphone in her direction. "Then it's not good enough," she said.

"Who's this?"

"Sheriff Brady, Mr. Blair," she replied. "Sheriff Joanna Brady. What day is today?"

"The second," he replied after a pause.

"And that would make the day after tomorrow July Fourth. Do you really think you'll have a technician willing to come down here on a national holiday, Mr. Blair? And what if he needs parts? Will any of your suppliers be open that day?"

"Sheriff Brady—" Blair began, but Joanna cut him off.

"The weather reports I've seen indicate this

weather pattern is going to continue for the next few days, so I'm giving you a choice, Mr. Blair. Either you have someone here to fix our problem prior to five p.m. today, or I'm calling someone else. Once they get us up and running again, they can send their bill to you. We'll just assume you've subcontracted the job out."

"We can't do that."

"Oh?" Joanna asked. "How are you being paid for maintaining our facility, Mr. Blair?" She knew exactly how much Anchor Air Conditioning was being paid on a monthly basis as an ongoing maintenance retainer. When the board had come up with that brilliant idea, she had argued against it—argued and lost.

"Monthly," Alex Blair returned.

"Right. Because the board of supervisors wanted to have a regular budgetary item they could count on rather than having occasional spikes, right?"

"Yes," Blair replied. "I believe that's correct."

"And how long have you had the contract?"

"Six months or so," Blair said.

"Seven," Joanna corrected. "I have it right here. It started in December of last year."

"Well, seven then," Blair admitted grudgingly.

"And how much time have you put in at our facility?"

Blair paused again. Through the phone Joanna

could hear him shuffling papers. "That would have been two months ago, when we came out to fire up the AC units and get them ready for summer."

"Seven months," Joanna said. "And your people have been here exactly once. As I said before, Mr. Blair, you'd better have someone here working on our equipment by five o'clock today. Otherwise, I'm calling in a pinch-hitter repair company and reporting you to the board of supervisors as well."

She punched the speakerphone button, ending the call, cutting Alex Blair off in mid-excuse.

"Do you think these clowns will actually show up, Sheriff Brady?" Tom Hadlock asked.

"They'd better," she said. "But if I were you, I'd call Sammy Cotton and give him a heads-up. Tell him if Anchor Air Conditioning isn't here by five, I want his crew here by five after."

"What if Sammy does the job and Anchor doesn't pay him for it?"

"Anchor will pay, all right," Joanna said grimly. "I'll see to it. Now tell me, what do we do in the meantime? I don't want to lose anyone—guards or prisoners—due to heat prostration."

"We can let the prisoners out in the yard, I suppose," Tom Hadlock said dubiously. "It's cooler outside in the shade than it is in here, but I hate to have that many people outside all at once. If there was any trouble . . ."

"Call Chief Deputy Montoya," Joanna said. "Have him come over. I need him to give me a hand."

Frank Montoya arrived at the jail a few minutes later. "What's up, Sheriff Brady?" he asked.

"What can we do about the prisoners?" Joanna asked. "We've got to let them cool off. Can we let them outside?"

Frank thought about it for a minute. "If everyone is loose in the yard at once, we should probably bring in some of the patrol deputies to back up the detention officers just in case there's trouble."

Joanna nodded. "Good idea."

"I'll get on the horn and see how long it'll take to get them here."

Joanna nodded and turned to Hadlock. "Before we let them into the yard, I want water out there—water and ice—plenty of it. Plenty of paper cups, too. Got it?"

"Right," the jail commander said. "I'll notify the kitchen right away. Anything else?"

"Yes. How do I make a jailwide announcement?"

Tom Hadlock motioned to an old-fashioned-looking microphone that stood on the credenza behind his desk. "Help yourself," Tom said. "Hold down that button and talk into the mike."

"What next?" Frank asked.

"I'm going to make an announcement over the

jail intercom," Joanna told him. "And, for the sake of our non-English speakers, you're going to translate.

"This is Sheriff Brady speaking," Joanna said. "As you have no doubt noticed, our air-conditioning units have gone out and won't be repaired until much later this afternoon. We have a choice here. You can spend the afternoon sweltering in your cells, or we can do something about it."

She passed Frank the microphone and then waited for him to translate before she continued. "At this point it's probably cooler outside than it is inside. We're willing to let people outside, but only if we can have some assurances that there won't be any difficulty."

Again she waited while Frank translated. "Once we have additional personnel in place, we'll be moving you out into the rec yards where we plan to have ice, water, and towels. We'll let you out. We'll do it in an orderly, careful fashion, but let me warn you—if there's any trouble, and I mean at the first sign of trouble—heat or no heat, you go back inside under full lockdown."

By the time Tom Hadlock returned to his office, Frank had finished translating the last segment of Joanna's announcement. "The kitchen will have the water and ice out there within the next fifteen minutes," Hadlock reported.

"It'll take more time than that to get our people here," Frank said.

"Okay," Joanna said. "Wait on the ice, and don't start emptying the units until we have backup on the scene, Tom. Frank will let you know when they're here."

"Fair enough," Hadlock replied. "You say the word, and we'll start moving 'em out."

"Did you call Sammy Cotton?" Joanna asked.

"Yes, ma'am. He says if we need him, he can be here with a crew at five-oh-five."

"Now that we've called Mr. Blair's bluff, that probably won't be necessary," Joanna said. "Anchor Air Conditioning has had a trouble-free ride up to now. I'm guessing Mr. Blair isn't going to want to screw that up."

Joanna and Frank left the jail complex and headed back across the parking lot. "Mind if I ask you a question?" Joanna said.

"What's that?"

"Have you ever heard of someone named Ada Lovelace?" Joanna asked.

"You mean that smart lady who's the mother of all computers?" Frank returned. "Sure, I know about her. Why?"

"Never mind," Joanna said irritably, chagrined that her male staff knew far more about this female computer pioneer than she did. "Forget it," she told Frank. "I'm going home for lunch.

Hopefully I'll be back before it's time to move the prisoners outside. Tell the Double Cs that I still want to touch base with them later on this afternoon. Before five o'clock today, I want to know exactly where we stand on the Mossman case."

"Will do," Frank said, "but I need to warn you. Word is out about all those dead dogs. I'm afraid we're going to take a hit on that subject once it's in the papers."

"What else is new?" Joanna asked.

Back in her office, Joanna found her devoted but as-yet-unnamed dog waiting just inside the door. The animal sprang to her feet and greeted Joanna as though the two of them were old friends. Looking at the dog, Joanna shook her head. "Maybe I'd better call Butch and give him a heads-up about you, old girl."

She picked up her phone and dialed High Lonesome Ranch. "Would you happen to have a couple peanut-butter-and-jelly sandwiches lying around if I were in a mood to come home for lunch?" she asked when Butch answered.

"If you'll give me ten minutes, I can probably do better than that."

"Good. I'll be there. How's Lucky doing?" Joanna asked.

"Fine. At least I guess he's fine. I've hardly seen him. He's been with Jenny all morning. They're evidently bonding. The good news is that so far Tigger hasn't bitten the little guy's head off."

"I had to go by Animal Control this morning . . ." she began.

Somehow Butch Dixon knew instinctively where she was going. "No," he said at once. "You didn't. Not another one."

"I had to," Joanna said. "She's such a sweet little thing. And her time was almost up. By tomorrow morning, if no one took her, they'd have put her down. Wait till you see her."

"Well, all right then," Butch said. "I suppose that makes us even."

"Even?" Joanna asked. "What do you mean?"

"I invited your mother and George over for dinner tonight. I thought it would be better if the two of us were together when we drop the big news that we're pregnant."

Joanna thought about that for a few seconds. "Right," she agreed at last. "I guess that does make us even."

An hour later she was back from lunch with the dog once more stowed under her desk when Kristin came to tell her the extra deputies had been deployed in and around the jail complex. Unbidden, the dog emerged from her cave and greeted Kristin with effusive tail-wagging.

"I thought you were going to leave her at home this afternoon."

"So did I," Joanna said ruefully. "But as soon as

she saw Butch she started jumping and bucking so hard, I could barely hold on to her leash. With him there, I would have had to bodily drag her into the house, so I ended up leaving her in the garage all through lunch. Jeannine Phillips warned me that the dog doesn't like men, but this is more than not liking. You should have seen her, Kristin. The poor thing was scared to death."

"What are you going to do?" Kristin asked. "Take her back to the pound?"

"I offered to, but Butch said no. He says he'll figure out a way around her, but he thought it would be better for everybody concerned if I brought her back to work this afternoon. So I did. Obviously the dog is fine with you, Kristin, but you should probably let Frank, Jaime, and Ernie know she's here so they don't barge in un-expectedly."

"I'll tell them," Kristin said. "By the way, Tom Hadlock said to tell you that the guy from An-chor called. They've hired Sammy Cotton's crew to come work on the air-conditioning. They'll be here by three this afternoon."

"Good enough," Joanna said. "Sounds like a win-win situation to me."

She hurried outside. She and Chief Deputy Montoya watched as the prisoners were allowed out of their cells and into the sun-drenched, razor-wire-surrounded rec yard, which, at this time of day, was at least partially shaded from direct sunlight by the jail itself. The inmates, apparently grateful to be allowed out of their ovenlike cells, helped themselves to paper cups of ice water and then moved in an orderly fashion into the long narrow sliver of shade beside the building or sat on the covered concrete picnic tables that lined the yard.

"The prisoners will be fine," Joanna said. "They have some shade. It's the detention officers and extra deputies I feel sorry for. None of them have any shade at all. Let's make sure they have plenty of water, too. I'd hate to protect the prisoners and lose one of our deputies to heatstroke."

"I'll have Tom Hadlock take care of it right away."

It wasn't long before the blazing sun drove Joanna herself back into the relative cool of her office. With the dog curled contentedly at her feet, Joanna spent the next two hours dealing with routine paperwork. At three-thirty, her phone rang.

"Detectives Carbajal and Carpenter are here," Kristin announced. "I told them you'd see them in the conference room."

"Right. By the way, any sign of the air-conditioning crew?"

"They've been here for almost an hour now," Kristin said.

"Great," Joanna replied. "Sometimes it pays to be the squeaky wheel."

Ernie Carpenter and Jaime Carbajal were already in the conference room. Frank Montoya arrived at the same time Joanna did. "Okay, guys," Joanna said. "What do we have so far?"

"Doc Winfield says Carol Mossman was struck by two bullets—one in the gut and one in the shoulder. The wound to the midsection was the one that actually killed her. She bled to death," Ernie Carpenter added. "No surprises there. All the shots, including the ones that missed the victim, were fired into the back door of her mobile home. The door was locked at the time from the inside, with her and all of her dogs . . . all but one of her dogs," he corrected, "inside the house with her."

"Why were they inside?"

"That I can't say. There were food bowls everywhere. The victim may have brought them into the house to feed them, but there was no food in any of the dishes. Either the dogs ate it or she hadn't finished feeding them before the killer arrived. We don't believe her assailant ever gained access to the house. After being shot, Carol Mossman managed to drag herself as far as the living room. We think she was trying to reach the phone, but she passed out and died a few feet shy of it."

"Wait a minute," Joanna said. "I thought someone told me last night the electricity was turned off at the Mossman place. Now you're saying the phone was still working. How's that possible?"

Beetling his thick eyebrows into a frown, Ernie nodded. "It's one of those old-fashioned Princess phones. Hard-wired. Unlike the new cordless phones everyone has these days, the old ones worked even with the power off. Not that it did Carol Mossman any good."

"Time of death?"

"She was shot at seven twenty-eight yesterday morning," Ernie said, consulting his notes. "Doc Winfield says she died some time after that, maybe as much as two or three hours."

"Seven twenty-eight?" Joanna asked. "How were you able to pinpoint the time of the attack?"

"There was evidently a clock hanging on the wall behind her. When she went down, she took the wall with her and knocked out the clock's battery."

"Did you pick up any pertinent information from Carol Mossman's neighbors?" Joanna asked, turning her attention to Jaime Carbajal.

"I talked to a Rhonda Wellington. She has a place off the Charleston Road about half a mile away. She's evidently the neighbor who called

Animal Control two weeks ago to report that Carol Mossman's dogs were running loose. Believe me, there's no love lost there."

"Is Wellington a possible suspect?" Joanna queried.

"I doubt it," Jaime answered. "She says she was scared to death of Carol Mossman's dogs and wouldn't go anywhere near them. She said she reported them when they showed up loose on her property and chased her horses. She claims that a couple of times she had to run into her house to get away from the dogs. I doubt she would have gone over there on her own."

"Maybe she would have if she'd been armed," Joanna suggested.

Jaime shook his head. "I'm telling you, she was scared of the dogs, and with that many of them, one gun wouldn't have done much good. Rhonda did claim to have heard what sounded like shots. She said she was outside hanging laundry on her clothesline when she heard a whole series of pops. With the Fourth of July coming up, she decided it was kids setting off firecrackers and didn't give it another thought. It corroborates the time, though."

"In other words," Joanna said, "Rhonda Wellington is a busybody who made a police report about loose dogs and ignored a flurry of gunshots."

"Exactly," Jaime agreed. "I checked with the other neighbors. So far, no one else saw or heard anything. When I finished that, I went out to Sierra Vista and talked to Alberto Sotomeyer, who owns the Shell station where Carol Mossman worked. He says she worked a double shift two days ago—her regular shift, which was four to midnight, and then she worked graveyard as well, from midnight to eight. Sotomeyer said she had some kind of important appointment yesterday and needed to have the whole day off."

"Yesterday was the deadline for having her dogs vaccinated and licensed," Joanna suggested. "Maybe she took off work so she could have that done."

Jaime jotted himself a note. "I'll check around with the local vets and see if she had an appointment," he said.

"Has either one of you talked to Edith Mossman yet?" Joanna asked.

Both detectives shook their heads. "Not enough time," Ernie said. "We'll try to get to her first thing in the morning. How come?"

"I was just thinking about something she told me last night," Joanna said. "She claims to have no idea where her son is."

"Carol's father?" Ernie asked.

"Right. I believe his name is Edward."

"That's what you put on the information you

gave us earlier. You also mentioned that Edith and the son are estranged."

Joanna nodded. "Her words, which she didn't bother to mince, were something to the effect that if he were to turn up dead, she'd be ready and willing to take a leak on his grave. What I find interesting, however, is that it doesn't sound as though she's estranged from any of her grand-daughters—from her son's children. Maybe we should find out what that's all about."

The phone rang. Frank Montoya reached around to answer it. "Conference room," he said. A moment later he passed it over to Joanna. "It's Tom Hadlock," he said. "Needs to speak to you right away."

"What's up?" Joanna asked.

"The air-conditioning guys expect to have us up and running in another hour, but once they turn the switch back on, it's going to take time to cool the place off again—a couple of hours at least. Ruby's wondering if she should make sand-wiches so the inmates can eat out in the yard."

Ruby Starr, a former restaurateur and chef, had been in the Cochise County Jail on a domestic-disturbance charge some three years earlier when the jail's previous cook had absconded with that year's supply of holiday turkeys. Ruby had been drafted directly out of her jail cell and into the kitchen. While still officially listed as one of the jail's inmates, she had set about whipping the

nearly derelict kitchen into shape. Under her supervision, sanitation had improved immeasur-
ably, as had the quality of the food. Upon her
release, she had stayed on as chief cook, now as a
paid employee.

"Good thinking," Joanna said. "Tell her to
make enough sandwiches for the guards and the
extra deputies as well. In the meantime, Frank,
liberate some money from petty cash and go get a
load of chilled watermelons from Safeway.
Everyone seems to be behaving themselves. Why
not reward them? And, since we seem to be having a jailwide picnic anyway, it might just as well
include some genuine picnic fare."

Frank gave Joanna a questioning look, complete with a single raised eyebrow that meant he
didn't necessarily agree. "Okay, boss," he said.
"If that's what you want, I'll get right on it."

Half an hour later, Joanna was back in her office. Watching the clock edge toward five, she realized the day had slipped away without her ever
calling her best friend, Marianne Maculyea, to
deliver the earth-shattering news that Joanna
was pregnant. She reached for the phone but
then put it down again without dialing.

**Butch is right. Better not tell anyone else un-
til after we tell Mother.**

"Come on, whoever you are," she said to the
dog. "It's time to go home and face the music."

FIVE

Leaving Chief Deputy Montoya to oversee the outdoor jail operation, Joanna took her family's latest canine member and headed home right at 5 p.m. It surprised her a little to realize what she was doing. In those first frantic months after being elected sheriff, she had hardly slept whenever her department had been sucked into a homicide investigation. Wanting to be more than a figurehead sheriff, she had thrown herself into each and every case. No one had placed greater demands on Joanna Brady than she herself had.

That was still true now, she realized. She had personally been to the scene of Carol Mossman's murder, but it pleased her to realize that she no longer had to be there in person in order to keep her finger on the pulse of every aspect of the investigation. Gradually she was learning to delegate. She was also learning to separate her personal life from her work life. In that regard, she had her stepfather, George Winfield, to serve as an example.

As Cochise County Medical Examiner, George dealt with many of the same cases Joanna did and more besides, doing doctor- and relative-requested autopsies for deaths where the victims had not died as a result of foul play. But when George Winfield wasn't actively at work, he lavished his wife—Joanna's mother, the demanding Eleanor—with devoted attention. He did his work at work and he left it there. Just because he had to deal with dead bodies during the day didn't mean he couldn't go to a classical music concert in Tucson that evening. Not only go— but go and enjoy as well.

For years Joanna hadn't left her office without a briefcase full of homework, but soon after their wedding Butch had raised an objection.

"Look," he had said, "you work long hours, and I don't mind that. And I don't mind that you get called out evenings and on weekends. But when you're home, you should be home. When it comes to getting your attention, Jenny and I shouldn't always have to be last in line."

And then George Winfield himself had pushed her over the edge. He and Joanna had been doing dishes after Easter Sunday dinner when he brought it up.

"You work too hard," he said.

Joanna had paused, dish towel and glass in hand. "Who put you up to saying that?" she asked. "Butch or Eleanor?"

"Neither," he had said. "I came up with the idea on my own."

"How come?" she asked.

"When I was a young doctor in private practice, I was ambitious as hell and wanted to be the very best there was. I wanted to make plenty of money so I could support Annie and Abigail in style. But then, once I lost them both, I found out the money didn't mean a thing, Joanna. Not a damn thing! Life doesn't always give people second chances, but it seems to me you have one. And now you have to make some decisions. You can spend all your time at work, but who's going to benefit from that? Once you've missed out on time spent with your family, you don't get it back—not ever. Once it's gone, it's gone. I'm glad to have my work right now. It's rewarding and I'm good at it. But I'm also glad to have your mother. I have no intention of neglecting Ellie the way I did Annie when I was so busy chasing after the almighty dollar."

Joanna had thought about George's comments all Easter Sunday night. What he had said wasn't exactly what a visiting out-of-town detective, J. P. Beaumont, had told her during their brief encounter last fall, when he had advised her to pay attention to what was important, but the advice was close enough. And close enough to hit home, as well.

Joanna had already lost Andy. Nothing could mend the quarrels they'd had when she and Andy had fought over things too unimportant to remember. Nothing could bring back the years when they had both been working so hard at their two separate jobs that, other than sleeping together in the same bed, their paths had barely crossed on a daily basis. Joanna could see now that too much of her precious time with Andy had been frittered away on things that meant nothing. Now, like George with her mother, she had a second chance—with Butch and Jenny. And soon there would be another little someone to take into consideration.

So Joanna had been working on it. Daily she made a conscious effort to leave her work at work—to put it behind her when she drove out of the Justice Center parking lot. Of course, with the campaign heating up, that wasn't always possible, but when she did come home from her latest rubber-chicken banquet, she didn't duck into her home office and open a brimming briefcase. And she didn't turn on her home computer, either.

Now the five-mile drive from work to home served as a very real decompression chamber.

Once again it worked its magic as she let go of her worries about the prisoners eating their picnic dinner in the rec yard and concerns about solving this latest homicide. As she turned up the newly bladed drive and saw their rammed-earth house nestled in among the brilliant greens of Clayton Rhodes's towering cottonwood trees, Joanna felt truly at home.

Tigger came dashing down the road to greet her. Lucky trailed fifty feet behind Tigger, running as fast as his short legs would travel. Seeing the other dogs outside the car, the new dog went nuts. She jumped excitedly between the front and back seats. The sharp yipping sounds she made were loud enough to make Joanna's ears hurt.

She stopped the Civvie outside the garage door and removed Blue Eyes's leash. "Okay, girl," she said. "Let's see how you do with your new pals. If they're loose, you should be, too. That way everybody will have a fighting chance."

She got out and opened the rear door. The Australian shepherd piled out. After a few stiff-legged, growl-punctuated moments of sniffing, the two big dogs raced off in a huge circle, with the puppy once again eagerly chugging along behind.

"I see you've already made the necessary introductions," Butch observed, coming out through the garage door. "Obviously she likes Tigger a whole lot more than she does me."

"She'll learn," Joanna said with a laugh. "After all, you talked your way around me, didn't you? What's for dinner?"

"Steak," Butch said. "Baked potatoes, homemade bread straight out of the bread machine, salad, and homemade ice cream for dessert. Considering the news we're about to drop, I figured it was time to kill the fatted calf. No doubt your mother's going to be fit to be tied, but don't feel like the Lone Ranger, Joey. My mother most likely will react the same way."

"Where's Jenny?" Joanna asked.

"Where do you think?" Butch returned, nodding in the direction of the corral, where a cloud of dust showed that Jenny and Kiddo were once again racing around a set of barrels. Closer at hand, the dogs were still chasing one another in ever-widening circles. "Should we bring them inside?" Butch added. "What if the new dog decides she doesn't like it here and takes off?"

"I think she'll be all right," Joanna said. "We'll put out food and water. What time are George and Eleanor due?"

"Seven."

"It's too hot to stand out here talking," Joanna said. "I'm going inside to change."

Inside, the rammed-earth home with its thick

walls, high ceilings, and state-of-the-art air-conditioning was pleasantly cool. Joanna hurried down the long bedroom-wing corridor, shedding her uniform as she went. After a quick shower she returned to the kitchen, where the tantalizing smell of baking bread wafted from Butch's well-used bread machine. Butch was working at the center island, tearing and spinning lettuce for salad.

"How'd it go today?" he asked.

"Not much progress on the Mossman homicide," she told him, snagging a baby carrot off the granite-tiled countertop and munching away. "Had to empty the jail this afternoon because the AC went out. I ended up raising hell with the AC contractor to get him to have it fixed today."

"You emptied the jail?" Butch asked. "What did you do with all the prisoners?"

"Right about now they're all out in the rec yard having a picnic. The AC's back on, but it's still too hot to put the prisoners back in their cells."

"Isn't that dangerous, having all of them out at once?" Butch asked.

"They're mostly misdemeanors," Joanna responded. "Besides, we brought in extra personnel to help out. It's fine. Now what can I do to help?"

"Sit," Butch said. "Take a load off. Have you told Marianne and Jeff the news?"

After years of being childless, Joanna's friend, the Reverend Marianne Maculyea, and her husband, Jeff Daniels, had finally adopted twin babies from China, Ruth and Esther. Months after losing Esther to a fatal heart condition, they had been surprised and delighted to learn that Marianne was pregnant. That baby, a boy named Jeffrey Andrew, was a fifteen-month-old red-haired handful, while Jeffy's big sister, Ruth, would head for kindergarten in the fall.

"Not yet," Joanna admitted. "I haven't told anyone, not even Eva Lou and Jim Bob."

Jim Bob and Eva Lou Brady, Joanna's former in-laws, were still very much a part of her and Jenny's lives and of Butch's, too. "I decided that the best way to keep peace in the family was to tell Mother first, although I did mention it to Frank."

"What did he have to say on the subject?"

"I told him about our idea of giving Marliss an exclusive. He didn't like it much."

"Maybe we should listen to him," Butch said. "After all, he's in charge of media relations."

"But it's our baby," Joanna objected. "And we're doing this our way."

Butch chuckled. "Our way or the highway."

Which sounded fine, right up until dessert was served, which is when Joanna finally screwed up her courage enough to drop the bomb.

"You're not!" Eleanor Lathrop Winfield exclaimed at once, pushing aside her untouched dish of homemade ice cream.

Joanna nodded. "I am," she said.

"What are you going to do, then, drop out of the race? Resign?"

"Neither one," Joanna answered. "I'm going to run for reelection and hopefully win."

Eleanor immediately appealed to Butch. "Surely you're not going to let her do this."

"Let?" Butch asked mildly. "This isn't up to me, Eleanor. It's up to Joanna."

"George," Eleanor said. "You tell them. It's just not possible to be a new mother and sheriff all at the same time."

"Why not?" George asked, carefully spooning his ice cream.

"Yes," Jenny agreed. "Why not?"

"Who's going to look after the baby?" Eleanor demanded.

"I am," Butch said.

"Have you ever taken care of a baby before?"

"Never," Butch said. "But that's the way it usually is with first-time parents—on-the-job training. I'm pretty sure I can handle it."

"He cooks a mean steak," George Winfield offered. Eleanor answered her husband's comment with a scathing look.

"Jeff Daniels takes care of Jeffy and Ruth,"

Jenny said. "Don't you think he does a good job?"

"That's different," Eleanor scoffed. "Marianne is a minister. She isn't out being shot at and beaten up by all kinds of riffraff."

"I'm not either," Joanna said quietly.

That was one of the many differences between Joanna and her mother. When Eleanor was upset, her volume went up. Joanna's went down.

"Oh?" returned Eleanor sharply. "I suppose that scar on your face is some kind of birth defect?"

Joanna felt her face flush, knowing when she did so that the long scar on her cheek, a souvenir from an encounter with an enraged suspect's diamond ring, would stand out that much more clearly.

"With all these working mothers, it's no wonder we're having such problems with juvenile delinquents."

Joanna knew that the statistics on the incidence of juvenile delinquency were down, not up, but now was no time to insert actual facts into Eleanor's diatribe.

"What would have become of you if I'd been gallivanting off to a job every day from the moment you were born?" Eleanor demanded.

Before Joanna could reply, Jenny beat her to it. "What about me?" she asked. "Mom's been working the whole time I've been around. I've turned out all right, haven't I?"

The phone rang just then. Glad for any excuse to escape the escalating dining room battle, Joanna hurried to answer it.

"Sheriff Brady?" an agitated Tom Hadlock said.

"Yes," Joanna replied. "What's up?"

"We've lost one," Hadlock replied.

"One what?"

"A prisoner. Richard Osmond."

Joanna was stunned. "What do you mean, you lost him? Did he go over the fence, or what?"

"No," Hadlock said. "He's dead. We did a roll call once we had everyone back inside, and Osmond was missing. We found him outside, lying on one of the picnic table benches. He was hidden in a shadow. Nobody knew he was there."

"Somebody knew," Joanna said grimly. "They just aren't telling. I'm on my way."

"Tica Romero's trying to get hold of Doc Winfield," Hadlock continued.

"Tell her not to bother. He's here with me. I'll bring him along when I come. She's calling out one of the Double Cs?"

"That's right," Hadlock answered. "I believe she said Ernie's on call. I'm really sorry about this, Sheriff Brady. We had guards and deputies all over that yard the whole time the prisoners were out there. I can't imagine how something like this could have happened."

"Was he stabbed, beaten up, what?" Joanna demanded.

"There are no apparent wounds, no sign of foul play," Hadlock said. "He's just lying there on his back, peaceful as can be, like he fell asleep. We didn't move him, though, so there could be something on his back that isn't showing."

"We'll find out when we get there," Joanna said. "Is the jail under lockdown?"

"Yes, it is," Hadlock replied. "It's a shame to have to do that. I mean, other than this, no other unfortunate incidents at all."

"If you'll pardon my saying so, Mr. Hadlock," Joanna said tersely, "finding a dead prisoner is unfortunate enough for me."

Joanna put down the phone and returned to the dining room. The people gathered around the table were quiet. They all looked at her expectantly. "I guess you heard, then," she said. "There's a problem at the jail. We have to go, George. You can ride with me."

Nodding, the ME wiped his face with his napkin, folded it, and then pushed his chair back. "Do you want me to drive you home first, Ellie?"

"I'm perfectly capable of driving myself," Eleanor returned.

George paused long enough to give her a peck

on the cheek. "All right, then," he said. "See you at home."

Butch, in the meantime, gave Joanna a raised-eyebrow look that said volumes about his being left alone to deal with Eleanor. All Joanna could do was give him a shrugged apology.

When she opened the door that led to her garage, the three dogs were all inside. Tigger greeted George happily. Lucky went up and dribbled a stream of pee on George's highly polished loafer while the Australian shepherd skittered away. When Joanna opened the outside door, she disappeared into the night.

"Where did all these dogs come from?" George asked. "Isn't that little one the pup you were carrying around last night at the Mossman crime scene?"

"That's right," Joanna said. "And I adopted the spooky Australian shepherd from the pound this morning."

"It's a good thing Ellie didn't see the new dogs earlier when we drove up," George said. "It would have been that much more grist for her mill."

"Will be," Joanna corrected.

They got into the Crown Victoria and started down the road. Worried that the dogs might try to follow her out to the highway, Joanna kept a close eye on the rearview mirror. She turned onto Highway 80 without seeing any sign of pursuit.

"Where did this happen?" George Winfield was asking. "In one of the cells?"

"No. Out in the rec yard. The air-conditioning broke down earlier this afternoon. I had all the inmates moved out into the yard while they were working on it. I didn't want anyone dying of heatstroke."

"You had all the prisoners in the yard at once?" George asked.

"We had extra personnel on duty. I didn't think anything would happen."

"But it has," George said.

"And it's not going to look very good, is it," Joanna replied. "It seems like it's one thing after another. First all those dogs died, and now this."

"You'll probably take more flak because of the dogs," George predicted.

"I'm sure that's true," Joanna said. They were nearing the turnoff to the Justice Center. "Do you want to stop here first, or should I take you by the house so you can pick up your van?"

"I'd better have the van," he said. "We're going to need to get that body out of there." He was quiet for a minute. "There's something else," he said.

"What's that?"

"Remember when we were working the Constance Haskell murder a few months back? Remember how Maggie MacFerson tried to make a big deal out of the fact that you and I were related?"

Maggie MacFerson, the murder victim's sister, happened to be **the** Maggie MacFerson, a well-known investigative reporter for the major Phoenix daily, **The Arizona Reporter.** She had been more than happy to imply that Sheriff Joanna Brady's stepdaughter relationship with the Cochise County Medical Examiner had somehow caused irregularities in the handling of and investigation into Constance Haskell's murder.

"Of course I remember," Joanna returned. "But there was nothing to it."

"You know there wasn't anything to it, and so do I," George Winfield said. "But this is different. Here we have an inmate who died while being incarcerated in your jail facility, Joanna. And he died in a situation that, however well-intentioned, wasn't business as usual."

"While they were out in the yard at my direction," Joanna muttered grimly.

"Considering all the possible ramifications, not the least of which is liability, we're going to have to be very careful."

"You mean there could be possible conflict-of-interest problems if you investigate Richard Osmond's death?"

"Precisely. This is a situation where neither one of us can afford the smallest margin for error."

"Are you saying you want to call in another ME?"

"I think it's wise, don't you?"

Joanna sighed and picked up her microphone. "Tica," she said when the dispatcher answered. "I need you to contact the Pima County Medical Examiner's office. Tell them what we've got down here, and see if we can borrow an ME. We'll pay, of course. Nobody expects them to work for free."

She put down the mike and turned back to George. "You know they're going to charge us an arm and a leg."

"No matter what they charge," George Winfield said, "it'll be cheap at twice the price."

Joanna dropped George next to his Dodge Caravan and then drove back to the Justice Center alone. Tom Hadlock intercepted her in the parking lot.

"The guys are pissed about the lockdown," he said. "They all say they didn't do a thing."

"Right," Joanna said. "Everybody's as innocent as the day they were born. That's why they're all in the slammer. Now, what's the story on Osmond? Who is he? What did he do?"

"He was serving ninety days for drunk and disorderly. He should have been in longer. He was up on a domestic-violence beef, but his lawyer plea-bargained it down to D and D."

"How old is he?"

"Thirty-six."

"How long's he been in?"

"Forty-five days."

"Did he cause any trouble?" Joanna asked.

"Not that I know of," Hadlock answered. "At least nothing that got written up. No difficulties with his cell mates, no calls to the infirmary, nothing."

"Who are his cell mates?"

"Brad Calhoun, a DUI from Willcox, and John Braxton, another D and D from Sierra Vista."

"Any reports on either of them?" Joanna asked.

Hadlock shook his head. "Braxton's only been here a couple of days, and Calhoun hasn't been any trouble either. That's why I try to put the drunks together. When they're not drunk, they mostly don't cause much trouble." Hadlock paused. "You want to go see him?"

"Not yet," Joanna said. "Doc Winfield and Detective Carpenter are both on their way. We should probably wait until they get here. Who found the body?"

"Lloyd did," Hadlock replied, referring to Lloyd Rolly, the assistant jail commander. "When we turned up one prisoner short, I sent him back out looking."

"Did he move anything?" Joanna asked.

Hadlock shook his head. "Lloyd checked for a

pulse and then called me. I called the EMTs, but he was gone."

George Winfield's Dodge Caravan pulled into the parking lot, followed immediately by Dave Carpenter's Econoline van.

"Good news," George said, hurrying toward them. "I just heard from Pima County. They're sending Fran Daly. She's leaving Tucson right now and will be here as soon as she can. That way she can take charge of the body to begin with rather than our having to do transfers back and forth."

Joanna had worked with Fran Daly on several other cases. Fran was a no-nonsense type who was an expert at dating long-dead corpses through the succession of bug and larvae found on the rotting flesh. Other than that, she was a fairly nice person.

"We could have done worse," Joanna said.

"That's what I thought," George Winfield agreed.

With Tom Hadlock in the lead, they made their way through the remotely controlled locks of the jail complex and out into the razor-wire-lined rec yard, which was lit up as brightly as the Warren Ballpark playing fields. Richard Osmond's body lay on the bench of a concrete picnic table. His hands were folded across his chest. Joanna was forced to agree that the dead man did indeed appear to be sleeping.

George cocked his head to one side and studied the body. "I'm guessing it's either an OD or natural causes. Anybody want to place bets?"

"Leave me out of it," Ernie Carpenter grumbled. "You always win."

Joanna turned to the jail commander. "Does his rap sheet show any drug convictions?"

"Not that I noticed," Hadlock replied.

"Does he have a wife?" Joanna asked.

"Live-in girlfriend," Dave Hadlock said. "Her name's Marla Gomez. We're trying to track down an address for her. Their apartment in Bisbee was in Osmond's name. Once he ended up in jail, Marla and the kid moved out. They may be staying with her parents, who live in Douglas."

"They have a child?" Joanna asked.

Tom Hadlock nodded. "A boy. He's four or five."

"You'll let us know as soon as you have the address?"

"Right," Tom said.

Dave Hollicker showed up then, camera in hand, and was directed to the picnic table bench. As the CSI began snapping crime scene photos, Ernie Carpenter shook his head.

"How many people were out here this afternoon?" he asked.

"Counting prisoners, detention officers, kitchen trustees, and deputies, right around a hundred."

"We're not likely to find much as far as physical evidence is concerned, mostly because we're going to find too much," Ernie said. "Our best bet will be to talk to the people who were there—guards and prisoners both. Maybe, while we're waiting for Fran Daly to show up, we could start interviewing some of those folks, beginning with Osmond's cell mates."

Joanna nodded. "Sounds good," she said as the hulking Ernie strode away.

"As for me," George Winfield said when he and Joanna were left alone, "since I'm taking a pass on this case, I believe I'll go on home. I'll have a word with your mother—or, rather, I'll let her have a word with me on the other major topic of the evening." He gave Joanna an understanding smile. "But again," he added, "congratulations. Ellie's comments notwithstanding, you and Butch and the baby will be just fine."

By the time Joanna had walked back across the parking lot and let herself into the Justice Center conference room, Frank Montoya had shown up as well.

"This isn't good," he said. "I've already had two calls—one from **The Bee** and another from **The Tribune** out in Sierra Vista. The reporters heard about it before I did. How's that possible?"

"It's all politics," Joanna said. "And in politics, anything goes. What did you tell them?"

"That I'd check things out and let them know."

Briefly Joanna brought him up to speed. By the time she finished, Tom Hadlock was leading a handcuffed man down the hall toward the interview room, where Ernie Carpenter was already waiting. Joanna and Frank followed them into the room. "This is Brad Calhoun," Tom said, shoving the man into a chair. "He's one of Richard Osmond's roomies."

"Look," Calhoun said, "I have no idea what happened to Richard, but whatever it was, I had nothing to do with it. I swear to God."

"Go ahead and remove the cuffs," Joanna told Tom Hadlock. "We're just talking here. I'm Sheriff Brady, Mr. Calhoun. This is Chief Deputy Montoya, and this is Homicide Detective Ernie Carpenter."

Calhoun was holding out his hands so Tom Hadlock could unlock the cuffs. When he heard Ernie's name and title, his jaw dropped. He waited until Tom Hadlock had taken the cuffs and left the room.

"Did you say homicide?" Calhoun asked. "You mean somebody's dead? I thought Richard just took off somehow. That he'd figured out a way to go over the fence—that he'd waited until everybody else went back inside and then away he went, know what I mean?"

"Mr. Osmond didn't go over the fence," Ernie told him somberly. "He's dead, and we're wondering what, if anything, you might know about that."

"Do I need a lawyer?" Calhoun asked.

"You tell us," Ernie returned. "When's the last time you talked to Mr. Osmond?"

"Right after dinner," Calhoun answered hurriedly. "Right after we finished up the watermelon."

"What was said?"

"Richard said he was tired, that he thought he'd take a nap. Didn't surprise me none. We were all wore out. The heat really takes it out of you. The AC in the jail went out last night, you see, and it was too hot to sleep—for me, anyway. It was just plain miserable."

"So you didn't think it was odd when Richard Osmond said he needed a nap."

"Naw. It was so ungodly hot that we were all beat. I was a little surprised, though, when he nailed that whole bench for himself. I didn't see him again after that, and I didn't think about it either—not until John and me got back to the cell and Richard wasn't there. We figured out he was missing about the same time the guards did, and then all hell broke loose. They figured he'd escaped somehow, and they put the whole place on lockdown."

"Did Mr. Osmond do drugs?" Ernie asked.

Calhoun grinned. "Around our cell, alcohol is the drug of choice, ma'am. I'd have to say Richard had been . . . well . . . maybe not sober, but dry at least, ever since they locked him up. Same goes for me and John Braxton, too."

"You don't think it's possible Osmond might have gotten himself some contraband drugs?"

"Not that I know of," Calhoun said, "but we weren't like, you know, best buddies. He wouldn't have told me if he had."

There was a knock on the door. Tom Hadlock pushed his head inside the room. "I've got the girlfriend's parents' address down in Douglas—Mr. and Mrs. Gabriel Gomez. Should somebody from the jail handle this?"

"No, Tom," Joanna said. "We will." She looked at Frank Montoya, who nodded, stood up, and headed for the door.

"I'll take care of it," he said.

Joanna stayed in the interview room for the remainder of Calhoun's interview and for John Braxton's as well. Fran Daly arrived in less than an hour and a half after being summoned. Once Dr. Daly went out to the rec yard to take charge of the body, Joanna headed home. Butch was in bed, reading, when Joanna walked into the bedroom.

"Where's everybody?" Joanna asked.

"Tigger and Lucky are in Jenny's room."

"You didn't leave the puppy loose, did you?" Joanna asked.

"Do I look that stupid? Of course he's not loose. Jenny and I rigged up a temporary crate to use until we can get a real one."

"Good," Joanna said. "What about the other one?"

"Lady's over there," Butch said, nodding toward Joanna's side of the bed. "See for yourself."

The Australian shepherd lay curled into a tight ball on the rug between the bed and the wall. She looked up as Joanna came around the side of the bed. Her tail thumped tentatively on the floor, but she made no effort to raise her chin off her paws.

"Did you say Lady?" Joanna asked.

"Yup," Butch replied. "Jenny picked it. She said she was dainty and ladylike, so that's what she's going to be called—Lady."

Joanna went over and patted the top of Lady's head. "How did you get her to come in here?" Joanna asked.

"Don't ask me. Jenny's the one who finally persuaded her to come into the house. She found your side of the bed all on her own."

"Smart dog," Joanna observed.

"Opinionated," Butch corrected. "She's fine as long as I don't get anywhere near your side of the bed."

Joanna undressed and then crawled into bed herself, sidestepping the dog as she did so. "You owe me," he said.

"With Mother, you mean?" Joanna asked.

"I'll say."

"Sorry," she said.

"I calmed her down eventually, but it took all of my considerable skill and charm."

"I can make it up to you," she offered, snuggling closer.

"Good," Butch said. "I thought you'd know how. What's the word on murder and mayhem?"

Right that minute, Joanna Brady didn't want to think about Richard Osmond and how he had died. "Do you mind if we talk about this in the morning?" she asked.

"No problem," Butch replied. "No problem at all."

SIX

Fran Daly and George Winfield stood with their heads close together, leaning over something just out of Joanna's line of vision. "The needle went in right here," Fran was saying. "Just at the base of the skull. He never felt a thing. Death would have been almost instantaneous."

Joanna held back, not wanting to see what they were looking at. The air around her was thick with nauseating odors. She could barely breathe, and yet she felt compelled to move forward, to make her way around to where she could see the naked figure lying there exposed beneath the harsh, bright lights. She expected to find the naked dead man lying exposed on Doc Winfield's autopsy slab to be Richard Osmond. Instead, it was Butch Dixon.

She awakened from the nightmare and scrambled out of bed. In her race for the bathroom, she stepped on Lady and almost fell in a tangle of legs and dog. Heaving, she made it to the bathroom in time, but only just barely. Seconds later, Butch was there as well, standing behind her with one hand on her shoulder.

"Are you all right?" he asked. "Is there anything I should do?"

Joanna was embarrassed to be found kneeling in front of the toilet and puking. "Go away," she mumbled impatiently through chattering teeth. "Go away and leave me alone."

He did. Finally, having survived that first powerful fit of nausea, Joanna showered, then pulled on a robe. Lady, waiting just outside the bathroom door, got up and followed Joanna through the house, trailing behind her like a four-footed shadow. The overhead skylights in the hallway shed a hazy gray glow as Joanna and the dog made their way to the kitchen. Butch was already there. The clock on the microwave read five-thirty as she hitched herself up onto one of the barstools positioned along one side of the island.

Butch looked up at her. "Are you all right?" he asked. She nodded. "Coffee's almost done," he added. "Do you want some?"

Just the smell of Butch's freshly brewed coffee made Joanna's queasy stomach turn flip-flops. She shook her head. "I think I'll have tea," she said.

"Tea?" Butch objected. "You don't even like tea."

"I do when I'm pregnant," she told him. "The same thing happened when I was pregnant with Jenny. I couldn't drink coffee the whole time."

Obligingly Butch filled the teakettle and put it on a burner. "This is going to take some getting used to," he said. "What do you eat for breakfast when you're pregnant?"

"No juice," Joanna said quickly. "English muffins with peanut butter and nothing else usually works."

"Coming right up," he said.

Joanna huddled miserably in her robe while Butch bustled capably around the kitchen. Usually Joanna's nightmares dissipated a few minutes after she awoke. This time the disquieting image of Butch laid out in the harsh lights of the ME's examining room stuck with her and wouldn't go away.

"Joanna?" Butch asked. "Are you listening?"

"Sorry, I must have been woolgathering. What did you say?"

"I asked what you're up to today."

"We'll have to deal with what happened to Richard Osmond at the jail yesterday," she told him. "But I'm also hoping we'll make some progress on the Mossman case."

"Sounds busy," Butch said. "Will you be having lunch with Marianne?"

Friends since junior high, Joanna and the Reverend Marianne Maculyea tried to have lunch together at least once a week. On the surface, they were just two old friends enjoying each other's company. But there was more to their weekly get-togethers than that. As two women working in nontraditional jobs and living in nontraditional families, each served as the other's primary support system. Other than Marianne, there weren't all that many women clerics working in Bisbee, or in Cochise County, either. And, as far as Joanna knew, there were no other female sheriffs anywhere.

"We probably will meet up," Joanna said dubiously. "But the way I feel right now, I'm not so sure about eating lunch."

"Isn't there something you can take for morning sickness?" Butch asked, putting a plate containing two peanut-butter-spread English muffins on the counter in front of her.

Joanna shook her head. "Too many antinausea drugs have the potential of causing birth defects."

"So we just have to wait it out?" Butch returned.

Joanna nodded. "Grin and bear it," she said.

While Joanna nibbled tentatively at her English muffins, Butch went into the laundry room and began distributing dog food. At the first clatter of dog dishes, Tigger came racing from the far end of the house, followed by the puppy. Butch put the food in the garage and then opened the door, but only Tigger and Lucky went out. Butch had to leave the door open and then come all the way back into the kitchen before Lady sidled into the laundry room and then on into the garage.

"I'd like to beat the crap out of the guy who hurt that dog," Butch said after she left. "I don't think she actually hates men. She's just scared to death of us—probably with good reason."

Jenny came into the kitchen about then, rubbing her eyes and frowning. "What's happening?" she asked. "Why's everyone up so early?"

"It's due to your mother's delicate condition," Butch said with a chuckle. "I have a feeling we're all going to be early birds for the next little while."

It was one of the few times ever that Sheriff Brady beat Frank Montoya into the office. When he came to see her a little later, he carried his usual cup of coffee. Again, the very smell of it made Joanna turn green.

If I'd only waited long enough to smell the coffee this morning, Joanna thought miserably, **we wouldn't have had to waste any money on the pregnancy test. Do you suppose that's what**

Dear Abby meant when she said, "Wake up and smell the coffee"?

"Is something the matter?" Frank asked. "You don't look very well."

"I'm all right," she said. "It's nothing that having a baby won't fix."

"Oh, that," Frank said. "I see." But, since he was a confirmed bachelor, Joanna wasn't convinced he did.

"What's on the agenda today?" she asked. "Did you have any luck tracking down Marla Gomez?"

Frank nodded. "Yes, unfortunately. It wasn't pretty."

"She was upset?"

"I'll say, and who could blame her? The thing is, she wanted to know what we'd done to Richard. I told her we hadn't done a thing, but she didn't believe it. Her father was there, and he wasn't much help, either. You do know who the father is, don't you?" Frank asked. "Gabriel Gomez?"

"I heard the name last night," Joanna said. "It sounded familiar, but at the time I couldn't place it. Who is he?"

"Gabriel Gomez is an attorney in Douglas. Specializes in immigration law. By the time I left their house last night, he was threatening to sue the department for wrongful death on his daughter's behalf."

"How can they do that?" Joanna asked. "We still don't have any idea of who or what killed Richard Osmond."

"You know that, and I know that, boss, but Papa Gomez is an attorney. You don't really expect him to wait around for the dust to settle, do you? His strategy is to sue first and ask questions later."

"Great," Joanna said. "That's just what I need to hear first thing in the morning."

The door to Joanna's office shot open and Joanna's secretary bounded into the room, brandishing a copy of **The Bisbee Bee** over her head.

"Why didn't you tell me?" she demanded. "Were you planning on keeping it a secret?"

"Keeping what a secret?" Joanna asked.

"That you're expecting. It says so right here. In Marliss Shackleford's column."

Kristin held out the paper, and Joanna snatched it out of her hand. **The Bee** was already opened to Marliss's column, "Bisbee Buzzings." For Frank Montoya's benefit, Joanna read the item aloud.

> An unnamed source close to Cochise County Sheriff Joanna Brady tells us that the sheriff and her husband, Butch Dixon, could be in a family way. There's no telling how the potential patter of little feet will affect Sheriff Brady's current

bid for reelection against former Cochise county deputy sheriff, Kenneth W. Galloway.

Motherhood, apple pie, and baby showers could get in the way of politics as usual, but at this point Sheriff Brady evidently has no intention of dropping out of the race.

That was all there was to the item, but by the time Joanna finished reading the two paragraphs, her voice was choked with fury. So much for her plan of giving Marliss Shackleford the kind of well-aimed, exclusive piece that might have allowed Joanna to control both timing and content. Here it was, set loose into the world in a way that was bound to do as much damage as possible. The general public would probably assume, just as Kristin Gregovich had, that Joanna had intended to keep her condition secret up to election day or even longer.

Livid, Joanna turned her ire on Frank. "You didn't give her this, did you?" she demanded.

"No, ma'am," Frank said. "Absolutely not. I didn't breathe a word of it."

"I didn't think so. Unnamed source, my ass. It has to be my mother, then. Eleanor's the only other person Butch and I have told. Too bad for me, she and Marliss have always been the best of pals."

With words of congratulation dying on her lips, Kristin retreated from Joanna's office. Frank Montoya followed, closing the door behind him as he went. The door was barely shut by the time Joanna had the telephone receiver in hand and was dialing George and Eleanor Winfield's number.

"Mother?" Joanna said stiffly as soon as Eleanor answered the phone.

"My goodness, you're certainly up and about early this morning," Eleanor responded brightly.

"I'm calling about the piece in the paper," Joanna said, struggling to keep her voice level.

"What piece is that?" Eleanor asked. "I brought the paper in from the porch, but I haven't had a chance to read it yet. I usually save that for after George goes to work."

"You know what piece I mean," Joanna retorted. "It's the part of Marliss Shackleford's column that talks about my being pregnant. How could you do that to me, Mother? How could you?"

"Do what?"

Eleanor's tone of affronted innocence made Joanna that much angrier. "Come on, Mother. Don't play games. How could you go behind my back and talk to Marliss that way? Other than Jenny, you and George were the first people Butch and I told. Did it ever occur to you that maybe we'd like the opportunity of sharing the news with a few other people in person before you hauled off and put it in the paper for everyone to read over their morning coffee?"

"Before **I** put it in the paper?" Eleanor repeated.

"Yes. It's this morning's lead item in Marliss Shackleford's column."

"So you think that as soon as I got home from your house last night, I called Marliss and told her about this?" Eleanor demanded. "You think the idea of my daughter being pregnant and running for office at the same time is something I'd be in a hurry to brag about?"

"Are you saying you didn't tell her?" Joanna asked.

"Of course I didn't tell her," Eleanor declared heatedly.

"Who did, then?"

"How should I know?" Eleanor returned. "All I can say is, Marliss didn't get it from me. It hurts me to hear you'd even **think** such a thing."

"You and Marliss have always been good friends," Joanna pointed out.

"Yes, but that doesn't mean I have to go to her to air our family's dirty laundry."

That brought Joanna up short. "It's not dirty," she said finally. "Remember, Mother? I'm a married woman. My husband and I are expecting a baby together."

"Then what are you so upset about?" Eleanor shot back. "Why are you calling me and giving me such a load of grief over it? Now, if you don't mind, I believe I'll get back to my breakfast. Good-bye."

With that, Eleanor hung up, leaving Joanna sputtering into thin air. Moments later, Joanna slammed her own phone back into its cradle. That was the thing that made Eleanor Lathrop Winfield so damned exasperating. No matter what happened, Joanna was **always** in the wrong.

Still seething, Joanna picked up the paper and turned it back to the front page. There she found a long article on the Carol Mossman murder, and a short piece about an unidentified inmate of the Cochise County Jail who had been found dead in the recreation yard. The paper had been printed late enough the previous night for the item about Joanna's pregnancy to make it into Marliss Shackleford's column. Wouldn't it also have been late enough to mention the jail fatality by name as well?

Maybe Mother didn't leak the story to Marliss after all, Joanna thought. **But if not Eleanor, who?**

Joanna was still staring unseeing at the newspaper when there was a discreet tap on her door. She looked up to see Kristin peeking warily into the room.

"It's all right," Joanna said. "It's safe to come in. I've stopped throwing things now."

Kristin came forward apologetically. "I'm so sorry, Sheriff Brady," she began. "I didn't mean to upset you."

"Don't worry about it," Joanna said. "I was surprised, is all. I didn't expect the news to show up in the paper quite this soon. It's like somebody having to read about the death of a family member before we have a chance to do a next-of-kin notification. There are a few other people I would have preferred hearing the news from me in person rather than having them read about it in the paper."

"Believe me," Kristin said, "I understand about that, but you are happy about this, aren't you, Sheriff Brady? Not about it being in the newspaper, but about the baby, I mean?"

"Of course I'm happy," Joanna answered. "It's a surprise, but Butch and I are both delighted. The lesson here is, no matter what the clever ads say on television, the Pill's not one hundred percent foolproof, especially if you happen to skip one at just the wrong time."

Which is probably exactly what happened, Joanna thought, although she didn't say it aloud.

"Oh," Kristin said. "That's okay then. It's just that you were so upset . . ."

"I'm still upset," Joanna corrected. "Marliss

could have had the common decency to check
out the story with me before she put the piece in
the paper. And if Madame **Bisbee Bee** should
happen to show her face around here anytime today, you might advise her to steer clear of me. If
she gets too close, I might be tempted to pull out
a handful of her peroxided locks. As long as I
can't see her, I'll be fine."

Joanna paused and, for the first time, noticed
that Kristin was carrying several handwritten
messages. "So what's up?" Joanna added.

Kristin nodded self-consciously. "Detective
Carpenter says he's going to Tucson for the Osmond autopsy. He'll be gone most of the morning. Also, Edith Mossman is coming here for an
interview with Detective Carbajal. Ernie says
Jaime will probably need someone to sit in on
that with him."

"All right," Joanna said. "If Frank Montoya
can't do it, I will. Anything else?"

"There were two other calls that came in while
you were on the phone. One was from Reverend
Maculyea and the other from Eva Lou Brady. I
told them you'd call them back."

Damn Marliss Shackleford anyway! Joanna
thought savagely. She said, "I will call them
back, Kristin, so when you go back out, please
shut the door."

For the next half hour, Joanna made a series of

calls. Conversations that should have been happy ones announcing her pregnancy ended up being chores instead. Joanna spent most of the time on the phone apologizing to one person after another, including her best friend, Marianne Maculyea, and her former mother-in-law, Eva Lou Brady, both of whom had already read Marliss's column. By the time Joanna's chief deputy returned for the morning briefing, Joanna welcomed the interruption.

"We'll have to make this quick," Frank told her. "I've got a news conference scheduled in a little while. It's primarily to go over the Richard Osmond situation, but if they ask, what do you want me to say about you?"

"About my delicate condition?" Joanna asked.

Frank nodded.

"Tell them I have no intention of dropping out of the race for sheriff. If daddies can be soldiers and sheriffs, so can mommies."

"Do you think that's the best way to couch it?" Frank asked. "With potential voters, I mean."

"It may not be the best way," Joanna told him. "But it's my way, and you can quote me on that. If you're going to be busy with a press conference, who's going to back up Jaime Carbajal when he questions Edith Mossman?"

"I guess it's up to you," Frank said.

Joanna nodded. "Okay. Speaking of Edith

Mossman, how's she getting here from Sierra Vista? We're not expecting her to catch a cab from there to Bisbee, are we?"

"No," Frank said. "I believe one of Edith's granddaughters—the one who lives here in town—is picking her up and bringing her to the department."

"Good," Joanna said. "I'm glad to hear it."

When the briefing ended, Frank left her office and Kristin entered once more, bringing with her that day's first load of correspondence. Joanna had managed to get a good start on dealing with the paper jungle when her intercom buzzed. "Sheriff Brady?" Kristin said. "Mrs. Mossman is here."

"She and Detective Carbajal are in the conference room?" Joanna asked.

"Right."

"Okay," Joanna said. "I'll be right there."

To reach the conference room, Joanna had to walk past Kristin's desk and through a small reception area. Seated on the love seat, thumbing through an old copy of **Arizona Highways,** was a large woman with mousy brown hair who looked to be about Joanna's age. She wore shorts, an oversize T-shirt, and thongs.

It was only midmorning, but already the office was heating up. Dressed in her uniform, Joanna couldn't help but envy the other woman's casual attire, but not the strained expression on her face. It was the despairing, empty look in the eyes that gave Joanna her first clue. She had seen that look far too many times before in the eyes of grieving survivors—the people left behind in the wake of violent and unexpected deaths. This had to be one of Carol Mossman's sisters.

Joanna stopped in front of the love seat and held out her hand. "I'm Sheriff Brady," she said. "You must be Stella Adams."

"Yes," the woman murmured softly. "Yes, I am."

"Please accept my condolences."

Stella nodded. "Thank you," she replied.

"And thank you for bringing your grandmother here for the interview. We're a little shorthanded at the moment. Otherwise I would have sent one of my detectives to bring her into town."

"It was no trouble," Stella said.

Just then a young boy of fifteen or sixteen came sauntering down the hall. The crotch of his pants hung almost to his knees. So did the tail of his shirt. A scraggily thin bristle of goatee protruded from the bottom of his chin. Stella Adams gave the new arrival a hard look. "There you are, Nathan," she said. "What took you so long? I thought I told you to park the car and come right inside."

Without glancing in Joanna's direction, the boy

slouched into a nearby chair. "Come on, Mom. Lay off. It's hot. I drove all around looking for some shade to park in."

"Mind your manners," Stella growled at him. Then, to Joanna, she said. "This is my son, Nathan. Nathan, this is Sheriff Brady."

Scowling, the boy stood up. "Hello," he said grudgingly. "Glad to meetcha." His handshake was limp. "Is there a Coke machine around here somewhere?" he asked.

"Just off the lobby," Joanna told him.

Nathan turned to his mother, who was already fishing a handful of change out of her purse. "Come right back," she admonished as he turned to go.

Joanna watched the transaction in silence. If Nathan was allowed to drive by himself, he had to be at least sixteen. And if Stella Adams was anywhere near Joanna's age—somewhere in her early thirties—then she would have been only fourteen or fifteen when Nathan was born, years younger than Joanna herself had been when she gave birth to Jenny.

"He may not look like it," Stella said to Joanna as her son walked away, "but Nathan's a good kid. It's hard to raise good kids these days."

"Don't I know it," Joanna agreed. "Especially once they become teenagers. Now I'd better get going."

She hurried into the conference room. "Good,"

Jaime Carbajal said, reaching for the tape recorder once Joanna had taken a chair. "Now we
can get started."

Jaime began the interview. Edith answered his
questions in a surprisingly steady voice, only occasionally biting back tears.

"Tell us about your granddaughter, Carol
Mossman," Jaime began.

"What do you want to know?"

"It's always helpful to know as much about the
victim as possible," Jaime said gently.

"Carol didn't have an easy life," Edith said
sadly.

"Why's that?"

"She had to live with my son, for one thing,"
Edith replied. "Carol's mother, Cynthia, died in
childbirth when Kelly was born. Carol was the
oldest. She was ten at the time her mother took
sick and twelve when Cynthia died in childbirth.
A lot of the burden of taking care of her sisters
fell on her. That's a terrible responsibility for
someone so young," Edith added. "Terrible!"

"Where was this?" Jaime asked.

"In Mexico. Obregón," Edith answered. "Eddie wasn't much of a student. He never finished
high school. He went to work for Phelps Dodge
the minute he was old enough. Working underground, he made good money for a while. Then,
in 1975, when PD closed down its mining opera-

tion, the company would have transferred him somewhere else. Instead, he quit and took his family to live in Mexico."

"I know Phelps Dodge had operations in Cananea," Jaime said. "But I don't remember any near Ciudad Obregón."

"That's because there aren't any," Edith replied shortly. "Eddie got himself mixed up with some cockamamy religious group called The Brethren. Their headquarters is on a ranch outside Obregón. Eddie and Cynthia took the three girls and went there because they could live on the ranch rent-free. I'm convinced that's why Cynthia died, by the way. She had M.S. and never should have gotten pregnant that last time. But if she'd been in a hospital here in the States, being treated by a properly trained doctor, she might still be alive to this day.

"At the time, and for a long time afterward, I didn't know any of this. Eddie and I don't exactly get along, you see, and we didn't stay in touch. Then, one day, out of the blue, a letter came from Carol—a postcard, really—asking if she and her sisters could come live with me. Just like that. And I said, 'Of course. Whatever you need.'"

"When was that?" Joanna asked.

"When the girls came home?" Edith asked. Joanna nodded. "Seventeen years ago or so,"

Edith said. "Carol had just turned twenty. She told her sisters that she was bringing them home for a visit. Kelly didn't want to come, and Carol couldn't make her change her mind. Once they got here, the girls stayed with me and never went back."

"What happened then?" Jaime asked.

"Well," Edith said, "Grady was already gone by then, so I did what I could. The girls didn't have much of an education—only a lick and a promise, so I saw to it that they all got GEDs. Andrea took to schooling like a duck to water. She got her AA degree from Cochise College in Sierra Vista and then went on to the U of A. She's working on a Ph.D. in psychology and works as a secretary in the Chemistry Department. They give employees a good discount on tuition, you see.

"Stella wasn't much of a student, but she had a baby to support, so she got a job waiting tables at PoFolks in Sierra Vista. That's where she met Denny, her husband. Couldn't have met a nicer guy, as dependable as the day is long. He drives a FedEx truck. He and Stella got married when Nathan was three. Denny's the only father little Nate has ever known."

"And Carol?" Jaime asked.

A pained expression crossed Edith Mossman's face. She shook her head sadly. "Carol never quite managed to cope," she said. "She bounced from one bad job to another, and no matter where she lived, she always ended up taking in a pack of dogs. It's hard to find a decent place to live when you have five or six or seven dogs living with you."

"You mean she's done this before—gathered up a bunch of stray dogs?"

Edith nodded. "And then she'd get evicted and the next thing I knew she'd have lost her job and she and the dogs would be living on the streets or in her car. That's how come I finally let her move into Grady's and my mobile. That way I could be sure that, no matter what kind of mess the place turned into, at least she'd have a roof over her head."

"In other words," Joanna said, "whenever Carol got into some kind of financial or legal difficulty, she came to you for help."

"There wasn't anyone else for her to turn to."

"Including two weeks ago, when she received the citation about this latest batch of dogs?" Joanna asked.

"That's right. And, like I said to you the other day, I told her I wouldn't be able to help out until after the first of the month, when my social security check showed up. In the meantime, she called me from work one afternoon and told me not to worry about it—that she'd made arrangements to get the money from someplace else."

"Did she say where this money was supposed to come from?"

Edith shook her head. "No. At least not to me she didn't."

"So even though she told you she had the situation covered," Joanna said, "you came on out to her house with your checkbook at the ready anyway. How come?"

"Because when Carol said she didn't need the money anymore, I didn't necessarily believe her," Edith replied. "You see, she wasn't a person who was always one hundred percent truthful. She was more than happy to tell lies when it suited her or when she was trying to save face. Carol may not have had much else going for her, but I'll tell you this much—she did have her pride. When it comes to that, Carol was a Mossman through and through."

So is pride what killed her? Joanna wondered. **Being poor and proud can sometimes be a lethal combination.**

SEVEN

The interview with Edith Mossman went on for sometime after that, but Joanna had a difficult time concentrating. Her early-morning English muffins had long since worn off. Her stomach was growling so loudly that she worried Edith might hear it.

The questions droned on and on. Did Carol have any enemies? No. Boyfriend? If Carol had a boyfriend, Edith knew nothing about it. How long had she worked in her present position? About six months. Had Carol had any difficulties at work, either with supervisors, fellow employees, or customers? Not that she had mentioned to Edith.

Taken individually, the answers to all of Jaime's questions seemed inconsequential. Together, they formed a picture of who Carol Mossman was and who her associates had been. The hope was that one or another of those slender threads would help lead investigators to the killer. When Edith finally complained of fatigue, Jaime immediately offered to break for lunch.

"You mean there's more?" Edith demanded. "What else can you possibly want to know?"

"We need to know everything," Jaime told her. "Everything you can tell us."

"It'll have to wait, then," Edith said. "I'll go over to Stella's house and take a little nap. I'm no spring chicken, you know. If I don't get my rest, I'm the next best thing to worthless. Maybe, after that, I'll feel up to talking some more. Right now I'm completely worn out."

Me, too, Joanna thought.

"Sure thing," Jaime said. "Later this afternoon will be fine."

Twenty minutes later, Joanna slid into a booth at Daisy's, across the table from where Marianne Maculyea was already sitting.

"How are you doing?" Marianne asked.

"Fine until I smelled the food," Joanna said.

"Queasy?"

"You could say that."

"Try the chicken noodle soup," Marianne suggested. "When I was pregnant, chicken noodle was one of the few things that didn't bounce back up the moment I swallowed it."

"I take it you've forgiven me for not telling you first thing?" Joanna asked.

Marianne grinned at her. "Let's just say I'm

over it," she said. "I'm thrilled to know Jeffy is going to have someone to play with."

"You may be over it, but I'm not," Joanna said. "I'm still pissed at Marliss."

Even as she said it, Joanna knew she was putting Marianne in a difficult situation, since Marliss Shackleford was also a member of the Reverend Maculyea's flock at Tombstone Canyon United Methodist Church.

"Don't be," Marianne advised. "Marliss was just doing her job. Or what she sees as doing her job."

Daisy Maxwell, owner of Daisy's Café, approached the booth with pad and pencil in hand, ready to take their order.

"Good afternoon, Sheriff Brady," she said with a smile. "And congratulations. What'll it be, now that you're eating for two?"

Word is definitely out, Joanna thought.

"My friend here recommends the chicken noodle soup," Joanna replied. "I guess I'm having that."

"And you?" she asked Marianne.

Once again, Marianne favored Joanna with an impish grin. "Well," she said, "since I'm not the one who's expecting, I'll have a hamburger. With fries!"

Forty-five minutes later, Joanna was back in her office when Ernie Carpenter knocked on the doorjamb. "Back from Tucson already?" she asked.

He nodded, came into the room, and eased his portly frame into one of the chairs. "If the jail's still under lockdown," he said, "I think you can tell Tom Hadlock to ease up."

"How come?" Joanna asked. "What's the verdict?"

"Fran Daly's preliminary conclusion is that Richard Osmond died of undiagnosed pancreatic cancer."

Joanna closed her eyes and whispered a small prayer of thanksgiving that George Winfield had wisely suggested bringing in an unbiased third-party medical examiner. The same information coming from Joanna's own stepfather would have been far easier to view with skepticism.

"Undiagnosed?" she asked. "You mean Richard Osmond was that sick and no one had any idea?"

Ernie nodded. "According to Doc Daly, that's the way pancreatic cancer works sometimes. It's like a time bomb that goes off with zero advance warning. Even if doctors find it, Fran says there's not that much that can be done about it."

"What I want to know is whether or not **we** had any warning," Joanna declared, emphasizing the first person plural pronoun. "Whether the Cochise County Sheriff's Department had any warning."

"What do you mean?"

"According to Frank, Richard Osmond has a child with a girlfriend whose father is a litigious kind of guy. Before Frank even finished doing the next-of-kin notification, Gabriel Gomez was already threatening us with a wrongful-death lawsuit. I want to know for sure that we're covered on this, Ernie. I want you to check the jail records and find out if Osmond ever asked to go to the infirmary on a sick call or asked to see a doctor. I also want you to check with the two guys in his cell; what are their names again?"

Ernie hauled out a pad of paper and checked his notes. "Brad Calhoun and John Braxton," he supplied.

"I want you to see if Osmond ever complained to either one of them about not feeling well. I want those interviews conducted immediately, properly witnessed and recorded. Understand?"

"Got it, boss," Ernie replied. "What's Jaime up to right now?"

"As far as I know, he's waiting for Edith Mossman to wake up from her nap so he can finish doing her second interview. Maybe you can squeeze in talks with Braxton and Calhoun before that happens."

Ernie nodded. "We'll get right on it," he said.

As Ernie rose to do her bidding, it occurred to Joanna that she owed this man, some twenty-five

years her senior, the courtesy of personally in-
forming him about what was going on.

"By the way, Ernie," she said, "I'll probably
have Frank put out an official bulletin, but
there's something I need to tell you."

"About the baby, you mean?" he asked.

Joanna nodded.

"Not to worry. Rose read me the article from
the paper this morning. I should have mentioned
it earlier. I guess congratulations are in order."

Marliss strikes again, Joanna thought.

"Thank you," she said.

Ernie frowned. "You're not planning on quit-
ting, are you?"

"No. Definitely not."

A slow smile crossed Ernie Carpenter's broad
face. "Good," he said. "Glad to hear it. I'm just
getting used to working with you. It'd be a shame
to lose you now."

As soon as Ernie left her office, Joanna picked
up her phone. "Frank," she said, "I think we
should send out a special department-wide bulletin as soon as possible. We need to let people
know what's going on vis-à-vis my pregnancy."

"I'm on it," Frank told her. "I've got a rough
draft almost ready to go."

"You're a mind reader," Joanna said. "I'm free
whenever you are."

She was working on her never-ending pile of

paperwork several minutes later when David Hollicker came rushing through her door. "What's up?" she asked.

"You're not going to believe it."

"What?"

"NIBIN just got a hit on the Mossman casings."

It took a moment for Joanna's brain to sort the acronym into actual words—the National Integrated Ballistics Information Network. Once the ballistics information was entered into the computer, it didn't matter where the weapon was used next. A match was a match.

"Where?" Joanna demanded.

"In a double homicide near Road Forks," Hollicker said. "In Hidalgo County, New Mexico."

"What do you know so far?" Joanna asked.

"Just that there's a match. When it comes to talking to other departments, I thought it might be better if someone other than a lowly CSI made the call."

In less than a minute, Joanna was on the phone with Sheriff Randy Trotter in Lordsburg, New Mexico.

"I understand we have a joint ballistics hit," Joanna said.

"So I hear," Sheriff Trotter returned. "I was about to call you."

"What's the deal?" Joanna asked.

"Two Jane Does," he told her. "One a white female, early forties, maybe. The other could be Hispanic. Mid-to-late twenties. They were found late yesterday afternoon, stripped naked and shot to death off the road between Road Forks and Rodeo."

"Any possibility that the guy who reported it is the killer?" Joanna asked.

"I doubt it. He's a history professor from the University of New Mexico. He's devoting his summer to riding a bike to historical sites all over the state. The Circle B Ranch is about ten miles north of Rodeo. There's a well there along with a stock tank and a couple of trees. The professor had written permission from the rancher allowing him to camp there. He set up camp and then went off toward a stand of yucca, looking for a place to . . . well, relieve himself. He found the bodies about twenty yards from the stock tank and called 911 from his cell phone. From the looks of the victims, they'd been out there for a while—a day or so, anyway."

"What about autopsies?" Joanna asked.

"With tomorrow being the Fourth," Trotter said, "we probably won't have those before Monday at the earliest."

"Monday," Joanna echoed. "Can't you do better than that?"

"Hey, our ME's out of town. Went to a class

reunion in Ames, Iowa. What do you expect? Do you think I'm going to do them myself? I tried getting a pinch-hitter in from another county, but that costs money, and the budget doesn't allow—"

"You don't have to tell me about budget problems," Joanna interrupted. "We're dealing with one of our own. Whenever your ME gets around to doing the autopsies will be fine, but you're saying there's no identification?"

"That's right. None. No purses. No ID. No clothing. No jewelry."

"What about sexual assault?"

"No sign that we could see offhand, but again, we have to defer to the ME on that. What's the situation with your case?" Trotter asked.

Quickly Joanna related what she could about the Carol Mossman case.

"No suspects?" Trotter asked when she had finished.

"Not so far."

For a moment there was silence on the other end of the phone. "I'm wondering if maybe we're dealing with a serial killer," Sheriff Trotter said at last. "Somebody who's on the move and targeting women. The big question: Is this guy traveling east or west?"

"We'll know that better when we have an approximate time of death on your victims,"

Joanna returned. "Depending on whether your victims died earlier or later than ours, we may be able to tell the general direction the killer's heading. You haven't heard about similar cases from any other jurisdictions that might be related, have you?"

"Not yet, but my detectives are checking."

"I'll have mine do the same," Joanna said. "Have your guys work to the east; I'll have mine work west."

"Fair enough. No sense in duplication of effort," Trotter said. Then, after a momentary pause, he added, "Do you think the guy would be be stupid enough to use the same kind of ammo three times in a row?"

"Beats me," Joanna said. "Antique bullets made in 1917 are pretty distinctive."

"I'll say," Trotter agreed. "Where the hell did they come from?"

"Good question. Maybe they were stolen from a firearms museum somewhere or from a collector. Who knows? Maybe the gun and the bullets are all the same age."

"That would be something, wouldn't it?" Trotter asked.

Hollicker raised his hand. "I've already tried checking with Colt," he said. "They had a warehouse fire years ago. Unfortunately, their records don't go back this far."

Joanna relayed that information to Sheriff Trotter. "What do you think about going public with some kind of warning?"

"I think we should," Randy said.

"But what kind of warning can we give?" Joanna asked. "We've got no suspect. No vehicle. Our victim was shot while standing inside the back door of her own home. Where yours were gunned down is anybody's guess."

"Well, then," Sheriff Trotter replied, "the best we can do is to tell women living or traveling alone to be on the lookout. Since the killer's presumably already crossed at least one state line, we should be able to ask for help from the feds. If nothing else, they can help us with profiling."

"But only if we have more to give them," Joanna cautioned.

"**When** we have more to give them," Trotter said. "Tell you what, Sheriff Brady. We have the crime scene photos, and we did pick up a few tire casts and a few footprints. The casts are from big tires, probably from an SUV or a pickup truck. The footprints look to be about a size eight or so and our CSI says that whoever made them was carrying a pretty heavy load. How about if I package up copies of what we have here and courier all of it over to you with one of my deputies. Your guys can package up whatever you have on your end, and send it back to me.

Trading copies back and forth won't screw up any chains of evidence."

"Sounds good to me," Joanna said. "When will your deputy be here?"

"Give me a couple of hours, but it won't be late. Everybody who can is planning on taking tomorrow off."

Lucky them, Joanna thought. If a serial killer was on the loose and stalking unsuspecting women in New Mexico and southern Arizona, many of Joanna's people wouldn't be enjoying a leisurely Fourth of July holiday.

"This is critical," Joanna told Dave once she was off the phone. "Whoever this guy is, we've got to get him off the streets. I'm putting you in charge of making up the evidence packet we send over to Hidalgo County."

"All right, Sheriff," Dave said dubiously, "but I don't know how much good it's going to do. The killer never gained access to Carol Mossman's residence. We have some tire casts and a couple of footprints, too, and Casey picked up one set of prints from the doorknob on Carol Mossman's front door, but that's about it. Other than the things I just mentioned, the brass, and the bullets I dug out of the wall paneling, our crime scene stuff is pretty thin."

"Ours may not be worth much," Joanna pointed out, "but it's possible Trotter's people picked up something important. We'll be better off sending everything we have, usable or not, in hopes of getting something good back from them."

"Okay, Sheriff Brady. I'll get right on it."

As Dave walked out the door, Joanna's private line rang. "Did you eat lunch?" Butch said.

"Yes." Joanna was glad to hear his voice. Glad to have something bringing her back from a world in which serial killers traveled the countryside murdering whatever unfortunate women happened to cross their paths. "I had chicken noodle soup. Marianne had a burger and fries."

"Did the soup stay put?" Butch asked.

"So far, so good. What's up?"

"I'm calling to let you know you're on your own for dinner."

"Why's that?"

"Because Jenny and I are on our way to Tucson," Butch said. "We're hoping to make it to Western Warehouse before it closes."

"How come? I don't remember anybody saying anything about going to Tucson today."

"That's because it isn't exactly a pre-planned trip," Butch replied. "In fact, it came up just a couple of minutes ago, when I found Lucky under Jenny's bed chewing up one of her cowboy boots."

"It's wrecked?" Joanna asked.

"Totaled. She's got to have boots for the barrel race tomorrow, and her old pair is so small she can't squeeze into them anymore. So we're leaving right now. I'm going to put Lucky in the garage—in your garage—where there's nothing else for him to chew up." Butch paused. "How about that Marliss," he said finally.

"You saw the article?"

"No, but I heard about it. One of Jenny's friends called her."

"Great," Joanna said. "Couldn't be better. Mother and I already had words about it."

"How come?"

"I suggested maybe the leak came from her."

"I doubt it," Butch said. "Even if Eleanor had called Marliss the moment she left our house, I don't see how she could have beaten the **Bee**'s press deadline."

"You could be right," Joanna agreed. "So someone else besides my mother might be the culprit."

"You should probably apologize then," Butch suggested.

"I will," Joanna said. "When I get around to it. Now drive carefully," she added.

"I will," Butch returned, "but I have one more very important thing to say."

"What's that?"

"Whatever you do, don't bring home any more animals."

"Right," Joanna agreed with a laugh. "I promise."

"And you be safe, too," he told her.

Joanna let Butch hang up without mentioning that there were now two possibly related murder victims across the border in New Mexico. It was a glaring omission, and she wasn't sure exactly whom it was she was trying to protect—Butch Dixon or Joanna Brady.

After the call ended, Joanna forced herself to turn her attention to her desk. Wanting to leave it in some kind of reasonable order, Joanna tackled her daily grind of paperwork. Dealing with the constant barrage was much like the thankless task of doing housework—it could be completed on a temporary basis but it was never actually finished.

In the course of the late afternoon, she tried several times to check with the Double Cs. Unfortunately, her detectives remained in the conference room conducting back-to-back interviews. She was still sorting papers when Kristin called to say Deputy Roy Valentine of the Hidalgo County Sheriff's Department was waiting outside.

"Send him in," Joanna said. "Tell Dave Hollicker that Deputy Valentine is here and ask him to come to my office with the Mossman packet. And please see if Frank and the Double Cs can join us as well."

Deputy Valentine was young and seemed ill at

ease as Kristin ushered him into Joanna's office. She directed him to a chair by the small conference table at the back of the room. "If you don't mind, Deputy Valentine, I've asked some of the others to join us as well."

"Sure," he said. "No problem."

Once Valentine was seated, Joanna assembled enough chairs to go around. The others arrived one by one, and Joanna introduced them to Valentine. Only when they were all gathered did he undo the string fastener on the packet he carried and slide the collection of grisly crime scene photos onto the smooth surface of the cherrywood table.

Four years earlier, the sight of pictures of bloodied corpses would have sent Joanna Brady scurrying for the nearest rest room. Today, even with her rebelliously queasy stomach giving her trouble, Joanna was able to gaze at the photos with the dispassionate eyes of a professional. Just as Sheriff Trotter had said, the two female victims, lying on their backs, were both completely naked. The bloodstains on the bodies and apparent lack of same on the ground told their own complicated stories.

"This isn't where they were shot, is it?" Joanna asked Deputy Valentine as she passed the first photo along to Ernie Carpenter.

The visiting deputy gave her a somewhat

quizzical look before answering. "That's right," he said. "We think they were shot over by the stock tank. That's where the brass was found, but we didn't find much blood there. Sammy— that's Sammy Soto, our CSI—says he thinks they were shot there and then dragged away from the stock tank to where they were found. If the guy on the bike hadn't needed to take a dump—"

Embarrassed, Valentine broke off without finishing.

"But you don't know that for sure?" Ernie asked.

"No. We didn't find enough blood at the scene to place the shooting there for sure. It's a stock tank, you see," Valentine explained. "A herd of cattle came through the scene to drink several times between the time the victims were shot and when the bodies were found. They stirred up the dirt around the stock tank pretty good. We were damned lucky to find the brass and even a few footprints."

"Is it possible they were inside a vehicle when they were shot?" Ernie asked. "That would explain the lack of blood at the stock tank, but the shooter would be left with a hell of a mess in whatever he was driving. Or maybe they were all in the stock tank skinny-dipping."

Joanna knew Ernie Carpenter had just pulled Deputy Valentine's leg. Valentine, on the other hand, had no idea. "I doubt that's possible," he objected with a frown.

Shaking his head, Ernie continued to ask questions. "Any tire tracks?"

Valentine shrugged. "Some. And we made casts of what there were, but we don't know for sure the vehicle belonged to the killer. And, like I said, it's a stock tank. There were probably lots more tire tracks at some point, but by the time we got there, the cattle had obliterated all but that one set."

"So we don't know if the victims were inside or outside a vehicle when they were shot, but they are both naked. Any sign of sexual assault?"

"None that we could see. We won't know for sure until after the autopsies."

"Did your CSI say whether or not he thought the women were naked when they were shot?"

Valentine looked surprised. "He didn't say. Why?"

Ernie shrugged. "This kind of deliberate posing and sexual assault usually go together. Now when are those autopsies due again?"

"Sheriff Trotter already gave me the bad news on that," Joanna interjected, answering before Deputy Valentine had a chance. "Because it's a holiday weekend, Monday is the soonest their ME will be available."

"Too bad," Ernie said, shaking his head.

"We'll be losing a lot of precious time." He passed the first photo along and reached for another. "What's this?" he asked.

"Those are the casings," Deputy Valentine said. "Four of them. Two shots each. There seem to be prints on the casings but we haven't had time to process them yet. Sheriff Trotter said we'll get those to you as soon as possible."

"Good," Joanna said.

Together they sorted through one photo after another, twenty or so in all—photos taken before and after the bodies were removed from the scene, along with enlarged photos of shell casings with their telltale antique markings. Joanna was disappointed in the material. She had hoped for something definitive. Other than some footprints and the possibility of fingerprints, the New Mexico authorities didn't have any more to go on in this case than Joanna's people had in the Carol Mossman case. Even so, when they had finished with Deputy Valentine's packet of photos, Dave Hollicker passed along the flimsy collection of Mossman material.

"I don't think we're dealing with a terribly sophisticated or organized perp," Frank Montoya theorized as Valentine thumbed his way through the new set of crime scene photos. "If he was, he never would have left his brass lying around like that, to say nothing of brass with prints on it."

"I agree," Ernie said. "He may not be organized this minute, but at the rate he's going, he won't stay disorganized for long."

"Right," Jaime Carbajal added. "It could be he's somebody who's been thinking about killing people for a long time and he's only just now started."

"But he's off to a big start," Ernie said. "Right this minute the death toll stands at three. If he keeps up the pace, I'd hate to think how much damage he might do between now and Monday morning."

"And he may not have started here," Joanna put in. "Sheriff Trotter is having his people check points east looking for cases with similar MOs. I told him we'll look west of here. If we can come up with any other recent cases that might be connected, we'd at least have some idea of what direction he's going in."

Valentine finished sorting through the Mossman material and then stuffed it into the now empty folder he'd brought with him. "I'd better take this and head home," he said.

"Sorry there's not more," Joanna told him.

"That's okay. It's better than nothing."

"Well, guys," Joanna said, turning to her officers once Deputy Valentine had left the room. "What do you think?"

"Sounds like we've got a big problem," Jaime Carbajal said.

Ernie nodded. "The sooner we find this guy, the better. The trouble is, we spent a big chunk of today dealing with Richard Osmond when we should have been chasing Carol Mossman's killer."

Joanna nodded in agreement. "That's what I think, too. This is too serious to let sit fallow over a three-day weekend. Overtime or not, we have to have people tracking on this tomorrow and Saturday both."

"Count me in," Jaime said.

"Wait a minute," Ernie objected. "Don't the Coyotes have a big game tomorrow?"

Jaime Carbajal coached a Little League team called the Copper Queen Coyotes. Pepe Carbajal, Jaime's twelve-year-old son, was the Coyotes' star pitcher.

"Yes," Jaime said, "but not until mid-afternoon. Why?"

"I'll tell you what," Ernie said. "The Fourth of July is for kids. I'll take your on-call. You spend the day with Delcia and Pepe. I'll come in and work."

"Thanks, Ernie," Jaime said, "but phone me and keep me in the loop."

"Don't thank me," Ernie added gruffly. "I'll see to it that we even up eventually."

Joanna appreciated the effortless way in which the two detectives sorted out the scheduling arrangements.

"Now tell me," she said. "Did you finish the Calhoun and Braxton interviews?"

"Sure did," Ernie said. "And it looks like we're in the clear on those. Osmond never said a word to either one of his cell mates about not feeling well. We've got no notations of him asking to see a doctor or of his going to the infirmary, either. I'm guessing the situation just snuck up on him. Took him by surprise same as it did everybody else. And, if you ask me, it's a pretty good way to go. Not in jail, mind you, but to just lie down to take a nap like that and . . . poof . . . you're out of there."

"I have a feeling that Marla and Gabriel Gomez won't necessarily share your benign view of the situation," Joanna said. "You'll have transcripts for me?"

Ernie nodded. "ASAP," he said.

"And what about Edith Mossman? Did you find out anything more in talking to her this afternoon?"

"Not really," Jaime Carbajal answered. "We're making arrangements to interview the two sisters who live in the States—Stella, here in Bisbee, and Andrea, the one who lives in Tucson. Andrea is supposedly coming down to see Edith over the weekend. I'll try to interview her while she's here. Since Stella lives in Bisbee, I can talk to her sometime next week if I don't catch up with her sooner than that."

"What about the sister who lives in Mexico?" Joanna asked.

"Kelly," Jaime answered. "I asked Edith about whether or not she had let Kelly know what had happened. She said no, because as far as she knows, there's no phone service out to where they live. I spoke to an officer named Enrique Santos in the Ciudad Obregón Police Department. He knows about The Brethren—that's what they call themselves. Santos agreed to send someone out there in person to notify Kelly and her father of Carol's death and to ask them to call me either here in the office or on my cell phone."

"Good enough," Joanna said. "Does that do it then?"

There were nods all around. "All right then. See you tomorrow."

The Double Cs headed for the door. Jaime turned back from the doorway. "About the baby, boss. If it's a boy, you're going to name it after me, right?"

Joanna glanced at Frank. "I guess that means the bulletin went out?"

"Yes, ma'am."

"Right, Jaime," Joanna replied with a grin. "We'll call him Carby, short for Carbajal." She could hear Ernie and Jaime laughing as they made their way down the hall. Joanna turned back to Frank. "Remember, you're on call tomorrow, too. I'm going to be all over God's creation."

"Don't wear yourself out," Frank cautioned.

Joanna shook her head. "I'm pregnant, Frank. That doesn't turn me into some kind of invalid."

"But you're not Wonder Woman, either," he told her.

Back at her desk, Joanna's calendar lay open to July 4. **Oh, yeah?** she thought, glancing down through the jumbled notations of appointments to be kept. **Prove it**.

It was not yet dusk and still very hot when she drove up to the house on the expanded High Lonesome Ranch. Tigger came to greet the Crown Victoria. Lucky shot out of the garage the moment she opened that automatic door. Lady hung back until she was sure Joanna was alone, then she came crawling toward the car, groveling on the ground.

"Somebody really did mistreat you, didn't they, girl," Joanna said soothingly.

The dog's tail wagged tentatively. Joanna had to coax her to come back into the cool interior of the rammed-earth house. She took off her weapons and put them away, then she stopped in the laundry room long enough to fill dog dishes. Butch had decreed that feeding the dogs in the garage would help cut down on the mess, so that's what she did.

Once the three dogs had finished mowing through their food, Joanna let them outside. Then she pushed the button that closed the automatic garage door. Back in the laundry room, she closed and locked the door to the garage as well. As she did so, she couldn't help thinking about Carol Mossman. She, too, had closed and locked the doors to her home, thinking those barriers would somehow keep her safe and protect her dogs as well. But nothing could have been further from the truth. She had locked death inside her tumble-down mobile home rather than keeping it out.

Thoughtfully Joanna extracted the small notebook and stubby pencil she kept in her pocket. "Why were dogs inside?" she wrote.

Still pondering the question, she walked through the house. In the bedroom she changed into a T-shirt and shorts. Back in the kitchen, she poured herself a glass of lemonade from the fridge.

With Butch and Jenny both gone and with the dogs outside, the house was unnaturally quiet. Taking her glass with her, Joanna went into the family room and settled on the couch to watch the evening news. Peter Jennings had no more than opened his mouth when Joanna fell sound asleep. She was awakened much later by a chorus of barking dogs and the sound of the door opener operating on Butch's garage. Except for the flickering light from the television set, the whole house was dark. When Joanna switched on a lamp, she was astonished to discover it was almost nine o'clock. She had slept for nearly three hours.

The door from Butch's garage opened, and all three dogs careened into the family room. Lady sidled up on the couch, where she cuddled next to Joanna.

"There you are," Butch said as he and Jenny walked into the room. "When we didn't see any lights, Jenny and I decided you still weren't home."

"I was tired and fell asleep," Joanna said. "Did you get some boots?"

"We're booted," Butch replied. "What about dinner? We ate, did you?"

"Haven't, but I will," Joanna told him, heading for the kitchen. "I'm famished."

"You're feeling all right, then?" Butch asked.

She paused long enough to give him a kiss. "It's called 'morning sickness' for good reason," she told him.

He studied her face. "You look upset."

"I suppose I am," she agreed. "At least four people are dead so far. On three of them, we're making very little progress."

EIGHT

Early the next morning, the smell of Butch's coffee brewing in the kitchen sent Joanna scrambling out of bed and into the bathroom. A miserable half hour later, when she finally dragged her body into the kitchen, Butch took one look at her pale face and shook his head. "You look like hell," he told her.

"Gee, thanks," she muttered. "I can't tell you how much better that makes me feel."

"Do you think it's worth it?" he asked.

"Being pregnant?" she returned. "Ask me that again in a month or so when I'm no longer barfing my guts out."

Butch came across the room to give her a gentle squeeze. "I have water on for tea. Want some?"

"This morning, tea doesn't sound any better than coffee."

"If you're not careful," he warned, "you'll go into caffeine withdrawal, and then you'll really be in trouble—headaches, mood swings . . ."

Joanna hitched her way up onto one of the barstools at the kitchen counter and then glowered at him. "I'm **not** having mood swings," she retorted.

"Oh, really?" Butch said with a grin. "In the meantime, as requested, here are your English muffins, madame."

After delivering her breakfast, Butch turned back to the cooktop. Using only one hand, he expertly cracked two eggs at a time into a heated frying pan. While Joanna watched, he deftly flipped the eggs in midair and then, after a few more seconds over the heat, slid the over-easy result, with yolks perfectly intact, onto a waiting plate. A former short-order cook, Butch Dixon was disturbingly adept in the kitchen, enough so that watching him at work made Joanna feel inadequate. She herself had attempted that midair egg-flipping trick on only one occasion—with disastrous results for both egg and cooktop.

"I wish I could come with you today," Butch said thoughtfully, placing his own plate on the counter and settling on the stool next to Joanna's. Worried about the state of her innards, Joanna kept a close eye on her remaining muffin.

"The problem is," Butch continued, "I promised Faye that I'd help out at the booth. She's concerned that the girls will need some male-type extra muscle while they're setting up."

Faye Lambert was the leader of Jenny's Girl Scout troop. The girls, working on raising money for their second annual end-of-summer trip to southern California, had made arrangements to sell sodas and candy bars during Bisbee's Fourth of July parade and at the field-day events to be held later in the afternoon at Warren Ballpark.

"Jenny's shift in the booth ends at noon," Butch added. "That'll give us plenty of time to come home, have lunch, change clothes, load Kiddo into his trailer, and head for the fairgrounds in Douglas."

"You don't mind doing all this?" Joanna asked. "The booth, horse wrangling, and all that?"

Butch shook his head. "Not at all," he said. "When I was growing up, I always wanted to be a cowboy and a dad. Now I'm getting some practice in both with Jenny. Sort of like a preview of coming attractions," he added with a smile. "But tell me, Joey, are you sure you'll be okay, driving all over hell and gone by yourself?"

Part of Joanna relished Butch's husbandly concern, and part of her resented it. "I'll be fine," she reassured him. "I'm scheduled to be one of the lead vehicles in both parades. That means I'll be done with each of those events with enough time to get to the next one. I may be a little squeezed hustling between the two picnics, but I should make it with no problem."

"Did you say 'squeezed'?" Butch asked. "I don't think that quite covers it."

When she went out to get in the Civvie, she discovered Butch had left an unopened package of saltine crackers on the roof of the car.

Smiling at his thoughtfulness, Joanna settled into the driver's seat. As she drove toward the department in her dress uniform, she wondered how long she'd be able to fit into it. She stopped by the Motor Pool garage long enough to have her Crown Victoria gassed up and washed to get rid of the layer of fine red dust that was the natural shade of any vehicle making daily trips up and down the pavement-free road to High Lonesome Ranch.

She stopped by her office and checked with Dispatch to make sure nothing out of the ordinary needed her attention. Well before eleven she took her place as the second vehicle in Bisbee's Fourth of July parade, positioned directly behind the Bisbee High School marching band. The parade started fifteen minutes late and then took another forty-five minutes to make a leisurely circuit of Warren's onlooker-lined streets. Immediately after reaching the Cole Avenue starting point, Joanna headed out of Bisbee. The fifteen-minute delay in the first parade's starting time caused her to arrive in Sierra Vista too late to be at the front of the pa-

rade there. That meant she was even further behind schedule as she drove the twenty-plus miles
from Sierra Vista to the first community picnic in
Benson.

Driving with complete concentration, she was
startled when her cell phone rang just shy of the
junction at I-10. The out-of-area number on the
phone's readout wasn't one Joanna recognized.

"Sheriff Brady here," she answered.

"Happy Fourth of July," her brother's cheerful
voice boomed at her. "What are you up to?"

"On my way from a parade to the first of two
picnics," she told Bob Brundage. "From the second of two parades, actually. How about you?"

For most of her life, Joanna Brady had thought
of herself as an only child. Slightly less than four
years earlier, Joanna had discovered that her parents had had an earlier and previously unmen-
tioned, out-of-wedlock child. The infant boy
had been given up for adoption long before D. H.
Lathrop and Eleanor Matthews's eventual marriage, and years before Joanna's subsequent
birth. Bob Brundage had come searching for his
birth mother only after the deaths of both his
adoptive parents. A career military man, Bob
had arrived in Joanna's life as a full bird colonel
in the United States Army.

For some people, learning about a parent's
youthful indiscretions can serve as a unifying ex-

perience between parent and child. It hadn't
worked that way for Joanna Brady and Eleanor
Lathrop Winfield. Finding out about Bob
Brundage's existence had left Joanna feeling be-
trayed, and her lingering resentment stemmed
from far more than Eleanor's long silence about
her own history.

For years Eleanor Lathrop had berated her
daughter for being pregnant with Jenny at the
time Joanna and Andy had married. The circumstances surrounding their shotgun wedding had
given rise to years of never-ending criticism
from Eleanor. Never once in all that time had
Eleanor mentioned that there were similar skele-
tons in her own closet. That was what bothered
Joanna the most—her mother's blatant hypocrisy.
Despite Joanna's best efforts, she had yet to come
to terms with the situation, and because she had
not yet taken that first important step, forgive-
ness remained impossible.

"We're in Hilton Head with Marcie's folks,"
Bob answered. "Just hanging out. July's a good
time to be as far away from D.C. as possible."

In the course of the last few years, Joanna had
seen her brother several times when he had come
to Bisbee to visit with Eleanor. She and Bob
weren't close, but Joanna had to admit that he
was a pretty sharp and likable guy. Usually, when
Joanna spoke to Bob Brundage, it was by phone,

mostly on holidays and mostly on her home telephone line. The fact that he knew her cell phone number came as something of a surprise and made her slightly apprehensive.

"So what's up?" she asked.

"I heard from Eleanor today," Bob said casually.

By mutual agreement, when Joanna Brady and Bob Brundage spoke of their mother, both of them referred to Eleanor by her given name. It was easier—a way of avoiding the emotional minefield of their shared-but-absent family history.

Suspicions confirmed, Joanna thought. **No wonder you have this number.**

"What about?" she asked innocently.

"Eleanor happened to mention that you and Butch are expecting," Bob replied. "Congratulations. I've never been an uncle before. Unless it's a girl, that is. I suppose then I'll end up being an aunt."

It was an old joke, and Joanna wasn't disposed to be amused. "We'll be sure to let you know which one you turn out to be," she returned.

"That is why I called, though," Bob went on with all trace of joking around excised from his voice. "Eleanor wanted me to talk to you about this."

"About what?"

"About your being pregnant and running for sheriff at the same time."

"I suppose she expects you to talk me out of it?" Joanna demanded. "She's bringing you in because you're her big gun. She's convinced that as soon as you say the word, I'll fold?"

"Something like that," Bob admitted. "I tried to explain to her that this is none of my business."

You've got that right, Joanna thought. **So why are we having this conversation?**

"But I did promise her that I'd call," Bob continued. "I'm worried—"

"Don't waste your breath," Joanna interrupted, running out of patience. "Please don't worry about me, Bob. I'm more than capable of taking care of myself, and I certainly don't need you telling me what to do."

"I meant I was worried about Eleanor," Bob put in patiently.

"You don't need to worry about her, either," Joanna said. "She's tough as nails."

"But she seemed really upset."

"Of course she's upset," Joanna fumed. "She's **always** upset. She disapproves of everything I do. It's been that way my whole life. Now that I'm pregnant, she wants me to pull out of the election, go home, put on an apron, and play housewife. That's not me, Bob. It never has been me."

"I don't think she's upset because you're pregnant," Bob said. "At least not totally so. It's partially because you accused her of leaking the information to some reporter. What's her name?"

"Marliss," Joanna said. "Marliss Shackleford. Maybe I was wrong about that, but Eleanor and Marliss have always been bosom buddies. Based on that, I can hardly be accused of leaping to conclusions."

"I suppose not," Bob agreed. "But I do think you need to take a look at this whole situation."

By now Joanna had pulled into the parking lot at Benson High School and was sitting with the car parked but idling in order to keep the air-conditioning running. "What situation?" she asked.

"Eleanor's jealous," Bob answered.

"Jealous?" Joanna repeated. "Of me?"

"That's right," Bob Brundage said. "Think about it. Eleanor based her whole life on all those old rules, the ones she grew up with. I was born pre–women's lib; you were born after. First, she lost me because, back then, being pregnant and unmarried just wasn't done, not by good girls from good families."

And what does that make me? Joanna wondered.

"Eleanor Matthews had a rebellious streak," Bob continued, "but society—in the form of her parents—ran roughshod over it. Her family made her conform and forced her to give me up for adoption. She told me once that losing me broke her heart, and I'm sure it's true. From then on, she decided she was through with breaking rules. She set about conforming, and she did it up brown. When the sexual revolution came along, she ran in the opposite direction. While other women her age were out burning their bras, Eleanor decided to go home and stay there, looking after her husband and raising her daughter. Did you know that, at one time, Eleanor wanted to be a fashion model?"

Joanna was stunned by this astonishing revelation. To those growing up in the cultural backwater of Bisbee, Arizona, a career as a fashion model would have been beyond the realm of possibility.

"You're kidding!" Joanna exclaimed. "Eleanor Lathrop a fashion model? You mean a real, honest-to-goodness fashion model, in someplace like New York?"

"Or Paris," Bob added.

Joanna was unconvinced. "That's a little far-fetched. It sounds about as likely as her wanting to grow up to be a stripper. Besides, she never mentioned a word about it to me."

"She did to me," Bob returned.

Naturally, Joanna thought bitterly. **Of course, she told her fair-haired boy and not me . . .**

"So what happened?" Joanna asked with more than a trace of sarcasm in her voice. "If she wanted to become a model so badly, why didn't she do it?"

"Because, after she had me, her mother convinced her that models who had damaged their bodies with babies were all washed up in the fashion biz."

"So she decided to become a housewife instead?"

"That's right. She stifled her own career ambitions, first because of me and later because of her husband and you. But now, Joanna, take a look at what you're doing. It's not just that you're not following Eleanor's blueprint for life. Instead, you're designing a whole new ball game. Eleanor Matthews Lathrop had two children—you and me. It's pretty clear to me that between the two of us we cost her everything."

Speak for yourself, Joanna thought.

But Bob continued. "You have one child, soon to be two, but you're living in a whole new era. From Eleanor's point of view, society is letting you off easy. You can do whatever you want. You don't have to pay the same kinds of prices Eleanor had to pay. As far as she's concerned, you're not having to give up anything."

The cell phone next to Joanna's ear was hot, but so was she. She sat there steaming, saying nothing but doing a slow burn. Bob Brundage had a hell of a lot of nerve analyzing what, if anything, Joanna Brady was having to give up.

"Joanna?" Bob asked at last. "Are you still there?"

"I'm here," Joanna said stiffly. "Tell me something. Did you think all this up on your own, or did Eleanor ladle it to you one word at a time?"

"On my own," Bob answered. "I swear, every word of it."

"So what are you then, some kind of psychologist?"

"I have an advantage you don't have," Bob replied.

"What's that?" Joanna asked pointedly. "Age?"

"That, too." Bob's reply to Joanna's blunt question was pleasantly evasive. "But not just that," he added. "I have the benefit of perspective, and perspective only comes with distance. You're too close to see it."

"As in too close to the forest?"

"Something like that."

Across the parking lot, Joanna could see the Benson mayor's aide, Martha Rogers, checking her watch and glancing anxiously around the parking lot. A look at the clock on the dashboard told Joanna why. It was two minutes away from the time to introduce visiting dignitaries, one of whom was scheduled to be Joanna Brady, sheriff of Cochise County.

"You still haven't said what you want me to do about it," Joanna said to her brother.

"Just be aware of it, is all," Bob said. "And cut Eleanor a little slack now and then."

"Does that mean you're not going to tell me to drop out of the race for sheriff?"

"Are you nuts?" Bob asked with a chuckle. "I get all kinds of points around the Pentagon when I tell my coworkers that my kid sister is a sheriff out west in Arizona. They always want to know whether or not you carry a gun. And when I tell them you're almost as good a shot as I am, they're impressed."

Joanna laughed, too. "Next time you're out to visit," she warned him, "you and I will do some target practice. We'll see then who's the better shot. Right now, I've gotta go. Someone's looking for me. Tell Marcie hi for me."

It was a thoughtful Joanna Brady who made her way through the parking lot toward the red-white-and-blue-festooned podium. Joanna had always despised what she had dismissed as Eleanor's perpetual social climbing. Now she wondered how much those social-climbing tendencies had to do with Eleanor's own thwarted ambitions—the hopes and dreams Eleanor Matthews had put aside in favor of marriage, motherhood, apple pie, and the American way. It was likely that her thwarted ambitions had determined the kind of mother Eleanor had turned out to be.

In Joanna's opinion, she and her mother had been locked in a perpetual state of warfare that dated from the very beginning—from Joanna's first conscious memories. Rather than supporting her daughter, Eleanor had always been the one standing in Joanna's way, blocking her progress and attempting to turn Joanna into someone far different from who she really was. But maybe Bob was right. Maybe the constant bickering with her mother was an outgrowth of a simple case of mother/daughter jealousy. And if Bob was right about that, maybe he was correct in something else as well. Maybe Joanna Brady was too close to the situation—so close that she hadn't had a clue it even existed.

Minutes later she was standing on a makeshift podium welcoming people to the Benson Community Fourth of July picnic. She kept her remarks short and nonpartisan, then she spent the next forty-five minutes working the crowd, shaking hands and doing what she could to drum up support for her campaign. Later, after the short ten-minute drive from Benson to St. David, she did the same thing again—a short speech followed by another session of glad-handing all around. Everywhere she went she was offered food, none of which appealed to her in the least.

After the St. David appearance, Joanna headed home. She sailed past the Cochise County Justice Center without even turning on the Civvie's directional signal. Had anything been wrong, someone would have summoned her. She took the relative silence of radio chatter to mean that even the crooks were taking a holiday. At the Double Adobe turnoff, however, she glanced at her watch. It was twenty after three. The barrel-racing competition would start after a four o'clock performance by Sierra Vista High School's junior girl's rodeo drill team. Joanna figured that would give her time enough to get out of her dress uniform and into something a little more comfortable for sitting in the dusty stands at the fairgrounds. With that, she stepped on the brakes, and headed for High Lonesome Ranch where, in addition to changing clothes, she might be able to find something decent to eat.

It took Joanna a couple of minutes to negotiate the ecstatic dog greeting committee that met her at the front gate. Tigger was beside himself, and Lucky was so thrilled that he managed to pee on Joanna's pant leg and dribble into her shoe. That meant the uniform would have to go to the cleaner's after all. Lady showed even stronger signs of being happy to see her. Sadie's loss was still a fresh memory, but it was a little easier to bear the bluetick's absence now that there were other dogs to take the old hound's place.

Once in the house, Joanna changed into jeans and a long-sleeved denim shirt. She knew better than to brave the late-afternoon sun with her fair complexion and short sleeves. Finding a banana on the counter, she downed that along with a glass of ice-cold milk. Then, settling a straw Stetson on her head, she hurried outside and back into the now-roasting Civvie. Butch had left a note saying that the Outback was in the garage if she wanted to take that, but she felt more at ease in the Crown Victoria. That way, if duty called and her services were needed, she wouldn't be driving in a vehicle without two-way radio capability.

Sticking strictly to the posted speed limits, Joanna arrived at the rodeo grounds just as the sixteen-member drill squad galloped into the arena. Shading the sun from her eyes, Joanna spotted Butch, Jim Bob, and Eva Lou Brady sitting high in the stands. Excusing herself, Joanna made her way up to them. She was grateful to realize that their backs were to the sun.

Butch greeted her with a kiss. "Glad to see you," he said.

Joanna settled into the seat beside him and actually let herself relax as she watched the end of the drill team's performance. Joanna couldn't help but be impressed by the talented troop of elaborately costumed and synchronized riders as they galloped around the relatively confined space on swiftly moving horses. Each rider carried a banner that stood out straight behind her, whipping in the wind. As horses and riders careened around the enclosure, Joanna held her breath. At every turn it seemed as though two or more of them were bound to crash into one another with disastrous results, but they never did. It made Joanna grateful that when Jenny's turn came, there would be only one horse and one rider in the ring at a time.

As the drill team finished up and filed out to tumultuous applause, Joanna turned to Butch. "I thought Eleanor was going to be here."

"She called and canceled at the last minute," Butch replied. "She said she had a splitting headache."

Eleanor's got a headache, all right, Joanna thought. **It has nothing at all to do with Jenny's rodeo appearance and everything to do with me.**

Eva Lou Brady reached over and squeezed Joanna's knee. "Congratulations again, Joanna," Eva Lou said. "Jim Bob and I are both so happy for you."

Joanna looked at her former mother-in-law. For some inexplicable reason, her eyes filled with hot tears. Jim Bob and Eva Lou Brady were and always had been the embodiment of unconditional love. They, too, might have come up with any number of excuses for not going to the hot fairgrounds, but they were in attendance that afternoon, interested and uncomplaining, to support Jenny's foray into the world of rodeo riding.

When Joanna had announced her engagement to Butch Dixon, they had accepted her choice without a hint of disapproval. From the beginning, they had treated Butch with unfailing kindness and grace. And sitting there under the hot afternoon sun, Joanna knew, without question, that Jim Bob and Eva Lou would accept this new child—Joanna and Butch's child—as though he or she were their own flesh-and-blood grandchild.

"Thank you," Joanna murmured.

"Are you nervous?" Eva Lou asked.

Joanna didn't know if Eva Lou was asking about Jenny's upcoming ride or about the pregnancy. She simply nodded yes.

As the first barrel racer pounded into the arena, Joanna's attention was riveted. The girl looked to be much older than Jenny, and the horse, a palomino, was utterly splendid. Leaning into the curves as one entity, horse and rider skidded around the three equally spaced barrels. Watching their seemingly breakneck pace, Joanna couldn't help but hold her breath.

As the PA system broadcast the first rider's

time, Joanna's cell phone rang. The distinctive rooster-crow ring echoed through a suddenly silenced grandstand. Joanna dived for her purse to stifle the noisy thing. With many nearby spectators glaring at her in disapproval, Joanna glanced at the readout. She recognized the number at once—Dispatch.

"Sheriff Brady here," she said tersely into the phone. "What's up?"

"I thought you'd want to know that we've got a serious roll-over accident on Highway 80 out by Silver Creek," Tica Romero answered. "A coyote-driven SUV with twenty or so undocumented aliens riding in it. We've got injured UDAs everywhere and at least two confirmed fatalities. Multiple units, ambulances, and an Air-Evac helicopter are all on the way."

"What about Chief Deputy Montoya?"

"He's at the site of a reported road-rage shooting west of Huachuca City. It'll take him at least an hour to get to the other side of the county."

"Fair enough," Joanna told her. "I'm on my way." **God help me, I'm on my way!**

She glanced up in time to see the second barrel racer charge into the arena. She hoped for a brief moment that it possibly might be Jenny, but of course, it wasn't.

Butch looked at her questioningly.

"There's been a multiple-fatality accident east

of here on Highway 80," she told him. "I've got to go."

Butch nodded. "Okay," he said. "Drive carefully. See you at home."

"Are you sure you can't stay long enough to watch Jenny ride?" Eva Lou asked, reaching out to stop Joanna. "It can't be more than a few minutes before it's her turn. Barrel racing doesn't last all that long."

"Sorry, Eva Lou," she said. "Jenny will just have to understand."

As Joanna threaded her way down through the grandstand, she hoped fervently what she said was true and that Jenny would indeed forgive her.

At the far end of the parking lot where she'd left the Civvie, Joanna paused long enough to open the trunk and slip on a Kevlar vest, then she vaulted into the front seat. In her glove box she fumbled blindly around until she located the spare spiral-bound notebook she kept there. Once she'd stuffed that into the pocket of her jeans, she turned the key in the ignition. She switched on her flashing lights the moment the engine started, but she didn't activate her siren until she was well away from the fairgrounds.

"Okay, Tica," Joanna said into the radio as she turned onto Highway 80. "Tell me again what's going on."

"A Border Patrol unit in New Mexico saw an

old GMC Suburban headed northbound toward Animas. He signaled the driver to stop, but the driver didn't pull over. Instead, he jammed his foot on the gas and drove straight past. The Border Patrol went after the guy, but when the Suburban's speed exceeded ninety miles per hour, the agent broke off pursuit. He notified the New Mexico Department of Public Safety. One of their officers headed down from I-10, expecting to intercept the fleeing vehicle, but before he could make contact, the Suburban had crossed into Arizona north of Rodeo. A unit from the Arizona Department of Public Safety had been called and was responding when word came of the crash."

"Where exactly is it?"

"Silver Creek. The vehicle smashed through a Jersey barrier at a construction site and plowed into the wash. Hold on, Sheriff Brady," Tica added. "I'll have to get back to you."

While she waited for Tica, Joanna thought about Silver Creek, a mostly dry, sandy creek bed that meandered through the Perilla Mountains. The community of Silver Creek may have been little more than a blip on even the best road map, but when it came to smuggling, the tiny community had a long and colorful history.

Joanna's father, an amateur historian, had delighted in telling Joanna the story of how, in the

early days, prior to Arizona's statehood, Texas
John Slaughter had once decoyed a Border Patrol
detail to Silver Creek, telling them some notori-
ous smugglers were on their way through. While
the hapless Border Patrol agents waited in vain
for the nonexistent smugglers to appear, Slaughter himself brought a herd of illicit cattle across
the line from his own ranch in Old Mexico. By
the time the Border Patrol agents wised up and
returned to Slaughter's ranch, the illegal cattle
were mingled in with and totally indistinguish-
able from Slaughter's home herd in the States.

Years earlier, while Highway 80 had still been a
main thoroughfare for cross-country traffic, Silver Creek had boasted a celebrated steakhouse.
Since the completion of Interstate 10 forty miles
north, both traffic and business had migrated
there. For decades the old highway had been left
to languish in neglect. The steakhouse, having
opened and closed in various incarnations, was
now permanently shuttered.

In the past several months, however, the Arizona Department of Transportation had em-
barked on an ambitious program to rehab
Highway 80 between Douglas and the New
Mexico border. A mile or two at a time, the roadway was being widened and straightened. De-
crepit bridges and worn-out culverts were being
replaced and widened as well.

Approaching Silver Creek from the west, Joanna was surprised at how abruptly the relatively straight and flat roadway suddenly evolved into a series of steep dips and blind curves just as the orange road-construction signs began appearing on the shoulder. No wonder the speeding Suburban had come to grief.

An ambulance came barreling into sight in Joanna's rearview mirror. She pulled over to let it pass, then sped up and kept pace behind it. She hated to think of the dead and wounded scattered across the desert floor in the searing afternoon heat. Driving in air-conditioned comfort, she found it easy to ignore how hot it was outside, but with temperatures hovering in the low hundreds, the injured were as likely to die of heat and dehydration as they were of their injuries.

And so, since there was nothing else to do as she drove, Joanna Brady went ahead and prayed. "Please, God," she whispered aloud. "Be with those poor people. Comfort the injured and the dying, and guide all those who would help. Amen."

NINE

I t was just after five when Joanna, still driving behind the ambulance, rounded the last curve and saw a clutch of first-responder emergency vehicles lining the road. From where she was, though, the accident scene itself remained invisible. The sun had dipped behind the tall cliffs that topped the rugged Perilla Mountains, casting the whole area into shadow. Joanna parked her Civvie and then hurried to a spot where a shattered wall of Jersey barriers spilled down the rocky cliffs onto the baked-sand floor of Silver Creek.

It wasn't until Joanna was standing directly over the newly constructed culverts that she was finally able to see the smashed SUV. Looking like the work of a suicide bomber and crushed beyond recognition, the Suburban lay upside down in the midst of what appeared to be a scatter of brightly colored rags. It took several moments for Joanna's mind to come to terms with the awful reality. Those scattered bits of colored cloth weren't rags at all—they were pieces of clothing with dead and injured people still inside them. Uniformed officers—some of them EMTs—and a few concerned civilians crouched here and there, offering aid to the victims, some of whom moaned and whimpered softly while others shrieked in agony. A few of the victims, lying still as death, had either been abandoned as beyond help or were as yet untended and uncomforted.

Rushing back to the Civvie, Joanna grabbed one of the several jugs of bottled water she kept there. Then she plunged down the rocky bank toward the nearest victim. **This isn't an accident scene,** she told herself grimly. **It's a damned war zone!**

The first person Joanna reached was a man who appeared to be in his mid-thirties. A streak of bright red blood dribbled from one corner of his mouth and disappeared into the equally red bandanna he wore around his neck. His pencil-thin mustache was neatly trimmed, even though his dusty, threadbare shoes and the rank odor of sweat told her that in his effort to cross the border, he must have walked across miles of scorching desert.

Kneeling beside him, Joanna picked up his limp arm and felt for a pulse. Finding none, she let his wrist drop back to the ground. Knowing there was nothing she could do for him, she rose and moved on to someone else. This one was an older man in his fifties or sixties, with his left leg crumpled unnaturally under the right one. The skin on one whole half of his face had been scraped away, leaving behind a raw, seeping wound.

His eyes fluttered open as soon as she touched his hand. **"Agua, por favor,"** he whispered weakly. **"Agua."**

She helped him raise his head and then held the bottle of water to his parched lips. He gulped a long drink and then sank back gratefully. **"Gracias,"** he murmured.

"Don't move," she told him in her awkward textbook Spanish. "It's your leg."

He nodded and motioned her to move on. "The others," he said. "Help the others."

With a screech of its siren, yet another invisible ambulance arrived on the roadway above her. A new team of EMTs scrambled down the bank carrying a stretcher and cases of equipment. "Over here," she shouted, waving at them. "This man needs help."

As Joanna stood up to move out of their way, Deputy Debbie Howell, who had been the first Cochise County deputy on the scene, appeared at Joanna's elbow. "How bad is it, Deb?" Joanna asked.

Deputy Howell's face was grim. "Five dead so far. We've counted twenty-three injured and several of those are critical. The Air-Evac helicopter should be here soon. We've alerted hospitals in Douglas, Willcox, Bisbee, and Tucson."

Joanna was dumbfounded. "You're telling me there were twenty-eight people crammed in that SUV?"

Debbie nodded. "Twenty-nine, counting the driver."

"Where is he?" Joanna demanded. "Dead, I hope?"

Debbie Howell shook her head. "No such luck. He's evidently the only one who was wearing a seat belt. As far as we can tell, he isn't here."

"You mean he took off?" Joanna demanded.

"Exactly."

"Call Dispatch," Joanna ordered. "Tell them to get the K-9 unit out here on the double. That man's a killer, and I want him found!"

"Right away, Sheriff Brady," Deputy Howell answered. She turned and headed back toward the roadway.

"Wait a minute," Joanna called after her. "Who's in charge?"

Debbie nodded impatiently toward a group of uniformed officers who stood near the damaged Suburban. Joanna recognized one Department of Public Safety uniform and three from Border Patrol. "Beats me," she said. "It looks like those guys got here first, but with any kind of luck, you're the one in charge."

Joanna hurried over to the officers, most of whom she knew personally. When she had first arrived on the scene, the other officers had been scattered among the victims, checking them out and, in some cases, administering whatever aid they could. Now, though, with the arrival of several more EMTs, the four uniformed men stood wrangling among themselves, arguing about how best to proceed with the investigation. Jurisdictional considerations aside, Sheriff Joanna Brady outranked them all, and the accident was on her turf.

"What's going on, gentlemen?" she asked.

She was answered by Officer Bill O'Dea of the Arizona Department of Public Safety. "Oh, hello, Sheriff Brady," he said. "We're discussing who pays."

"Who pays?" Joanna repeated.

"For the medical care," O'Dea answered. "For the dispatched ambulances, the air ambulance, everything. Ed Coffer here of the Border Patrol was first on the scene."

Ed Coffer nodded in agreement but said nothing.

"UDAs are a Border Patrol problem," O'Dea continued. "I talked to my captain on the radio.

He says Border Patrol needs to step up and take responsibility for this situation."

The momentary anger Joanna had felt toward the missing SUV driver now coalesced and focused in laserlike fashion on that invisible captain who, far removed from the bloodied and broken bodies, was interested only in protecting his department's bottom line.

"This is everybody's problem," Joanna snapped. "People are hurt. How about if we take care of the victims first and worry about the medical bills afterward? Since the driver took off, I've got a K-9 unit on the way. Does anyone know which way he went?"

More than happy to let Joanna take charge, the other officers breathed a collective sigh of relief.

"Somebody said he took off in that direction," O'Dea told her, pointing to the left of the roadway.

"I want that man caught," Joanna declared. "Bill, how about driving up the road a mile or so to look for him. My guess is that sooner or later he'll be back on the highway trying to hitch a ride."

"Yes, ma'am," O'Dea responded. "Will do." He set off for his waiting patrol car at a fast trot.

Behind her, a woman screamed out in a torrent desperate Spanish. **"¿Dónde está mi niño? Mi niño . . . mi niño . . . ¿Dónde está mi niño?"**

Joanna turned toward the EMT, who was fitting the woman with a back and neck brace. "Did she say something about a baby?"

The medic nodded grimly. "That's right. She's looking for her baby."

Joanna turned at once to the three remaining Border Patrol officers. "Has anyone seen a baby around here?"

The three officers looked blankly from one to another, shrugging and shaking their heads. "Not so far," Ed Coffer said.

"If she says there's a baby, there's a baby," Joanna growled at them. "How about if you three go look for him?"

As the Border Patrol agents set off, Joanna once again scanned the scene in time to see the man with the broken leg and flayed face being strapped to a stretcher and then carried up the steep embankment. Then, for the first time, Joanna noticed a middle-aged Anglo woman in shorts and sandals sitting on a nearby rock. With her face buried in bloodied hands, she was sobbing uncontrollably.

Joanna hurried up to her. "Excuse me," Joanna said. "Are you hurt?"

When the woman removed her hands, her face, too, was stained with blood, but it was the vacant expression in her eyes that provided an answer all its own.

"Who, me?" the woman replied dazedly. "No, I'm not hurt. I'm fine, but I've never seen someone die before. I was holding him—that man over there." She pointed at the still and bloodied form of yet another man.

Little more than a boy, really, Joanna thought. A teenager.

"I asked him if he was okay." Her body shook as though she had just emerged from a pool of icy water. "But just then he stopped breathing," the woman continued. "I learned about giving mouth-to-mouth years ago. I tried to help him. I did my best, really I did, but there was so much blood coming out of his mouth . . . You've gotta believe me, I tried, but . . . but he died anyway. I've never felt so . . . useless." She broke off into another fit of sobs.

Joanna crouched down next to the woman and put an arm around her shoulders. "You did what you could," she said. "Nobody can fault you for that."

The woman nodded vaguely, but she didn't stop crying. Or shaking.

"Would you like a drink?" Joanna asked, offering her the water. While the woman stopped weeping long enough to gulp some water, Joanna realized that although this innocent passerby wasn't physically injured, she, too, was wounded.

"You should probably use some of the water to wash off," she suggested as the woman finished drinking.

The woman looked down in amazement at her bloodied clothing and hands. Using the remaining water, she began to sluice off. "Your face, too," Joanna added.

As the woman doused herself with water, Joanna pulled the notebook and pencil out of her pocket. "You saw the accident?" she asked gently.

The woman shook her head. "No," she said. "But I was right behind it, by only a minute or so. When I came around the curve and saw it, the dust was still flying. I couldn't believe it. That idiot had passed me a mile or so back, out while we were still on the flat. I was doing seventy. He came tearing up behind me like I was standing still and almost ran me off the road. He must have been doing ninety when he went flying past. Then when he hit the first set of curves, I don't think he even slowed down. At least I never saw any brake lights."

Finished with the water, the woman looked questioningly at Joanna's notebook. "Who are you?" she asked.

"Sorry I didn't introduce myself," Joanna said. "My name's Brady. Sheriff Joanna Brady of Cochise County. When the call came in, I was at a rodeo waiting to see my daughter's first barrel race. Who are you?"

"Suzanne Blake," the woman answered.

"Are you from around here?"

Suzanne shook her head. "From Douglas originally, but I live in Las Cruces now," she said. "My folks still live in Douglas. I come down once a month to check on them."

"You'll need to be interviewed," Joanna told her. "So if you could give me your parents' names and numbers . . ."

For the next several minutes Joanna gathered Suzanne Blake's pertinent information, including the exact time of the accident and where and when she had been passed by the speeding Suburban. "If you want to continue on your way," Joanna said as she returned her notebook to her pocket, "one of my investigators will be in touch with you tomorrow."

"Fine," Suzanne said. "And you're right, I should go. I called my parents when I left Cruces. My father knows exactly how long it takes to drive from my house to his. He timed it with a stopwatch once. He'll be worried sick."

As a still shaken Suzanne Blake tottered off, Joanna glanced around at what were now several teams of EMTs from various jurisdictions who were busy carting loaded stretchers back up to the roadway. An Air-Evac helicopter, returning after its first run, hovered overhead, looking for a place to land and receive the next load of injured patients.

Joanna had no idea how much time had passed since her own arrival on the scene, but now the sun was definitely setting. It was still hot, but in the increasingly dark shadow of the mountains it was already noticeably cooler.

The K-9 unit arrived and sought Joanna out. "We're here, Sheriff Brady," Terry Gregovich announced. "Now what can Spike and I do to help?"

"Find the asshole driver who caused this mess," Joanna ordered. "According to witnesses, he was wearing a seat belt, so he wasn't ejected along with everyone else. I'm told he took off into the desert, and I want him found."

Nodding, Terry headed for the wrecked Suburban with Spike. Not wanting to interfere with their work, Joanna let them go. Instead, she walked to the far end of the debris field, hoping that, by looking at the trajectory the vehicle had followed through the Jersey barriers, she would gain a better understanding of exactly how and why the accident had occurred.

As she turned around to examine the scene, her eye was drawn to a splotch of white barely visible beneath a nearby mesquite tree. She hurried over and was appalled to see a child lying there—the wounded woman's missing baby. Pushing her way through the mesquite, Joanna saw that the toddler wore a diaper and nothing else. One look at the unnaturally still body and at the blood pooled around the back of his dark-haired head was enough to tell Joanna that he was probably beyond help. Dropping to her knees, she felt for a pulse, but there was nothing—not even the smallest flutter.

For a few moments, Joanna wavered in a maelstrom of indecision. The boy was dead. In terms of crime scene investigation procedure, dead victims are to be left where they're found until the scene can be properly documented—measured, photographed, and recorded—before being packed off to the icy chill of a morgue.

But the desperate cries of the injured woman as she had called for her missing child still echoed in Joanna's heart. Dead or alive, that mother wanted her child—needed her child—to be with her. As a police officer, Joanna was obliged to leave the dead baby where he was. As a woman and mother, she wanted to return him to his mother. A fierce skirmish shook Joanna's very soul. In the end, motherhood won out.

Gently, Joanna lifted the limp child. With one arm supporting the boy's bloodied head, she carried his still body through the rocky underbrush and stumbled with him up the steep embankment.

"Where's the woman with the baby?" she demanded of the first EMT she saw. He gave her a blank shrug and a dismissive look that made Joanna wish she were still wearing her uniform. And her badge. She went on to the next EMT and to the next and to the one after that. Finally she found a medic she had never seen before but who at least knew what she meant.

"Oh, her," the medic said. "I think she took off in that last helicopter. They're taking her to Bisbee."

"Call them back," Joanna said.

"But, lady . . ."

"My name's Brady," Joanna snarled back at him. "Sheriff Joanna Brady, and I said call them back! Do it **now!**"

The EMT backed warily away from her and reached for his radio. After his summons, the helicopter was back within minutes. By then Joanna's shoulders ached from the strain of holding the lifeless form, but she was unwilling to relinquish her burden to anyone else. When the door of the helicopter flew open, she alone carried the little boy through the sand and grit raised by the whirling blades. With muddied tears streaming down her own face, she handed her precious burden over to his mother's outstretched arms and then fled from the helicopter. She didn't want to be within earshot when the mother learned her baby was dead.

But at least, Joanna thought as she darted once more through the whirling sea of dirt and grit, **at least she can hold him one last time. At least she can say good-bye.**

Moments later Joanna found herself leaning heavily against the front fender of the nearest ambulance, barfing into a clump of sun-dried verbena that had grown up along the edge of the pavement. Somehow she knew that this wave of sour banana nausea had nothing at all to do with her own baby. She was still heaving when someone laid a sympathetic hand on her shoulder.

"Joanna?" Frank Montoya asked. "Are you all right?"

She wiped her mouth on her shirttail. "Not really," she managed. "You wouldn't happen to have any water on you, would you? Mine's all gone."

Her chief deputy disappeared and returned a moment later with a bottle of water.

"The blood on your arm looks pretty bad," he said. "Are you hurt?"

Joanna looked down at her bloodied arm and thought about Suzanne Blake. "My heart's hurt," she said softly. "There was a two-year-old baby in that car, Frank. A baby whose mother was willing to risk death for both of them to bring him here. They came on the Fourth of July, for God's sake! I'm sure she thought she was giving her son a chance at a better life. Instead, she's hurt and he's dead."

Frank nodded. "Somebody told me there were five dead."

"Six," Joanna corrected. "Counting the baby."

Frank studied her face for a long moment. "Look, Joanna," he said at last, "my car's right over there. Maybe you'd better come sit down for a couple of minutes."

Any other time, Joanna Brady might have argued the point. With a docility that surprised them both, she allowed herself to be guided to Frank's Crown Victoria and placed in the rider's seat while he stood outside.

"I talked to Officer O'Dea of DPS a couple of minutes ago," Frank told her. "I met up with him on my way here. He said to tell you that so far there's no sign of the driver."

"That figures, but we'll find him," Joanna declared. "Terry and Spike are out combing the desert for him right this minute."

Frank nodded in agreement. "Jaime and Ernie just pulled up," he added. "I'll go see if they have what they need."

"I'll come, too," Joanna said.

"I don't think so," Frank said. "Not right now. Sit tight for a couple of minutes."

"But . . ."

"Nobody's keeping score, boss," Frank told her. "Lighten up. Give yourself a break."

Joanna nodded. "All right," she agreed.

She sat in the car and leaned her head against the seat back, but when she closed her eyes, all she could see was the little boy lying in the dirt with his shattered skull oozing blood. Minutes later, and against Frank's advice, she was down in the dry bed of Silver Creek watching Jaime Carbajal shoot crime scene photos. The bodies of five of the victims remained where they had fallen. The sixth one was missing, but Joanna refused to feel any sense of guilt about that. When the time came, she led Jaime and Ernie Carpenter to the clump of mesquite where she had found the dead child.

"Was the boy alive when you found him?" Ernie Carpenter asked, his pen poised over his own notebook.

Joanna looked her investigator straight in the eye. "Would I have moved him if he hadn't been?"

Ernie's thick eyebrows knotted into a frown, but he said nothing. Joanna was grateful he was willing to let it go at that. It helped that George Winfield came scrambling down the bank into the creek bed just then. His timely arrival provided Joanna with a welcome change of focus.

He glanced around the scene and shook his head. "Hell of a way to get out of Ellie's annual fireworks party," he said. "Where do we start?"

Joanna was still at the crime scene forty-five

minutes later, when Deputy Howell came to announce that the K-9 unit had just radioed in for assistance. Deputy Gregovich and Spike had located the driver, who, in a futile effort to escape the dog, had fallen down a cliff and injured his ankle.

"Too bad he didn't break his neck and save us all a hell of a lot of trouble," Joanna told Debbie Howell. "Take a team of EMTs and go get him, but don't bring him back here. If he comes too close, I'm as likely to shoot him as look at him."

Five more hours passed before Joanna finally crawled back into her Civvie and headed home, having missed her evening appearance in Willcox. She was drained and tired and, surprisingly, hungry. She let herself into the darkened house and stopped off in the kitchen long enough to make herself some hot chocolate—not the instant stuff where you add hot water and stir. No, she hauled out a saucepan and made the old-fashioned kind. The recipe, learned at her father's knee, came complete with canned milk, chocolate syrup, salt, sugar, and vanilla. She was just sprinkling sugar and cinnamon onto a piece of buttered toast when a bathrobe-clad Butch appeared in the kitchen.

"How was it?" he asked, pouring the remaining half cup of cocoa for himself.

"Bad," Joanna told him. "A speeding Suburban

full of UDAs turned over at Silver Creek east of Douglas. The department of public safety investigator estimates the guy was doing at least eighty when he slammed through the Jersey barrier at a construction site. Six dead, including a two-year-old boy. Twenty-some injured, some of them critical."

"Six dead and twenty-some injuries," Butch repeated. "How many people were in the car?"

"Thirty."

Easing himself onto a stool beside her, Butch whistled. "They must have been stacked inside like cordwood."

Joanna nodded. "They were," she said dully. "The driver was wearing a seat belt. Naturally the son of a bitch walked away unscathed."

"How are you, Joey?" Butch asked after a pause.

He knew her well enough to ask. Joanna didn't dodge the question. "Not so good," she admitted, biting her lip. "I'm the one who found the baby."

"I'm sorry," he said. "That had to be pretty rough."

"It was. He couldn't have been more than two, Butch. And he ended up dead in a clump of mesquite with the back of his head bashed in."

Joanna's voice quivered audibly as she spoke. Butch reached over, put an arm around her shoulders and pulled her over so she was leaning against his chest.

"That's not all."

"What else?"

"I'm a sworn police officer, but I deliberately disturbed evidence at a crime scene."

Butch's carefully placed his empty cup on the granite-tiled surface of the counter. "You did what?" he asked, keeping his voice low.

"The boy was dead when I found him, Butch," Joanna confessed. "I know I should have left him where he was, but I didn't. I couldn't. Instead, I picked him up and carried him to his mother. She was in a helicopter on her way to the hospital in Bisbee, but I called it back. I gave her the boy's body—so she could hold him one more time, so she could say good-bye. I know I shouldn't have, Butch, but with all the other bodies lying everywhere, I didn't think it would hurt . . ."

Joanna's voice trailed off into a stifled sob. Butch pulled her close and let her weep into the shoulder of his terry-cloth robe.

"It's okay, Joey," he said soothingly. "It's okay. It sounds like this was one of those times when you had two choices, both of them right and both of them wrong. You did what you had to do."

Butch and Joanna sat that way for several minutes. Finally Butch pushed her away. "With all this going on," he said, "I'm sure you'll have to go into the office tomorrow, right?"

Sniffling, Joanna nodded. "Probably."

"Well, then, come on. It's late. We'd better go to bed and try to get some sleep."

Taking Joanna by the hand, Butch led her into the bedroom. It wasn't until she was lying in bed next to Butch that she finally thought to question him about the results of Jenny's barrel-racing performance.

"She did all right," Butch answered.

"All right?" Joanna asked.

"Jenny didn't bring home a ribbon, if that's what you mean," Butch said. "But she was out there making the effort. She and Kiddo did a good job, but remember, it was also their first time out. Not only that, Jenny was by far the youngest competitor in the bunch. Don't worry. She can hold her head up."

"Was she upset that I wasn't there?"

"I don't think so," Butch said. "Jenny knows you have a job to do, Joey. We both do."

"I wanted to be there. I meant to be there."

"I know you did, but allow me to let you in on a little secret. You can't be in two places at once. Now hush up and go to sleep."

Within seconds, Butch had turned over onto his side and was snoring softly. With the day's events taken into consideration, Joanna expected to lie awake, tossing and turning, but she didn't. Within minutes she, too, was sound asleep.

In her dream, the SUV driver was on his knees, cowering in front of her. She was holding a gun in her hand. Not one of her little Glocks, but her father's old .357-magnum. "Please, lady," the guy begged. "I didn't mean for it to happen. It was an accident. I was just doing my job."

"Those people didn't have a chance," she told him scornfully. "And neither do you."

With that she pulled the trigger and the back of his skull exploded. He fell onto his back. As a pool of blood spread out beneath him, Joanna turned and walked away, still carrying the .357.

TEN

The horror of the nightmare woke her up. Shaken, Joanna reached across the bed, hoping to find Butch Dixon's comforting presence, but he wasn't there. His side of the bed was empty. With one hand over her mouth to stave off the retching, she piled out of bed. By then, Lady knew the drill and was smart enough to scramble out of the way as Joanna once again raced for the bathroom to deal with that day's worth of morning sickness.

She was still pale and shaken when she made her way into the kitchen. "How long is this going to last?" Butch asked as he handed her a mug of tea.

Joanna shrugged. "Last time I was fine for the first month, sick as a dog for the second, and fine again after that—except for drinking or smelling coffee." That was when she noticed that the coffeepot next to the sink was empty. "No coffee for you this morning, either?"

He held up a stainless-steel covered mug. "Iced," he answered. "Made from yesterday's coffee. I thought if you didn't have to smell me making it, maybe you wouldn't get sick. Obviously that didn't work."

"It was nice of you to try," she said, smiling wanly.

"Maybe I should start marking off days on the calendar," Butch said. "And how long do you go on eating mostly peanut butter? It's not what I call a balanced diet."

"No," Joanna agreed, "but I'm sure I won't starve."

"Lucky chewed up another one of Jenny's boots yesterday," Butch mentioned in passing.

"Not one of the new ones!"

"Yes, one of the new ones. And the right one, just like the other pair. If he'd chewed up the left-hand one, she'd still have two boots to work with even if they weren't a pair. I tried to explain to her that, with a puppy in the house, she can't leave anything lying around untended. I don't think she got the message."

"Will she this time?" Joanna asked.

Butch shrugged. "Maybe," he said. "Especially if this pair of boots comes out of her own pocket." He came over and settled onto the stool next to Joanna's. "By the way," he said, "your mother called late last night."

"What about?"

"I'm not sure. She said she was looking for George and wondered if you were home."

"That wasn't it," Joanna said. "I'm guessing she really wanted to find out if her calling out the big gun had any effect on me."

"What big gun?" Butch asked.

Joanna told Butch about Bob Brundage's call. Butch listened to the story in thoughtful silence and shook his head when she finished. "Eleanor just doesn't get it," he said.

"Get what?"

"The idea that you're all grown up and able to make your own decisions."

"You're right," Joanna said. "And I doubt she ever will."

An hour later, when Joanna drove into the Justice Center parking lot, she noticed an Arizona DPS van that was parked in front of the gate to the razor-wire-surrounded impound lot where the wrecked remains of the Suburban had been hauled and deposited for inspection. It had been decided the night before that this would be a joint-operation investigation, and Joanna was glad to see someone from the Department of Public Safety was already on the job. So was Dave Hollicker.

"Finding anything important?" Joanna asked as she joined the two clipboard-carrying officers who were conferring earnestly just to the left of the Suburban's smashed driver's-side fender.

"This is Sheriff Brady," Dave said, seeing her for the first time. "And this is Sergeant Steve Little of the DPS."

"Glad to meet you, Sheriff Brady," Sergeant Little said. "The biggest question in my mind is why this old crate was still on the road in the first place. No way it should have been doing ninety miles an hour. The brakes are shot. The shock absorbers are rusted out, and, with as many people as he had in there, the vehicle was grossly overloaded."

"Who's it registered to?" Joanna asked.

"A guy in Tucson who says he sold it last week to a Hispanic guy who paid him a thousand bucks in cash and said he needed it for his landscaping business. He used it for landscaping, all right. Turned it into a bulldozer."

"Do we have any idea who 'he' is?" Joanna asked.

Dave Hollicker shook his head. "No idea. The driver was carrying a fake ID and a fake driver's license. He won't answer any questions, but he's asking for a court-appointed lawyer. Says he wants to be deported back to Mexico."

Joanna thought for a moment of the dead and bloodied baby she had cradled in her arms. "That driver's not going home anytime soon," she declared determinedly. "Not if I can help it."

Leaving the impound lot in her Civvie, Joanna was surprised at the number of vehicles pulling into the Justice Center parking lot. On Saturdays, when court wasn't in session, the public parking arca at the front of the complex was usually deserted. Last in the line of arriving vehicles was a battered Camry. A magnetic sign bearing the **Bisbee Bee**'s distinctive logo was plastered on the driver's door.

As passengers began spilling out onto the hot pavement, Joanna assumed they had nothing to do with her and headed for her reserved and shaded parking place behind the building. Inside her office, she used her phone to call Lupe Alvarez at the reception desk in the public office.

"What's going on out front, Lupe?" Joanna asked. "Did someone schedule some kind of tour or activity that I don't know about?"

"Beats me," Lupe replied. "From here all I can see is a bunch of people milling around in the parking lot, lots of them waving signs. It must be some kind of demonstration."

"What do the signs say?" Joanna asked.

"One of them said A-W-E," Lupe returned. "Any idea what that means?"

"AWE? Not the slightest," Joanna answered. "What about the people? Do any of them look familiar?"

"No, but most of their backs are to me right now. They seem to be posing for photos in front of the door. Right, I just saw a flash, so someone did take a picture."

"Why don't you give Chief Deputy Montoya a call," Joanna suggested. "Maybe he knows something about this."

"Right away, Sheriff Brady."

Joanna put down her phone. While she waited for Lupe to call back, she turned on her computer to check her e-mail in-box. She had twenty-seven new messages, most of them offering her ways to earn money by working at home, or quick fixes for the latest computer virus. One by one she deleted those without even opening them. She was down to the last eleven seemingly real messages when her phone rang again.

"Chief Deputy Montoya is on his way in," Lupe reported. "It'll take him about twenty minutes to get here. He's scheduled a ten o'clock press briefing, so maybe some of the vehicles are reporters coming for that, but he doesn't have a clue about a demonstration."

"Great," Joanna said. "Well, then, since he's not here and I am, I'd better go out and see what's happening."

Since it was Saturday and Joanna had planned on spending the entire day in the office, she had come to work wearing jeans and a wrinkled but comfy linen blazer. If a newspaper photographer was outside snapping pictures, it was likely that a less-than-wonderful photo of Sheriff Brady would end up appearing in print.

Eleanor Lathrop was nowhere around, but Joanna had a fair idea of how their next conversation would go. "How could you possibly go to work dressed like that," her mother would ask, "looking like something the cat dragged in? What about that nice uniform you wore in the Fourth of July parade?"

Walking toward the door, Joanna smiled grimly to herself, imagining the reaction if she came right out and told Eleanor that the uniform was out of commission due to an encounter with puppy pee. An answer like that wouldn't be well received.

Opening the front door, Joanna stepped out onto the shaded veranda where a shorts-clad blonde with short-cropped hair was speaking earnestly to Kevin Dawson. Kevin, the **Bisbee Bee**'s ace reporter and photographer, was also, by some strange coincidence, the son of the newspaper's publisher and editor in chief.

As the door closed behind Joanna, one of the nearest sign-wielding demonstrators spotted her. "There she is," he shouted to the others, pointing in her direction. "That's Sheriff Brady."

Interviewer and interviewee turned to face Joanna while a series of boos and catcalls erupted from the group of demonstrators gradually coalescing at the foot of the stairs. As they moved closer, Joanna managed to catch a glimpse of some of the signs. SHAME ON SHERIFF BRADY, said one. CCSD UNFAIR TO ANIMALS, announced several others.

Animals? Joanna wondered in confusion. **What animals?**

Considering the events of the night before, she more than half expected the demonstrators outside to be human rights activists protesting the maze of conflicting international policies that had resulted in the terrible human carnage at Silver Creek. In fact, considering the dead boy whose bloodied body Joanna had held in her arms, Sheriff Brady herself might have been sorely tempted to join such a protest.

Then she saw another sign that clinched it. SEVENTEEN TOO MANY.

That's when Joanna tumbled. The people in the parking lot weren't the least bit concerned about dead and injured illegal immigrants. Callous about human casualties, the jeering group of protesters on the doorstep of the Cochise Justice Center had come to express their outrage over the heat-related deaths of Carol Mossman's dogs.

Joanna stifled an inward groan. "Who's in charge here?" she asked.

The woman with the short-cropped blond hair who looked to be about Joanna's age gave Sheriff

Brady a scathing look. "I am," she announced crisply.

A man with a video camera on his shoulder shoved his way through the crowd and pushed a microphone in Joanna's face.

"And you are?" Joanna asked, ignoring the cameraman.

"Tamara Haynes," the woman replied. "That's H-A-Y, not H-A-I," she added for the reporter's benefit as he dutifully took notes.

"May I help you?" Joanna asked.

Her question was drowned out by a new series of jeering catcalls. Despite her best intentions, Joanna felt her temper revving up.

Her second question was far less welcoming. "Who exactly are you?" she demanded. "And what are you doing here?"

"I already told you," the woman replied. "My name is Tamara Haynes." A diamond tongue-stud glittered as she spoke. Her ears were pierced a dozen times over. Her belly button, visible on a bare midriff, sported its own set of piercings, and her upper arms and shoulders were covered with a series of tattoos.

"I'm the local chapter president for AWE."

"Which is?" Joanna prodded.

"A-W-E," Tamara said. When Joanna exhibited no sign of recognition, the woman added, "Animal Welfare Experience."

"And you're here because . . . ?"

"You're in charge of Cochise Animal Control, are you not?" Tamara Haynes asked.

"Yes," Joanna said, "I am at the moment. Why?"

"Well," Tamara returned, her voice dripping contempt, "we're here to serve notice that the members of AWE hold you personally responsible for the deaths of all those poor animals out by the San Pedro. If you and your department had simply responded to the situation in a more efficient and timely fashion, none of those unfortunate dogs would have died."

With great effort Joanna kept her response reasonably civil. "Those dogs died in their owner's overheated mobile home—a home with no electricity and no air-conditioning," she added. "They died after their owner was murdered, shot to death by an unknown assailant through a locked back door. If anyone is responsible for the deaths of those animals, it's Carol Mossman's killer. And that's what my department is doing right now—searching for her murderer."

But Tamara Haynes wasn't someone whose opinion could be easily swayed by the presentation of mere facts. She grew shriller, making sure her voice carried beyond the front line of demonstrators. "If you and your people in Animal Control had been doing the job properly,

Sheriff Brady, Carol Mossman never would have had the opportunity to amass that many animals in the first place."

"That's right," one of the men shouted, waving his hand-lettered sign in the air. "Way to go, Tammy. You tell her!"

Joanna's temper edged up another notch. Her voice, unlike Tamara Haynes's, actually decreased in volume. "Ms. Haynes, I'm in charge of a department that handles public safety for an area eighty miles wide and eighty miles long. A total of one hundred thirty people report to me. Four of them are in Animal Control.

"As I'm sure you know, Animal Control officers enforce ordinances having to do with animal licensing. They collect stray and injured animals. They supervise animal adoptions and attend to the ones they've impounded. They respond to calls involving wildlife, which sometimes include marauding javelinas as well as human encounters with rabid skunks and coyotes. When Game and Fish officers aren't available, my people are responsible for trapping and relocating rattlesnakes and other wildlife that pose threats to public safety.

"In other words, Ms. Haynes, Animal Control has its hands full. My Animal Control officers are doing an excellent job despite limited resources and severe budget cuts. If you really care about animal welfare, Ms. Haynes, you and your sign-wielding friends here should be out at the pound volunteering your time shoveling doggie-doodoo and arranging adoptions instead of staging a protest on my doorstep. Now, if you'll excuse me—"

"So that's it?" Tammy Haynes objected before Joanna could step back inside the building. "You're just going to give us a line of excuses and that's the end of it?"

"I'm not giving you excuses," Joanna said tightly. "I'm giving you a dose of reality. In case you've been too busy being an animal activist to notice, seven human beings have died in Cochise County in the past several days, including a two-year-old boy who died in a senseless automobile accident, to say nothing of the owner of those seventeen dogs who was murdered in the sanctity of her own home. You're going to have to pardon me, Ms. Haynes, if I put those dead dogs on a back burner in favor of attending to my other duties.

"It's Saturday morning. You're here because you want to be, and so are my people. Paid or not, I expect most of my investigators will be on duty today, working hard to solve the cases I just mentioned to you. Protest all you like, but we have a job to do here. If you'll excuse me now, I'll go to work."

"What about us?"

Tamara Haynes sounded like a petulant child. "What about you?" Joanna returned. "You're welcome to stay here as long as you wish and as long as there's no disruption of traffic in or out of the building."

"We have every right to be here," Tammy Haynes whined. "I'll have you know this is a peaceful protest."

"Good," Joanna returned, "I'm glad to hear it. And if you know what's good for you, you'll keep it that way."

With that, Joanna turned away. Most of her part of the discussion had been conducted in a voice so low that only the nearest of the protesters had heard what she said. As she let herself back into the building, a new outburst of jeering rose up from the crowd. Frank Montoya was waiting just inside the door.

"They don't sound happy," he observed as the closing door stifled the noise. "What the hell is that all about?"

"They're pissed about Carol Mossman's dead dogs."

"They're that upset about the dogs?"

"Right," Joanna said. "I don't think any of them noticed that Carol Mossman also died. For some reason, that's beside the point."

"How long are they going to be here?" Frank asked.

"Most likely until hell freezes over. Why?"

"Because what happened last night at Silver Creek has happened three other times in the past year and a half," Montoya returned. "Each incident has resulted in up to a quarter of a million dollars' worth of unreimbursed medical costs to nearby hospitals, putting a further burden on overtaxed trauma care all over the state."

"So you're telling me there's a lot of statewide interest in this case."

Frank nodded grimly. "I've scheduled a press briefing for later this morning. In a little over an hour the place will be crawling with reporters and photographers."

"Great," Joanna said. "The press will get their money's worth this morning—a twofer—a press briefing and an animal rights protest." She turned from Frank Montoya to the receptionist's desk. "Lupe," she said, "do you still have that Out of Order sign we had to put up on the rest room door two weeks ago?"

Lupe frowned. "Yes, ma'am," she said. "But as far as I know, Sheriff Brady, the rest room's fine now—"

"No," Joanna said, "I don't believe it is. I believe someone mentioned to me that they heard a strange gurgling sound in one of the drains, so until we can get a plumber in here to check it out on Monday, I'm declaring the public rest room off limits. If the reporters or anyone else with legitimate business here needs to use the facilities, direct them to employee rest rooms. Everyone else, especially the demonstrators outside, are out of luck."

A smile of comprehension passed over Lupe's face as she went searching for the sign. Meanwhile Joanna walked over to the Coke machine in the rest room alcove and calmly pulled the plug on the soda machine. "Oops," she said. "I think this is on the blink, too."

Following her, Frank shook his head. "Are you sure antagonizing them is a good idea?"

"Probably not, but ask me if I'm enjoying it."

"But, Joanna . . ." Frank began.

"Look," she said, "those people have their noses out of joint because of the way Animal Control handled the Mossman case, but as far as I'm concerned, Officers Ruiz and Phillips went by the book on that one. True, they're shorthanded at the moment. We all are, and budget constraints keep me from adding any more officers—not to Animal Control and not to Patrol, either. Should I beef up Animal Control by sidelining regular deputies into Animal Control? Not on your life, not when we're inundated with everything else. And if those people in the parking lot think coming out here and waving signs and yelling at me is going to change my mind on that, they're nuts."

Joanna and Frank had walked into Joanna's office. Closing the door behind them, Frank tried to reason with her. "But is locking them out of the rest rooms a good idea?"

It wasn't lost on Joanna that the public-contact section of her police academy training was where she had earned some of her lowest marks. Years into the job, she realized that anger management was still one of her biggest challenges.

"If their only choice is to go pee behind a bush, maybe they'll pack it in and go home," she said. "If they were out there protesting the death of that two-year-old, I might feel differently about it. In fact, I'd probably be out in the parking lot waving my own sign. But those yahoos don't have the foggiest idea about what we do here, and the sooner they leave, the better."

"This is an election year," Frank reminded her.

"I'm well aware of that," Joanna returned. "But I'm not going to change my mind."

"So be it," Frank said, giving up. "I guess I'll go get ready for that briefing."

Frank left then, and Joanna turned to her desk. With everything on her plate, it would have been easy for her to feel totally overwhelmed that morning, but she didn't. Somehow the confrontation with the protesters had cleared Joanna's head and renewed her sense of purpose. She had a job to do, and she set about doing it.

As reports and information came across her desk, she sorted them into three separate piles. One stack was for the Richard Osmond case. Another was for Carol Mossman and the two murdered women in New Mexico. The third stack was for the vehicular homicide incident at Silver Creek.

Osmond and Mossman, Joanna thought. Sitting side by side, the two names were spookily similar, and yet there was real irony in how the two people had died. Osmond, a jail inmate who could easily have been the victim of jailhouse violence, had actually died peacefully and of natural causes in his sleep, while Carol Mossman had been gunned down in the privacy—and presumed safety—of her own home.

How come nobody's protesting that? Joanna wondered.

Jaime Carbajal came in a few minutes after Frank's departure and handed Joanna a computer-generated printout. "What's this?" she asked.

"It's a tentative list of last night's victims," he said. "The ones with hospital notations are still hospitalized, or were the last time we heard. Several of the less seriously wounded have already been released."

"To whom?" Joanna asked.

"What do you mean?"

"If they were released, who took charge of them? Does Border Patrol have them in custody?"

"I doubt it," Jaime returned. "INS doesn't want to get dinged for anybody's hospital bill. If they're taken into custody, that's what'll happen."

Joanna recalled the officers she had heard arguing the previous evening. Joanna had thought the medical-bill buck-passing had been limited to that one Department of Public Safety captain. Clearly the problem was far more widespread than that.

"So Border Patrol just let them go?"

"That's right. That way the hospitals don't get paid, and the illegals are granted free entry to disappear into the wilds of the good ol' U.S. of A."

"What about the driver? You'd better not be telling me that somebody turned him loose."

"Don't worry, boss. We've got him and his bill both. He's in the Copper Queen Hospital. I've been assured that they'll only release him into our custody."

"Fair enough," Joanna said. "If I have to, I'll pay his bill out of my own pocket. That guy's going to jail."

She studied the list Jaime had given her until she located the name of a woman. Maria Elena Maldonado had also been admitted to the Copper Queen Hospital. Then she cross-referenced that name with the list of fatalities. Finally she found a name that matched—Eduardo Xavier Maldonado.

"Eduardo?" Joanna asked. "That's the name of the little boy who died?"

Jaime nodded.

"What about the mother? Is she going to be all right?"

"I talked to Dr. Lee about her," Jaime answered. "Her internal injuries are more extensive than they thought. She'll be transferred to TMC for more surgery later on this afternoon."

"Is she going to make it?"

Jaime shrugged. "With the injuries she has, the doc tells me her chances are about fifty-fifty," he said.

"What about the other victims?" Joanna asked. "How serious are their injuries?"

"Five of them are still in ICUs."

Joanna went back to studying the list. "What are your plans for the day, Jaime, and what's Ernie up to?"

"Ernie's back out at Silver Creek working with the DPS accident site investigation team. They'll be interviewing locals who were on the scene. As for me, the woman you interviewed, Suzanne Blake, is due to show up any minute. After I talk to her, I'm not sure what I'll do next."

Joanna put down the two separate lists. "Here's the deal, Jaime," she said. "It sounds as though, as soon as these patients are well enough, INS will let them walk out of hospitals free as birds, just like they did the others. When you're finished with the Blake interview and after Frank finishes with his press conference, I want the two of you to hit the trail. I want you to find and interview as many of those hospitalized UDAs as possible. Explain to them that we need their help so we can find the coyotes who did this. I want to put those guys out of business before any more people die. Wherever possible, I want taped sworn statements."

"I don't understand," Jaime objected. "What's the point of doing interviews, boss? As you said, once the injured UDAs are released from treatment, they'll disappear. None of them will stick around long enough to testify against the driver."

"Of course they won't," Joanna returned. "That's why I want you to interview them now—today!"

"But if they're not here to testify at the trial, the tapes won't be admissible."

"True," Joanna agreed. "And much as I'd like to nail that bastard, getting the driver isn't the point. He's a little fish and entirely expendable by both sides. I'm after somebody bigger than he is, Jaime. I want the people running this ring— the ones making the big bucks."

"How do you plan to catch them?"

"The driver's scared to death. That's why he won't give his real name. He knows he killed all those people. I'm hoping we can use those statements to put the squeeze on the driver's **cojones** long enough for him to lead us to someone higher up the chain of command."

"I suppose it could work," Jaime conceded doubtfully, "but if his lawyer gets wind of it—"

Joanna refused to be dissuaded. "We won't find out if we don't try," she said, cutting Jaime off in mid-objection and abruptly changing the subject. "Now, tell me about the autopsies on the Silver Creek victims. Any idea when those will happen?"

"Monday," the detective told her. "Doc Winfield says he'll schedule them pretty much back-to-back."

Detective Carbajal left a few minutes later, and Joanna spent the remainder of the morning mowing through a mountain of incoming reports and evidence. The results of the SUV driver's routine Breathalyzer check came back negative. That was no surprise. Driving drunk had never been an issue. Driving crazy was. A preliminary on-site analysis by DPS officers indicated that the Suburban had been traveling in excess of eighty miles per hour when it crashed through the Jersey barrier. That report would later be verified and/or fine-tuned by a computerized analysis.

A while later a faxed copy of Dr. Fran Daly's preliminary autopsy results on Richard Osmond appeared on Joanna's desk. That, along with the interviews Ernie and Jaime had conducted with each of Osmond's current and previous cell mates, indicated that Osmond had died of natural causes resulting from a previously undiagnosed and untreated form of cancer. The evidence appeared to exonerate Joanna Brady's department from all blame with regard to Osmond's death, but she knew that what seemed cut-and-dried to her would become far more murky in the hands of an attorney bent on pursuing a wrongful-death claim.

She was still considering that thorny issue when her phone rang.

"Sheriff Trotter here," her caller said. "I'm not surprised to hear you're hard at work this morning, Sheriff Brady. Me, too. If our guys had been a little quicker on the draw, that mess at Silver Creek would have happened on my turf instead of yours. Sorry about that."

"Sure you're sorry," Joanna returned. "And the word 'mess' doesn't come close to covering what happened out there."

"I know, and I know, too, that you've got your hands full today, and I'm about to add to it by sending more trouble your way."

"How's that?"

"For one thing, we've got tentative IDs on our two Jane Does. Their names are Pamela Davis and Carmen Ortega, freelance television journalists from L.A. Diego Ortega, Carmen's brother, is a pilot. He's flying into Lordsburg later on today to give us a positive ID."

"Television journalists?" Joanna asked.

"That's right. Pamela was the on-screen talent. Carmen ran the camera and tech stuff. They worked with a production company called Fandango Productions that sells in-depth pieces to outfits that specialize in female-oriented programming. You might know who they are, but since I never watch that kind of stuff, I hadn't ever heard of them."

Joanna liked Randy Trotter and had worked with him on numerous occasions. Even so, she couldn't help being slightly irked by his automatic assumptions about her.

"I'm not big on watching TV of any kind," she told him. "I don't have time, so I don't know them either."

Sheriff Trotter hurried on. "According to the brother, Carmen and Pamela won some big cable award a year or so ago for a piece they did on the pedophile scandal in the Catholic Church. They were going to Tucson to do a new series of interviews."

Joanna thought about what Edith Mossman

had said about Carol Mossman's shaky fi-
nances—about how she had first asked her
grandmother for financial help in having her
dogs vaccinated. Later she had told Edith that
help was no longer necessary—that she had
somehow come up with another way of laying
her hands on the money.

"Does the production team pay for interviews?" Joanna asked.

"Pay?" Trotter repeated.

"You know," Joanna said. "Like the tabloids
do. Do they buy exclusive rights to people's stories?"

"I wouldn't know about that," Trotter replied,
"but the brother might."

"What time is Diego Ortega due in Lordsburg?" Joanna asked.

"Sometime around two," Sheriff Trotter said.
"Why?"

Joanna looked at her watch and considered her
options.

"Tell you what," she said. "My investigators
are all up to their ears in work this morning, but
all I'm doing is clearing paperwork. If I leave
right now, I should be able to be in Lordsburg by
the time Mr. Ortega arrives."

"Thought you might want to have someone on
hand to talk to him," Trotter agreed. "I sure as
hell would if I were in your shoes."

As soon as she got off the phone with Sheriff Trotter, Joanna left word with Lupe Alvarez about where she was going. After stopping at the Motor Pool long enough to gas up, she headed out of the Justice Center compound. Demonstrators still milled in the parking lot and a few of them rapped on the windows of her Civvie as she drove past.

Peaceful, all right, she thought as she goosed the Crown Victoria forward and left the demonstrators behind. Two miles down Highway 80, she realized that the ratty clothing that had been inappropriate for her newspaper photo wasn't going to work any better for a next-of-kin interview, either. Rather than driving by the Double Adobe turnoff, she headed home to High Lonesome Ranch to change.

Butch was sitting at the kitchen counter with his laptop open in front of him when Joanna walked in the back door. "You're home early," he remarked. "What happened?"

"I need a change of clothes," she explained. "I'm on my way to Lordsburg to interview a next of kin. My in-office grubbies aren't going to hack it." She disappeared into the bedroom and emerged minutes later wearing a summer-weight khaki uniform. "The dress one has to go to the cleaners," she told Butch. "Lucky peed on it."

"Great," Butch said. "Whose next of kin?"

"Randy Trotter has a tentative ID on the two women killed north of Rodeo. The brother of one of them is flying into Lordsburg this afternoon."

"When will you be back?" Butch asked.

"Five or six. Why?"

"Just wondering. By the way, Eva Lou invited us over for meat loaf after church tomorrow. I told her I'd check with you first. I said I didn't know if your tummy would tolerate meat loaf."

"Sounds good right now," Joanna said. "Where's Jenny?"

"Off riding Kiddo," Butch answered. "This afternoon she's going swimming with Cassie, and she's planning on spending the night."

Cassie Parks, Jenny's best friend, lived a few miles away in a former KOA campground that her parents had rehabbed into a private RV park. The park, catering mostly to winter visitors, was underutilized in the summer, giving Cassie and Jenny a clear shot at the park's swimming pool.

"So it'll be just be the two of us for dinner tonight?" Joanna asked.

"That's right. I might make something special then," Butch added. "We haven't exactly celebrated our new addition. Drive carefully, but don't be late. I've learned my lesson. I'm not starting dinner until I see the whites of your eyes."

From High Lonesome Ranch, the most direct route to Lordsburg, New Mexico, was on Highway 80 through Douglas, Rodeo, and Road Forks. It also meant returning to Silver Creek. If time hadn't been an issue, Joanna might have been tempted to drive the long way around, just to avoid revisiting the site of the deadly accident, but her dread proved to be mostly unfounded. By the time she arrived, few signs remained of the previous day's horrors. The Highway Department had already sent out a crew to reposition the displaced Jersey barriers. A few scraps of yellow crime scene tape still lingered here and there, marking spots where the bodies of dead and injured had come to rest.

There may have been little to see, but, driving alone in her Crown Victoria, Joanna heard once again the frantic voice of the injured mother calling for her baby. It was a voice and a sound she would never forget, any more than she'd be able to wipe away the memory of carrying the terrible burden of that dead child up the embankment and into the waiting helicopter. Yesterday Eduardo Maldonado's deadweight had been a burden for her arms and shoulders. Today he was a burden for her heart.

Snap out of it, she ordered herself when a blur of tears clouded her eyes. **That was one job. This is another**.

With intermittent radio traffic chattering in the background, Joanna forced herself to review everything she knew about the Carol Mossman case. If she could establish a definite connection between Carol's death and the two murders in New Mexico, then perhaps there was something else at work here other than simply an opportunist killer targeting susceptible women.

She had crossed the border into New Mexico and was heading north when her cell phone rang. "Hi, Frank," she said. "Where are you?"

"Jaime and I are on our way to University Medical Center in Tucson to do the interviews you wanted," Frank Montoya answered. "How about you?"

"Between Rodeo and Road Forks on my way to Lordsburg. What's up?"

"I thought you'd like to have a little of the inside scoop on the lady in charge of the Animal Welfare Experience folks. It occurred to me that it was too much of a coincidence that AWE would show up with all those sign-waving demonstrators within minutes of the time I had scheduled the press briefing."

"Right," Joanna agreed. "The timing was impeccable."

"I wondered if someone had tipped them off about when the briefing was to happen, so I did some research."

"And?"

"Tamara Haynes and Marty Galloway were roommates together at Northern Arizona University."

"Tamara and Ken Junior's wife were roommates?" Joanna blurted. "Are you telling me that whole demonstration thing was nothing more than an election campaign stunt?"

"That's how it looks, although maybe that's not entirely true," Frank said. "AWE does exist. Nationally, it's a legitimate organization, but the local group has surfaced just in the last few days. And there's a good chance today's demonstration was a put-up deal, aimed at garnering free publicity for them at your expense, to say nothing of boosting Ken Junior's chances in the upcoming election."

"In other words, Ken Junior isn't above using Carol Mossman's dogs as political fodder."

"And neither is Tamara Haynes, who's something else, by the way."

"What do you mean?"

"I've taken a look at her rap sheet. During the week she teaches Women's Studies courses at the Sierra Vista campus of Cochise College. On weekends, she's a political activist. She's been picked up twice for demonstrating at the Nevada Test Site, twice at the Palo Verde Nuclear Plant at Gila Bend, and twice at demonstrations at the front gate at Fort Huachuca. So far, she's got two disorderly conduct convictions and one interfering with a police officer—all of them with suspended sentences."

"What do you think we should do about it?" Joanna asked after several moments of reflection.

"I'm not sure," Frank began.

Suddenly her chief deputy's voice disappeared into the ether. Then there was nothing. Frustrated, Joanna checked her phone and saw that she had crossed into a no-service zone. She tossed the phone down in disgust.

There was no sense in wondering how Tamara Haynes and AWE had hooked themselves up to Frank Montoya's press briefing. Ken Galloway no longer worked inside the department but he still had plenty of friends there. Looking for the leak would serve no useful purpose.

Joanna was offended to think her opponent would stoop so low as to use Carol Mossman's dead dogs to make political hay.

Which is exactly why Ken Galloway isn't worthy of being sheriff, Joanna told herself determinedly. **And it's why, baby or no baby—Eleanor or no Eleanor—I'm staying the course, and I'm going to win!**

ELEVEN

The Hidalgo County Sheriff's Department was located in a single-story cinder-block building in Lordsburg's small downtown area. Hard-to-come-by tax money had been spent on the new jail and communications center two blocks away, but Randy Trotter's humble two-phone-line office reminded Joanna of her father's old office. When D. H. Lathrop had been the sheriff of Cochise County, his department—office, jail, and all—had been located behind barred windows in the art deco courthouse up in old Bisbee. That, too, had been a two-phone-line office. Here, though, the iron bars with their brightly painted Zia symbols were more decorative than utilitarian.

Sheriff Trotter, carrying a cup of steaming coffee, emerged from a back room and greeted Joanna. In his late forties, Trotter had the bowlegged, scrawny, sunbaked look of a man whose preferred mode of transportation remained a horse and saddle. Joanna remembered hearing from someone that Sheriff Trotter's family had once lived in the Bisbee area, but they had left there before he was born. Long before Joanna was born, too, for that matter.

"Coffee?" he asked, offering Joanna a stained mug full of thick, brackish brew.

Just the smell of it was enough to make her queasy all over again. "No, thanks," she said, shaking her head. "I'm off coffee at the moment."

"You're not one of those anti-coffee health nuts, I hope."

Joanna thought about her answer for a moment. "Not anti-coffee," she said. "I'm pregnant."

Trotter was old enough that he hailed from a time when women in law enforcement had been anything but commonplace and pregnant women had been rarer still. Joanna expected some kind of comment. All she got right then was a raised eyebrow. "Water, then?" he asked. "Or a soda?"

"Water would be great."

"Come on into my office," he said. "The place isn't much, but it works for me. Have a chair."

Joanna followed him into his private office, where the wooden desk and creaky chair reminded her even more of her father's old digs. Randy Trotter walked into the adjacent room and removed a bottle of water from a small refrigerator. He handed it over as Joanna sat down on a battered and lumpy brown leather chair that seemed to swallow her whole body.

"Sorry about that," Randy apologized. "When push came to shove, there was money enough for a new refrigerator or a new chair. The fridge won." He glanced at his watch. "Johnny Cruikshank, my homicide detective, is out at the airport now. As soon as Mr. Ortega's plane lands, Johnny will bring him here to the office. Then, once we make arrangements, we'll take him to the morgue—what we call the morgue, anyway. It's really nothing more than a couple of rooms the county leases from a local funeral chapel."

Sipping her water, Joanna nodded. "Fine," she said.

Trotter eyed her curiously. "If you're pregnant, are you still going to run?"

"Absolutely."

"Do people well . . . you know . . ." He paused awkwardly.

"You mean, do they know I'm pregnant?" It was Sheriff Trotter's turn to nod. "They do," Joanna continued. "You know how small towns work. I haven't had my first prenatal checkup yet, but the pregnancy is already hot news in the local paper."

"So how's it going then?" he asked, studying her over the rim of his coffee cup.

"My pregnancy or the reelection campaign?"

"Reelection." He grinned.

Thinking about the demonstrators banging on her car windows and doors as she drove through the Justice Center parking lot, Joanna decided to underplay her hand. "All right, I guess," she said with an indifferent shrug. "Yours?"

"About the same," he agreed. "I just wish politics weren't so dirty. You think about that poor guy out in Kentucky, the one who was allegedly gunned down by one of his opponent's henchmen a while ago . . ." He paused. "I mean, when one candidate for sheriff puts out a contract on the other guy's life, it kind of defeats the whole idea of law and order, wouldn't you say? Makes you wonder if it's worth the time, effort, and trouble."

Joanna nodded. **You've got that right,** she thought.

"I think I've heard, but remind me," Trotter continued. "What's the name of the guy who's running against you?"

"Galloway," Joanna answered. "Kenneth Galloway."

"That's what I thought," Sheriff Trotter said. "Is he one of the old Jiggerville Galloways?"

That brought Joanna up short. Jiggerville was a Bisbee neighborhood that had been dismantled in the early 1950s to make way for Lavender Pit.

One by one, houses from places like Jiggerville and Upper Lowell had been removed from their foundations, loaded onto axles, and then trucked to other locations in newly created subdivisions around town. Joanna had heard her father talk about those old parts of town, but for Joanna herself they were pieces of local history and lore rather than places rooted in actual memory.

"I think Ken's from Saginaw," she said.

"Right," Trotter agreed. "That's where Phelps Dodge put the Galloway house when they moved it. And, from what I've heard, Ken's pretty much a chip off all those old Galloway blocks."

Joanna looked at Sheriff Trotter in surprise. "You know Ken Junior then?" she asked.

"Not directly, but I know of him and of his family by reputation, if nothing else," he added. "There was a whole clan of Galloways living in Jiggerville back when my grandparents lived there. Grandpa Trotter was a shift boss—a jigger—in the mines in Bisbee, and Jiggerville was the residential area where most of the shift bosses lived. My dad used to tell stories about living there as a kid—about exploring caves, getting in all kinds of hot water, and pole-vaulting all over God's creation on agave sticks.

"Dad is one of those old-time, Andy Griffith-type storytellers," Trotter continued. "The wonderful thing about his stories is that he never edits out any of the bad stuff he did, including all the scraps and scrapes. And I remember that whenever someone named Galloway showed up in one of Dad's stories, you could bet he'd be tough as nails and mean as hell."

Joanna gave a wan smile. "Sounds like Ken's right in there with the rest of them," she said.

Randy Trotter grinned. "That's something Grandpa Trotter always used to say. 'The apple doesn't fall very far from the tree.'"

It seemed strange for Joanna to be sitting a hundred miles away from Bisbee and hearing about her town's history.

"According to my father," Randy continued, "Jiggerville was paradise on earth and the Garden of Eden all rolled into one. It was full of shade trees and fruit trees and lush gardens because back then people could still use the mineral-rich water they pumped out of the mines. There was a trolley stop and a playfield where Dad and his pals played pickup games of baseball and football. Dad said when they had to leave there to move to Lordsburg, he hated it."

"Why'd he leave?"

"His mother, Grandma Trotter, came from Lordsburg originally. When her mother, my Great-Grandma Clementine Case, took sick, Grandma and Grandpa came back here to look after her. Grandpa had worked in the mines for quite a while, but he got on with Southern Pacific—Sufferin' Pacific, as he called it—and he worked there until he retired. They built a house next door to Clementine's. That's where my dad and uncles were raised. Now, with my mother gone and my father retired from teaching, he lives in Clementine's House, as we call it. My wife and I live next door."

"Your father taught school?"

"That's right. He taught social studies and coached football and basketball right here in Lordsburg. Grandpa said he wanted his sons to work with their brains instead of their brawn, so he made sure they all went to college. It worked, too. Came out with a college professor, a high school principal, and my dad. Then there's the black sheep of the family, my Uncle Ned. He owns the Ford dealership up in Silver City and probably makes as much money as the other three put together."

Just then the outside door opened, and two people walked in—a man and a woman. The man was short and dark but fine-featured and handsome. Despite the heat, he wore a starched white shirt and a carefully knotted tie under an expensive lightweight blue silk blazer and exquisitely tailored camel-colored slacks. On his feet were a pair of hand-tooled snakeskin cowboy boots that Joanna estimated could easily have set him back five hundred bucks.

The woman, two or three inches taller than

Joanna, was pushing forty and good-looking. Her hair was pulled back in a long smooth pony-tail. She wore dangling silver-and-turquoise ear-rings. Silver rings, heavy with chunks of turquoise, decorated several of her fingers. She was dressed far more casually than the man in what looked like freshly pressed Levi's topped by a cowboy shirt and a Western-cut jacket. She might have been modeling Western attire if it hadn't been for her boots. Unlike the man's highly polished snakeskin footwear, the woman's worn Judson's bore the dusty sheen and telltale marks of someone accustomed to working in barns and corrals and dealing with the business end of horses and cattle.

Randy Trotter stood to greet the new arrivals. "You must be Mr. Ortega," he said, holding out his hand. "It's very good of you to come all this way on such short notice. And this is Sheriff Joanna Brady," he added, gesturing in Joanna's direction. "She's from Cochise County, Arizona, our neighboring county to the west."

Mr. Ortega shook hands first with Sheriff Trotter and then with Joanna. "Glad to meet you," Diego Ortega said gravely.

Randy Trotter continued with the introductions. "And this is Detective Cruikshank, Sheriff Brady."

Until that moment, it hadn't occurred to

Joanna that Detective Johnny Cruikshank was a woman rather than a man. The two women sized each other up briefly. Then, after nodding in Joanna's direction, Detective Cruikshank retreated into the other room and returned pushing two additional desk chairs in front of her.

"We won't be able to get into the morgue for another half hour," she explained. "Dr. Lawrence didn't want to pay any more overtime than absolutely necessary. He told me not to call Bobby Lopez to let us in until after Mr. Ortega was here."

"Is Bobby on his way?" Sheriff Trotter asked.

Johnny nodded. "Yes, but he's out at the ranch. He says it'll take him that long to get here."

"Thanks for bringing the chairs, then," Randy said to his detective. "I guess we should all take a load off."

"It was very kind of you to send Miss Cruikshank to pick me up," Diego Ortega said, settling himself onto one of the two rolling chairs and carefully easing the knees of his trousers so as to avoid bagging them and spoiling the crease

"Under the circumstances, it's the least we ca do," Trotter returned.

"My coming was an absolute necessity," Die Ortega replied with a grim smile. "Otherw my mother would have killed me. Carmen's baby—the youngest. And yesterday was M birthday. Carmen travels a lot. At times Mama may not hear from her for weeks on end, but when it came to birthdays, no matter where she was, Carmen was always the first to call, usually first thing in the morning.

"By noon yesterday, when Carmen still hadn't called, Mama was worried. By six o'clock last night she was frantic and on the phone to my brother, Carlos, who happens to be a lieutenant with the LAPD. He's the one who entered the missing-persons report. Even though it was a holiday, someone from LAPD got through to Fandango Productions. They told us Carmen and Pamela were in Arizona. They also said Carmen and Pamela were expecting to interview Carol Mossman—"

"Who's also been murdered," Joanna put in.

Diego Ortega nodded. "So I've been told," he replied. "Once we knew Carol Mossman was dead, it was the weapon connection Sheriff Trotter told me about that brought me here. I told Mama I'd fly out today and make sure, one way or the other. I think not knowing is harder on her than knowing will be. And since I fly my own plane, I didn't have to mess around with airline schedules. Flying into someplace this small . . ."

Joanna knew that Lordsburg, New Mexico, like Bisbee, Arizona, was a long way off the map for any regularly scheduled flights. The two cities' tiny municipal airports were good for little else than serving as bases of operations for local general aviation enthusiasts.

"Tell me about Fandango Productions," Joanna said.

Diego Ortega studied Joanna appraisingly. "It's a woman-owned and -operated outfit," he explained. "It's run by the well-connected daughters of several old-time television producers. They sell original material to cable channels like Oxygen and Lifetime. That's where Carmen and Pamela met. A year or so ago, they were assigned to do a story together on pedophile priests. They met at work, and they've been partners ever since."

"In life and work?" Johnny Cruikshank asked.

Diego Ortega nodded. "That was pretty tough for my mother to accept at first. She's pushing seventy, and she's pretty old-fashioned about things like that. But when she finally realized Carmen was happier living with Pamela than she'd ever been in her whole life, Mama just sort of got over it. We all did."

"I know from Carol Mossman's grandmother that Carol was always short of cash," Joanna said. "So did Fandango Productions pay for the interview with her?"

"That's how we first learned Carol Mossman's name," Diego replied. "It was on a check requisition that Pamela put in prior to their leaving for Arizona—a check for five thousand dollars. Pamela had the check in her possession when they came to Arizona. As I understand it, the check wasn't found with the bodies, but as far as anyone knows, it has yet to be cashed."

Joanna Brady let her breath out. That was why she had come to Lordsburg—to find out if there was some other connection, beyond the ballistics report, between the New Mexico victims and the homicide in her jurisdiction. With Diego Ortega's revelation about the existence of the missing check, that possible connection moved from theory to reality.

"Do you know where your sister and Pamela Davis were staying?" Joanna asked.

"The Willows Inn in Sierra Vista," Ortega answered. "I talked to Candace Leigh, the CFO from Fandango about that. She was kind enough to check the transaction records on their company credit cards. They checked into The Willows on Sunday night and booked the room for a whole week. Although they haven't been seen back at the hotel since Tuesday morning, the hotel clerk said no one was particularly worried about them since it appeared the room continued to be occupied with luggage, clothing, and the like. When they checked in, they said they were working on a story and would be in and out. The last credit card transaction is dinner Monday night at a place called The Brite Spot. They had breakfast at the hotel on Tuesday morning. After that, nothing."

"We'll need records of all phone calls made from their hotel room," Johnny Cruikshank said. "I'm assuming they both have cell phones?"

Diego nodded.

"We'll need those records, too," the detective added.

Diego Ortega nodded. "Of course," he replied. "Ms. Leigh may not have all the information you need at her fingertips, but she'll be able to find someone who will." When he gave Johnny Cruikshank a list of Candace Leigh's telephone numbers, Joanna jotted them down as well.

"What kind of stories did they work on?"

"Pam and Carmen more or less specialized in children's sexual-abuse cases—that and child pornography. It was something they both had in common."

"Child pornography?" Randy Trotter asked.

"No, no. Sexual abuse. Carmen was victimized by a parish priest when she was a little girl, although we didn't find out about it until much later. And Pamela was abused, too, by an older relative, I think. An uncle, maybe, or perhaps a cousin. I don't know the details. But that's why, when they were assigned to work the pedophile priest story, they really clicked together. On any number of levels."

Randy Trotter looked at Joanna. "Do you have any information that Carol Mossman was involved in that kind of thing?"

"Not really," Joanna replied. "I know she had a troubled family life and that, as an adult, she had a hard time keeping it together. Periodically her grandmother would have to pitch in and help out. At the time Carol Mossman was murdered, she was living rent-free in her grandmother's mobile home."

"Hey," Detective Cruikshank objected, "I live rent-free in a place my grandmother owns. What's wrong with that?"

The last thing Joanna wanted to do was offend the detective. "Nothing," Joanna said quickly. "Nothing at all."

She was saved by the ringing of a telephone. Randy Trotter reached over to answer it. "Sure enough, Bobby," he said. "We'll finish up here and be at the morgue in ten minutes or so. Thanks for coming all the way into town for this. It's a big help."

It was only a matter of blocks from Randy Trotter's office to the morgue. After a short discussion, they decided to walk. A hot, dusty wind blew in their faces, but off to the south Joanna spotted a bank of clouds building on the horizon. The summer rains had missed Bisbee's Fourth of July fireworks display, and so had Joanna Brady; but it looked as though the monsoons might come—sooner rather than later.

The Hidalgo County Morgue consisted of two rooms carved out of a basement corner of the Lordsburg Funeral Home. "Hello, Bobby," Sheriff Trotter said to the middle-aged man waiting just inside the front door. "This is Mr. Diego Ortega. We believe he knows both victims. One of them is believed to be Mr. Ortega's sister."

Bobby Lopez nodded gravely. "Are you ready?" he asked.

"Yes," Diego said softly, squaring his shoulders. "Let's get this over with."

Bobby Lopez opened a door to usher them into an interior room. Joanna hung back. "Are you coming?" Randy asked.

Joanna shook her head. "Identifying victims isn't a spectator sport," she said. "And Mr. Ortega doesn't need an audience. If you don't mind, I'll wait right here."

"Good thinking," Randy said. "I believe I'll join you."

Detective Cruikshank and Diego Ortega, looking decidedly pale, were back in the lobby in less than a minute. "It's them," Diego said shakily. "It's Carmen and Pam. Now, if you'll excuse me for a moment," he added, taking a cell phone from his pocket, "I need to call my mother. From the descriptions, we were pretty sure, but she's back home in Garden Grove hoping against hope that we were wrong."

He turned back to Bobby Lopez. "Any idea when the bodies will be released so my mother can start planning a funeral?"

The ME's assistant shook his head. "Dr. Lawrence will perform the autopsies on Monday. It'll be several days after that."

"I understand," Diego said. Holding the phone to his ear, he stepped outside. Joanna and the others stayed where they were.

"We'll need the other victim's next of kin as well, Sheriff Trotter," Bobby Lopez said.

"Right," Randy said. "We'll try to get it for you."

Diego remained outside for several long minutes. Joanna was more than happy to be out of earshot. It was bad enough to have seen the despair on Diego's face as he emerged from the morgue's back room. She didn't want to bear witness to the phone call that would finally shatter all of a grieving mother's hopes and dreams for her daughter.

When Mr. Ortega returned to the waiting room, he seemed to have regained control. "All right," he said. "What next?"

"We'll need to gather some more information, if you don't mind," Johnny Cruikshank said. "There's a little coffee shop just around the corner. Maybe we could go there and talk."

Esther's Diner was a long, dingy place with a counter on one side and a string of booths on the other. At mid-afternoon on a Saturday, the place was virtually deserted. Even so, Johnny led them to a booth in the far corner. With no peanut butter anywhere on the menu, Joanna settled on ordering a tuna sandwich. Johnny Cruikshank ordered key lime pie, while Randy Trotter and Diego Ortega had coffee.

"Please tell us about your sister," Johnny urged Diego once their gum-chewing waitress had departed with her order pad.

Diego's eyes dimmed with tears. "She was always such a cute little kid," he said. "She was what my mother called an afterthought—one of those babies that come along when women think their childbearing days are over. My brothers and I were all in high school or college when Carmen was born. My parents were good Catholics. They wanted to have a whole bunch of kids, but after I showed up, Mama had several miscarriages in a row. The doctor told her she'd never have another child, but he was wrong. When Mama was forty-two, along came Carmen.

"When she was born, things were different

from the way they had been when the rest of us were little. For one thing, Dad was making good money by then. We older kids always had to make do with secondhand clothes and hand-me-downs. But then we were all boys. so that made a difference, too. Everything Carmen got was brand-new, from her crib to her clothing.

"The truth is, I think my brothers and I all resented her a little—thought she was spoiled rotten. And she was, too, but it wasn't her fault. Dad and Mama just worshiped her and wanted her to have the very best. Which is how Carmen ended up going to St. Ambrose, a private Catholic school, while all the rest of us went to public schools. One of the parish priests at St. Ambrose is the one who molested her."

"But she didn't tell the family about it right away," Johnny Cruikshank put in.

"Of course not," Diego agreed. "That's not the way child abuse works. When it came time for Carmen to go to high school, Mama and Dad were ready to enroll her in another private high school, but she wasn't having any of it. She wouldn't go. In fact, she absolutely refused. About that same time, she stopped going to church, too. She wouldn't attend mass or go to confession. It broke my mother's heart. But Mama's never been one to take something like that lying down. She insisted that they go to counseling. That's when she first learned that Carmen was . . . well . . . different."

"You mean that she was a lesbian?" Johnny asked.

Diego nodded. "It's also where Carmen first told our mother about what had happened to her all those years ago when she was in second grade. Mama was furious. She went to the bishop and found out that the priest had been transferred to another parish—one right here in New Mexico, I think."

"Right," Randy Trotter said. "It's common knowledge that for a long time the Catholic Church used New Mexico as the dumping ground of choice for pedophile priests."

"Sure enough, the priest was still up to his old tricks," Diego Ortega continued. "Mama hired a lawyer and took her case first to the bishop and then to the cardinal. I think she would have gone all the way to Rome itself, except the Church settled. It was one of the early settlements, the ones that came complete with a nondisclosure agreement. In other words, they paid, but the terms of the deal kept all parties from revealing the amount of the settlement or even that a settlement existed."

"Hush money," Joanna murmured.

Diego nodded again. Their food order came then. Joanna's tuna sandwich was surprisingly good, but she had to edge herself into the far corner of the booth to keep from smelling everyone else's coffee.

"The settlement was large enough that it paid for Carmen's education, with some left over, but Mama always said it wasn't enough. She's convinced the abuse Carmen suffered is what made her turn out the way she is. I don't think that's true, and neither does . . ." He paused and took a deep breath. "Neither **did** Carmen," he corrected. "She told me once that she always knew she was different. But Mama's set in her ways, and none of us are about to try convincing her otherwise."

Joanna nodded. "Good plan," she said.

"So, anyway," Diego continued, "when Fandango wanted to do a piece about the pedophile priest scandal, Carmen went knocking on their door and begged them to let her work on it. She had done some other freelance work for them prior to that. They hired her for the project and teamed her up with Pamela. Carmen told me that when she and Pam met, it was love at first sight for both of them."

"Tell us about Pamela Davis," Johnny Cruikshank urged. She had finished her key lime pie and was taking detailed notes.

"Her father, Herman Davis, was an executive for one of the big studios," Diego Ortega said.

"Herman died of a stroke years ago, but I understand he was one of the off-screen movers and shakers behind launching that first **Star Trek** series. Her mother, Monica Davis, is in her eighties now. In her heyday, before she married Herman, she made a decent living as a bit actress in B-movies."

"Do you know how we can get in touch with her?"

Diego nodded. "She lives in an assisted-living facility in Burbank. It's called Hidden Hills, and it's exclusively for movie and television folk. I can get you the number if you want, but I'm not sure it'll do you any good. She's an Alzheimer's patient, and she's pretty well out of it. If you contact her, she probably won't know who you're talking about."

"But the facility may have a list of other people—other relatives of Pam's—who should be notified," Johnny persisted. "And don't worry about the number. I'm sure I can get it from directory assistance."

"Did Ms. Leigh say what kind of a story Pam and your sister were working on here?" Joanna asked. "Not more pedophile priests, I hope."

"Bigamy," Diego Ortega answered.

"Bigamy?" Johnny Cruikshank demanded.

"They spent the better part of two weeks up in northern Arizona, in both Page and Kingman.

Ms. Leigh said they made several trips to a place called the Arizona Strip investigating a break-away Mormon group called The Brethren. From what I understand, The Brethren practice bigamy quite openly."

What Joanna Brady knew about the Arizona Strip came from Arizona Sheriffs' Association meetings where Mojave County Sheriff Aubrey Drake had complained at length about trying to enforce the law—any kind of law—in the part of his jurisdiction that lay north of the Colorado River. Relatively inaccessible, it was a haven for people who had a penchant for wide-open spaces and a lack of law enforcement oversight. It was an open secret that bigamy was practiced among some of the reclusive people living on ranches in and around some of the more remote communities.

"They're not," Johnny Cruikshank announced abruptly.

"Not what?" asked Sheriff Trotter, looking at his detective with a puzzled frown.

"The bigamists aren't real Mormons any more than the 9/11 terrorists are real Muslims. They're jerks who've decided to use religion to justify any kind of outrageous behavior."

Not even the dim lighting of Esther's Diner concealed the two angry red splotches that had suddenly appeared in Johnny Cruikshank's tanned cheeks. **So she's a Mormon,** Joanna realized.

Joanna turned her attention to Diego Ortega. "I've heard of The Brethren," she said. "Edith Mossman, Carol's grandmother, mentioned that her son Eddie, Carol's father, belonged to a group by that name."

Diego Ortega's eyes hardened. "Have you talked to him yet?"

"No," Joanna said. "We've been trying to contact him, but as far as I know, he's still in Mexico."

"If I were you, I'd do more than just contact him," Ortega said.

"Why?"

"Because," he replied, "Carol Leigh told me that Carmen and Pam made contact with a second group, one that calls itself God's Angels. It's made up of women who have escaped from bigamy situations. The whole purpose of God's Angels is to help other women do the same thing—escape. Within two days of making contact with that group, Pam received a threatening e-mail that she forwarded to Candace Leigh at Fandango Productions."

"Do you have any idea what it said?" Joanna asked.

Diego reached into the inside pocket of his suit coat and pulled out a folded piece of paper. "I can do better than that," he said. "I can show you. Look."

He unfolded the paper and placed it on the table. The message was short: "Leave my daughters alone" was all it said. It was signed Edward Mossman.

"At the time, no one at Fandango took it seriously, not even Carmen and Pam," he said quietly. "Nobody believed it was a death threat. Unfortunately, now we know it was."

TWELVE

An hour later, when Joanna finally emerged from Esther's, she found herself in the strange half-darkness of a full-fledged dust storm. The humidity had shot up, making the heat that much worse. Off to the south, but far closer now, thunder rumbled in unseen clouds. It was the oncoming storm that had finally brought the joint interview with Diego Ortega to a halt. He was hoping to take off and fly north far enough to escape the brunt of the wind and rain.

"Are you sure you want to head home in this?" Randy Trotter asked as he walked Joanna back to her Civvie.

"I'll be fine," she said. "Most of the culverts on Highway 80 have been replaced. And usually there's not that much runoff from the first summer storm."

Famous last words. The rain hit just as she turned off I-10 onto Highway 80 at Road Forks. The wind-driven rain had so much dust mixed in with it that the water turned to blinding mud on her windshield. For the better part of an hour she crept along at twenty and thirty miles per hour. By the time she finally made it as far as Rodeo, the roadside ditches and dips were beginning to run. The storm let up for a while, then returned with renewed vigor about the time she hit the curves at Silver Creek. One after another, the newly replaced culverts were running with deep reddish-brown, foam-flecked water, spreading from one sandy bank to another. The place where the speeding Suburban had crashed off the road and landed upside down was totally underwater.

Joanna breathed a quick prayer of thanksgiving. **If that accident had happened tonight rather than last night,** she thought, **those people would have drowned. It could have taken months just to find the bodies.**

Once she was inside radio range she checked in with Dispatch. "How are things?"

"This is a major storm," Tica replied. "Two cars washed away in the dips between Double Adobe and Elfrida. Everyone's safe, but we still have units on the scene, including Chief Deputy Montoya."

"I'm almost home," Joanna told her. "Have Frank call me when he finishes up out there."

It was still raining when she finally reached

High Lonesome Ranch. Water more than a foot deep partially covered the road that led to their old house. If she had been going there, she would have had to abandon the car and walk. As it was, she was able to drive to the new house with no difficulty. When she finally pulled into the garage, the door from the laundry room opened and three dogs shot out, followed immediately by Butch.

"I'm really glad to see you," he said. "I was worried. How was it?"

"The drive was wet," she told him as she divested herself of her weapons and locked them away. "But I'm glad I went. We've got a positive ID on the two New Mexico victims and a definite connection between them and Carol Mossman. How was your day?"

"I made real progress," Butch replied. "I was sitting on the couch in the living room when the first clap of thunder rolled overhead. Lady was over under the dining room table, but as soon as she heard the thunder, she came streaking out of there and landed in my lap. She was so petrified, I ended up holding her for the better part of an hour."

Joanna laughed. "Does that mean you and Lady are friends now?" She laughed.

Butch shook his head. "I think it means any port in a storm. The funny thing is, Lucky slept right through the worst of the thunder. Is it possible he's deaf?"

"Deaf?"

Butch nodded. "He comes when he's called, but that may be because he's mimicking what the other dogs do."

Joanna thought about it. "I wonder if that's how he ended up being left behind at Carol Mossman's house. Maybe when she called the other dogs, he wasn't with them."

Butch grinned. "As you said, lucky for him. But how do you go about training a deaf dog?"

"Sign language, maybe?" Joanna asked.

"Remind me to check with Dr. Ross and see what she says," Butch said thoughtfully.

"Where's Jen?"

"At Cassie's, remember? I thought I told you that she's staying the night. I called to make sure they were out of the pool as soon as the thunder and lightning started. The big news of the day is that one of the girls from school is planning a slumber party that's supposed to be the social event of the summer. Both Jenny and Cassie are hoping for invitations."

"What about parental supervision?" Joanna asked.

"How about if we don't worry about that just yet," Butch advised. "First let's see if Jenny's invited or not."

"Fair enough."

"Hungry?" Butch asked.

"Not very. I had a tuna sandwich a while ago. Why? What's for dinner?"

"Roast-beef hash," Butch answered.

"In that case, the tuna sandwich was hours ago and I'm starved."

"By the way," Butch added, "Dr. Lee called today. Tommy said that his feelings are permanently hurt that he had to read all about your pregnancy in the **Bee**. He wants to know when you're going to show up at his office for your first prenatal checkup."

Dr. Thomas Lee, a Taiwanese immigrant, had come to Bisbee right out of medical school. He had planned to stay long enough to pay off his student loans. Ten years later, he was still there. Joanna had known him first as patient to doctor, but through his friendship with Jeff and Marianne Maculyea he had become friends with Joanna and Butch as well. Tommy Lee was also an exceptional cook who had set out to teach his group of new friends the fundamentals of Chinese cooking, which they were all still learning.

"What did you tell him?"

"That you'll call for an appointment next week."

"Fair enough." Joanna went into the bedroom and slipped into shorts and a T-shirt. More comfortable now, she returned to the kitchen. "Anything else?" she asked.

"Nothing much. You remember we're having dinner with Jim Bob and Eva Lou after church tomorrow?"

"Thanks for the reminder," she said. "I had forgotten all about that."

After dinner Joanna and Butch enjoyed a quiet evening together. Joanna Brady reveled in just watching TV, while several of Butch's O-gauge trains chugged around and around the room on the shelf that had been built for them just over the tops of the windows and doors. Frank Montoya never called her, and for a change Joanna resisted calling him. If there was nothing that pressing demanding her attention, she was better off lying low. And tomorrow or the next day would be time enough to write up her reports and pass along to her investigators the information she had gleaned from her trip to New Mexico. The past few days had been hell for her department. She figured they all needed a bit of a break.

At nine-thirty, though, the phone rang. It was late enough that Joanna was tempted not to answer, but when she saw the call was coming from Jeannine Phillips of Animal Control, Joanna took it.

"What's up?" she asked, worried that some of

the AWE activists had decided to picket the Animal Control offices.

"How's Blue Eyes?" Jeannine asked.

"You mean Lady?" Joanna returned. "Jenny renamed her, and she's settling in fine. She's great with the other dogs, and she's even starting to accept Butch."

"Good," Jeannine said awkwardly. "That's good."

There was a long pause. "Is that all you wanted?" Joanna asked. "To check on the dog?"

"Well, not really."

"What then?"

Jeannine took a deep breath. "I just wanted to thank you," she said. "For what you said about us—about Animal Control. It was nice. When I saw it on the news, I felt like . . . well . . . like somebody had finally noticed what we're doing here. And how."

"You're welcome, Jeannine," Joanna said. "You are doing a good job."

There was another strained pause. It seemed as though there was something else Jeannine Phillips wanted to say, but she couldn't quite bring herself to do it.

"It's about hoarders," Jeannine said. "We used to call them collectors. Now we call them hoarders. What exactly do you know about them?"

Joanna gathered her thoughts. "As I understand it, it's a kind of mental disorder, an obsessive-compulsive disorder that causes people—women, mostly—to gather animals in hopes of taking care of them, of protecting them. The disorder can be controlled with medication and it comes back without it."

"But do you know what causes it?"

"No," Joanna said. "Not really."

"The women almost always have one thing in common," Jeannine Phillips said.

"Really. What's that?"

There was another long pause. "They almost always have a history of childhood sexual abuse."

For a moment Joanna had nothing to say.

"If I didn't have this job, Sheriff Brady, I'd be one, too," Jeannine added softly. "In fact, I guess I am one. It's just that I don't take the animals here to my own place. It's why I do what I do, Sheriff Brady. But it's important for me to know that you think I do a good job anyway, and I wanted to say thank you."

"You're welcome, Jeannine," Joanna murmured as she put down the phone.

"Who was that?" Butch asked. "Not an emergency, I hope."

"No," Joanna said. "Believe it or not, it was someone calling to say thank you."

Joanna and Butch went to bed early that night.

Butch went right to sleep. Joanna lay awake for a long time, thinking about what Jeannine Phillips had said and what she had left unspoken.

Having been saved from the thunder and lightning by Butch, Lady was ready to switch her loyalties. For the first time the dog curled up on Butch's side of the bed rather than on Joanna's, which made it easier the next morning when it was time for Joanna's daily hand-over-mouth race to the bathroom.

"Didn't take as long this morning," Butch observed when she came into the kitchen for her single cup of tea.

"Maybe I'm getting used to it," Joanna returned.

After breakfast, Butch and Joanna stopped by Cassie's house to pick Jenny up and take her along to church. On the way into town Joanna was amazed to notice that less than twenty-four hours after that first drenching downpour, the long-bare stalks of ocotillo were already showing a hint of green as a new crop of round leaves poked out of what, for months, had seemed to be nothing more than a bundle of dried thorn-covered sticks. In another day, six-inch-long clumps of red tube-shaped flowers—the kind of flowers hummingbirds loved—would pop out along the top of each of those newly leafed branches.

"That's why I love ocotillos so much," Joanna said.

"Why's that?"

"Because it takes so little rain and time for them to spring back to life. It always seems like a miracle to me."

"I feel the same way about you," Butch said.

She smiled, took his hand, and squeezed it.

When they stepped out of the Subaru in the parking lot at Tombstone Canyon United Methodist Church, the sky overhead was a brilliant washed-clean azure with a few puffy white clouds perched on top of the surrounding red-and-gray hills. But with the onset of the rainy season, the humidity was also on the rise—so much for Arizona's supposedly dry heat.

Church that morning was warm and awkward, too. Marliss Shackleford was there, front and center, along with her fiancé, Richard Voland, a man who had once been Joanna Brady's chief deputy and whose resignation she had been forced to engineer and accept. Out of law enforcement, he now worked as one of Cochise County's few private investigators.

Marliss Shackleford and Richard Voland had been engaged for some period of time with no hint of whether or when they would take the plunge and marry. During the time of sharing, however, Marliss ended all speculation by standing up and announcing that they had recited their marriage vows in a private ceremony on Saturday of the previous week and that the wedding cake to be served during the social hour after church would be part of an informal reception.

Sitting several pews back, Joanna was stunned by this news. Her ongoing difficulties with Marliss and the complications surrounding Richard Voland's resignation made her relationship with the bridal couple strained, to say the least. She resented the idea that she was being coerced into attending a surprise wedding reception. All through Marianne Maculyea's sermon, Joanna stewed about the upcoming social hour and made up her mind to leave as soon as the last hymn was sung. That plan was foiled by Jenny's disappearing into the basement for cake and punch before Joanna had a chance to stop her.

Taking Butch's arm, she allowed herself to be led into the social hall with about as much enthusiasm as a prisoner being led to execution. A beaming Marliss, with Richard Voland at her side, waited at the door, greeting each new arrival.

As Joanna approached, Marliss leaned over and whispered in Joanna's ear, "Love **is** lovelier the second time around—but then I guess you and Eleanor already figured that out."

Marliss's first husband and high school sweetheart, Bradley Shackleford, had been out of the picture almost as long as Joanna could remember. Under her cloud of unruly and newly frosted curls, Marliss looked so undeniably happy that Joanna couldn't help but soften a little.

"Yes, we did, Marliss," Joanna agreed. "Congratulations to both of you."

Wandering through the social hall with paper cups of punch in their hands, Joanna and Butch were the recipients of their own greetings and well-wishes. Regardless of how they had learned of Joanna's pregnancy, everyone there made some comment about the news. Finished with her punch, Joanna was standing to one side of the room and waiting for Butch to finish a conversation with Jeff Daniels when Richard Voland sidled up next to her.

"How's it going?" he asked.

Joanna looked at him warily. Everyone knew that, in the aftermath of his divorce, Voland had fallen victim to drinking too much, but no one other than Butch knew that the real reason behind Richard Voland's resignation from the sheriff's department had been his unrequited crush on Joanna Brady. She had seen him occasionally since then in social settings. Basking in this new romance with Marliss, Voland appeared to have overcome his personal demons and his feelings about Joanna, too, but she was nonetheless leery of spending too much time in his presence.

"All right," she said. "And you?"

"Couldn't be better," he replied. "Business is picking up a little, and you know Marliss. She keeps me hopping."

"Yes," Joanna agreed. "I'm sure she does."

"There is one thing we don't agree about, though," Voland added.

"What's that?"

"You."

"Richard . . ." Joanna began as a blush started forming at the base of her neck. "Really, I—"

"About the election," Voland added quickly. "Marliss is anything but unbiased when it comes to Ken Junior, and I think she's wrong. Pregnant or not, you really are the best man for the job."

Across the room, Marliss noticed Joanna and Richard Voland standing together. Tossing her mane of curls, she caught her husband's eye and summoned him with a come-hither finger. Joanna's blush, which had started for one reason, finished for another.

"Thank you, Richard," she said. "I really appreciate that."

Butch appeared at her side half a minute later. "Ready?" he asked.

"Yes," Joanna said gratefully. "More than ready."

"And what was that all about—the thing with Richard Voland?"

"I'm not sure," she replied, "but I think he just gave me one of the biggest compliments of my life."

Once Joanna and Butch had retrieved Jenny from the puzzle-and-game corner where she'd been involved in a killer game of Chinese checkers, they headed for Jim Bob and Eva Lou Brady's duplex on Oliver Circle. As Jim Bob welcomed them inside, the whole house was filled with the delectable aroma of Eva Lou's old-fashioned meat loaf.

Butch and Joanna's former father-in-law went out to Jim Bob's workshop to discuss one of the older man's woodworking projects, while Joanna and Jenny ventured into Eva Lou's undisputed domain, the kitchen. "Anything I can do to help?"

Her face red with exertion, Eva Lou was energetically mashing potatoes. "Not a thing. Joanna, you sit down and relax. Jenny, do you mind setting the table?"

Without argument, both mother and daughter did as they were told. While Jenny pulled out plates and silverware and carried them into the dining room, Joanna sat at the kitchen table and gratefully kicked off her high-heeled shoes. She sighed with relief as she wiggled her liberated toes.

"What does your mother have to say about all this?" Eva Lou asked.

"She's not exactly thrilled," Joanna allowed.

Eva Lou laughed. "No, I don't suppose she is, but what about you?"

"I'm thrilled, and so is Butch."

"That's all that matters then, isn't it?" Eva Lou asked. "I learned a long time ago that if you spend your whole life worrying about what other people think, you're not going to get anywhere."

Just like Eleanor, Joanna thought. **Worrying about other people's opinions and not doing anything on her own.**

"How come I can't have you for a mother?" she asked.

Eva Lou looked at her and smiled. "Well, you do," she said. "I'm just another mother. Now when exactly is this baby due? You and Butch aren't the only ones with plans to make. Jim Bob and I have some things we want to do, too."

That afternoon, Eva Lou's down-home cooking hit the spot—meat loaf, mashed potatoes, fried okra, and freshly made biscuits, followed by fresh peach pie. As soon as dinner was over, Jenny retreated to the spare bedroom which was her special domain at the Brady household. As Butch, Eva Lou, and Jim Bob sipped their coffee, conversation turned to work.

Before Andy's death, Jim Bob Brady had always expressed more than a passing interest in whatever cases his son, the deputy sheriff, had been involved in. Now that same curiosity was focused on Joanna's cases, and she was happy to oblige. She had found that sometimes, in the process of explaining a case to a law enforcement outsider, she was able to gain a new perspective on it herself.

With regard to the Mossman/Ortega/Davis murders, Jim Bob homed in on the ammunition. "The casings all come with the same stamp?" he asked.

Joanna nodded. "Initial **S** for Springfield, Massachusetts, and 'seventeen' for 1917. So we know where it came from, and obviously it still works. The question is, where has it been all this time?"

Jim Bob frowned. A faraway look came into his eyes. "I wonder," he said.

"Wonder what?"

"You know what was going on around here in 1917, don't you?"

"World War One?" Joanna offered tentatively.

Jim Bob shook his head. "No, that was over in Europe. Around here, the big news that year was the Bisbee Deportation."

"I remember now," Joanna said. "Something about union activists being run out of town on a rail."

"In boxcars, actually," Jim Bob corrected. "A bunch of company-organized vigilantes rousted over a thousand men out of bed at gunpoint, marched them down to the Warren Ballpark, and then loaded them into boxcars that left the men standing for hours ankle-deep in manure. After some back-and-forthing, they finally dropped them off in the desert near Columbus, New Mexico, before the U.S. Cavalry finally showed up to take charge of them. Some came back eventually, but others never did."

"You seem to know a lot about this," Butch observed.

"Sure thing," Jim Bob said, nodding sagely. "When I went to work in the mines after the Korean War, the Deportation was still big news around here. Back then, considering whatever company you were keeping, if you came down on the wrong side of the Deportation, you were likely to get your ass kicked."

"Jim Bob," Eva Lou admonished, "watch your language. Jenny might hear."

Joanna could picture Jenny lying on the floor, with her eyes closed and the earphones to her Walkman clapped to her ears.

There's a good chance the language on the CD is a lot worse than that, Joanna thought.

Joanna had heard pieces of the story all her life. Butch, hearing about the Bisbee Deportation for the first time, listened with avid interest. "So if the vigilantes were company men . . ."

"Deputized by Sheriff Wheeler," Jim Bob interjected.

". . . who were the deportees?"

"Where's that book of mine?" Jim Bob asked. **"Bisbee Seventeen,** it's called. That tells the whole thing."

"It's out in the garage," Eva Lou replied. "Along with all the other books you boxed up because you were going to build a new bookshelf, remember?"

Jim Bob grimaced. "Wobblies," he said, in answer to Butch's question. "The IWW. International Workers of the World. They called a strike in July of 1917. According to the company honchos, they were undermining the war effort. The real problem was, the IWW recruited minority members. Back then, Mexicans weren't allowed to work underground, and they received less pay. Same goes for the European immigrants. They were allowed to work underground, but they were limited to lower-paying jobs. Now it sounds like the IWW had the right idea, but back then what they were proposing must have been pretty outrageous."

He stopped then and slammed his open palm on the table with enough force to make the cups and saucers rattle. "That's it!" he exclaimed. "I'm sure it is."

"What's it?" Joanna asked.

"The ammunition. The weapons. All of the vigilantes were armed with guns the company bought and paid for. In fact, a couple of people were actually shot and killed in the process of the roundup, but afterward everybody turned their weapons back in, and most of 'em ended up stored in a safe up in the old General Office in Bisbee."

"The ammunition, too?" Joanna asked.

"I think so," Jim Bob replied.

"So where's that arms cache now? Is it still there?"

"No. Somebody opened the safe and found them when Phelps Dodge was shutting down its Bisbee operation in the mid-seventies. They just divvied the stuff up among the people who worked there. Whoever wanted some, gathered up a gun or two and took them home."

Joanna's mind was already blazing on ahead. She had spent part of the night thinking about what Diego Ortega had said about the bigamy-practicing group called The Brethren, the same group Edith Mossman had mentioned several days earlier with regard to her estranged son, Eddie. It was also the group Pam Davis and Carmen Ortega had been investigating. Was it possible Eddie Mossman had murdered his own daughter in order to keep her from telling her story, whatever it was, in front of a camera?

Joanna put down her napkin. "Excuse me," she said. "But I need to go make a phone call." And she went outside on the Bradys' front porch to do it.

At three o'clock in the afternoon, tall columns

of cumulus clouds were rising over the hill with its distinctively heart-shaped top that generations of Bisbee kids had called Geronimo. With any luck, there would be another late-afternoon thunderstorm today, and the summer rainy season would be well under way. But right that minute, Joanna's mind wasn't on the weather.

She reached Frank Montoya at his newly purchased home in Old Bisbee. "What's up, boss?" he asked when he heard Joanna's voice.

Briefly she summarized what she had learned from her trip to Lordsburg the day before as well as what she'd just discovered about the Bisbee Deportation from Jim Bob Brady.

"What do you want me to do?" Frank asked.

"We need to know whether or not Eddie Mossman had access to any of those weapons. If he worked in PD's General Office, it's possible he was given some of them."

"That was a long time ago," Frank said dubiously.

"Twenty-five years, at least," Joanna agreed.

"So finding out could be tough. The people who worked there are likely to be in their sixties, seventies, and eighties. It doesn't sound likely that some old coot in a nursing home would let himself out and then start plugging people with a weapon that's older than he is."

"What about a son or a son-in-law?" Joanna suggested. "Or maybe even a grandson?"

Frank thought about that. "Still," he said, "I'd say the odds aren't good."

"How many people would have been working there?" Joanna asked. "Thirty-five? Forty? Once we have the names, we'll at least have a place to start, and it could be, when we start talking to them, one of them might be able to tell us something we need to know."

"All right," Frank agreed finally. "I'll contact PD headquarters in Phoenix first thing tomorrow morning to see if I can track any of this down, but don't hold your breath."

"Do we know if the cops in Obregón had any luck contacting Mr. Mossman about his daughter's death?"

"I'll check on that, too," Frank said.

"How did the interviews go in Tucson?" Joanna asked.

"All right, I guess," Frank replied. "At least we have some. Whether what we have will be enough to put the squeeze on the driver, I don't know."

"And the little boy's mother?" Joanna asked.

"We never had a chance to talk to her," he said. "She had undergone surgery for a ruptured spleen and other internal injuries. The doctor says that it's going to be touch-and-go for her for the next several days. She may not make it."

"With her baby dead, she may not **want** to make it," Joanna observed.

"That, too," Frank agreed. "If that's all, I'll get on the horn and see who I should call in the morning when offices open up. It'll be easier if I know where to start."

Jenny popped her head out the door. "Mom, can't we go home soon?"

"In a while," Joanna replied. "But first I want to help Grandma Brady with the dishes. What's the hurry?"

Joanna made a face. "It's boring here," she said. "Besides, Cassie and I want to go riding."

At thirteen, Jenny was taller than her mother, although her fast-growing string-bean limbs had yet to fill out. It seemed only days ago when nothing had made Jenny happier than spending a long summer afternoon in the company of her paternal grandparents. Those days were gone.

Joanna glanced at the sky, where the threatening clouds had grown even darker while she had been on the phone.

"You can't go riding, Jenny. It's going to rain."

Jenny sighed, made another face, and flounced back into the house. When Joanna returned to the kitchen, she discovered that Butch had beaten her to the punch as far as doing dishes was concerned. The dishwasher was loaded and he was cleaning the last of the pots and pans by hand.

"Looks like I dodged KP," she said.

"Again," Butch said.

They went home shortly after that. Jenny, still in a huff, closeted herself in her room. Butch and Joanna spent the remainder of Sunday afternoon in relative quiet. They were halfway through **60 Minutes** when the phone rang.

"Here we go again," Butch said as he rose to answer it. "I knew this was too good to last. Oh, hi there, George," he said into the phone. "No, hang on. She's right here."

"What's going on?" Joanna said to Doc Winfield.

"We've got a problem with Ed Mossman."

"Ed Mossman?" Joanna said. "Carol's father? I thought he was in Mexico. As far as I know, he hasn't even been notified."

"He's been notified, all right," George Winfield observed. "And he's on the warpath."

"What about?"

"According to the grandmother, she was Carol's next of kin. At her direction, I had made arrangements for the body to be released to Higgins Funeral Chapel in the morning. Edith wants Carol to be buried here in Bisbee. Ed Mossman claims he's making arrangements to ship the body back down to Mexico. Not only that, when he called here to the house, he was rude to your mother and downright abusive to me. He even threatened his own mother."

"He threatened Edith?"

"That's right. He said she's already caused enough trouble between him and his daughters and he's not going to stand for her keeping him away from Carol now that she's dead. He wants her buried next to her mother in the family plot in Obregón."

"Wanting to bury his daughter next to her mother is fine," Joanna said. "Threatening Edith Mossman isn't. What did you tell him?"

"To come by the office tomorrow morning. He said he'd be there at nine."

"I will be, too," Joanna said.

"There is one other thing," George Winfield added.

"What's that?"

"Speaking of next of kin, has anyone done anything to locate Carol Mossman's child?"

"What child?" Joanna asked.

"I take it you haven't read my autopsy report?"

"I've been a little pressed for time," Joanna returned. "What child?"

"Carol Mossman bore at least one child," George said. "It was delivered by C-section. She also had a complete hysterectomy. From the scarring, I'd say both the C-section and hysterectomy were done at the same time by a surgeon who wasn't exactly the head of his class."

"It was bad?"

"Let's just say it was unskilled," George said.

"And as bad as the hysterectomy was, it's likely that the child didn't survive, but we should clarify the situation just to be on the safe side. If you want me to, I can call Edith Mossman and ask her."

"No," Joanna said. "She's been through enough. I'll ask Eddie Mossman about it myself in the morning."

She put down the phone. Butch had muted the television set. Andy Rooney's mouth was moving, but no words could be heard.

"A looming funeral battle?" Butch asked.

Joanna nodded.

Butch shook his head. "I hate it when that happens. Funeral fights are the worst. My grandparents both wanted to be buried in Sun City. Gramps hated Chicago. He told me once that the last thing he wanted was to spend eternity buried under drifts of Chicago snow and ice. He asked me, over and over, to make sure that didn't happen, and I promised him I would.

"He and Grandma died within weeks of each other. The minute Gramps was gone, my mother and aunts and uncles came riding into town on their broomsticks. They had Grandma's casket dug up and then they shipped both Grandma and Grandpa back home to bury them. It's years later, Joey, and I'm still pissed about it. That's one of the reasons I haven't gone back home to visit. I'd as soon punch my aunts' and uncles' lights out as look at them."

"I never knew any of that," Joanna said quietly.

"No," Butch agreed. "I don't suppose you did. I'm still ashamed of myself for letting him down—for not putting up more of a fight. But I was only the grandson. No one was interested in listening to me."

Joanna reached over and put a comforting hand on Butch's leg. "I'm sure you did the best you could," she said quietly.

"Right," he said bitterly. "Sure I did, but it wasn't good enough."

With **60 Minutes** over, Joanna went into the den, turned on her computer, and wrote up a report on everything she had learned during her trip to Lordsburg. When she finished, she e-mailed it to Frank Montoya at the office. That way, even if she didn't go in right away in the morning, the report would be there.

"Reports come first," D. H. Lathrop used to say. "If you're not doing the paper, you're not doing the job."

Twenty-four hours late, Dad, she said to herself. **But the paper's there.**

THIRTEEN

Good as her word, Joanna was at the Cochise County Medical Examiner's office by eight forty-five the next morning. Busy on the phone, Nell Long, the ME's receptionist, waved Joanna toward George Winfield's open office door.

"Any sign of Mr. Mossman?" Joanna asked, peering around the doorjamb into her stepfather's office.

"Not so far," George replied. "But I have an idea he'll be here shortly. Have a chair. How are you feeling?"

"I'm still a puking mess every morning," Joanna returned. "I'm hoping that'll settle down in a few weeks. At least that's how it worked when I was pregnant with Jenny."

"I never had a chance to say anything about the other night—with Ellie, I mean," George Winfield said. "I thought she was way out of line, and I told her so. In other words, if it's any consolation, Joanna, I think she's as provoked with me right now as she is with you."

"The old misery-loves-company routine," Joanna said with a hollow laugh. It was easier to make light of Eleanor Lathrop Winfield's rantings and ravings when she was well out of earshot.

"Something like that," George agreed.

"Well, don't worry about it. I've known Mother a lot longer than you have, George. She'll get over it eventually." Joanna made the statement with more conviction than she felt. There were some things Eleanor Lathrop **never** got over.

"What about you?" George asked.

"I'm going to go ahead and do what I do," Joanna told him. "Eleanor will have to like it or lump it."

"Good girl," George said. "Way to go!"

The telephone rang. Nell answered it. A moment later, her voice sounded on George's intercom. "Edith Mossman is on the line."

"Great," George said. "Just what I need. I love being caught in the cross fire between battling relatives." He picked up his phone. "Good morning, Mrs. Mossman. What can I do for you?"

There was a pause. A frown appeared on George Winfield's brow. The longer Edith Mossman talked, the deeper grew the lines on George's forehead.

"Yes, that's true. He is coming in this morning. I'm expecting him in the next few minutes. And no, I'm not sure who notified him. Someone from the sheriff's department, I should imagine."

Another pause. "No, I'm really not involved in all that. I release the body to the mortuary. After that, it's up to the family to handle things from there."

There was another long silence on the medical examiner's part. Joanna couldn't make out any of the words, but the angry buzz of Edith Mossman's shrill voice hummed through the telephone receiver and out into the room.

"Really, Mrs. Mossman, that's not up to me. You'll need to discuss it with Norm Higgins and with your son. I'm sure if you'll just sit down and talk, you and he will be able to sort all this out—"

Suddenly, a dial tone replaced the sound of Edith Mossman's voice.

"She hung up on me," George said, staring first at the phone and then at Joanna.

"I don't think she liked what you had to say."

"No kidding! But it's true. My job is to release the body to the mortuary. It's up to the family to figure out who takes charge from there."

"Mr. Mossman to see you," Nell Long announced over the intercom.

"Saved by the bell," George Winfield said, raising an eyebrow as he rose to greet the newcomer Nell Long showed into his office.

Somehow Joanna had expected there to be more to Eddie Mossman than what she saw. He was a pint-size bantam rooster of man, only an inch or two taller than Joanna's five feet four. Wiry and tanned, he had a bottle-brush mustache and piercing blue eyes. For some reason, he seemed familiar, even though Joanna doubted she had ever seen him before.

"Dr. Winfield?" Mossman asked.

George nodded. "That would be me," he said. "And this," he added, indicating Joanna, "is Sheriff Joanna Brady."

Edward Mossman wasn't interested in pleasantries. "As I told you on the phone, I'm here for Carol's body."

"And as I told you on the phone, it hasn't been released yet," George returned evenly. "I haven't yet prepared the death certificate. When it's finished, I'll be releasing the body to Norm Higgins at Higgins Mortuary and Funeral Chapel. I believe your mother has already discussed arrangements with them. If you want to change those, you'll have to discuss it with them and her."

"I've already been to see Norm Higgins. Tried to, anyway. Since Mother has already made a deposit on those 'arrangements,' as you call them, no one at the Higgins outfit will give me the time of day. I want the body to go to someone else. I've contacted a mortuary over in Nogales that's accustomed to transporting bodies in and out of Mexico. I want you to release Carol's body to them."

"I'm sure Norm Higgins could assist you with that as well," George Winfield replied. "In the meantime, I think it would be more to the point if you and your mother met and sorted this whole thing out before you involve some other mortuary in an already complicated situation. Your mother—"

"My mother's an interfering old lady," Ed Mossman said. "She has no right to usurp my authority like this. After all, I am Carol's father. Doesn't that give me some right to decide about things like this? And who the hell are you to say that I don't? If I have to go back there, find Carol, and carry her out of here myself, my daughter's body is coming back to Mexico with me. Understand?"

With that and still bristling with anger, Ed Mossman slammed his doubled-up fist on the top of George's desk. The Tiffany crystal clock Eleanor had given her new husband as a wedding present skittered toward the edge of the desk. George caught it in time and returned it to its original place.

Thinking things had gone far enough, Joanna stepped into the fray. "Excuse me, Mr. Mossman," she put in. "If you'll allow me—"

"Allow you what? I believe I was speaking with Dr. Winfield here," Mossman growled at her. "I don't remember anyone asking for your opinion."

"No one asked because they don't have to. I get to give my opinion, because it happens that my department is investigating your daughter's murder," Joanna returned evenly. "Like it or not, that means you'll be speaking to me and to my investigators. In the meantime, Mr. Mossman, I would advise you to have a seat and adopt a less threatening demeanor. If not, I'll be forced to call for backup and throw you in jail for disturbing the peace. Is that clear?"

"I'll try to keep that in mind," Ed Mossman sneered, but he did settle himself into a chair.

"Good," Joanna said. She reached into her purse, removed her cell phone, and used her one-touch dialing system to reach Dispatch. "Are either Detective Carbajal or Ernie Carpenter in yet?" she asked.

"Jaime's here at the office," Larry Kendrick said. "As I understand it, Ernie's on his way."

"I want them both here at Doc Winfield's office as soon as possible," Joanna said. "There's someone here who needs to give them a next-of-kin interview."

She paused. If they were going to interview Ed Mossman, the two detectives needed to know that Pamela Davis and Carmen Ortega had been prepared to pay good money for whatever Carol Mossman had to say. Jaime and Ernie also needed to know that the two murdered reporters had been on the trail of Ed Mossman and his fellow Brethren.

"Try to turn Ernie around and have Jaime check in with Chief Deputy Montoya before he comes here," Joanna told Larry. "I faxed my report from Saturday to Frank last night. I want the Double Cs, both Ernie and Jaime, to know about it before they do the next-of-kin interview."

"Who's that?" Ed Mossman asked once Joanna ended the call. "Who are the two guys you just asked to come here?"

"Detectives Carpenter and Carbajal are my homicide detectives," Joanna replied.

"Why do they need to interview me?" Mossman demanded. "I wasn't anywhere around when Carol was murdered."

"Did I say you were a suspect?" Joanna asked.

"No, but——"

"In homicide investigations we routinely question everyone connected to the victim. Since that person is already dead, we talk to friends and relatives in order to gain a better idea of who all might be involved. You are Carol's next of kin, aren't you?"

"Yes," Mossman answered. "I already told you. Of course I am."

"So my detectives need to interview you."

"But it's just routine then, right?" Mossman asked warily.

"Absolutely. They're just minutes away, so it won't take long for them to get here. In the meantime, would you mind telling me how you heard about Carol's death? I know one of my deputies contacted the police in Obregón, and they agreed to do the notification, but—"

"My daughter called me," Mossman interrupted.

"Which one?"

"Does it matter?" Mossman said. "The point is, one of them did. And, once I knew Carol was dead, I came here to do something about it."

Joanna Brady had spent only a few minutes with Eddie Mossman, but already she had some idea of why the man's own mother held him in such contempt. He was pushy and obnoxious, but there was something else about him, something about his carriage and attitude that she didn't like. And now, as he disregarded her question, little warning bells jangled alarmingly in her head. Suddenly it seemed vitally important for her to learn exactly where Ed Mossman had been when he first learned of Carol's murder, but Joanna didn't want to give that away. Instead, she smiled what she hoped to be her most convincingly sincere smile.

"Of course it doesn't matter, Mr. Mossman," she assured him. "It doesn't matter at all."

Across the desk from her, George Winfield's eyebrows shot up in surprise. Obviously he recognized the lie for what it was. Joanna was grateful, however, that the ME managed to keep his mouth shut about it.

"Is there anyone else you'd like us to notify?" Joanna continued disarmingly. "Besides your daughters and your mother, that is. Any spouses, former spouses, or boyfriends?"

"I don't know of anyone else," Mossman grumbled. "Notifying my mother first was bad enough."

"Actually, your mother found out about Carol's death all on her own," Joanna told him. "She came to your daughter's place shortly after Carol's body had been discovered by one of my officers. Carol was evidently in dire financial straits, and your mother was coming to offer help. You wouldn't know anything about your daughter's financial situation, would you?"

"I don't know anything. Carol and I stopped speaking years ago," Ed Mossman said. "It happened about the same time my mother encouraged Carol and two of my other daughters to run away."

"So your mother and you aren't on what you'd call the best of terms."

"I believe I did mention that."

"And you were estranged from Carol, too?"

Mossman glowered at her. "Carol was always

headstrong and irresponsible, even when she was little. And the fact that my mother was always willing to step in and bail her out didn't help matters any. If she had run away all on her own, I probably wouldn't have worried. She was twenty by then—a grown-up. But she took off with her two younger sisters in tow. I do blame my mother for that. If she hadn't stepped in to help them back then, none of this would have happened."

"So you're saying your mother is ultimately responsible for Carol's death?"

"Absolutely," Ed Mossman said with a decisive nod. "That's exactly what I'm saying."

Joanna's phone, still in her hand, let out a sharp little crow. Looking at the readout, Joanna saw her mother's number. For once Joanna Brady was thrilled at the idea of an Eleanor Lathrop interruption. It gave her a much-needed reason to escape the confines of George Winfield's office.

"If you'll excuse me," she said, heading for the door, "I need to take this call."

The phone rang twice more before Joanna made it through the outside door and answered. "Oh, there you are," Eleanor said. "I was about to leave a message."

"I had to come outside to answer."

"Well," Eleanor huffed, "if it's inconvenient

for you to talk to me right now, I can always call back later."

"No, please. It's fine. I can talk for a few minutes. What is it?"

"George thinks I was out of line," Eleanor began uncertainly. "He thinks I owe you and"—she paused—"Butch an apology." As long as Eleanor had known her son-in-law, she had made clear her preference for his given name, Frederick. Even now the word **Butch** seemed to stick in her throat.

"You don't have to apologize, Mom," Joanna said. "We just have different ideas about how the world works, that's all."

"It was unfair of me to enlist your brother's help. It's just that I so wanted you to listen to reason, which I'm sure you won't."

Since that was true, Joanna said nothing.

"George tells me that it's a whole new century with different rules and roles for everyone, but I can't see a grandchild of mine being raised by a . . ."

"By a what, Mom?" Joanna asked.

"By a novelist, I guess," Eleanor said lamely. "And a male novelist at that. It strikes me as wrong, somehow—unseemly."

What about Jenny? Joanna wanted to ask. **Butch is doing a fine job of raising her, isn't he?** But just then Ernie Carpenter, driving his own Mercury Sable, pulled into the parking lot. Hoping to head off the arriving detective was the real reason Joanna had rushed outside to take her phone call.

"Mom," Joanna said. "Sorry to interrupt, but something's come up. I've got to go."

"See there?" Eleanor said. "Even when I'm calling to apologize, you can't spare me even a moment of attention. You don't have the time— you don't **take** the time—to listen. It's hopeless."

"Mom, I really do have to go. I'll call you later."

She hung up just as Ernie walked over to her. "What's up, boss?" he asked.

"Did you have a chance to go over my report?"

"Jaime just called and gave me a rundown," Ernie replied. "You picked up a lot of information. You think the guy in the ME's office, the father, is a suspect?"

"I'm not sure," Joanna replied. "He could be."

"Do we need to Mirandize him?"

Joanna shook her head. "Not right now. He's not an actual suspect at this point. When you and Jaime talk to him, keep your questions to next-of-kin issues for right now. Pick up as much information and as many details as you can that we might be able to use later to trip him up in case he does turn into a suspect."

"Like what?" Ernie asked.

"I think we can get away with asking him about

when and how he learned of his daughter's death. Ask him that, but don't ask him where he was at the time she was murdered. We also need to figure out a way to keep him around long enough for us to decide if he is a suspect. Once he goes zipping back home to Mexico, we'll never see him again."

"What's the deal here?" Ernie asked. "Mossman's not really a suspect, but he may turn into one, so you want us to keep him here. Do we have any solid evidence that makes him a likely suspect in any of these murders?"

Joanna shook her head. "I'm not necessarily convinced that he actully killed any of the women, but I have a feeling he has something to do with it."

Ernie shook his head. "Great," he grumbled. "Another one of your **feelings**. Those don't exactly count as probable cause."

"Exactly," Joanna agreed. "That's why you're doing a next-of-kin interview and nothing else."

Just then a green-and-white cab pulled into the parking lot and stopped in the handicapped parking area in front of the door. While Joanna watched in amazement, the back door opened and Edith Mossman clambered out and then hobbled forward on her walker.

"You wait right here," she ordered the cabbie. "I'll be out in a few minutes."

Joanna hurried up to her. "Mrs. Mossman," she said. "What are you doing here?"

"I came to see that son of mine," Edith Mossman wheezed. "I'm not armed, so I can't shoot him, but if I can get close enough to hit him with my walker, I'll beat him to a bloody pulp."

"Please," Joanna said, "you can't do that. If you struck him, my officers would have to arrest you for assault."

"If that's what it takes to keep him from taking Carol's body back to Mexico, so be it. Lock me up if you have to, but hitting him will be worth it," Edith Mossman declared grimly. "Beating the crap out of him won't change a thing, but it'll make me feel a lot better."

"Really, Mrs. Mossman," Joanna said. "I can't allow you inside if you're planning a physical assault, but if you simply want to talk to your son—"

"I don't want to talk to him."

"But telling him how you feel might do you as much or more good than hitting him." Joanna took Edith by the arm. "Come on," she added. "I'll take you to where he is."

With Ernie trailing behind, Edith allowed herself to be led first into the building and then on into George Winfield's office. As soon as Ed Mossman glimpsed his mother's face, he was outraged.

"What the hell is **she** doing here?" he demanded. "Get her out of here."

"Don't talk about me as though I'm deaf or dumb, Eddie," Edith ordered. "I'm perfectly capable of speaking for myself. I came here to tell you that you're scum. That if I ever had a son, I don't any longer."

"The feeling's mutual there, I'm sure," Ed Mossman fired back at her. "You don't have a son and I don't have a mother. That makes us even."

"And if you even attempt to take Carol back to Mexico with you, I swear, I'll . . ."

"You'll what?" Mossman demanded. "You'll disown me? You already did that. So what?"

"I'll take you to court, Eddie," Edith vowed. "I'll fight you down to my dying breath and down to my last penny. I may not have a lot of money, but I'll bet I have more than you do."

As she spoke, slamming her walker on the floor with every step, Edith had moved across the room toward her son. She stopped when their faces were bare inches apart. Worried that Edith might still make good on her threat, Joanna moved closer as well, just in case she needed to separate them.

For almost a minute, Edith Mossman stared at her son, saying nothing. When she did speak, it was in a hoarse whisper.

"I'm so grateful your father didn't live long

enough to see what a monster you've become, Edward Mossman. What you did to those girls is utterly unthinkable!"

With that, Edith turned on her heel and banged her way back out of the room. In the long silence that followed Edith's exit, Joanna once again heard Jeannine Phillips's voice, telling her about animal hoarders—about who they were, where they came from, and why.

"I'm one, too," Jeannine had said.

Jeannine Phillips had been a victim of child abuse. In a flash of clarity illuminated by Edith Mossman's righteous anger, Joanna realized that the woman's murdered granddaughter had also been victimized. As had her sisters. By their own father.

George Winfield's office was suddenly too small. The walls closed in on Joanna until she could barely breathe. "I'd better go check on Mrs. Mossman," she managed.

Out in the parking lot, the cabbie was already helping Edith into the backseat. "Please, Mrs. Mossman," Joanna said, "I need to talk to you. Let the cab go. I'll give you a ride back home when we finish."

Edith looked briefly at Joanna. "All right," she said, then reached for her purse and wallet. She gave a handful of bills to the driver. "Thank you for getting me here in such a hurry, young man," she said. "And thank you for waiting. I really appreciate it."

The cabdriver counted through the money and then beamed back at Edith. Clearly she had given him a sizable tip. "Anytime, ma'am. You call the dispatcher and ask for me personally. I'll be glad to take care of you."

It took several minutes to help Edith Mossman into the car. Once she was settled, Joanna went back into the building. By then Jaime Carbajal had arrived on the scene. Joanna brought him up to speed. "You two handle Eddie," Joanna told him. "In the meantime, I'm giving Mrs. Mossman a ride back to Sierra Vista."

Once in the driver's seat of the Crown Victoria, Joanna glanced in Edith Mossman's direction. She sat slumped in the passenger's seat, staring stonily ahead at nothing in particular.

"Are you all right?" Joanna asked.

"I'm a failure," Edith said quietly.

"A failure?"

"At motherhood. If I'd done a better job, Eddie wouldn't have turned out the way he did."

"If your son turned out to be a child molester, it's not your fault. It's his."

Edith turned sharply and stared at Joanna. "I never said that," she said.

"No, you didn't," Joanna agreed. "You didn't have to, but it is true, isn't it?"

Edith shut her eyes. Two fat tears dribbled slowly down her bony cheeks. Finally she nodded. "Yes," she whispered brokenly. "Yes, it is."

"Would you tell me about it?"

"It's too late. It's over and done with."

"It's not over," Joanna said quietly.

"What do you mean?" Edith asked.

"Two other women were murdered last week over near Rodeo, New Mexico," Joanna said. "Pamela Davis and Carmen Ortega were independent television journalists doing a story on a group called The Brethren."

Joanna let the last word fall into the conversation like a pebble into a deep well. It took a long time for her to hear the answering splash.

"The same group Eddie's involved with," Edith Mossman breathed at last.

Joanna nodded. "Pamela Davis and Carmen Ortega left California with a check for five thousand dollars from their production company, Fandango Productions, made out to Carol Mossman. They were going to pay her to tell her story, Edith. Somebody murdered them and your granddaughter, too, in order to keep Carol from going public."

"And you think my son did that?"

"It's possible."

"If he did," Edith said fiercely, "then you have to lock him up and throw away the key."

"You'll help us then?"

"Absolutely. Just tell me what to do."

"You'll need to talk to my detectives again."

Edith nodded. "All right," she said.

"Why didn't you mention any of this to them the other day when you talked to them the first time?"

Edith shrugged. "I guess I didn't think it was important. And Carol never wanted to talk about it. At least she never did before. I thought I was respecting her wishes. But now . . . Of course I'll talk to them, but there's something else I need to do first."

"What's that?"

"I need to talk to a lawyer. I want someone to go to court for me to keep Eddie from taking Carol's body away."

"You don't have an attorney of your own?" Joanna asked.

"I used to," Edith said. "Augie Deming, out in Sierra Vista. He's the one who did Grady's and my wills, but that was years ago. Augie died a few years after Grady did. I haven't used an attorney since."

While they talked, Joanna had started the car and driven down Tombstone Canyon as far as the downtown area. Now she pulled into a parking place. "Tell you what," she said. "Burton Kimball's office is just over there." She pointed toward the entrance to a long red-brick building. "Burton's an attorney. He's also a friend of mine. He's done some work for me over the years. I'm not sure what, if any, grounds he could use to keep your son from taking charge of Carol's body, but if it can be done, he's the one to do it."

"Do I need to have an appointment in order to see him?" Edith asked.

"Just a minute," Joanna said. "I'll find out."

Joanna used her cell phone to make sure Burton Kimball was available, then she escorted Edith as far as the office door. "You go inside and talk to him," Joanna told Edith. "I'll be waiting here when you're done."

As soon as Edith disappeared inside, Joanna hurried back to the Civvie, and called Frank Montoya.

"I guess the morning briefing's been canceled due to lack of interest," he said derisively.

"Not lack of interest," Joanna corrected. "Lack of personnel." As quickly as possible, she explained everything that she had learned so far that morning.

"As long as Ernie and Jaime are meeting with Eddie Mossman," Joanna finished, "he's not going anywhere. And I'm relatively certain that he'll stick around town long enough to try to wrest Carol Mossman's body out of Edith's grasp. But we have to move fast. If he once figures out he's becoming an actual suspect, I'm afraid he'll disappear back into Mexico."

"So what do you want me to do?" Frank asked.

"First, I want you to call down to the police department in Obregón and find out whether or not they made a next-of-kin notification. I also want to know when and how Eddie Mossman traveled from there to here."

"Got it," Frank said. "If he was involved in his daughter's death, he wouldn't need to be notified."

"Exactly. I also want you to get on the phone to Fandango Productions."

"Right. The television production company Pamela Davis and Carmen Ortega worked with. I saw that in your report."

"Talk to Candace Leigh, the CFO. Have her send you to whoever you need to talk to. Find out if they have any details on Pamela Davis and Carmen Ortega's activities once they left there for Arizona. Diego Ortega said something about their being the target of one or more death threats. He even read me one that was purportedly from Ed Mossman. But it could have been sent by someone else. We need to know everything about that threat and any others that might have been received. If any police reports were made in regard to the threats, I want copies of those. And if Pam and Carmen sent any e-mails that contain notes or information, I'd like to have access to those as well. Somewhere along the way, they crossed paths with Carol Mossman's killer. I want to know where and when that was."

"Anything else?" Frank asked.

"Yes. Hidalgo County's medical examiner is doing the two autopsies today. Call over there and let them know that I need preliminary results as soon as possible."

"How come?" Frank asked. "They were shot, weren't they? What's an autopsy going to tell us that we don't already know?"

"I want them to pinpoint the time of death as closely as possible. I want to know if they were murdered before or after Carol Mossman died."

"So you're thinking Ed Mossman murdered the two women in New Mexico and his own daughter as well?"

"The thought had crossed my mind."

"What if he skips out and goes back to Mexico before we pull together enough pieces to have probable cause?"

Joanna was quiet for several moments as a tiny chip of an idea began to take shape in her head. "At this point, we don't know for sure that Ed Mossman is a suspect. But I do know he's been threatened. In fact, his own mother was all set to assault the man this morning."

"So?"

"We tell him that, because we believe his life may be in danger, we're putting him under a police guard. Have one of the deputies on hand when Jaime and Ernie finish their next-of-kin interview. Tell him that because we've been notified of what we believe to be a credible threat to his life, we're offering him protection. Tell him if we didn't do that, there's a possibility we'd be held liable in case anything happened to him."

"That's stretching it a little, isn't it?" Frank Montoya asked.

"Whatever works," Joanna returned.

"Okay," Frank said. "So I have my marching orders. Anything else?"

"That's all I can think of at the moment. No, wait. Any luck with Phelps Dodge on the General Office employees?"

"Not yet. What do you think I am, some kind of miracle worker?"

"Pretty much," she told him.

Frank Montoya wasn't amused. "So while I'm busy making my next set of phone calls, what are you up to?" he asked.

"I'm going to be picking Edith Mossman's brain," Joanna said. "Trying to get the goods on her son."

"Nice," Frank said. "Call me a wimp if you want to, but I'll stick to making phone calls. Getting a nice little old lady to turn state's evidence against her own son sounds a little underhanded to me."

"Maybe," Joanna agreed. "But if Eddie Mossman is the kind of creep he seems to be, I'm in favor of doing whatever it takes to get him off the streets."

FOURTEEN

When Edith Mossman emerged from Burton Kimball's office, Joanna hurried forward. She helped the older woman into the car and stowed her walker in the backseat. Once Joanna's seat belt was fastened, she glanced at Edith. The older woman sat motionless. Her head was thrown back against the headrest; both eyes were closed.

"Are you all right?" Joanna asked.

"Tired," Edith returned. "I'm very tired."

"Have you had anything to eat?"

Edith shook her head. "Knowing that Eddie was coming here to make trouble upset me so much that I couldn't eat a thing."

"Let's go have some lunch then," Joanna offered. "You'll feel better after you have some food."

"I don't think so," Edith said hopelessly. "I don't think anything is going to make me feel better ever again, but I suppose I do need to keep up my strength."

"Did Burton think he could help you?"

"Mr. Kimball wasn't sure," Edith replied. "He said we could probably slow things down some, but he didn't know if we can stop Eddie from taking Carol's body away altogether. He said that if Carol were a minor or incapacitated in some way and I had been appointed her guardian, then it was more likely he could fix this. Or if I had some kind of written document, like a will or something, specifying her wishes, then that would work, too. As it is, Eddie, as her father, is officially considered to be her next of kin."

"Your son can't take Carol's body anywhere if he isn't going there himself."

Suddenly, despite her lack of food, Edith Mossman straightened in her seat and came to full attention. "What are you saying?" she asked sharply.

"If someone were to file criminal charges against your son, if he ended up going to jail or prison rather than returning to Mexico, he wouldn't be able to take his daughter's body anywhere. It's my understanding that when it comes to shipping caskets containing human remains across the international border into Mexico, it's customary to have a relative of the deceased ride along to accompany the body."

"You're saying, if Eddie doesn't go back to Mexico, then Carol's body doesn't go either?"

Joanna nodded. "It's not one hundred percent, but it might work."

"Tell me what I need to do," Edith said.

"First you're going to have some lunch. Then we'll talk."

Joanna pulled into the last open parking place at Daisy's Café. Junior Dowdle, Daisy's adopted developmentally disabled son, met them at the door with a wide smile and a pair of menus. "Booth or table?" he asked.

"Booth, please, Junior," Joanna told him.

Junior led them to an empty booth and deposited their menus on the table. As he waddled purposefully away, Edith Mossman eyed him suspiciously. "Why would a restaurant hire someone like that?" she asked.

"It's his mother's restaurant," Joanna explained. "A few years ago, Junior's guardian abandoned him over in St. David. Moe and Daisy Maxwell took him in. First they were just his foster parents. After the death of Junior's biological mother, Moe and Daisy officially adopted him. They also taught him how to work here."

"Oh," Edith said, relenting. "I suppose that's all right then."

When Daisy appeared, pad in hand, Joanna ordered a roast beef sandwich while Edith settled on a cheese enchilada. As soon as Daisy walked away from their booth, Edith turned her full attention on Joanna.

"Now what can I do to help?" she asked.

Joanna herself had been mulling that very question. "Did any of your granddaughters' abuse occur while they were still in the States?" she asked.

Edith shook her head. "I don't think so. According to Carol, it started happening after they moved to Mexico. Cynthia, my daughter-in-law, was terribly ill ever before she became pregnant with Kelly. She never should have gotten pregnant that last time, but Eddie insisted. That's one thing The Brethren do believe in—that they should go forth and multiply. Eddie believed in multiplying in a big way. And so, when Cynthia was too sick to . . ." Edith paused, searching for the proper word. ". . . to accommodate his needs any longer, he came to Carol looking for . . . sexual gratification."

For several seconds, while Edith Mossman struggled to regain her composure, Joanna had to battle her own sense of outrage. A terrible revulsion assaulted her—a sickness that had nothing to do with current physical reality.

How could someone do that to his own child? a shaken Joanna wondered. **How could he?**

"Carol told me Eddie came to her bed late one night a few months after Cynthia became ill,"

Edith Mossman continued at last. "With Cynthia confined to her sickbed in the room next door, he woke Carol up and forced himself on her. He told her that since Cynthia could no longer perform her wifely duties, they were now Carol's responsibility. He said that her mother needed Carol to take her place. He claimed that was what Cynthia **wanted!**"

Edith paused again while her eyes brimmed with tears. "So, of course Carol complied. What choice did she have?"

In her years as sheriff, Joanna Brady had encountered more than her share of ugly situations. A year earlier she had struggled to come to terms with the murder of a pregnant and unwed teenager. Dora Matthews had been a sexually precocious classmate of Jenny's, and it had been tough on Joanna to realize that children Jenny's age were already sexually active. But the tale Edith Mossman had just related was far more appalling.

When Joanna tried to speak, the question she was asking stalled in her throat. "How old was Carol at the time?" she managed finally.

"She'd just turned ten," Edith answered.

Months earlier, when thirteen-year-old Jennifer Ann Brady had crossed the critical line of demarcation that separates girlhood from womanhood, Joanna had responded to the situation by taking her daughter out to dinner alone so they could have a private woman-to-woman discussion of the intricacies of human sexuality. To Joanna's dismay, Jenny had wasted no time in derailing her mother's best intentions.

"Come on, Mom," Jenny had told her with a dismissive shrug. "I already know all that stuff. They teach us about it at school."

Being told about the birds and the bees by your mother or by a respected teacher at school was one thing. To be routinely raped by your own father from age ten on was something else.

"How long did the incest continue?" Joanna asked.

"Until Carol was fourteen," Edith answered. "As soon as she had her first period, she got pregnant. When it came time to deliver, she was too small and the baby was too big. The doctor did a cesarean, but it was too late to save the baby. He died. Later on the doctor told Carol that her female organs had been damaged and that she'd never be able to have children."

Joanna thought about what George Winfield had told her about his autopsy findings. "They'd been damaged all right," Joanna put in. "Dr. Winfield, the medical examiner, told me that he thought a complete hysterectomy was performed on Carol right along with the cesarean."

"A hysterectomy?" Edith Mossman gasped. "Carol never mentioned that."

"Maybe she didn't know," Joanna suggested.

"They did that to her at age fourteen? That's criminal."

"Yes," Joanna said quietly. "I couldn't agree more, but go on. What happened then?"

"Carol said Eddie left her alone after that. She always thought it was because the scar made her too ugly—because the other girls were prettier than she was. I think it's because my son is a pervert, Sheriff Brady. Fifteen was too old for him. He went right on down the line—from Carol to Andrea, and from Andrea to Stella."

"And Kelly?"

"I suppose he abused her, too. I don't know for sure because I've never talked to her about it."

"And she's still there," Joanna said. "In Mexico."

Edith nodded. "I believe Eddie married her off to one of his middle-aged Brethren buddies. She couldn't have been more than twelve or thirteen at the time."

"I know you told me the other day, but I don't remember. How old was Carol when she finally ran away?"

"Twenty."

"Do you have any idea why?"

"You mean, after ten years of living in hell, what finally provoked her to leave?"

Joanna nodded. "Something like that."

"She heard her father making arrangements to

marry her off. To someone up in northern Arizona."

"In one of the bigamist communities on the Arizona Strip?"

It was Edith Mossman's turn to nod. "Somewhere up there," she agreed. "I don't know exactly, but that's the thing. People like my son treat their wives and children—especially their daughters—like chattel. They make all the decisions and no one else is allowed any input. They marry them off to men twice and three times their age, and the girls have no say whatsoever."

"You said wives?" Joanna interjected. "As in plural?"

Again, Edith nodded.

"And your son has more than one?"

"He had three the last I heard, but that was a long time ago. He could have more by now. The last one I knew about was thirty years younger than he is."

"The same age as Kelly?" Joanna asked.

"Younger," Edith answered. "And that's what he was going to do to Carol—marry her off to an old buzzard in his sixties who already had four or five wives and a whole raft of children. Eddie told the guy Carol was good at looking after other people's kids. Somehow Carol overheard the conversation. She must have been eavesdropping. That's when she wrote and asked for my help. Not just for herself, but for her sisters, too. She was afraid her father would send her away and the three younger girls would be left completely unprotected—as much as she could protect them, that is."

"So you made arrangements for the girls to come live with you."

"That's right. I managed to wire money to her. She bought train tickets and away they came with nothing but the clothes they were wearing."

"But Kelly wouldn't leave," Joanna added.

Edith nodded. "Kelly was the baby and she truly was spoiled. She refused to come along, and it broke Carol's heart. I don't believe she ever forgave herself for going off and leaving Kelly there alone."

Daisy delivered their plates of food. "Sorry it took so long," she said. "The kitchen was a little backed up."

In fact, Joanna and Edith had been so deep in conversation that they hadn't noticed the passage of time. And, considering the subject under discussion, the arriving food no longer seemed nearly as appetizing as it had appeared on the menu.

"Tell me about those other two dead women," Edith said at last "You say they were going to interview Carol and put it on television?"

"That's what we believe," Joanna returned.

"One of my investigators is checking on that right now."

"And they were going to pay her for doing this interview, whatever it was?"

Joanna nodded. "That's right. They had brought along a check for five thousand dollars."

"Carol must have known that payday was coming," Edith mused. "That's why she no longer needed my help."

Joanna nodded again. "But I don't think the interview ever took place, or, if it did, the money never changed hands. Pamela Davis and Carmen Ortega left California with a company check payable to Carol Mossman in their possession, but no such check has been found—not at your granddaughter's mobile home and not at the crime scene in New Mexico, either."

"But who were they?" Edith asked. "What did they want with Carol?"

"Before they came here, they had been in northern Arizona looking into The Brethren," Joanna said.

"Oh," Edith Mossman said.

"Diego Ortega, Carmen's brother, said something about a group called God's Angels. Have you ever heard of them?"

"Oh, yes," Edith said. "Of course, I know about them. They're wonderful."

"What do they do?"

"They're a support group, sort of like the old Underground Railroad. When women run away from those situations . . ."

"From their bigamist husbands," Joanna supplied.

". . . they leave with nothing. They have no money, no job skills, nowhere to go. They've left everything familiar behind—their families, their homes, and often their own children."

"Their religion?" Joanna asked.

"That, too," Edith agreed. "And they need a lot of help as they start over. For one thing, they've led terribly sheltered and mostly isolated lives, so they don't know much about the outside world. That's where God's Angels come in. They have programs for fleeing wives and for fleeing children, too. I believe that's the one Andrea is most involved with—the one for children."

"Your granddaughter is part of this group?"

"Andrea has always been the smart one in the family. She has a full-time job and goes to school part-time. But on the side, she volunteers as a God's Angels sponsor. That means she counsels individual women and whatever children they may have brought with them when they ran away. She tries to help the women gain a toehold on life away from their former lifestyle. Otherwise they're in danger of going back."

"They're like refugees," Joanna observed.

"Pretty much," Edith agreed.

There was a short pause in the conversation during which both women concentrated on their food. Joanna moved her sandwich around on the plate rather than eating much of it.

"If Andrea is part of that group," Joanna began, "what about Stella?"

"Oh, no. Not Stella. She found herself a husband—a very nice husband, by the way. She's always been the strong one. She's not big on support groups, either. Once she made up her mind to, she put all that other business behind her. I think Andrea tried to get her to help out with some of the God's Angels programs, but Stella wasn't interested. She said she was over it, and she wanted to stay that way."

Joanna decided to switch subjects. "What did your son do for Phelps Dodge when he worked there?" she asked.

"Drove a truck," Edith answered at once. "Those big dump trucks they used to haul waste from the pit out to the tailings dump."

"He never worked in the General Office?"

"Oh, no. Are you kidding? Eddie Mossman never had an office job in his life. He didn't have the education for a desk job, to say nothing of the mind-set."

"What about your daughter-in-law?"

"Cynthia? The poor girl was a mousy little

thing who never worked outside the home. If she had—if she'd had a job and money of her own— maybe she could have left Eddie just like some of those other women are doing, but back then, there wouldn't have been anyone like God's Angels to help her. As far as Cynthia was concerned, Eddie was the head of the family, and his word was law. She did as she was told. If I'd had any idea about what was really going on, I would have tried to do something, but I didn't know. Not at the time. Not until it was too late to do any good. But why are you asking about Eddie's job? What does his job with PD have to do with any of this?"

Joanna wasn't prepared to reveal details about the unusual weapon information that had telegraphed the connection between Carol Mossman's death and the murders in New Mexico.

"Just wondering," she said. A moment later she added, "When did you first hear that your son was in town?"

"Yesterday," Edith said. "Yesterday afternoon. He phoned and ordered me to call the mortuary and tell them that Carol's body should be released to him rather than to me. I told him to go fly a kite, that I'd already made the arrangements. He said I couldn't do that, that she was his daughter and he'd have the final say. I told him to go ahead and try."

"Did he happen to mention how he found out about Carol's murder?"

"No."

"Or when he came to town?"

"No. He didn't tell me that, either. You have to understand, Sheriff Brady, it wasn't a pleasant phone call. He was yelling at me the whole time, and I was yelling right back."

It was time for Joanna to ask the critical question straight out. "Mrs. Mossman," Joanna said, "do you think it's possible that your son murdered his own daughter?"

"You mean, do I think Eddie killed Carol?" Edith shook her head. "No, I doubt that's possible, but I almost wish he had. At least that way, I'd have the satisfaction of seeing him shipped off to prison for the rest of his life, the way he deserves. You see, Sheriff Brady, I wrestled with that same question myself all last night. If Eddie was the one who murdered Carol, why on earth would he come back here to try and claim her body? Why not just go straight back to Mexico and stay there? Nobody's going to bother going all the way down to Obregón to bring him back. Eddie's stupid, but surely he's not **that** stupid. Besides, what would be his motive to kill her?"

"Maybe he didn't want Carol to go public with her story," Joanna suggested.

"Why would he object to that?" Edith asked.

"Eddie's proud of the way he lives. He doesn't think he has anything to be ashamed of. As far as he's concerned, he's right and everybody else is wrong. And since the people he hangs around with all hold the same beliefs, why would he care?"

"Maybe some of them care," Joanna said. "There are other Brethren, aren't there? Maybe some of the ones who live in this country aren't interested in being quite so blatant about it. Maybe one of them wanted to keep the interview from taking place."

"I suppose that's possible," Edith said, pushing her plate away.

"Wasn't the enchilada any good?" Daisy asked when she came to pick up their dirty dishes. "I'd be glad to get you something else."

Edith shook her head. "The food was fine," she said. "For some reason, I seem to have lost my appetite."

Daisy looked at Joanna's plate. "You, too?" she asked.

"Me, too," Joanna said.

She paid for their virtually uneaten lunches and was helping Edith Mossman into the Civvie when her cell phone rang. Joanna answered the call while stowing Edith's walker in the backseat. "Just a minute, Jaime," she told Detective Carbajal. "Let me start the engine. As hot as it is, I can't leave Edith Mossman sitting there with no air-conditioning."

"Okay, boss," Jaime said when she returned to the phone. "Here's the deal. We've turned Mr. Mossman over to Deputy Howell. She'll keep an eye on him. He wasn't thrilled about having a bodyguard hanging around, but when we told him his life had been threatened, he warmed up to the idea. Just exactly how serious is this threat?"

Joanna glanced at Edith Mossman sitting quietly in the front seat of the idling Civvie. She probably wasn't particularly dangerous at that point.

"Let's just say I consider it serious," she said. "And credible. Tell Debbie not to let him out of her sight."

"Good enough."

"Did you learn anything useful?" Joanna asked.

"Other than Eddie Mossman's a total creep? He came up from Mexico because his daughter's about to become engaged to some guy from up near Kingman."

"But I thought Kelly Mossman was already married," Joanna objected.

"Kelly?" Jaime said. "I don't know anything about Kelly. I'm sure Mossman said his daughter's name was Cecilia."

Joanna's stomach tightened. Knowing that Eddie Mossman had yet another at-risk daughter made what little roast beef Joanna had managed to swallow threaten to stage a rebellion.

"Did you find out how he learned about Carol's death?" she asked.

"Sure did. He said that another daughter, Stella, called to let him know."

"Called how?"

"On his cell phone," Jaime answered.

"Did you get the number?"

"Yes, ma'am."

"Good. Tell Frank I want incoming and outgoing call records for that phone."

"But the phone is from Mexico."

"That's all right. All that means is that Frank Montoya will have to work a little harder than he usually does to retrieve the information. He may have to pay a little **mordida** to get it. What are you doing next?"

"Heading into the office to get organized and to see what Frank may have for us."

"Good enough. Tell him I'm taking Mrs. Mossman back to Sierra Vista. We'll have to have our morning briefing when I get back."

Joanna stowed her phone and clambered into the driver's seat, grateful to be out of the heat and the rising humidity.

"Anything important?" Edith asked.

"No," Joanna said. "Just touching base with some of my people."

They drove through town in relative silence. It was only when they emerged from the other side of Mule Mountain Tunnel that Joanna resumed her questioning. "You've told me about Carol," she said. "And a little about Andrea, but you've barely mentioned Stella."

"I don't like her much," Edith said abruptly. "Of all the girls, she's the one who's most like her father. I was surprised that she offered to come get me the other day and bring me to town when your detectives needed to talk to me. She doesn't usually come across all sweetness and light."

"Considering her history, I'd be surprised if she did," Joanna said.

"Yes," Edith agreed. "That's why, with Stella—with all the girls, really—I've always been willing to let things slide."

"So what's her story?" Joanna asked.

"She came along with Carol, but once she got here, she wouldn't do a thing I told her. She was just as wild as she could be, but she grew out of it. She married herself a nice young man, and she seems to be doing all right now."

"I met her son," Joanna said.

Edith shot Joanna a questioning glance.

"He's nice, too," Joanna said.

"Yes." Edith Mossman sighed. "I suppose he is."

"And who's Cecilia?" Joanna asked.

"Cecilia who?" Edith asked.

Right that moment, Joanna wasn't prepared to tell Edith Mossman that she had yet another granddaughter, a possible half sister of Carol, Stella, Andrea, and Kelly, who was now also in jeopardy.

"Never mind," Joanna said at last. "I'm probably mistaken."

After that, Edith Mossman settled back in her seat. Seconds later she was snoring softly. In the relative silence that followed, Joanna thought about Carol Mossman and her three victimized sisters. It was one thing for a ten-year-old child to take over the household responsibilities—the care and feeding—of three younger siblings, but for Carol to be unable to protect any of them, herself included, from their own father . . . That was, as Edith Mossman had said, unthinkable! No wonder that, as an adult, Carol had turned to animals for comfort and companionship. Compared to what the human race had dished out to her, dogs must have seemed amazingly uncomplicated.

Joanna's phone crowed. She reached for it quickly, afraid the sound might disturb Edith, but the snores continued unabated.

"Yes," Joanna said quietly.

"Where are you right now?" Frank Montoya asked.

"On my way to Sierra Vista to take Edith Mossman back to her place. Why?"

"And that's at the Ferndale Retirement Center?"

"That's right."

"You've hit the jackpot then," he said. "So far, nobody at PD up in Phoenix has been able to come up with a list of General Office employees, but according to the guy I talked to, we've got something just as good. Does the name Bob Mahilich ring a bell?"

"Sure," Joanna said. "He's the Bisbee boy who made good and went on to become some bigwig for Phelps Dodge up in Phoenix."

"That's right," Frank Montoya agreed. "Went to college on a full-ride PD scholarship and went to work for them as soon as he graduated from the Colorado School of Mines. Now he's their VP for Operations."

"What about him?" Joanna asked.

"When the person I was talking to found out what I wanted, she referred me to Bob, since she knew he was from Bisbee originally. I figured it was going to be another dead end, but I called him anyway and got lucky. His grandmother, Irma Mahilich, worked in the General Office here in Bisbee from the time she graduated from high school until she retired in 1975. According to Bob, Irma's memory isn't so sharp when it comes to telling you what she had for breakfast, but as far as what she did during her working years, she's an encyclopedia."

"He thinks she'd remember who worked in the General Office way back then?"

"Right, since she hired most of them. And you'll never guess where she lives."

"Where?"

"At the Ferndale Retirement Center. For all I know, she may live right next door to Edith Mossman."

"You want me to talk to her?" Joanna asked.

"Either that or I can send Jaime and Ernie."

"No. They have enough to do. When it comes to dealing with LOLs, I'm every bit as good as they are."

"That's what I thought," Frank agreed.

Joanna glanced at Edith Mossman, who hadn't stirred. "Any other news?"

"Yes. Ernie's been in touch with Fandango Productions. They're checking with their attorney to see whether or not they can give us access to the two victims' company e-mail files. Otherwise, we'll have to go through the pain of sending someone over there and serving them with a warrant."

"Let me know what happens on that score."

Joanna's phone buzzed in her ear. "I've got another call, Frank. I have to go."

"Joey?" Butch Dixon asked. "Where are you?"

"On my way to Sierra Vista. I'm just crossing the San Pedro. What's up?"

"You'll never guess who just called."

Joanna was too tired to want to play games. "Who?" she asked.

"Drew," Butch replied excitedly.

Drew Mabrey was the literary agent who, for the last year, had been trying to sell Butch's first manuscript, **Serve and Protect**. In the intervening months, Butch had worked on the second book in the series, and he had also done a good deal of physical labor on their new house. But as time had passed with no word of acceptance on the manuscript, Butch had become more and more discouraged.

"And?"

"Remember that editor, the one who had expressed interest in the book and then ended up turning it down? Something to do with Marketing not liking it?"

"Yes. Didn't she move to another publishing house or something?" Joanna asked.

"That's right," Butch said. "And this morning she called Drew to see if **Serve and Protect** is still available. Drew is pretty sure she's going to make an offer after all."

"Butch, that's wonderful!" Joanna exclaimed. "When will you know?"

"Probably sometime later this week."

Edith stirred. "What's wonderful?" she asked.

"I have to go, Butch," Joanna said. "Congratulations. We'll talk more later. That was my husband calling," Joanna explained to Edith, once she was off the phone "He just had some very good news. He's written a book, and someone may be interested in buying it."

"I'm glad," Edith said. "It's nice to hear that someone has good news."

Looking at Edith Mossman's weary, grief-ravaged face, Joanna was immediately awash in guilt and resolve as well. Carol Mossman had been murdered, taking with her huge chunks of her grandmother's heart.

We'll find out who did it, Joanna vowed silently. **I promise you that**.

FIFTEEN

Twenty minutes later, having escorted Edith Mossman to her Ferndale Retirement Center apartment, Joanna presented herself at the reception desk in the lobby. "Can you tell me the room number for Irma Mahilich?" she asked.

"One forty-one," the receptionist answered without looking up. "But Irma's not in her room. She's over there, working a jigsaw puzzle."

Joanna glanced around the lobby. The attractively furnished and brightly carpeted room resembled an upscale hotel lobby rather than what Joanna would have expected in an assisted-living facility. Several seating areas were ranged around the reception desk. A large-screen television blared unwatched in one of them. Two women, both in wheelchairs, sat reading newspapers in another. In a third—one lined with book-laden shelves—a solitary woman sat hunched over the bare outline of a round jigsaw puzzle so large that, once completed, it would cover much of the massive table. It wasn't until Joanna approached the table that she realized the woman was studying the pieces with absolute intensity and with the aid of a handheld magnifying glass.

"Mrs. Mahilich?" Joanna asked.

Irma Mahilich's shoulders were stooped. Thinning white hair stood on end in a flyaway drift. She wore dentures, but the lower plate was missing. The bottom left-hand portion of her mouth turned down, betraying the lingering effects of a stroke.

"Yes," Irma said, lowering the magnifying glass. "Who are you?"

"I'm Sheriff Brady, Sheriff Joanna Brady."

"That's right. I remember now. Aren't you D. H. Lathrop's little girl?" Irma asked, peering up at her visitor.

Surprised, Joanna answered, "Yes. He was my father."

"I'm the one who hired him to work for the company, you know, back when I was running the PD employment office. When he showed up there, your father had never done a lick of work in a mine. Everybody else said he wouldn't last, but I had a good feeling about him. And he stuck in there—right up until he decided to go into law enforcement. When he ran for office, I was proud to vote for him. Did that every time he ran.

D. H. Lathrop was a nice young man. It's a shame he got killed the way he did. Now, what do you want?"

Joanna was taken aback, both by Irma Mahilich's abrupt manner as well as by her unexpectedly detailed memories of D. H. Lathrop.

"I suppose you're here to ask me more questions," Irma continued. "They send that social worker around from time to time to bother me. She's so young she looks like she should still be in high school. She asks me things like who's the president of the United States and other such nonsense. I don't know who the president is because I don't care anymore. Those politicians are all just alike anyway. But it's like she's trying to find out how much I know about what's going on around me. If I knew everything, then I wouldn't need to be in a place like this, now would I?"

"No," Joanna agreed. "I don't suppose you would."

"So what do you want?" Irma demanded again. "For Pete's sake, spit it out, girl. And while you're at it, have a seat. I don't like it when people hover over me."

Joanna sat in a chair on the opposite side of the table with a clear view of the lid to the two-thousand-piece puzzle that featured a stained-glass window in brilliant primary colors—jewel-tone blues, greens, reds, and yellows. Just looking at the tiny, intricate pieces was enough to give Joanna a headache. The round-edged border was all in place but not much else.

"We're working on a case," Joanna said quietly. "A homicide case. I'd like to ask you some questions."

"What homicide?" Irma asked. "Somebody here?"

"No."

"Good. That's a relief then. So who died?"

"Three women, actually. A woman was murdered over by the San Pedro last week. Two additional victims were found in New Mexico the next day."

With her hand trembling, Irma picked up a piece of the puzzle and put it unerringly in the proper spot, sighing with satisfaction as it slipped neatly into place.

"That lets me out then," she said as she resumed studying the other loose pieces. "I've been shut up in here for years, so I can't possibly be a suspect."

"No," Joanna agreed, "you're not a suspect, but we thought you might be able to help us find the killer. Your grandson thought the same thing."

"Which one?" she asked.

"Bob."

"You mean Bob Junior," Irma said, nodding. "That boy's always giving me far more credit than I'm due." With that, Irma put down her magnifying glass and stared at Joanna. "Now tell me, how could I be of help?" she asked.

"All three women were murdered with the same weapon," Joanna answered. "They were shot with ammunition that dated from 1917. We have reason to believe that the ammunition, and maybe even the weapon, may have come from a cache of weapons that was once stored in the safe in the General Office."

"Oh, those," Irma breathed. "The ones from the Deportation. I remember telling Mr. Frayn, my boss, at the time they opened that safe—I remember saying, 'We need to get rid of those things, Mr. Frayn. Burn them if need be. They were bad news when they were used in 1917, and they're bad news now.' But Mr. Frayn—Otto Frayn, his name was—wouldn't hear of it. 'We'll just hand them out to whoever wants them,' he said, and that's what he did. Passed them along to the people who worked there."

"Which is why I'm here talking to you, Mrs. Mahilich," Joanna said. "We need to know who all was working there with you at the time."

"You should contact the company for that," Irma said, picking the magnifying glass back up and resuming her careful examination of the puzzle pieces.

"We already tried that," Joanna explained. "At the moment they're unable to locate any official records that date from as long ago as 1975, but your grandson suggested we talk to you. He said you'd probably remember who worked there. Maybe you can't remember all of them, but if you could put us in touch with one or two, perhaps those people can lead us to others."

"I don't suppose this can wait until after I finish the puzzle, can it?" Irma asked.

"No," Joanna said, glancing at the empty expanse of open puzzle. "I'm afraid we need what information you can offer a little sooner than that."

"Oh, all right," Irma said impatiently. "You might want to go over to the desk and get me some pieces of paper and a pencil. Meet me at that table over there." She pointed to a table in the still empty TV alcove. "That way we won't disturb any of the puzzle pieces."

While Joanna hustled off to the receptionist's desk, Irma produced a folded walker from under her chair. She was just tottering up to the second table when Joanna returned. Joanna reached to help Irma onto a chair, but Irma pushed her hand away.

"Leave me alone and turn off that TV set," she snapped. "With all that noise, I can barely hear myself think."

Chastened, Joanna located the remote and

turned off the television. Then she took a seat at the table and pushed paper and pencil in front of Irma. When she was seated, Irma once again stowed her walker, picked up the pencil and began to draw, frowning and biting her lower lip in total concentration. Joanna watched while Irma drew a series of shaky rectangles on the first sheet of paper. Then she began to label each of them.

"This is the way the desks were arranged when you first came into the building," she explained. "It's easier for me to remember where people were located than it is for me to remember their names. Nona Cooper sat here, for instance," Irma said, pointing at one of the first rectangles she had drawn. "And the door was right next to her, so you had to come in past her desk. She always had a picture of her little boy on her desk. I believe his name was Randolph, but she called him Randy, and he was cute as a button. He died, though. Got drafted into the army right out of high school and died in Vietnam in 1967. Poor Nona. She never got over it. She died in '76, just a year or so after she got laid off. Committed suicide. Can't say I blame her."

Joanna had her notebook out by then. Sorry she hadn't brought spare tapes and grateful to be proficient in shorthand, she made swift notes of everything Irma said.

"Would Nona Cooper have been given one of the weapons from the safe?" Joanna asked.

Irma shook her head. "Certainly not," she huffed. "Randy was killed by sniper fire. Nona wouldn't have had a gun in her house on a bet."

Joanna and Irma worked that way for the better part of an hour, with Irma drawing and labeling individual desks in the various rooms, all the while delivering thumbnail sketches of each desk's respective occupant. Irma had begun drawing the fourth and final room when Joanna's cell phone rang.

"What an annoying sound," Irma grumbled upon hearing the distinctive rooster crow. "You should get yourself a phone with a nicer ring than that."

Answering quickly, Joanna got up and moved out of earshot. "What's up?" she asked her chief deputy.

"Fandango's lawyer told them to go the search warrant route. Jaime's on his way to pick up a warrant right now, then he'll head for the airport in Tucson. He should be able to catch a flight out to L.A. this evening, but he'll have to stay over until tomorrow morning to execute the warrant."

"This sounds expensive," Joanna said. "Isn't there any other way to do it?"

"Not really," Frank said. "For one thing, Carmen Ortega had downloaded some of what she had filmed into an attachment and e-mailed it to Fandango. We don't have the equipment it would

take to download it. For another, Fandango has a
networked computer system for keeping track of
calendars and expenses. Again, you have to use
their equipment to access it. Not only that, if
any of the threats are there, we want them to be
admissible in court."

"Okay, okay," Joanna agreed. "I get it."

"Dr. Lawrence, the ME from Hidalgo County,
is faxing over his preliminary report, but Ernie's
been on the phone with him. Detective Carpenter is right here in my office. Do you want to talk
to him?"

"Sure," Joanna said. "Put him on." She waited
while Frank handed the phone over to Ernie. "So
what does Dr. Lawrence have to say for himself?" she asked.

"It's all pretty interesting," Ernie answered.
"Insect larval evidence would indicate that the
two New Mexico victims died a week ago tomorrow."

Joanna didn't like to think about how succeed-
ing generations of teeming maggots could be
used to estimate the shelf life of corpses that had
been left outside to rot in the elements, but she
appreciated the fact that the process worked with
uncanny accuracy.

"A week ago?" she asked. "On Tuesday, you
mean?"

"That's right," Ernie replied. "The same day
as Carol Mossman's murder. What's even more

interesting is this: Both victims were evidently fully clothed when they were shot. The doc found microscopic fabric fibers in the entrance wounds on both victims."

"You're saying they were stripped of their clothing after they were killed?" Joanna asked.

"Yes, ma'am, and, considering the extent of the entrance and exit wounds, whoever did that job must have had an iron-clad stomach," Ernie told her. "First they were moved—carried, most likely, rather than dragged—from where they were killed to where they were found. Then they were stripped and finally tied up."

"How weird," Joanna said.

"You've got that right," Ernie agreed. "But Doc Lawrence says that the rope-burn chafing on both victims' ankles and wrists is definitely indicative of postmortem injury rather than pre."

"And if they were carried as opposed to dragged . . ." Joanna began.

"Then the killer is one strong dude who wants us to think we're dealing with a sexual predator when we're really not."

Joanna thought about this last piece of information. "So we're not out of line in thinking they were murdered because they were interfering where they weren't wanted."

"Which takes us right back to The Brethren," Ernie agreed.

"I want you to get on the horn to the Mojave

County Sheriff's Department," Joanna said after a moment's consideration. "Talk directly to Sheriff Blake if you can. Let him know what we're up against, and see if he'll have his people send us everything they have on The Brethren."

"I doubt they'll have much," Ernie said.

"Maybe you're right, but we want whatever they **do** have," Joanna told him.

When she finished with the phone call, she turned back to the table where she had left Irma Mahilich, only to find it empty. Irma had returned to the puzzle table and her magnifying glass, having left behind a set of four completed office drawings. The last one contained seven or eight desks, but without Irma's commentary, the names meant little.

Joanna approached the puzzle table, carrying the drawings. "Oh, there you are," Irma Mahilich said. "I'm glad you're finally off the phone."

"Could you tell me a little about the people on the last drawing?" Joanna asked.

"No," Irma said. "I can't, not today, anyway. Thinking about all those people's names and what they did has worn me out completely. I need to go take a nap, but I didn't want to leave without telling you good-bye. Now if you'll be good enough to tell the receptionist that I'm ready to go back to my room, she'll call for one of the aides to come get me."

"I can help you," Joanna said. "I don't mind."

"It's not that," Irma said. "I'm a little slow and I can walk just fine, but I can't always remember what room I'm in. My neighbors get cranky when I go up and down the halls trying my key in all the doors until I find my own place. Short-term memory loss, they call it. Drives me batty sometimes."

Joanna looked down at the sheets of paper in her hand and at all the desk-placement arrangements and at the co-workers' names Irma Mahilich had summoned from that long-ago time. The old woman had been able to recall all kinds of pertinent details concerning her work life and her office mates from thirty and forty years ago, but in the present she was unable to remember the number of her own room.

"It's room one forty-one," Joanna said. "And I don't mind taking you there."

"Oh, no," Irma said. "You go on about your business. I'm fine."

Joanna nodded, and let Irma do it her way. "Thank you so much for all your help," Joanna said. "But is there a time when I could come back and talk to you again?"

"Anytime," Irma said. "I'm always here. You'll probably have to remind me of what this is all about, because I won't remember from one day to the next. And bring those pieces of paper along with you. It helps me to have something to look at, something physical. As Hercule Poirot might say, that helps get the little gray cells up and working."

Joanna went to the receptionist's desk and then waited while a young Hispanic aide in a flowered smock stopped by the puzzle table to accompany Irma Mahilich back to her apartment. Watching their slow progress across the lobby and down a long corridor, Joanna Brady had a sudden awful glimpse of her own future. She could only imagine the vital businesslike young woman Irma Mahilich had been when she held court inside the PD General Office years ago, first as a clerk in the employment office and finally as private secretary to Otto Frayn, the local branch's general manager.

Was Joanna doomed to have something similar happen to her? Would she one day come to a point when she'd be able to recall details of long-ago murder investigations from her days as sheriff and the names of all the investigators who had worked them while not being able to find her own way home? She hated to think about what a long, slow, debilitating decline like that would mean not only for her and for Butch, but also for her children—for Jenny and for the unborn child she carried in her womb.

And as she made her way to the Civvie she had left parked outside, for the first time it occurred to her that, tragic as her father's sudden death may have been, perhaps D. H. Lathrop had been lucky to go the way he did. Seeing Irma Mahilich made Joanna think that there were far worse alternatives.

It was a subdued and thoughtful Sheriff Brady who drove into the Justice Center parking lot forty minutes later. She stepped into the lobby outside her office long enough to let Kristin know she had arrived, then she returned to her desk and started sifting through stacks of loosely organized papers.

She had barely made a dent in the first pile when there was a tap on the door. She looked up to see the hulking figure of Detective Ernie Carpenter filling her doorway. The grim set of his mouth told her something was wrong.

"What is it?" she asked.

"Just had a call from University Medical Center," he said, shaking his head. "Maria Elena Maldonado didn't make it."

"The little boy's mother?"

Ernie nodded. "She died a little over an hour ago. They just now got around to letting us know."

"Where's Jaime?" Joanna asked.

"On his way to Tucson to catch his plane," Ernie replied. "Why?"

Without answering, Joanna picked up her

phone and dialed Frank Montoya's extension. "Meet Ernie and me over at the jail interview room ASAP," Joanna told her chief deputy after passing along Ernie's news. "The three of us are going to have a little chat with our friendly neighborhood SUV driver. You might want to bring along your tape recorder and a fresh tape."

"Wait a minute," Ernie said as he followed Joanna down the corridor. "If we're going to ask him questions, shouldn't we call his attorney?"

"Who said anything about questions?" Joanna returned. "We're going to give that son of a bitch a message. He's still jailed as John Doe, isn't he?"

Ernie gave her a somber, questioning look before nodding. "That's right, boss. We ran his prints through AFIS and came up empty."

Once at the jail, Joanna detoured long enough to stop by the booking desk before she met up with Frank and Ernie inside the jail's stark interview room. Joanna took Frank's proffered recorder and handed it over to Detective Carpenter.

"I'll talk," Joanna said. "Frank will translate. Ernie, you listen."

They were standing, ranged silently around the perimeter of the interview room, when the shackled prisoner, walking with the aid of crutches and with his left foot in a cast, was led inside a few minutes later. The tape recorder, already running, sat on a table in front of Ernie Carpenter.

"Are you interested in having your attorney here?" Joanna asked as soon as the man was seated.

Frank translated the question, and the man shook his head. "I just want to go home," he said in Spanish. "Back to Mexico."

Joanna walked over to the table, stopping only when her face was no more than a foot away from the prisoner's. "Do you know another of your passengers has died?" Joanna asked as her emerald eyes, blazing with fury, bored into his. "The mother of the little boy you murdered," she continued. "Now she is dead as well."

"Not murder," the man objected, again with Frank translating. "An accident. It was only an accident."

"The deaths occurred in the course of your committing a crime," Joanna returned. "Smuggling illegal aliens into this country is a crime—a felony. I'm sure your attorney explained to you that when death occurs in the course of committing a felony, that results in an automatic charge of murder."

"No," the man said. "It was not my fault. The car was old—"

"Do you believe in heaven and hell?" Joanna asked, interrupting Frank's translation.

Frank paused before passing along her question, as though he couldn't quite believe that was what she meant for him to say.

"Go on," Joanna urged impatiently. "Ask him."

With a reluctant shake of his head, Frank did as he'd been told. Once he heard the question, the prisoner shot Joanna a quizzical look and then shrugged his shoulders dismissively as though the question didn't merit an answer.

"You're here as John Doe," Joanna continued. "You may think that because we don't know your real name, you can't be charged with a crime. And the truth of the matter is, because of jurisdictional considerations, we may not be able to hold you here much longer. Federal law may take precedence and you may very well end up being deported."

The prisoner smiled knowingly and began to nod as Frank neared the end of that translation. That was how the system usually worked. It was what the driver had expected to happen.

"You still haven't answered my question," Joanna said. "The one about heaven and hell. Do you believe or not, yes or no?"

"No," he said.

"But that's a lie, isn't it?" Joanna said, pulling a slip of paper out of her pocket. "I stopped by the property room," she said. "This is an inventory of your personal possessions, the ones that were taken away from you when you were booked into my jail. The second item here is listed as a crucifix. People who don't believe in God or in heaven or hell don't usually wear crucifixes."

The prisoner stared at the silently whirring pins in the tape recorder and said nothing.

"So even though I don't know your real name, God does," Joanna continued. "You can call what happened an accident if you want, but God knows better. He knows that the blood of all those people—including the blood of that little boy, Eduardo, and his mother, Maria Elena—is on your head and your hands."

Joanna paused after that and waited for a response that didn't materialize. "It may be true that you don't believe in God or in heaven or hell, but you might want to reconsider," she added several long moments later. "Because when you are deported, I'm going to let it be known among some of our friends in the **federales** that the reason we let you go is that you told us everything we needed to know about the people behind this coyote syndicate. We'll say you told us who they are and that we're just waiting for one of them to cross the border so we can arrest them and put them on trial."

The prisoner shifted in his seat. For the first time in several minutes, his eyes met Joanna's. "No," he objected. "You must not do this. It is a lie. I've said nothing to you about them. Nothing."

"We know that, you know that, and even God knows that," Joanna agreed with a slight smile. "Unfortunately, the people you work for will not know that. Call Border Patrol," Joanna added briskly to Frank. "Tell them to come get Mr. Doe and take him back to Mexico. It's too much trouble to keep him in my jail any longer."

The prisoner, who up to now had required a translator, suddenly burst into perfect English. "No, señora," he begged. "Please. You don't understand. If they think I have told you anything, they will kill me."

Joanna shrugged. "Too bad," she said. "That's your problem and God's, Mr. Doe, not mine."

"But what if I do tell you what you want to know?" he asked. "Then will you let me stay?"

"I can't say because it's not up to me," Joanna replied. "I suggest you call your lawyer and talk to him. Have him see what kind of deal he can negotiate. Your attorney may be able to help you. I can't."

Turning her back on the prisoner, Joanna walked as far as the door and knocked on it to summon the guard. "We're leaving now," she announced as the guard unlocked and opened the door. "If the prisoner wishes to speak to his attorney, let him use the phone."

"Wait," the prisoner called after her. "Señora, wait, please. My name is Ramón—Ramón Alvarez Sandoval. I will tell you whatever it is you want to know, but you must understand that the men I work for are evil. If they find out what I have done, they will kill me, and my family, too."

Joanna stared hard at the prisoner. She wanted to spit in his face and grind it into the ground. Here was a man whose wanton disregard for others had left a total of seven people dead. And yet he was, as she had told Jaime Carbajal earlier, very small potatoes. Drivers were entirely expendable—to both sides. What she really wanted was a list of the names of the people running the syndicate—the ones giving the orders and collecting their blood money while giving not the slightest consideration to the lives that might be lost in the process.

"You're right," Ramón added softly a moment later. "I do believe in God, and you do, too."

Slowly Joanna moved away from the door and returned to the table. Not taking her eyes off Ramón, she sat down across from him. "I am only a sheriff," she said quietly. "I'm not with INS or the FBI. I'm not a prosecutor. I can't make plea bargains, and I can promise nothing, but if you help us put the animals you work for out of business—if you will tell us what you know and agree to testify if they can be brought to trial—I will do what I can to help you. Do you understand?"

Ramón nodded. "Yes," he said.

Joanna looked at Frank Montoya. "Talk to the prosecutor's office," she said. "Check with Arlee Jones and see who all needs to be here to witness Mr. Sandoval's statement—in addition to Mr. Sandoval himself and his attorney, that is. Then set it up for tomorrow if at all possible."

"But, Sheriff Brady," Frank began. "There are all kinds of jurisdictional complications here."

"You're good at sorting out complications, Chief Deputy Montoya. You always have been. Does this meet with your approval, Mr. Sandoval?"

"Yes," Ramón said softly.

"Then you'd better talk with your attorney and clear it with him. If he advises you not to go through with this, or if you change your mind, you're to notify Mr. Montoya here at once. Do you understand?"

"You have given me your word, and I have given mine," Ramón Sandoval said. "I will not change my mind."

As Joanna left the jail to walk back to her office, she was not surprised to notice that the sky had darkened overhead. A stiff, cooling breeze took the edge off the July heat and kicked up puffs of dust devils that danced and jigged across the parking lot. Off in the distance, thunder rumbled. Joanna couldn't tell if the sudden lift in her spirits came from the possibility of breaking up a major illegal-alien-smuggling syndicate or from the desert dweller's hard-wired joy at the prospect of coming rain.

Fifteen minutes later Joanna was back at her desk when Ernie Carpenter once again appeared in her doorway. "How the hell did you pull that one off?" he demanded morosely. "Here we busted our butts to get all those UDA interviews, and you never even bothered to mention them."

"Didn't have to," Joanna said. "All I had to do was let him know God was on our side. Once Sandoval understood that, he knuckled right under."

"Whatever gave you the idea that God was on our side?" Ernie asked.

Sheriff Brady looked at her detective and grinned. "She told me so Herself," Joanna said.

"Right," Ernie Carpenter returned, shaking his head. "I walked right into that one, didn't I!" He was still shaking his head and muttering under his breath as he turned to walk away.

SIXTEEN

You're looking chipper," Frank Montoya said the next morning as he entered Joanna's office for the daily briefing, which would include the previous day's skipped briefing as well.

It helped that Joanna had gotten a decent night's sleep for a change. She had come home to find Butch and Jenny both excited about the prospect of a publisher's making him an offer on **Serve and Protect**. That good news, combined with a nice dinner and a rainstorm pounding down on the roof, had made for a restful night's sleep. And once again this morning's nausea hadn't been quite as rough as that on previous days.

"I'm feeling half-human for a change," Joanna replied with a smile. "Which reminds me, I have a doctor's appointment this afternoon at two for my first prenatal checkup. You'll be here, won't you?"

"Sure will," Frank said. "But I'll be busy. One o'clock is when the Sandoval meeting is scheduled to take place. That's the soonest I could gather everyone together."

"Where will you hold it?" Joanna asked.

"The conference room here," Frank answered. "There are too many people coming for them to all fit in the interview room at the jail."

"Have you talked to Sandoval's attorney?"

"Twice," Frank said. "Her name's Amy Templeton. I suggested she have Sandoval show up dressed the same way he would if he was going to court rather than in his jail jumpsuit. I also suggested that they ditch the translation pretense. Sandoval's English is fine, and dealing with a translator may wind up pissing off some of the people he needs to have in his corner. That's what I told her, but I probably didn't need to. She says her firm is already working on the details of a deal for Sandoval. She expects to have it pulled together in time for this afternoon's meeting."

"What firm?" Joanna asked.

"Gabriel Gomez, down in Douglas."

"The immigration attorney?" Joanna asked. "You mean Richard Osmond's girlfriend's daddy?"

Frank nodded.

"The one who's going to take us to court for Osmond's wrongful death?"

"One and the same," Frank replied. "But I think Gomez has changed his mind on that score. With an autopsy diagnosis of metastasized pancreatic cancer, it would be pretty hard to make a wrongful-death charge stick."

Joanna allowed herself a small sigh of relief. "When's Osmond's funeral?" she asked.

"Yesterday," Frank said.

"I suppose the department should have sent flowers."

"We did," Frank told her.

Joanna looked at her chief deputy in absolute gratitude. "I'm not sure how I'd ever get along without you, Frank."

"Good." Frank grinned. "It's nice to be indispensable. Let's keep it that way. Now how about getting down to business?"

Most of the items up for discussion were strictly routine, including the usual fender-benders and DUIs. The fierce storm that had marched through Cochise County the night before had caused numerous power outages. Running water on the road between Double Adobe and Elfrida had once again stranded several motorists who had required rescue for both themselves and their vehicles. A divorcing couple from Sun Sites had gotten into a domestic-violence beef over who would have custody of their Old English sheepdog, Casey. The husband

and wife were now both cooling their heels in the Cochise County Jail, while the dog had been taken into custody by Animal Control. In Bisbee Junction, a rancher's herd of cattle had gotten loose and had damaged gardens and fruit trees on three separate properties.

Only at the end of the session did Joanna pass along the information she had gleaned from her long discussion with Edith Mossman.

"Jeez!" Frank exclaimed when he heard about Eddie Mossman's long history of abusing his daughters. "And now there's another daughter involved?"

"That's right."

"I'd as soon shoot the bastard and put him out of his misery."

"I'd rather find a way to lock him up for good," Joanna replied. "And with any kind of luck, we will. Did Ernie come up with any information on The Brethren from Sheriff Drake?"

"Not so far," Frank said. "I'll let you know if and when he does."

Finally she handed over copies of Irma Mahilich's pencil drawings. "What are these?" Frank asked as he stared down at the rectangles with their spidery handwritten labels.

"They're road maps of the Phelps Dodge General Office in Bisbee circa 1975," Joanna told him. "Compliments of Irma Mahilich. She veri-

fied that the Deportation weapons were handed
out to whatever employees were interested in
taking them home. I've got shorthand information on all of the people listed, except for the
ones on this last page—the one that's marked
page four. I'll transcribe my notes, so whoever
goes looking for these folks to interview them
will have at least that much information at their
disposal."

"I recognize some of the names," Frank said,
examining the sheet. "Some of them still live
around here. Others"—he shrugged—"I've
never heard of."

Joanna nodded. "That's why I think we should
hand this job off to Ernie. As far as Bisbee's concerned, he's an old-timer, and these people will
talk to him. As soon as I finish with the notes, I'll
get them to him. And later on today, if I can, I'll
talk to Irma again and find out about the people
on page four. How are you doing on the phone
records?" she added. "I still want to know when
Eddie Mossman first heard about Carol's death."

"It's not easy getting phone records from Mexico," Frank replied. "But we know Mossman
said his daughter Stella is the one who told him.
So I've fallen back on my old pal at the phone
company, and I'm requesting information on
Stella Adams's phones as well."

Once Frank left her office, Joanna quickly

transcribed her notes, keying them into her computer. When she had printed copies in hand, she asked Kristin to deliver a set to Ernie Carpenter. Then she began wading her way through the paperwork jungle. She was deep into it when Jaime Carbajal called from California.

"We've hit pay dirt here," he said.

"How so?" Joanna asked. "Tell me."

"I got a look at the download of one of Carmen Ortega's film segments. It's dynamite. It shows a wedding ceremony between a horny old coot named Harold Lassiter and a twelve-year-old girl."

Joanna felt a clutch in her gut. "Cecilia Mossman?" she asked.

"You've got it," Jaime returned. "Mossman married his daughter off to a guy who has to be sixty if he's a day. Lassiter's other four wives were all there at the ceremony with him, waiting to welcome poor little Cecilia into the family while Eddie Mossman himself was proud to give the so-called bride away. It was enough to make me want to puke. Cecilia's there swimming in a wedding dress that must be five sizes too big for her. The poor kid looks like she's scared to death."

"Pam Davis and Carmen Ortega filmed the whole wedding?" Joanna demanded. "How the hell did they pull that one off?"

"I don't know how they did it, but they did. It's pretty damning stuff. If nothing else, we should be able to nail Mossman on transporting a minor across state lines for immoral purpose. It may be an international border, but it's still, by God, a state line. Is Deputy Howell still keeping an eye on Mossman?"

"As far as I know. I haven't pulled her off him, and I don't think Frank has, either."

"Well, good, let's keep him under observation long enough to arrest him."

"I still can't believe they got it on film," Joanna murmured.

"They must have had a contact inside the Lassiter family compound. They used a hidden, stationary camera," Jaime told her. "It's not great-quality film, but believe me, it's plenty good enough."

"And if someone found out about the filming later on, after the wedding, that would explain Eddie Mossman's death threat, because taking the film public would blow the cover off The Brethren's dirty little secrets. So is there any sign of that death threat in either Pam Davis's or Carmen Ortega's work e-mail accounts?"

"No. The Fandango Productions Web site has a link to their corporate generic e-mail account. They say that the receptionist checks that one and personally forwards mail to the proper department managers. That's where the threat showed up."

"So," Joanna said thoughtfully, "whoever sent them knew the victims' names and where they worked, but didn't take the time to figure out their personal e-mail addresses."

"Right," Jaime agreed. "It came through an ISP located in Mexico and from Ed Mossman's account, but that doesn't mean he was actually in Mexico when he sent it or even that it was sent by him personally." Jaime paused and then added after a moment, "Considering The Brethren's subsistence-style living conditions, it's amazing to think that they're even into computers and digital cameras."

Unlike her detective, Joanna found the technical end of things far less compelling than the people connections. "What I want to know is who put Davis and Ortega on the trail of all this?" Joanna asked. "Somebody must have clued them in about Cecilia's upcoming wedding and put them in touch with Carol Mossman."

"I believe I may have found an answer for that," Jaime Carbajal replied. "Remember Eddie Mossman's other daughter?"

"Andrea?" Joanna asked.

"That's the one. I found her name and address in Pam Davis's e-mail address book. Pam Davis evidently handled most of the business e-mail.

I've glanced through Carmen's e-mail correspondence and it's mostly personal—family-
and-friends kind of stuff. Pam Davis, on the
other hand, routinely deleted her e-mails as soon
as she read them, as though she was concerned
someone might go looking through her correspondence and find out something she didn't
want them to find. I'm checking into whether or
not any of those deleted messages can still be retrieved through Fandango's ISP. In the meantime, if I were a betting man, I'd say Andrea
Mossman is our missing link here."

"So would I," Joanna agreed, "especially in
view of what Edith Mossman told me about her
yesterday." She went on to relate what she knew
about Andrea Mossman's work with the support
organization known as God's Angels. There was
a long pause after Joanna finished her recitation.

"Three people are dead already," Jaime said finally. "What are the chances that Andrea Mossman is on the list of people to be taken out?"

"That thought occurred to me, too," Joanna
said. "I'll talk it over with Frank and decide what
we should do."

"There's one more thing," Jaime added. "I got
a look at Pam Davis's appointment calendar for
the first of July. She and Carmen were scheduled
to meet Carol Mossman at her mobile home at
eleven that morning. When he did the autopsy,

Doc Winfield estimated Carol's time of death as between eight and nine. I'm thinking that whoever killed Carol knew the reporters were coming and waited around to nail them as well."

"Sounds plausible," Joanna said. "But how did the killer know what was up? If The Brethren had a team of highly technical hackers, it's possible someone there might have accessed Pam's e-mail account or checked her calendar."

"If you'd seen the insides of that one house on the Lassiter compound," Jaime said, "you'd know that a compound-based hacker is highly unlikely."

"Then the simplest option is that someone who knew what was going on told someone else. And the person who has the most connections going in every direction would be Andrea Mossman. If she's been helping women and children once they escape the cult, she's the one most likely to still have connections inside it."

"I'm not going to be able to leave here much before late this afternoon," Jaime said. "Maybe Ernie could run up to Tucson and have a talk with Andrea Mossman."

Ernie's already booked, Joanna thought. **But I'm not.** "I'll see what I can do," Joanna said.

The moment she put down the phone, she punched the intercom button. "Kristin," she said, "I'm going to have to go up to Tucson for a little while. Please call Dr. Lee's office and see if he can reschedule my appointment for some time later this week—Thursday or Friday, maybe."

"What about Rotary?"

"Rotary?" Joanna asked.

"Yes. The San Pedro Valley Rotary Club luncheon. It's today at noon out at the Rob Roy Country Club. You and Ken Junior are both scheduled to speak."

"Ken's on his own then," Joanna said. "Work comes before politicking, and this is work. Please call them and explain."

"When will you be back?" Kristin asked.

"I'm not sure," Joanna said. "I'll let you know."

It was a two-hour, one-hundred-mile drive from the Justice Center to Tucson, and the long period of relative quiet gave Joanna time to think about what she would say once she located Andrea Mossman. **Is it best to show up with no advance warning?** Joanna wondered. **Or, since I'm accosting her at work, should I call to let her know that I'm on my way?"**

Eventually, she opted for the latter choice and used her cell phone's direct-connect feature to reach the Chemistry Department at the University of Arizona.

"Andrea Mossman," Joanna said.

"I'm sorry, Ms. Mossman isn't in today." The

female voice on the telephone sounded young, probably a student putting herself through school on a work/study program. "I believe there's been a death in her family."

"I know," Joanna responded, thinking quickly. "I'm with Grant Road Flowers. I have a bouquet for her. I was directed to bring it to her at work, but if you happened to have her home address available . . ."

"Of course," the young woman on the telephone said, falling for what Joanna considered to be a lame ploy. "If you'll wait a minute, I'll be glad to get that for you."

Half an hour later, Joanna pulled up in front of a small redbrick house on South Fourth Avenue in an old barrio neighborhood a few blocks from downtown. The tiny house, with its steeply pitched roof and old-fashioned front porch, looked as though it might once have served as a mom-and-pop grocery store. A sign in faded Chinese characters still lingered over the front door, which was inset into the right front corner of the building. Inside, the shades on all windows were pulled all the way down to the wooden sills. Parked in a space just to the left of the door was a bright green late-model VW Beetle.

With no sign of movement coming from inside the house, Joanna took the time to pull in behind the Bug and run the plates. The results were back within moments, confirming that Andrea Mossman was the VW's registered owner.

Her sense of apprehension growing, Joanna turned off the Civvie's engine and stepped out of her air-conditioned vehicle into Tucson's midday midsummer heat. The one-hundred-plus-degree temperature pounded into her head. Sunlight glared off the sidewalk with blinding intensity while, from somewhere nearby, the too-sweet smell of freshly baked bread filled Joanna's nostrils. Usually the scent of bread baking would be a welcome one, but not today. That odor, combined with the almost unbearable heat, teamed up to leave Joanna feeling more than slightly woozy.

There was no bell, so Joanna knocked on the door. When no one answered, she knocked again, hard enough to hurt her knuckles. Finally, just when she was considering whether or not she should call Tucson PD and ask for help, there was the smallest motion on the corner of a pull-down shade in one of the front windows.

"Who is it?" a female voice asked. "Go away. I don't want any."

"It's Sheriff Brady," Joanna replied. "From Cochise County. I need to talk to you about your sister's death."

"Show me your badge," Andrea Mossman replied. "Drop it through the mail slot."

Grateful to hear that Andrea Mossman was exercising some caution, Joanna did as she was told. Moments later, after a series of locks had been unlatched, the door opened and she was allowed inside.

Compared to the humble exterior the building showed to the world, Andrea Mossman's home wasn't at all what Joanna had expected. The tiny living room was a full thirty degrees cooler than the outside temperature, a feat performed by new and highly efficient air-conditioning equipment. The rooms Joanna could see had been fully remodeled and painted in bright colors paired with an assortment of mismatched but highly whimsical furniture. A hardwood floor, broken by thick rugs, gleamed underfoot. And, although shades remained drawn, the recessed lighting and well-placed lamps made the small room seem both bright and cozy, which was more than could be said for Andrea Mossman.

Joanna had never seen Carol Mossman in the flesh, but the resemblance between Andrea and her younger sister, Stella Adams, was downright spooky. Both had the same mousy light brown hair that must have come from their mother, Cynthia. Both had the same haunted-looking eyes, although Andrea wore glasses and Stella didn't. Andrea wore a faded cotton robe and carried a box of tissues. She looked as though she'd been crying.

"I had no idea Pam and Carmen were dead,"

she said, half sobbing. "Not until a few minutes ago, when Grandma called to tell me. I can't believe it. It can't be true."

"I'm sorry to have to say this," Joanna said gently, "but it is true, Ms. Mossman."

Andrea Mossman sank into an overstuffed easy chair covered in a fabric with a pattern of bright-pink peony blossoms and yellow butterflies. "I was about to get dressed and come to Bisbee to talk to you," she said. "But I'm glad you're here."

"May I sit down?" Joanna asked.

Andrea nodded woodenly and motioned Joanna onto a small bright yellow leather couch. On her way out of the office, Sheriff Brady had paused long enough to collect a pocket-size tape recorder. She pulled it out of her purse and set it on a nearby end table. Then she took out her cell phone and switched it off.

"Do you mind if I record this conversation?" she asked.

"No," Andrea said. "Go ahead."

Joanna switched on the recorder. After identifying herself and giving the time and date, she introduced Andrea Mossman. "And you know why I'm here?" she asked.

"Of course I do," Andrea replied. She stopped long enough to force down a sob. "It's because all of this is my fault."

"Your fault?" Joanna asked. "Why is that?"

"Because I'm the one who heard what Pam and Carmen were looking for," Andrea said in a rush. "One of my clients—one of the former Brethren women whose children I helped counsel and who ended up living in L.A.—somehow learned that Pam Davis and Carmen Ortega were looking for a way to do a story—an insider's story—on The Brethren and what goes on with them." Andrea paused and looked closely at Joanna's face. "You do know what goes on, don't you?"

Joanna nodded. "I have a pretty good idea," she said grimly. "Your grandmother told me some of it, but I'd like to hear what you have to say."

Andrea Mossman's face darkened. "Among The Brethren, women are nothing, and girls are less than that. They're pieces of property, to be traded back and forth. And abused. For some of the girls, it's the first thing they remember. For others, it's the first thing they forget.

"Pam had heard about me through that former client. She contacted me and asked if I would help her put together a story on The Brethren. That same client has a son named Josiah who still lives in the family compound up in northern Arizona—out on what they call the Arizona Strip. He helped his mother get out, and he's functioned as a spy for us ever since. Among The Brethren, boys are given far more freedom to come and go than women and girls are—it's a lot like the Taliban that way. Josiah has been able to smuggle messages in and out for us. It was through him that I found out about . . ."

"Cecilia's wedding?" Joanna suggested quietly.

Andrea glanced quickly at Joanna's face, then she nodded. "You know about that, too—about my father's other family?"

"Yes."

"I shouldn't have told you Josiah's name," Andrea said. "If anyone finds out he helped us . . ."

"He'd be in danger, too?" Joanna asked.

"What do you think?" Andrea broke off. After a minute or so, she went on. "If it hadn't been for Josiah, I wouldn't have known what was going on. I didn't think I could stop it, but Pam and Carmen convinced me that if they could film the wedding itself and make it public, maybe there would be enough publicity so we could bring Cecilia out of there and try to give her some kind of normal life. They said they needed enough damning evidence to blow The Brethren sky-high—something so compelling that even the mainstream media would be forced to pick it up."

"So you made arrangements for Josiah to help Pam and Carmen film the wedding."

Andrea nodded.

"And how did you contact them?" Joanna asked.

"Once or twice I e-mailed them, but usually I used a phone card and pay phones. I didn't want to have anything traceable back to me."

"One of my detectives found your e-mail address in Pam Davis's e-mail address book," Joanna said.

Andrea's face darkened. "I warned Pam about how dangerous these people can be," she said softly. "But I don't think she believed me."

"Tell me about Carol," Joanna urged. "I'm assuming you're the one who put Pam and Carmen in touch with her."

Andrea nodded again. "Everything I have—everything I own—this house, my education, my car, my independence—I owe to Carol. She's the one who saved us—Stella and me. She really did bring us out of the wilderness. If it hadn't been for her, I'd probably have been sold off into indentured servitude in some family compound the same way Cecilia has been. But Carol called Grandma and made arrangements for train tickets. Then she hustled us onto the train. She tried her best to get Kelly to come with us, but she wouldn't. That was awful for Carol. Kelly simply refused to go. If Carol had tried to take her by force, none of the rest of us would have gotten away. So the three of us left and Kelly stayed, God help her. She's twenty-five now. It breaks my heart to think of the kind of hell her life must be. It broke Carol's heart, too."

"So Carol saved you," Joanna breathed.

Andrea Mossman nodded as tears began to course down her cheeks. She dabbed at them fitfully with a tissue. "She saved us, but she couldn't save herself. Maybe it's because Stella and I were younger than Carol was. Somehow we were able to find our sea legs and go on. Once I got into school, I was so hungry to be educated, nothing could stop me. And Stella found Denny, but Carol never found anybody or anything."

"Except her dogs," Joanna offered.

"Yes," Andrea agreed. "Her dogs. They were always hungry and needy and mostly discarded purebreds, but she loved them to distraction. She always thought she could take one more, and then one more and one more after that, until it would get to be too much and the whole house of cards would come tumbling down. That's when Grandma would step into the breach again and fix whatever needed fixing."

"What about Pam and Carmen?" Joanna urged.

"When I found out they were willing to pay for some interviews with some of the women who had escaped The Brethren, I thought, why not put them in touch with Carol? Here was a woman—a potentially wonderful, capable woman—whose whole life had been torn apart by what my father and The Brethren did to her.

It's one thing to show a little girl being married off to an ugly old man. That's bad enough. But when I told Pam and Carmen about Carol, they were interested in doing a story about the long-term ill effects of what The Brethren do. They wanted to interview both Stella and Carol. I told them talking to Stella was a bad idea. I knew she wouldn't be interested, but Carol was in a bind for money."

"How did you know she needed money?"

"Carol always needed money," Andrea replied. "This time she had gone so far as to ask me to help, and I didn't," Andrea said hopelessly, tears welling up again. "I had some money set aside for a vacation next year, after I finally get my Ph.D. I wasn't willing to spend it on vaccinating that latest batch of stray dogs. And so I turned her down, but I put Pam and Carmen in touch with Carol instead. Call it guilt on my part, because it's true, but it was also a way for Carol to have the money she needed without my having to come up with it and without Grandma's having to do it, either. I thought I was helping, I really did."

Andrea paused and stared off into the middle distance. "What happened then?" Joanna urged.

Andrea swallowed hard. "Carol died. I didn't know exactly when Pam and Carmen were supposed to see her, so I fooled myself into thinking that Carol's death was just a random act of violence, that it had nothing at all to do with The Brethren, or with Pam and Carmen, either. And I believed that, right up until this morning, when I talked to Grandma. Then I knew."

"Knew what?"

"That my father killed them, and Carol, too," Andrea said quietly. "And now he wants to take Carol's body back to Mexico with him. It's like he's not willing to let any of us escape, not even in death. I'm afraid he'll come looking for me next, Sheriff Brady, and if he does—if he even so much as comes near me—I swear to God, I'll kill him myself."

Somehow Joanna understood this was no idle threat. "I wouldn't advise that, Ms. Mossman," she said. "We currently have your father under surveillance based on the fact that he's been the object of a previous death threat—one from your grandmother," she added with a slight smile. "And now one from you. I'm confident that we're going to find a way to charge him with something. That way he'll end up in jail rather than going back to Mexico, with or without Carol's remains. In the meantime, however, I believe it's possible that you yourself are in danger. Do you have anywhere you can go? Is there anyplace you can stay?"

"The people I work with have safe houses," Andrea said quietly.

"Go to one of them," Joanna urged. "Just for the time being. Give us a chance to find out exactly what happened to Carol and to Pam and Carmen. It's early in the investigations. We're in the process of sorting out the forensics and gathering evidence. Once we make our case, that will be plenty of time for you to come out of hiding."

Andrea nodded. "You're right," she said. "And I will. But you should probably talk to Stella, too. If I'm in danger, so is she." She paused. "But there is one thing," she added.

"What's that?" Joanna asked.

"If you can, don't mention to her that I'm the one who put Pam and Carmen in touch with Carol. Stella's done a better job than any of us at putting the past behind her and getting on with her life."

Joanna nodded. She switched off the tape recorder and then stood to go. Reaching into her pocket, she pulled out a business card. "Call me tomorrow and let me know you're okay and where you are so I can be in touch with you if I need to."

"I will," Andrea said. "I'll call as soon as I can."

Outside, early-afternoon Tucson temperatures scorched sidewalks, softened pavements, and made the door handle and steering wheel of the Civvie too hot to touch, but Joanna barely noticed. Her whole being simmered with contempt for a wormy little weasel named Eddie Mossman—a man whose betrayal of his daughters went against everything Joanna herself believed in and held dear.

"We'll get you, you lousy bastard," she vowed aloud once she eased herself down on the skin-searing seat. "One way or another, we're taking you down."

SEVENTEEN

On the hundred-mile drive back to Bisbee, a bank of beautifully mountainous thunderclouds, fat with the promise of still more much-needed rain, piled up over the mountainous silhouettes of the Chiricahuas and Dragoons. After only two days of summer monsoons, the shoulders of the highway were already tinged with green, as dormant seeds of grass and weeds sprang to life.

Ordinarily, Joanna Brady would have reveled in this summer miracle, but today she was as blind to the desert's annual transformation as, earlier, she had been unaware of Tucson's heat. With her mind focused totally on the job, her initially angry resolve to deal with Eddie Mossman gradually evolved into questions of strategy.

What was her duty here? What was her responsibility as sheriff, and what was required of her as a human being? Although as yet there was no physical evidence to support such a theory,

Andrea Mossman was clearly operating under the assumption that her father, Ed Mossman, had murdered his own daughter, Carol, and that he posed a danger to his other surviving children as well.

Andrea had asked Joanna to warn Stella. What kind of connection existed between Stella and her father? Were the two of them on better terms than he had been with Carol and Andrea? Ed Mossman claimed Stella was the one who had notified him of Carol's death. Stella might have placed calls from someplace other than her own home, but Joanna had little reason to doubt that Stella Adams's telephone records, once found, would back up that claim. Unless, of course, Ed Mossman had already been only too well aware of his daughter's murder.

How do you go about delivering this kind of news? Joanna asked herself. It was hard enough to tell someone that their loved one was some-how unexpectedly dead. What could she say—what should she say—to Stella Adams? And how could she go about warning Stella without necessarily revealing that Ed Mossman was coming into view as a prime suspect in three separate homicides?

The safety of Stella Adams and her family was important, but so was Joanna's responsibility—her duty—to bring a killer to justice. Her investigators were counting on Sheriff Brady to conduct herself in a fashion that didn't interfere with the successful resolution of the case. So were the voters of Cochise County. Now was no time for her to go Lone Rangering into a situation that might very well blow up in her face.

Joanna glanced at the clock on the dash. Two o'clock. That meant that both Frank Montoya and Ernie Carpenter might still be up to their eyeballs in the Ramón Sandoval meeting. This was no time to interrupt them, either.

She radioed into Dispatch. "See if you can hook me up with Deputy Howell," Joanna told Tica Romero. "I want to know how she's doing with keeping an eye on Ed Mossman."

When her phone rang a few minutes later, she thought it might be Debbie Howell getting back to her. Instead it was Butch. "Where are you?" he asked, sounding annoyed.

"Coming back from Tucson."

"You missed your appointment with Dr. Lee." It was a statement rather than a question. An accusation, really.

"Yes," Joanna admitted. "I did. I had to cancel it. Something came up—something important."

"This baby's important, too," Butch said. "Dr. Lee's office just called to verify that the appointment has been reset for tomorrow morning at ten. I told his receptionist that you'd be there on time if I have to bring you in myself."

"I'll be there," Joanna said. There was a long

pause. "Any word from Drew Mabrey?" Joanna added, more to fill up the uneasy silence than anything else.

"Nothing," Butch said. "But I've got better things to do than just hang out by the telephone waiting for it to ring."

That was when Joanna figured out that the annoyance in Butch's voice had far more to do with his case of nerves about what was going on with the manuscript than it did with his being upset about her missing a doctor's appointment. During the long months when Drew Mabrey had reported one rejection after another, Butch had resigned himself to the idea that the manuscript might never be sold. Now, with a glimmer of hope, the anxiety was excruciating.

"Will you be home for dinner?" he asked.

"Yes," Joanna replied, without mentioning the fact that she had missed lunch altogether. "I'll be home as close to six as I can make it."

Tica radioed back only seconds after Joanna finished the call with Butch. "Deputy Howell says to tell you Mr. Mossman has been holed up in his room out at San Jose Lodge all afternoon. She says she's been keeping an eye on him, and he isn't going anywhere without her."

"Great," Joanna said. "Tell her to keep up the good work."

By then the towering clouds had mounded ever

higher in the sky. When she came through St. David, a black curtain of rain had settled over the Dragoons, completely obliterating the mountain range from view. By the time Joanna started through Tombstone sixteen miles later, rain was pelting so hard against the windshield that the wipers barely made a dent in the water. Even at the posted limit of twenty-five miles per hour, she could hardly see to drive. At least an inch of water covered the roadway, and every passing vehicle raised a blinding spray in its wake.

Then, as suddenly as Joanna had driven into the cloudburst, she emerged on the far side of it into blazingly bright sunlight that turned the pavement surface a shimmering silver. Switching off the air-conditioning, she opened the windows and left them open. In the aftermath of the storm, outside temperatures had dropped a good twenty degrees. The distinctively refreshing smell of summer rain on sun-warmed creosote bushes washed through the Civvie. It wasn't enough to dispel all her concerns about the impending visit with Stella Adams, but it helped.

When Joanna reached the Divide outside Bisbee, the storm clouds had been replaced by bright blue, rain-washed skies. The pavement on the road was still slightly wet, while hundreds of tiny waterfalls cascaded down the rocky cliffs of the Mule Mountains. On both sides of the Divide, washes ran bank to bank with muddy, swiftly moving water. As a lifelong resident of southern Arizona, Joanna knew how treacherous those fast-moving floods of water could be. Every year someone, usually a hapless visitor from out of state, would drown after being surprised by floodwaters from a downpour that had happened miles away.

Ignoring the turnoff to the Justice Center, Joanna drove straight to Stella and Denny Adams's home on Arizona Street, just across from Warren Ballpark. There were no cars parked in the driveway or on the street in front of the low-slung iron fence, but Joanna parked along a concrete-lined drainage ditch. It, too, was running with several inches of swiftly moving water. Then she walked across a narrow footbridge, through a gate, and up onto the front porch, where she rang the doorbell.

Inside she heard the muffled sound of a television set tuned to something that sounded like MTV. Moments after the doorbell rang, the TV set was silenced. A few seconds after that, the door opened and there stood Nathan Adams. The sight of him was enough to take Joanna's breath away. When she had first seen Eddie Mossman, she remembered that he had looked familiar somehow, even though she was certain she had never seen the man before. Now she knew why. Nathan Adams looked just like Eddie Mossman—just like his grandfather.

Or was it also, Joanna wondered for the first time, **just like his father?** No one had said as much. No one had admitted that, at the time Carol Mossman had fled Mexico with her two younger sisters, Stella might have been pregnant with her own father's child. And the simple fact that no one **had** mentioned it made Joanna wonder that much more whether it was true.

"Yeah?" Nathan said. "Whaddya want?"

"Is your mother home?" Joanna managed. "There's something I need to talk to her about."

"She's not here."

"Do you know when she'll be back?"

Nathan Adams shrugged. "No idea," he said. "Could be an hour or two, maybe longer."

"What about your dad?" Joanna asked hopefully.

"He stays at an apartment up in Tucson during the week," Nathan explained. "He's usually only home on weekends."

"Oh," Joanna said. "I'll be going then."

"Want me to have her call you when she gets in?"

"No," Joanna said. "Don't bother. I'll talk with her tomorrow."

As Joanna walked back across the wide porch, the door slammed behind her. A moment later, the atonal thumping of MTV returned. Joanna retreated to the Civvie and then sat there for several long minutes without turning the key in the ignition.

Is that the truth? she wondered. **Is Nathan the product of an incestuous relationship between Stella and her father? And if so, does he have any idea about the truth of the situation?**

Joanna remembered Nathan as he had appeared when she had first laid eyes on him that day in the lobby of the Justice Center. He had struck her as a surly, smart-alecky teenager—typical, in other words. She had thought him spoiled, doted on, and more than a little obnoxious, but normal—utterly normal. But could you be a normal teenager if you knew that kind of awful truth about your parentage?

Kids exist in a herd mentality. They want to fit in—want to be just like everyone else. That's why they wear the same kinds of clothes, watch the same television programs, listen to the same music. But could you fit in if you knew that you existed because your mother had been impregnated by her own father?

It came to Joanna then in a flash of insight. "He doesn't know!" she almost shouted, pounding the steering wheel with her fist. "Nathan Adams has no idea!"

Joanna's hands trembled as she turned the ignition key and put the Crown Victoria in gear. Meanwhile the gears in Joanna's head were meshing as well. **And if Nathan doesn't know, that's because Stella's been keeping it a secret. And if Carol was going public, the secret was about to come out.**

There it was laid out before her so clearly that Joanna wondered why she hadn't seen it before. Andrea was convinced that her father was Carol's murderer, but this made far more sense. Here was motive—a protective mother's motive—understandable, utterly implacable, and absolutely deadly.

Joanna headed straight for the department. Without being aware of her speed, she found herself doing seventy down the Warren Cutoff. Taking a deep breath, she forced herself to pull her foot off the gas pedal and drive sensibly. She parked the Civvie behind her office and darted inside. As soon as she put her purse down, she hurried over to the door.

Kristin looked up from her desk, surprised to see her,. "What are you doing here?" she said. "I thought you'd go straight home from Tucson."

"Something came up. Where's Frank?"

"Still in the conference room with Ernie and those other guys," Kristin answered. "They must be having a great time in there. A few of them have come out for pee stops, but they're obviously still going strong." She gave Joanna a close look. "You seem upset," she said. "Is something wrong?"

"No," Joanna said, "nothing's wrong. But let me know as soon as Frank comes out. Tell him I need to see him. What about Jaime Carbajal? Has anyone heard from him?"

"Not as far as I know."

Joanna returned to her office and tried calling Jaime's cell phone. It rang several times, and she hung up without leaving a message. Frustrated, she stared at the mounds of untouched paperwork covering almost every square inch of her desk. Finally her eye settled on the last of Irma Mahilich's General Office drawings—the one marked page 4. The paper sat directly in front of her just where she'd left it. Something drew Joanna's eyes to the far-right corner of the paper where, although she hadn't noticed it before, a single name stood out: Adams—Anna Wakefield Adams.

Staring at the words written in Irma Mahilich's spidery script, a string of names tumbled through Joanna's mind: Stella Adams. Denny Adams. Anna Wakefield Adams. Joanna had known of Denny Adams. He had been younger than Joanna by several years, so they hadn't been in school together, but she knew the name. Now she wondered if Anna Adams and Denny were related. She looked up the number in the telephone directory and called the Ferndale Retirement Center.

"Irma Mahilich," she said to the person who answered.

"I'll ring her room for you."

"No," Joanna said. "Don't do that. Let me speak to the receptionist. The one at the front desk."

A moment later another voice came on the line. "May I help you?"

"This is Sheriff Brady," Joanna said quickly. "I'm trying to reach Irma Mahilich. Is there a chance she's sitting out in the lobby working on a jigsaw puzzle?"

"Yes," the receptionist said. "She's right there. If this is important, I could have her come take the call here at the desk."

Joanna let her breath out. "Yes, it is important," she said. "I'd really appreciate it."

After an interminable wait, Irma's voice rang over the phone. "I'm here," she said irritably. "Who is this? What do you want?"

"It's Sheriff Brady," Joanna said.

"I can't hear a thing. Wait while I fix my hearing aid. Now, who are you again?"

"I'm Joanna Brady. You know, D. H. Lathrop's little girl."

"Oh, yes. I remember you. You came to my house selling Girl Scout cookies that one year. I think I even bought some from you. Thin Mints,

I believe. Those were always my favorites. What can I do for you?"

"I was wondering about someone who used to work with you," Joanna said slowly. "Someone who worked with you in the General Office." Joanna picked up the drawing and studied it. "Her name was Anna Adams, and she worked upstairs. Her desk was just to the right of the stairs—between them and your office."

"Oh, yes, Anna," Irma said. "I remember her. Her husband ran off with another woman and left her to bring up her son on her own. Dennis, I believe his name was. Fortunately, she had her parents to fall back on, so she had a place to live and someone to help her look after the baby when she had to go to work. Once PD shut down, I don't have any idea what became of her. She probably transferred up to Silver City or over to Playas. Unlike the rest of us, Anna was way too young to retire."

"And when Mr. Frayn was passing out those guns," Joanna asked softly, "do you happen to remember whether or not Anna Adams took one?"

"Took one!" Irma practically whooped. "Are you kidding? When they handed out guns, that girl was first in line. She said she wanted one of her own. She said if that worthless husband of hers ever came nosing around again, she was going to plug him full of holes."

Irma paused. "Now wait a minute," she said. "Who did you say you were again?"

"Sheriff Brady," Joanna said. "Thank you so much for your help."

She put down the phone and sat there thinking about how a gun that had once been used by company-hired vigilantes to march union protesters to the Warren Ballpark had now, more than eighty years later, come home to roost in a house directly across the street from that very same ballpark.

The phone rang. When Joanna answered, Deputy Debbie Howell was on the line and fighting mad. "Some son of a bitch messed with my vehicle, Sheriff Brady," Debbie Howell stormed. "Mossman came out of his room, got in his car, and drove away. I had gone into the restaurant long enough to use the facilities. When I came out, he was getting into his car and leaving, so I hustled after him. He drove out to the highway and turned left like he was headed back into town. My Blazer started fine, but two miles down the road, just short of the junction with Highway 92, it conked out on me. It acts like it's out of gas, but I just filled it. I think maybe somebody put sugar in the gas tank."

"What kind of vehicle is he driving?" Joanna asked.

"A Hertz rental," Debbie replied. "A late-model white Ford Taurus. I passed the vehicle description and license info along to Dispatch so people can be on the lookout for it. I'm sorry I dropped the ball on this one, Sheriff Brady. I really thought I had it under control."

"How long ago did you lose sight of him?"

"Only about ten minutes."

"He can't have gotten too far then," Joanna said. "I'm sure we'll find him. What about you?"

"Motor Pool is sending a tow truck to bring me back to the department."

"See you here," Joanna said.

As she put down the phone, Frank Montoya sauntered into her office. Grinning, he held both thumbs up in the air. "I think you scored a bull's-eye, boss," he said.

"How's that?"

"Señor Sandoval knows more than anyone thought possible, and he's naming names that the feds want to hear—people on both sides of the border. The FBI is taking him into custody, so he'll be out of our bailiwick and into theirs. We're also handing over the interviews you had us do."

"Great," Joanna said.

Frank homed in on her lack of enthusiasm. "What's wrong?" he asked.

"I don't know where to start," she responded. "But maybe you should get Ernie in here before I do."

Frank and Ernie listened in almost total silence. When Joanna finished, Ernie nodded. "You could be right about all this," he observed. "It's not like it used to be in the old days. Now, having an out-of-wedlock child is no big deal, but this is incest. And if all of this is a result of Stella Adams trying to conceal the boy's real parentage, it might not be over yet. Who else would know?"

"The grandmother, Edith Mossman," Joanna replied. "Ed Mossman himself, and the sister, Andrea."

"You said Andrea was going into hiding."

"Most likely she's hiding from the wrong person," Joanna answered. "But, yes, I think she's out of harm's way for the moment."

"Should we send an officer to look after Edith?" Frank asked.

Joanna nodded. "Absolutely," she said. "The same goes for Ed, once we locate him again. What about the phone situation, Frank? Any luck there?"

"Not really," Frank replied. "It's a case of having too much information rather than too little. It turns out there are several phone calls going back and forth from Stella's home number to her father, both in the days and weeks preceding the three murders and in the days afterward. So there's no way we can point to a single individual call and say this one is significant. Mossman said

Stella called and told him about Carol's death sometime on Wednesday. He claims he doesn't remember the exact time. Unfortunately, there are several different calls during which that communication might have taken place."

Ernie's fingers drummed an impatient tattoo on the surface of Joanna's desk. "We've got plenty of suspicion, but zero probable cause," he said. "So far there's nothing that would merit getting a search warrant, so how about this? What if I track Denny Adams down in Tucson and find out if Stella could possibly be in possession of one of those old Deportation Colt forty-fives? If he works for FedEx, they'll have a local phone number and address for him."

"Good thinking," Joanna said.

"Anything else?"

"That's fine for a start."

"I'll get on it then," Ernie said, lumbering toward the door. "One other thing. Do we know when Jaime will be back?"

"Not so far. I've tried calling him, but I can't get through to him."

"Too bad. If we knew when he was coming in, we could have him go talk to Adams," Ernie said. "As it is, I guess I'll do it."

"You could always do a phoner," Frank suggested.

Ernie shook his head. "Not me," he said. "Phones work fine for some people, but I'd rather be eyeball-to-eyeball and belly-to-belly. I get a better feel for things that way, and better information, too."

Ernie went out and closed the door behind him. "I should have known," Frank said with a laugh. "I knew Ernie disapproved of computers, but this is the first I realized telephones are also suspect."

Joanna laughed. "Give the man a break, Frank. Ernie Carpenter's just an old-fashioned kind of guy."

Frank left, too, and since there was no other excuse to avoid the paperwork on her desk, Joanna knuckled under and went to work. A whole hour had passed before her phone rang again. This time it was her private line.

"I thought you said you were going to call me back," Eleanor Lathrop Winfield huffed. "That was days ago now."

Joanna's first instinct was always to grab hold of the guilt her mother was so willing to pass out, but for a change she caught herself. "It was only yesterday," Joanna said. "And I've been incredibly busy."

"If you're this busy now, how will you ever manage with a baby thrown into the bargain?"

"Mother," Joanna said quietly, "Butch and I are going to have this baby. And, if the voters are willing, I'm going to go right on being sheriff."

"In other words, like it or lump it."

"I didn't say that," Joanna countered. **Although it's exactly what I meant,** she realized. "I suppose that **is** what I mean. I want you to be happy about this with us. I want you to be involved, and George, too. But, Mom, you're going to have to get used to the idea that I'm a grown-up. This is my life, and I'm going to do things my way."

"That's almost exactly what George said," Eleanor replied tearily.

"George Winfield is a very smart man."

"All right," Eleanor replied. Then she paused, but only for half a beat. "So have you been to see the doctor yet? You shouldn't let that go too long, you know."

All her life, Joanna had reacted to her mother's interference with anger. When her mother pushed, she pushed back. Now, for the first time ever, she burst out laughing.

"What's so funny?" Eleanor demanded.

"You're hopeless, Mom. A minute ago you agreed to let me do things my way. Now, less than a minute later, you're telling me to go see the doctor."

Eleanor sighed. "I guess I just can't help myself."

"And, if it'll make you feel any better, I am going to the doctor," Joanna said. "I have a prenatal appointment with Dr. Lee tomorrow morning at ten."

"Good. I'm delighted to hear it. Well, I suppose I should let you go. You said you're busy," Eleanor replied.

"I am busy," Joanna agreed. "But there's one thing more."

"What's that?"

"I love you, Mom," Joanna told her. "I love you very much." For a moment, there was dead silence on the other end of the phone. "Mom? Are you still there? Did you hear what I said?"

"Yes," Eleanor replied, her voice strangely muffled. "I did hear you. And I think it's one of the nicest things you've ever said to me."

Joanna's desk was relatively clear when she left to go home at five-thirty. At seven, she and Butch were sitting at the kitchen counter with the three dogs flopped on the cool tile floor around them while she related the details of Eleanor's phone call.

"So she's not mad anymore?" Butch asked.

"Evidently, and I'm not mad, either."

"Then this is new ground for both of you," Butch said. "If you weren't off the sauce for the duration, I'd propose a toast."

Joanna raised her milk glass and smiled at him. "Go ahead," she said. "I'll drink to that."

She leaned over to kiss him, only to have Jenny appear in the doorway holding the cordless phone. "It's for you, Mom," she said. "Detective Carpenter."

"What's up?" Joanna asked.

"Denny Adams and I are on our way back to Bisbee right now. He's in one car. I'm in another. Turns out his mother gave him an old Colt when he graduated from high school. He says he's never fired it, but that he keeps it on the top shelf of his closet. He offered to check to make sure it's still there, so he called home. Stella was out, so Denny asked Nathan to go look in the closet to see if he could find the gun. Naturally it isn't there, and Nathan has no idea where his mother is. He says she went out today just after noon. She didn't say where she was going and hasn't been back since. I clued Denny in on what may be going on. He's coming down to Bisbee to be with Nathan."

Joanna took a deep breath. "Did you ask him about . . ." She looked toward Jenny, who was waiting to retrieve the phone as soon as her mother was finished. ". . . about the rest of it?" Joanna finished lamely

"Yes," Ernie said. "It's true. All of it. Denny has known the truth all along, but Stella swore him to secrecy. Denny Adams came into Nathan's life when the kid was just three years old. Denny's the only father the boy has ever known, and he'd like to keep it that way. I told him that was doubtful, but that we'd try. That we'd do our best." Ernie paused. "That's the one thing I hate about this job."

"What's that?" Joanna asked.

"Making promises I may not be able to keep."

"So what's the game plan?"

"We're going to the house to talk to Nathan and see if he can give us any idea of where his mother might be."

"Jaime hasn't shown up yet, has he?"

"No, ma'am, but we've heard from him. There was a security breach at LAX. They had to empty two terminals and re-screen all the passengers. He still doesn't know when he'll get here."

"In that case," Joanna said, "would you like me to meet you there—at Denny and Stella's house?"

"You bet," Ernie Carpenter returned. "I thought you'd never ask."

EIGHTEEN

By the time Joanna returned to the far end of Arizona Street, it was dark. Due to a Pony-tail League softball game, the glowing ball-park lights cast that whole part of town in a strange half-twilight. Cars were parked every-where, but all the drivers had observed the hand-stenciled No Parking signs that had been placed on both posts of the footbridge leading to Stella and Denny Adams's front gate.

Other than the hazy glow of a TV set some-where deep inside the house, there was no sign of life. The driveway was still empty, and Joanna saw no trace of Ernie Carpenter's Econoline van. She opened the car windows, turned off the en-gine, and settled in to wait. Across the street, a cheer went up from the crowd, and over the top of the fence Joanna saw someone use a long stick to change one of the numbers on the green and white scoreboard.

It seemed odd to be sitting there dealing with a

possible triple murderer while across the street carefree fans munched popcorn, sipped sodas, and cheered their respective teams. How could both things be happening in such close proximity at the same time? One was so normal and everyday, while the other was so . . .

Joanna glanced at the clock on the dash. The digital readout said 9:10. Ernie had called from the far side of Tombstone. Joanna had left the house immediately after the call, pausing only long enough to retrieve her weapons and her vest. Even so, Ernie and Denny should be close at hand by now. How many hours ago was it since Joanna had stopped by this house the first time? Then, she had been coming to warn Stella Adams that her father, Ed Mossman, might be dangerous—that he might pose a danger to his surviving children.

In the space of a few hours' time, that whole situation had changed. Now Stella was the one who seemed to pose the danger and it was her son, Nathan, who would need protection— maybe not from his mother but from the awful truth of his own squalid heritage. Who would break that ugly news to him? Probably Denny Adams—the only father Nathan had ever known.

The radio crackled to life. "Sheriff Brady?"

Joanna picked up the mike and thumbed it. "I'm here, Tica," she said. "What is it?"

"City of Bisbee has reported finding Ed Mossman's Taurus."

"Where?"

"Up at the far end of Tombstone Canyon, where the old road goes up over the Divide."

"Any sign of Mossman?" Joanna asked.

"I'm afraid so," Tica replied. "The officer reported what looked like blood dripping from the trunk. They popped it and found the body of a white male, fifty to sixty years of age, shot in the chest at close range. Mossman's driver's license was in the guy's wallet, so we're assuming that's who it is. Bisbee PD is wondering if we have anyone who could do a positive ID."

Stella strikes again, Joanna thought. She started to say, "I suppose I could, but—"

But Tica continued. "They also found two trash bags filled with what appears to be women's bloodstained clothing."

"Most likely Pam Davis and Carmen Ortega's," Joanna breathed.

"That's what City of Bisbee is assuming."

"All right, then," Joanna said. "I'm waiting for Ernie Carpenter, but as soon as—"

She broke off in midsentence as a yellow Dodge Ram pickup with a matching yellow camper shell drove slowly past the place where Joanna was parked. The driver peered out at Joanna through a half-open window. If it hadn't been for the ballpark lights across the street, Joanna never would have been able to make out enough details to recognize Stella Adams's face.

When Joanna's eyes met Stella's, an electric charge of recognition passed between the two women. With a squeal of tires that left a layer of rubber on the pavement, the Dodge sped off, heading south out of town, past what had once been the bus barn and on up the hill. Joanna dropped the mike, turned on the engine, and pulled a U-turn that sent the rear end of the Crown Victoria skidding back and forth across the street. Only when the in-grille lights were flashing and her siren blaring did Joanna retrieve the mike.

"I've spotted suspect Stella Adams," Joanna reported into the phone. "She's headed south toward Bisbee Junction in a yellow Dodge Ram pickup with a camper shell. I'm in pursuit, but I'm going to need backup from whoever can get here."

Tica said, "Just a minute."

Driving and unconsciously holding her breath, Joanna felt as though far more than a minute had passed before Tica's voice returned.

"City of Bisbee has two cars en route. Ernie Carpenter is just coming around the Traffic Circle. Do you have the suspect in view?" Tica asked.

"No, she went up and over the hill while I was turning around. I'm just topping the hill now. No, I still can't see her. When I saw her last she must have been going close to . . ."

As the road jogged slightly to the right, Joanna drove into a cloud of dust. When she came out the far side, a pair of glowing headlights slanted up into the air through the dust off to the right of the road.

"Hang on, Tica. I think she rolled it. The pickup is off the road."

"Any sign of the driver?"

Joanna peered through the dust. It was clearing enough that she could make out the truck sitting upside down on a berm, its wheels still spinning furiously. Joanna manhandled the Civvie's spotlight into position and aimed it at the wreckage. The front driver's door had disappeared completely. The draped remains of a deflated air bag and a seat belt spilled out through the opening and dangled, still swaying, in midair. But there was no sign of life inside the battered cab. Stella had either been thrown free or clambered out once the truck came to rest.

Joanna swung the circle of light back and forth across the ground. She searched with such total concentration that it took her a moment to tune back in to Tica Romero's voice.

"Sheriff Brady!" Tica demanded urgently. "Are you there? Please respond."

"I'm here, Tica. I'm okay."

"Any sign of the driver?"

"None. That's what I'm looking for."

Behind her a series of vehicles alive with lights and sirens came screeching over the crest of the hill and through the still-drifting haze of dust. Two uniformed City of Bisbee patrol officers trotted off and began putting lighted flares down the middle of the road. Seconds later Ernie Carpenter appeared at Joanna's window.

"Are you all right?"

Joanna nodded. "I'm fine, but Stella's gone. She got away."

Ernie looked back at the debris field. "She can't be far," he said. "It's a helluva wreck. The driver's door is gone completely. She might have been thrown clear at the same time the door flew off. I'm guessing that when we find the door, we'll find her, too."

A second man appeared behind Ernie. Tall and bony, he was in his late twenties and wore an Arizona Diamondbacks baseball cap along with a loose-fitting T-shirt. In the eerie glow of headlights and flashers, his face was deadly pale.

"Did you find her, Detective Carpenter?" he asked.

"Not yet, Dennis," Ernie said kindly. "We're looking for her."

As soon as Joanna knew who the man was, she let go of the handle on the spotlight and stepped

out of the Crown Victoria. "I'm Sheriff Brady,
Mr. Adams," she told him. "I was the first person on the scene. And, as Detective Carpenter
told you, so far there's no sign of your wife."

Denny nodded mutely. Joanna could see that he
was trembling as if from the cold and struggling
to hold back tears.

"I can't believe any of this . . . It's all so . . .
so . . ." His voice faded into a croak that was half
sob, half hiccup. Suddenly he blinked and
straightened his shoulders. When he spoke
again, his voice was surprisingly steady.

"Do you want me to try to talk to her?"

Joanna thought about that and then shook her
head. "You'd better go back to the house and be
with Nathan."

"When you find her, will you let me know?"
Dennis asked.

"Yes," Joanna said. "Of course we will."

Adams nodded. "All right then," he said. With
that, he turned and walked away.

Another emergency vehicle showed up, this
one an ambulance dispatched by the Bisbee Fire
Department. Across the desert, Joanna heard a
shout. "Hey," someone yelled. "The door is over
here."

Without a word, Ernie Carpenter loped away
in that direction. Joanna reached back into the
Civvie and collected the mike. "Tica," she or-

dered, "call out the K-9 unit. Everyone else thinks Stella Adams is lying around here dead someplace, but I'm thinking she did the same thing the Silver Creek driver did and walked away."

Fortunately, Terry and Kristin Gregovich's rented house was on Black Knob, the last street on the southernmost part of town. The K-9 officer and Spike were at the scene in less than ten minutes.

"What's up, Sheriff Brady?" Terry asked, after leaping out of an idling Blazer he had parked directly behind Joanna's Crown Victoria.

Joanna pointed toward the wrecked pickup. "The driver's missing," Joanna said. "I want you to find her."

Terry nodded. "Will do," he said.

Taking Spike, he walked down the embankment and over to the wrecked vehicle. Joanna was relieved to see that Spike was wearing his new custom-fitted Kevlar bulletproof vest. Joanna watched while Deputy Gregovich reached inside and removed something from the tangled interior. Hurrying behind him, Joanna was astonished to see Terry was holding a single tennis shoe up to the dog's nostrils.

"Where did that come from?" Joanna asked.

"It was wedged up under the dash. And that's the good news," Terry said. "If she took off with either one or both shoes missing, she's not going to be that hard to track down." Then, keeping a tight hold on Spike's leash, he gave the order. "Find it!"

For the next few minutes the dog, with his nose to the ground, went round and round in ever-widening circles. Ernie Carpenter reappeared at Joanna's side.

"Still no luck," he said. "We're looking on the ground, but if she was airborne, it's possible she could have been tossed up into one of these clumps of mesquite."

Suddenly Spike stopped circling. He stood stock-still, ears up, tail straight out behind him, sniffing the air. Then he dashed off to the west, with Terry Gregovich galloping along behind him.

"They need backup," Joanna said.

Ernie nodded and headed for Terry's Blazer. "Come on," he said. "I'll drive."

Joanna was barely in the passenger seat when Ernie flung the SUV into gear and they bounced away. Fifty feet from the wreck, Terry Gregovich and Spike paused briefly at a barbed-wire fence posted with an official-looking No Trespassing sign. They delayed for only a moment before Spike crouched and slid under it while Terry clambered up and over the top. Spike and Terry were well beyond the fence when Ernie stopped in front of it.

"What's the word, boss?" he asked. "Do you want to go look for a gate?"

"Are you kidding? Go through the damned thing!" she ordered. "We can always fix the fence later."

Ernie backed up a few feet. After putting the Blazer in four-wheel drive, he roared forward. For a time the wire seemed to stretch, then it broke, sending fence posts and coils of wire spiraling into the air as the Blazer rushed through.

"Cut the lights," Joanna ordered when they once again had Terry and the dog in view. "Now that we're away from the ballpark, there's enough moonlight tonight that, once our eyes get accustomed to it, we should be able to see just fine. If we keep our lights on, we're liable to blind them."

And let Stella know they're coming, she thought.

Without a word, Ernie cut the lights. It took only a moment before their eyes adjusted to the dark. Soon, though, the silvery light cast by a wedge of moon was enough to allow them to make out the movements of both the officer and his dog as they traversed a ghostly landscape.

Off to the left lay what looked like a pale layer of white earth. That was a long-abandoned tailings dam—waste left over from the copper-milling process—that covered acres of desert with a relatively flat layer of debris. To the right was the mound of steep hills that formed a backdrop to the neighborhood of Warren. The tops of the hills, tipped with silver, gleamed against the sky with the reflected glow from the ballpark lights where the softball game was still in full swing.

And straight ahead of them, at the base of those hills, crouching in shadow, lay broken hulks of buildings that had once, long ago, been a state-of-the-art ore crusher. Joanna remembered that she and her father had once spent hours exploring the ruin. The machinery and equipment that had been used to grind copper ore to dust had disappeared right along with the men who had once operated it. But Joanna knew that the concrete shells of those long empty buildings would offer shelter for a fleeing Stella Adams—shelter and cover.

"She has to be headed for the old crusher," Joanna said.

Concentrating on driving, Ernie could only nod in agreement. Joanna reached for the radio mike and barked into it.

"We think Stella Adams is headed for the old crusher on the southwest side of Warren," she told Tica. "We need backup officers to come from the west side of town, out past the Juvenile Detention Center, to rendezvous there. The K-9 unit is on the suspect's trail. Detective Carpenter and I are to the east of the old crusher. I don't want anybody caught in a cross fire. No weapons are to be fired under any circumstances until we positively locate the suspect and our guys are in the clear. Got that?"

"Got it," Tica Romero repeated.

"The suspect may be injured, and we believe she may have lost one or more shoes. But she's still to be considered armed and dangerous."

Something cold and wet trickled down Joanna's neck and into the cleavage of her bra. The afternoon rainstorm had left the desert surprisingly cool, but the sweat dribbling under Joanna's clothing had nothing to do with heat and everything to do with fear.

Another fence appeared out of nowhere. Stella Adams wasn't following a road; neither were Deputy Gregovich and Spike. Again, there was no time to go looking for a gate. Once again, Ernie backed off a few feet before gunning the Blazer forward. Around them breaking wires sprang apart with a screeching twang.

"Sounds like God just broke his guitar string," Joanna said to Ernie. A moment later, although it wasn't that funny, they were both laughing— laughing and driving and sitting in their own rank, fear-spawned sweat.

That's when they heard the shot. The single roar of gunfire crackled through the air and echoed off the surrounding hillsides and buildings. Ahead of them, Joanna saw both Terry and Spike dive for cover. At least she hoped they were diving for cover. Hoped that they had fallen of their own volition rather than because Stella Adam's single, well-aimed shot had found its mark. A moment later Joanna and Ernie, too, were on the ground, scrambling forward.

It probably took them less than a minute to reach the low rise where Terry Gregovich and his dog huddled behind a thick mound of creosote. "Looks like we found her," Terry muttered.

"Are you both all right?" Joanna demanded.

"Yes. We're fine, but this woman is a damned good shot. Watch yourselves."

"We didn't see where it came from." Ernie Carpenter was out of shape and out of breath. "Did you?"

Terry pointed. "Over there," he said. "Behind the wall of that first building. What the hell is this place?"

Remembering that the manufacturer called her Kevlar vest "bullet-resistant" rather than "bulletproof," Joanna managed to utter a one-word answer: "Crusher." Then she pulled herself together. "Okay, guys," she added. "Spread out. We'll be better off behind the wall than we are out here in the open. We move forward at the same speed. No one gets too far ahead, and no one drops behind."

"By the way," Terry said, "she's bleeding pretty good."

Joanna looked at the ground in front of her and saw the faint reflection of moonlight off droplets of moisture leading them forward. And Deputy Gregovich was right. It was more than mere droplets.

Weapons drawn, the three officers and the accompanying German shepherd inched forward, crawling on their bellies. They reached the relative shelter of the wall with no additional shots being fired.

"Stella," Joanna called. "We know you're in there. We also know you're hurt. Give yourself up. Throw out your weapon. Let us help you."

"I don't want help," Stella called back.

"Good work, boss," Ernie muttered. "You've made contact and got her talking."

"Think of your son," Joanna said. "Think of Nathan. He loves you and needs you."

"He doesn't. I've wrecked his life. It's spoiled. Everything I tried to do is gone. And it's all Carol's fault. And Andrea's. How could they do that—to me and to Nathan? Why couldn't they leave well enough alone? And why did Carol have to decide to go and open her big mouth?"

Stella's voice came from only a few feet away, from the other side of the roofless wall. Joanna thanked God for the thick concrete that separated them.

"Maybe she was tired of keeping secrets, Stella," Joanna said. "Secrets like that get to be too heavy over the years. They drag you down."

"I was doing fine. So was Nathan, but now . . ."

"Pam Davis and Carmen Ortega thought you were Carol, didn't they?" Joanna called softly. "They came to Carol's place for their appointment that morning, but Carol was already dead, wasn't she? You pretended to be her."

For a few moments, Stella Adams was silent. During the silence Joanna was struck by the peculiar intimacy of their conversation. They might have been girls off on a double date, sharing secrets between locked stalls in a ladies' rest room. "How did you know that?" Stella asked finally.

Because you all breed true, Joanna felt like saying. **Because all of Eddie Mossman's daughters look like twins. And his son looks just like him.**

Far ahead, Joanna caught sight of the winking flash of approaching lights. The additional officers she had summoned were coming toward them from the opposite direction. "Tell Tica we're talking to the suspect. Tell our backup to stay back until I give the word," Joanna ordered. Moments later Deputy Gregovich was relaying the information through the radio attached to the shoulder of his uniform.

Meanwhile Joanna turned her attention back to the suspect. Nathan was Stella Adams's Achilles heel, and that was where Joanna focused her efforts.

"Think about Nathan," she said. "Turn yourself in."

"That's what my father said, too," Stella returned. " 'Think about Nathan.' But I **am** thinking about him. Everything I did, I did for him. To protect him."

"Your father wanted you to turn yourself in?"

Stella erupted in a mirthless chuckle. "Right. That's what he wanted, but I told him, 'No way!' I told him he owed me—he owed us all—but he owed Nathan more than anybody. So, at first, when I asked him, he was willing to help. He agreed to send the e-mail to try to get Pam and Carmen to back off."

"You knew they were coming?"

"Sure, I did. Because they wanted to talk to me. After they finished talking to Carol, they were going to interview me, too. But the threat didn't work. They didn't back off. Pam and Carmen showed up anyway, so I got rid of them, and Carol, too. Dad was headed back to Mexico from Kingman. When I told him what had happened, he offered to move the bodies for me. He said he'd try to make it look like some pervert had done it."

That should have been easy for Ed Mossman, Joanna thought.

"So he moved them and stripped them and tied them up," Stella continued.

"You shot them?"

"Yes."

"Where?"

"In their car. What a mess! I didn't think I'd ever get all that blood washed off. It was everywhere."

"Where's the car, Stella?" Joanna asked. "The car you shot them in. Where is it?"

"I ran it off the road, somewhere the other side of Animas. Then I hitchhiked back. I told the guy who gave me a ride that my husband had beaten me up and that I was going back home to my parents. He believed me, too. Nice guy."

Her voice was softer now, with a funny dreamlike quality that made it sound as though she was struggling to concentrate and stay connected.

"Sounds like she's fading some," Ernie whispered. "I think she really is hurt."

"Are you all right, Stella?" Joanna asked. "Are you hurt?"

"I'm fine. Leave me alone."

"We can't leave you," Joanna returned. "Throw down your weapon and come out. Let us help you."

"No. If anyone comes near me, I'll shoot."

"Mom?"

The sound of Nathan Adams's voice coming from twenty-five or thirty yards away sent a surge of fear coursing through Joanna's body. Hair stood up on the back of her neck. Her hands tingled.

"Where'd he come from?" Joanna demanded. "What's he doing here, and where the hell is he?"

"Off to our right," Terry Gregovich returned, pointing. "I saw him a second ago. Now he's dropped behind some bushes. He must have followed the railroad bed out of town."

Joanna couldn't see Nathan Adams, but she could hear him as he dashed forward once more. He must have run the better part of the mile and a half to two miles from his house to the scene. As he drew closer, Joanna heard him panting with exertion.

"Nathan!" Joanna shouted. "Stop. Go back. It isn't safe!"

But Nathan Adams paid no attention. "Mom," he gasped. "What's going on? Are you all right?"

Stella, who must not have heard him the first time he spoke, did this time. "Nathan!" she exclaimed forcefully. "Get out of here! Go back to the house! This is none of your business."

"But it **is** my business," Nathan argued.

"Terry," Joanna ordered. "Ernie will cover you while I try to keep her talking. You and Spike go get that kid and do whatever it takes to get him out of here!"

Crouching low to the ground, Terry set off with Spike at his heels.

"I'm sure you don't want Nathan to get hurt," Joanna said. "Throw down your weapon, Stella. Let's finish this."

"It is finished," Stella returned. "It's over. There isn't anything more to do."

"Mom, let me be with you," Nathan pleaded. "Let me help. Please."

In the pale moonlight Joanna caught a glimpse of Nathan Adams as he tripped over some obstacle and fell to the ground. He started to rise, then crumpled again as Terry Gregovich and Spike tackled the boy and sent him sprawling. After a fierce but brief scuffle, the clump of milling figures lay still.

"No," Stella said, oblivious to the fact that her son had just been physically prevented from coming any nearer to her. "I don't want you here, Nathan. Go away."

"Mom, please."

"You're better off without me. Go!"

"Watch yourself," Ernie muttered in Joanna's ear. "Sounds like she's maybe gonna take herself out."

Joanna nodded. "I think so, too," she agreed. "How many people will she try to take with her?"

Suddenly the night was blacker. It took a moment for Joanna to realize that the softball game was over. There was a flicker as if someone had thrown a switch. Then the moonlight gleamed that much brighter. Off to the right she spied movement. As her eyes adjusted to the changed light, she was able to make out three figures—two human and one canine—moving back toward town as Deputy Gregovich and Spike hustled Nathan Adams to safety.

They disappeared from view behind a small rise, leaving the desert in an eerie nighttime silence that was broken only by the muted chatter of distant police radios.

"Stella?" Joanna asked finally.

"What?"

"Are you okay? We know you're hurt."

"I'm all right."

The woman's voice was definitely changed now, as though the effort of dealing with her son's unexpected appearance had weakened her somehow and left her exhausted.

"Four people are dead," Joanna said quietly. "Isn't that enough bloodshed?"

"No, it's not enough—not nearly."

Joanna Brady thought about the officers ranged around the buildings now, awaiting her order to move forward. They were young men and women—dedicated law enforcement officers—

with wives and husbands and children at home. She was one of those, too, with a husband and a teenager at home and with an unborn child sheltered inside her body. Joanna and the people who worked for and with her had everything to lose. On the other hand, Stella Adams, far beyond the possibility of hope, had nothing whatsoever left to lose.

Sheriff Brady turned to Ernie. "We're going to wait," she said.

"Wait?" he demanded. "For how long?"

"For as long as it takes."

The next two hours, waiting for a gunshot that never came, were the longest ones Joanna could remember, including the three hours she had spent in the delivery room when Jenny was born. She crouched next to the wall with Ernie Carpenter beside her. Sharp rocks poked into her knees. Occasionally some night-walking creature scrambled across her skin. Meanwhile, the unconcerned desert, oblivious to the human drama playing out nearby, resumed its natural nighttime rhythms. Meandering coyotes sent their mournful songs skyward. An hour into the process, Joanna was startled by a single long-eared jackrabbit who loped past within a few feet of where she was lying.

But throughout that long, long time, there was no response from Stella Adams—no further word. Joanna called out to the woman again and again without receiving any reply.

Eventually Deputy Gregovich and Spike returned.

"You took Nathan home?" Joanna asked.

Terry nodded. "His dad was pissed. Denny thought the kid was locked in his room. He had no idea Nathan had let himself out through a window. What's happening here?"

"Nothing."

"Do you want me to send Spike in?"

Joanna shook her head. She wasn't willing to risk Spike's life either. "Not yet," she said. "We'll wait a while longer."

Finally, just after midnight, she gave the word, and the K-9 unit moved forward. As Terry Gregovich and Spike disappeared from view, time slowed to an even more glacial crawl. Barely daring to breathe, Joanna listened to every sound. Finally Terry shouted out the words she had been waiting to hear.

"It's all clear," Deputy Gregovich called. "She's cut her wrists. She's dead."

Joanna gave the order to stand down, then she and Ernie Carpenter helped each other to their feet. They limped stiffly around the protecting wall, guided by the glow of Terry's flashlight. Stella Adams sat slumped against the wall just inside the empty doorway of a crumbling concrete building. She still wore a single tennis shoe on one foot. The other foot had been scraped raw in her desperate flight across the nighttime desert.

Stella's hands lay her in her bloodied lap, cradling the Colt .45 and a bloodstained Swiss Army knife. Joanna looked from Stella Adams to Ernie.

"Maybe you'll be able to keep your promise to Denny Adams after all," Joanna said softly. "At least Stella had the good sense to spare her son the shame of a trial."

NINETEEN

J oanna was home by two o'clock in the morning. At three she was still sitting on the couch
in the family room with Lady cuddled in her
lap, considering the mind-numbing series of
tragedies that had befallen the entire Mossman
clan. The seeds for that human disaster had been
planted by Ed Mossman himself, and Joanna
Brady had no sympathy for him. A fatal gunshot
wound to the chest was actually far better than
he deserved. But her heart ached for the others—
for the unwilling victims of Ed Mossman's
abuse, his own children—from Carol right on
down to Nathan and Cecilia.

Jaime Carbajal had described the film of Cecilia Mossman's supposed wedding. Joanna had
yet to see it, but she could well imagine the
frightened and reluctant child bride forced by
her father into a situation she could neither handle nor stop.

"Well, I'll stop it," she told Lady aloud. "Tomorrow morning I'm calling Sheriff Drake and telling him to go get her. With any kind of luck, Harold Lassiter will go to jail for child rape. If she's only twelve, that should work. Otherwise, they can nail him for involuntary servitude, if nothing else. Slavery's illegal in this country, even out on the Arizona Strip."

Butch, barefoot and clad only in a pair of shorts, came into the family room. "Who are you talking to?" he asked.

"The dog," Joanna said. "I'm telling Lady all about it."

"It's late," Butch said. "Shouldn't you come to bed?"

"I can't sleep."

He settled down on the couch beside her. Lady opened one eye and looked at him, but made no effort to move away. He put one arm around Joanna's shoulders and the other on Lady's hip. "Then maybe you'd better tell me about it, too," he said.

And so she did.

"Will it come out in public?" Butch asked when she finished. "The part about who Nathan's father really was?"

"Not if I can help it," Joanna said. "It'll be tough enough living down the fact that his mother was a murderer who committed suicide. As far as Nathan is concerned, Denny Adams **is** his only father. They'll both be better off if we can leave it that way."

Butch nodded thoughtfully. "What about the other little girl?"

"Cecilia?"

Butch nodded again.

"I've been thinking about her. For one thing, we've got Pam Davis and Carmen Ortega's film. I'm hoping that'll be enough to get the Mojave County sheriff off the dime. And Andrea Mossman told me she has at least one undercover contact inside the Lassiter compound. One way or another, we'll get that little girl out of there and pack Harold Lassiter off to the slammer. Cecilia's only twelve, for God's sake, Butch. She's a whole year younger than Jenny."

"Supposing you do rescue her from that situation, what will happen to her then?"

Joanna sighed. "I'm not sure. Child Protective Services will have to be called into play. I would imagine her mother is still in Mexico. The problem is, her mother is also hooked in with The Brethren."

"If you send her back home, she might be going from the frying pan into the fire."

"Exactly," Joanna said.

"So what are you going to do?"

"Talk to Andrea Mossman, and to Edith. Cecilia is Edith's granddaughter. And she's Andrea's half sister. They may be able to work with CPS and establish some kind of custody arrangement. That's probably about the best we can hope for."

Butch yawned and looked at his watch. "Wrong," he said. "The best we can hope for is an hour or two of sleep. Come on. We've got to go to bed now. You've done all you can for one day."

Joanna persuaded Lady out of her lap, then the two of them followed Butch into the bedroom. Butch was asleep again within minutes. So was Joanna. It seemed like only minutes later when he was shaking her awake. "Rise and shine or rise and barf," he said. "It's late. We're due at Dr. Lee's office in half an hour."

Joanna looked at the clock and was astonished to see that it said nine-thirty. "I'm late for work," she objected.

"No, you're not. I called Frank and told him you'd be in after your doctor's appointment. I know you. If I let you go into the office for even a minute, you'll forget."

Joanna would have argued with him about that, but there wasn't time. She had to race for the bathroom.

An hour later, with the physical part of the prenatal exam behind her, Joanna—now fully dressed—and Butch sat in Dr. Thomas Lee's office in the clinic portion of the Copper Queen

Hospital. Dr. Lee frowned in concentration as he consulted a calendar.

"From the date of your last period, I'd estimate your due date to be March 7. Of course, human pregnancy isn't an exact science," he added. "I can tell you the due date but the baby will arrive when it's ready—before or after, depending. Are you going to want to know in advance whether it's a boy or a girl?"

"Yes," Butch said at the same time Joanna was shaking her head no.

Dr. Lee laughed. "Welcome to parenthood," he said. "This is only the first of many things the two of you will need to discuss and decide on. Let me know next month, when you come in for your next appointment."

"What about morning sickness?" Butch asked.

"What about it?" Dr. Lee replied.

"Is there something she can take . . . ?"

"Never mind," Joanna put in quickly. "It's not **that** bad, and it'll probably go away in a few more weeks. It did last time."

Dr. Lee nodded. "If you can tough it out without taking medication, it's usually better for the baby. There can be side effects, you see . . ."

"I know," Joanna said. "I'll be fine."

For the next several minutes, Dr. Lee went over a list of general dos and don'ts. Finally he looked at Butch. "This is your first?"

Butch nodded.

"If you plan to be in the delivery room with her, you'll both need to sign up for a Lamaze class."

Butch looked at Joanna. "Is that what you want?"

"Of course it's what I want, silly. If you think I'm going through that all on my own, you're nuts."

"All right, then," Butch said. "Tell me where and when to sign up and I'm there."

It was close to noon by the time they finished up with Dr. Lee, so they stopped by Daisy's for lunch. Wednesday was Cornish pasty day, and Butch and Joanna split one of Daisy's massive, plate-sized meat pies.

"You're sure you don't want to know the sex in advance?" Butch asked.

"I'm sure."

"But that means we have to come up with two names—one for a boy and one for a girl."

"That's right," Joanna agreed. "So start thinking."

They had driven into town in separate cars. When lunch was over, Joanna kissed Butch good-bye in the parking lot. While he returned to High Lonesome Ranch, Joanna headed for the department. She felt slightly guilty about showing up late on a day when there was bound to be so much catch-up paperwork to do, but then again, she didn't feel **that** guilty.

She was at her desk and surveying the damage when Andrea Mossman called. "I heard about it on the news," she said. "I just got off the phone with Denny."

"How's Nathan?" Joanna asked.

"About how you'd expect. He's pretty broken up."

"And your grandmother?"

"She's a tough old bird," Andrea said. "She's doing remarkably well."

"I have a note here from my chief deputy," Joanna said. "Police officers in Obregón have been dispatched to the ranch to notify Kelly and . . ."

". . . and Dad's other wives," Andrea supplied.

"Do you have any idea what kind of arrangements will need to be made as far as your father's remains are concerned, once the autopsy is done and the body is released?"

"I don't care what happens to him," Andrea said. "And I doubt Grandma does, either. Talk to his other families. If they want him, they can have him—as long as they pay for shipping. I already discussed this with Grandma. She's not paying a dime, and I'm not either."

"What about Cecilia?" Joanna asked.

"Grandma and I have an appointment with a

CPS caseworker later on this afternoon. I wanted to talk to them **before** somebody brings Cecilia out of the Lassiter compound. Cecilia hasn't ever met me, and she probably has no idea her grandmother even exists. But if Grandma and I can help her, we will. I do have some experience with this kind of thing."

"What about the boy?" Joanna asked.

"What boy?" Andrea returned.

"Josiah. The one in the Lassiter compound who helped Pam Davis and Carmen Ortega film the wedding."

"We'll try to get him out at the same time," Andrea said. "If old man Lassiter figures out who was responsible, he'll make his life hell."

As if it wasn't already, Joanna thought.

After she got off the phone, the day turned into a marathon of paperwork. In addition to the usual day-to-day e-mail and correspondence, there were reports to be read—reports from Jaime Carbajal and Ernie Carpenter. And there were case-clearing phone calls and faxes back and forth between the Cochise County Sheriff's Department and Sheriff Trotter's office over in Hidalgo County. Joanna should have felt triumphant, but she didn't. Too many people were dead—too many lives ruined. Clearing cases under those circumstances made for hollow victories.

It was almost three o'clock when Kristin came into the office. "Sorry to interrupt, Sheriff Brady," she said. "But there are some people here to see you."

"Who?"

"They wouldn't give their names."

They would have if you'd tried a little harder, Joanna thought wearily.

Sighing, she rose and followed Kristin back out into the lobby. Outside her office, she found two Hispanic women—a young one and one much older—seated side by side on the love seat facing Kristin's desk. They were both dressed in black. The younger woman's hair was loose. The older one's hair was in a long gray braid that was wrapped around the top of her head like a silver crown. Over her head and shoulders she wore an old-fashioned mantilla.

The younger woman rose and stepped toward Joanna, holding out her hand. "Sheriff Brady?"

Joanna nodded.

"My name is Gabriella Padilla. This is my mother, Ramona Quiroz. Maria Elena Maldonado, the woman who died after that car wreck the other day, was my cousin, my mother's sister's child."

"Oh, yes," Joanna said. "Won't you come in?"

Gabriella went back to her mother and helped the old woman rise to her feet. Her hands and fingers were twisted and gnarled by arthritis. It was painful for her to walk and painful to watch her do it. Gabriella led her into the inner office while Joanna hurriedly pulled out a chair at the conference table, which was far closer to the door than the chairs in front of her desk.

"I'm sorry for your loss," Joanna said when they were seated. She waited while Gabriella translated.

"**Gracias,**" Mrs. Quiroz returned and then added something more in Spanish.

"She says it is God's will," Gabriella explained.

It has nothing at all to do with God's will! Joanna thought savagely.

"The funeral was this morning," Gabriella continued. "In Tucson. Maria Elena's husband, Tomas, is . . . well . . . if he tried to take them back home for a funeral, he wouldn't be able to return."

"He's illegal?" Joanna asked.

Gabriella paused and then nodded. "That's why they were coming—to be with Tomas. He paid for them to come. But since he can't go back, Maria Elena and Little Eddie will have to be buried here."

"I'm sorry," Joanna said again.

Gabriella's eyes filled with tears. She nodded. "I'm sorry, too."

There was a pause. During the period of silence, Joanna was aware of Ramona Quiroz's steady eyes examining her face with unblinking scrutiny. **What is she looking at?** Joanna wondered. **Is there something wrong with me—with what I'm wearing, with the way I look?**

Finally Gabriella continued. "I apologize for dropping in on you like this, but I work—in the tortilla factory in Barrio Anita," she said. "They let me have today off for the funeral. After the service, my mother insisted that I bring her here."

"Why?" Joanna asked.

"Mother spoke to Maria Elena in the hospital. Tomas was on his way, but Mother was the only one there. Maria Elena told Mother about you—about the red-haired woman who found Eduardo and brought him to the helicopter. You are that woman, aren't you?"

Joanna felt a lump constrict her throat. "Yes," she murmured. "Yes, I am."

"Maria Elena must have known she was dying. She asked Mother to come to you and ask you to please show us that spot. She wanted us to put up a cross for Eduardo—a single cross—but we would like to put up two—one for Eduardo and one for his mother as well."

Still Ramona Quiroz continued to stare. She said nothing, but when Gabriella stopped speaking, the old woman nodded almost imperceptibly.

"Would you take us there?" Gabriella finished.

"Yes," Joanna said at once. "Of course. Now?"

"Please. If it wouldn't be too much trouble."

Joanna stood and went to the door. "I'm going out, Kristin," she said.

"When will you be back?"

"I have no idea." Joanna turned back to the two women, where Gabriella was busy translating what had transpired.

"We can take one car or two, whichever you like," Joanna offered.

"The things we need are already in mine," Gabriella said. "So it would probably be better if we took that."

"All right," Joanna said. "But if you'd like, you could bring it around here to the back, to my private entrance. That way your mother won't have nearly so far to walk."

Gabriella left to fetch the car. When the door closed behind her, Ramona Quiroz spoke on her own for the first time. "You are very kind," she said. "Thank you."

"**De nada,**" Joanna replied.

"So you went out there with them?" Jenny asked. It was after dinner. Jenny was sprawled on the family room floor next to Tigger. Lucky, worn out with playing, was stretched out on

Jenny's other side. Both dogs were sound asleep. Joanna and Butch were on the couch and Lady, with one watchful eye on Butch, was tucked into a tight curl at Joanna's feet.

"Yes," Joanna answered. "The walls of Silver Creek are so steep right there, I didn't think Mrs. Quiroz could possibly make it down and back up again. But she did. She was very determined. And Gabriella had brought along everything they needed—two matching crosses, flowers, a shovel."

"And they put the crosses at the exact spot where you found the little boy?"

Joanna nodded. "Even with the storms we've had, I was able to show them where I found him. And that's where they put both crosses, under a clump of mesquite. If it rains as hard as it did the other night, it could be the crosses will be washed away, but that's where they wanted them."

"Why did they do that?" Jenny asked.

"It's a kind of remembrance," Joanna said. "And it seemed like a nice thing to do."

"Is the guy who wrecked the van even going to jail?" Jenny asked.

"I don't know," Joanna said. "I doubt it. I think the feds have made some kind of deal with him."

"That doesn't seem fair," Jenny remarked.

Joanna looked at her daughter. At thirteen,

Jenny still saw the world in terms of right or wrong, good or bad, black or white.

"It doesn't seem fair to me, either," Butch added.

Joanna sighed. "It's the best we can do. If we can put the heads of the syndicate out of business and hand some of them jail time, maybe we can keep some other poor families from being slaughtered the same way."

She stood up then. Her whole body ached. She was still paying the price for the three hours she had spent the night before lying on hard rocky ground. "I'm going to bed," she said. "I'm so tired I can barely hold my head up."

She went into the bedroom and slept so soundly that she never heard Butch come to bed. During the night she dreamed she was out on High Lonesome Road, attempting to plant a flower-covered cross in the middle of the road at exactly the same spot where she'd discovered Andy's helpless body all those years ago—where she'd found her husband unconscious and lying in a pool of his own blood.

Again and again she tried to pound the cross into the hard, unyielding ground. Again and again, the rock-hard caliche rejected it. When Joanna awakened, the sun was just coming up, and her face was wet with tears. She looked across the bed to the spot where Butch lay, snoring softly. It was a dream Joanna didn't understand, but she knew, whatever it meant, she probably wouldn't be telling Butch about it.

Lady lay on the rug on Joanna's side of the bed. The dog sensed Joanna was awake, and she raised her head warily as if she expected a mad dash to the bathroom, but it didn't come. For some reason, the nausea was in abeyance that morning. Joanna reached down and patted Lady's head, then she motioned for the dog to join her on the bed. Carefully, without disturbing Butch, Lady eased herself up onto the covers. Then, after circling three times, she nestled herself against Joanna's body and, with a contented sigh, fell back asleep.

Moments later, Joanna did, too.

TWENTY

On Friday morning, when Joanna arrived at the county offices for the weekly board of supervisors meeting, she was astonished to find the usually empty parking lot crammed full of vehicles, which forced her to park at the far end of the lot. On her way to the door she was greeted by a milling group of protesters, all of them carrying placards. board of supervisors unfair to animals several of them said. Others said seventeen too many. And then she knew. The folks from Animal Welfare Experience were at it again, only this time they were targeting someone besides her.

At the door to the building, Tamara Haynes was busy berating Charles Longworth Neighbors, the newest and Joanna's least favorite member of the board of supervisors. "Have you even been to Animal Control?" Tamara demanded. "Do you have any idea how short-handed they are?"

Joanna was gratified to see the AWE activist tackling somebody else for a change. And now that Sally Delgado, one of the first office clerks, had quit the department to work full-time on Ken Junior's campaign, Joanna was relatively sure her information leak had been plugged.

"Ms. Haynes," Neighbors began as Joanna edged past them, "you have to understand—"

But Tamara Haynes was on a roll, and she paid no attention. "And why did you deep-six that animal-adoption program they wanted to start— the one that would have taken strays to various shopping centers in hopes of finding owners? We need to get unwanted animals off death row, and if you think we don't vote, Mr. Neighbors, you're in for a rude awakening. Right, folks?"

The last comment was greeted by cheers all around.

For the first time, Joanna was forced to consider that perhaps Tamara Haynes did care about animals, after all. Perhaps the demonstration outside the Cochise County Justice Center had been something more than a strictly political plot to further Ken Junior's chances of winning the election.

"Really, Ms. Haynes," Neighbors was saying, looking decidedly uncomfortable, while his eyes remained focused on the little diamond sparkler winking at him from Tamara Haynes's very much exposed belly button. "As I said," he continued awkwardly, "I'm already late for a meeting. You'll have to excuse me."

He broke away from his interrogator then and dodged into the building right on Joanna's heels. "Who in the world are those people?" he wanted to know. "And why are they so upset with me?"

"What set them off was having all those animals die at the scene of that homicide last week," Joanna told him.

"That's certainly not my fault," Neighbors grumbled. "I don't see how they can hold the board of supervisors responsible for that."

"But they know Animal Control is short-handed," Joanna replied. "If we'd had enough personnel to keep an eye on hoarders like Carol Mossman, she might not have ended up with so many animals in her possession at the time of her death."

"What did you call her?"

"A hoarder," Joanna said. "Carol Mossman was what's called an animal hoarder. It's a mental condition."

"Really," Charles Longworth Neighbors said with a concerned frown. "I had no idea. And what's this about all that adoption nonsense?"

"It's not nonsense," Joanna returned. "The more pets we place in adoptive homes, the fewer we have to euthanize."

They were nearing the boardroom now. Charles Longworth Neighbors appeared to be lost in thought. "How many people do you think were out there?" he asked.

"Out in the parking lot? Fifty, I suppose," Joanna answered.

"On a Friday morning," he mused. "That's quite a few. Do you think they really do vote?"

In that moment Sheriff Joanna Brady understood exactly what was at stake. Charles Longworth Neighbors had been appointed to fill out someone else's unexpired term. Now he faced the prospect of running for election on his own and based on his own record.

In the years since her election, Joanna Brady had learned a little about politics herself.

"I'd be amazed to think they didn't," she said. "Vote, that is. And if they can summon this many folks for a Friday morning rally, who knows how many votes they can muster?"

This was news Charles Longworth Neighbors clearly found disturbing. "We should do something about this," he said.

"Yes," Joanna agreed amiably. "We certainly should."

"Do you have any ideas?"

Yes, Joanna thought, **like breaking Animal Control out of the sheriff's department and putting Jeannine Phillips in charge.**

"One or two," Joanna said.

"Good, good," Neighbors said distractedly as he held the boardroom door open for Joanna to enter. "Write up something on that and get it to me, would you, please? I'll put it on the agenda for next week."

"Sure," Joanna said. "I'll see what I can do."

She took her seat in the room and waited for the meeting to get under way. It was hard not to smile. After all, doing what it took to give the AWE vote to Charles Longworth Neighbors was also going to help Sheriff Brady.

Frank Montoya showed up just as the meeting was called to order. He leaned over to her and asked, "What's going on? You look like you just won the lottery."

"Tell you later," she said.

The meeting that morning wasn't as bad as meetings sometimes were, but when Joanna emerged just before noon, she wasn't surprised to see that the protesters had evaporated in the face of the hot sun. She checked her phone and found she had five missed calls. Scrolling through them, she discovered they were all from home. She called there immediately. Jenny answered on the second ring.

"Hi, Mom."

"What's going on?" Joanna demanded. "Is anything wrong?"

"No," Jenny said. "Everything's fine. Butch and I just got back from taking Lucky to the vet. Dr. Ross says Butch is right. Lucky is stone-deaf. She gave us the name of a book on sign language for dogs. She said we might be able to train all the dogs to respond to hand signals. Wouldn't that be neat?"

"Yes, it would. Is Butch there?"

"No. He's in town. He said that if you called, he'd meet you at Daisy's for lunch."

"Want to grab some lunch?" Frank asked, coming up behind her.

"Sorry," Joanna told him. "It turns out I'm having lunch with my husband."

As she drove to Daisy's, Joanna had to pull over at the traffic circle to let a funeral cortege go past. She knew whose funeral it was—Stella Adams's—and she was glad the windows in the limo following the hearse were dark enough that she couldn't see inside. She was glad not to see Denny Adams and his son, Nathan, coping with their awful loss. She had read in the paper that the services for Stella Adams would be private, but still, it seemed wrong that more people weren't there. This was a time when Dennis and Nathan Adams needed people around them— even if they didn't want them.

As the procession with its woefully few cars drove past, Joanna said a small prayer for Dennis and Nathan Adams and for all the remaining Mossmans as well.

It was a subdued Joanna Brady who arrived at Daisy's Café. Butch was seated in their favorite booth, the one at the far corner of the restaurant. He was grinning from ear to ear.

"What's up?" she asked as she slipped onto the bench seat.

"What makes you think something's up?" Butch returned.

"Your face, for one thing. You'd never make it playing poker."

"Drew called," Butch said, bubbling over. "Carole Anne Wilson is making me an offer. She wants **Serve and Protect** to be the first title in her new Hawthorn Press Mystery imprint. Can you believe it, Joey? It's not that much money, but it's a start."

He leaned across the table and kissed her full on the lips. A few nearby diners looked askance.

"Yeah," Daisy Maxwell added as she walked by, carrying a tray laden with glasses of iced tea. "You keep that up, Butch Dixon, and you'll make all the other women in here jealous."

But Butch's infectiously happy mood was catching.

"I can't believe it, Butch. This is wonderful!"

"You can't believe it," Butch returned. "Just wait until I tell my mother. She always told me

I'd never amount to anything. When she finds out I'm going to be published, she'll be amazed."

"I'm not," Joanna said with a smile. "When does it come out?"

"September of next year."

"Over a year away?" Joanna asked. "It takes that long? That's even longer than it takes to have a baby."

"I guess so," Butch agreed.

"So what are the love birds having today?" Daisy asked, stopping at their booth. "The special is all-you-can-eat **machaca** tacos, five ninety-nine. And for the tenderhearted . . ." she added, peering pointedly over her glasses at Joanna, "for them, I've got a nice new batch of chicken noodle soup."

Joanna looked at Butch and realized she was suddenly feeling better. "Today," she said, "I'm going for gusto and grabbing the **machaca**."

"Me, too," Butch said, beaming. "Whatever the lady's having, I'll have the same, and don't spare the salsa."

Minutes later, Joanna bit into the crunchy tortilla shell on the first of three delectable tacos. "So how did the board meeting go?" Butch asked.

"It was fine," Joanna said.

"Really?" Butch gave her a searching look. "After everything that's happened, for a change

Charlie Neighbors didn't give you too much grief?"

A lot had happened. In terms of Cochise County, the human death toll for the last week and a half was off the charts. As far as Charlie Neighbors was concerned, those deaths weren't worth mentioning. What counted for him were the votes that could be delivered to an opponent by the group protesting the deaths of Carol Mossman's dogs.

Ever since his appointment to the board of supervisors, Charles Longworth Neighbors had made Joanna's life miserable. Only today had she realized that he wasn't nearly as all-powerful as she had once assumed him to be. And the next time Sheriff Brady had to go up against him in defense of her department, she wouldn't be nearly as intimidated.

"No," Joanna said, giving her husband a thoughtful smile, "when it comes to grief and Charlie Neighbors, today was my day to dish it out."

After that, she lapsed into silence. "You're awfully quiet," Butch said finally. "What's going on?"

"Nothing."

"Come on, Joey. I know you better than that. Tell me."

"I drove past the ballpark this morning," she

said. "There's already a For Sale sign posted on the Adams place."

Butch shrugged. "Makes sense to me," he said. "If I were Denny Adams, I'd do the same thing. Take Nathan and go somewhere else—preferably someplace far enough away that nobody knows anything about what's happened. If Nathan tried to go back to school here in the fall, the other kids would eat him alive."

"Yes," Joanna agreed, "I'm sure you're right. And I'm sure, too, that's why Stella did what she did—to protect Nathan—to keep her son's friends from learning the truth about who he is and where he came from."

"You have to give the woman some credit," Butch said. "Regardless of who Nathan's father was, Stella Adams obviously loved her child more than she loved life itself. I'm not sure how that works, though," he added with a frown.

"How what works?"

"How is it possible that the process of becoming a mother can also turn someone into a killer?"

"It's not that hard to understand," Joanna told him. "Motherhood changes you. From the moment you hold that baby in your arms, you're a different person from who you were before. You turn into . . ." She paused, searching for words.

"A tigress defending her young?" Butch offered.

Joanna nodded. "Something like that," she said.

"You make it sound as though fathers have nothing to do with it."

"Ed Mossman certainly had something to do with it," Joanna said fiercely. "He had **everything** to do with it. All this happened because his daughters were trying to escape from the mess he created."

"Ed Mossman's dead," Butch reminded her gently. "He can't be punished any more."

Joanna thought about her jail-based conversation with Ramón Alvarez Sandoval. Confronting the driver of the SUV with his crucifix and forcing him to look at his actions through the prism of his own beliefs had helped tip the scales and convince him to turn state's evidence. It had taught Joanna something about her own beliefs as well.

"You're wrong there," she said at last. "Ed Mossman can be punished more."

"How?" Butch asked.

"He can rot in hell," Joanna told him, pushing her plate away and standing up. "And if there's any justice anywhere, he'll do just that."

AUTHOR'S NOTE

Hoarders like Carol Mossman exist in the real world. I wouldn't have known about them or written about them had it not been for my sister, E. Jane Decker, Director of Animal Control for Pinal County in Coolidge, Arizona. Like Carol Mossman, these unfortunate people have two things in common: an unending availability of unwanted dogs and cats and a chaotic and disturbed childhood that might include a history of sexual abuse, alcoholism, and profoundly unstable relationships with people.

What can we do to help? First, we must understand that when we take a cute, cuddly little puppy or kitten into our homes, it is a commitment of at least ten to fifteen years. We also need to understand that if the animal in our care has problems, we must go to experts for help and training to ensure the animal's well-being and to keep the animal from becoming unwanted and difficult to place. Next, we should spay and neuter our animals, and when we choose to welcome a new animal into our lives, we ought to avail ourselves of any one of the many pet rescue operations located throughout the country.

Finally, if we know of a hoarder in our neighborhood, we must notify our local animal control officers. Hoarders think they're helping, but the animals in their care are usually undernourished, unvaccinated, neglected, and unsocialized animals that become difficult to place after being removed from this unfortunate environment. Please consider helping in any way you can because animals cannot help themselves, and neither can hoarders.

The Humane Society of the United States (www.hsus.org) has valuable information on how communities can effectively respond to the animal and human problems associated with hoarding cases.